"Slade's debut presents a dark supernatural conflict with high stakes in a world where demons and angels possess humans and use them as tools in the unending fight between heaven and hell . . . [a] rich crossover urban fantasy." —*Publishers Weekly*

"Slade has created a world within our own. Sera and Archer are sincere characters who show that not every person, nor any love, is ever perfect, but it can survive with work. This is a thoughtful and emotional look into the paranormal world." —*Romantic Times*

"The tension between good and evil is well done. . . . It is a gripping, suspenseful story." —San Francisco Book Review

"*Seduced by Shadows* is a beautiful and inventive new series start with plenty of action and wonderful characters!" —Errant Dreams Reviews

"This compelling page-turner is action-packed and you are thrown into a battle between good and evil. Ms. Slade writes with a deft hand and beautiful description. This is a paranormal romance that will have you glued to your seat till the very end as you await the outcome." —Night Owl Romance

"*Seduced by Shadows* blew me away. . . . Slade creates a beyond-life-or-death struggle for love and redemption in a chilling, complex, and utterly believable world." —Jeri Smith-Ready, award-winning author of *Wicked Game*

"*Seduced by Shadows* is wonderfully addictive!" —*New York Times* bestselling author Gena Showalter

TEMPTED

She held herself taut against the hard plane of his chest. "Is that a hammer in your pocket, or are you just glad to see me?"

His soft laughter warmed her cheek and still made her shiver. "Yes."

Something coiled deep in her, and it wasn't any demon. A demon would be easy to banish in comparison. "Let me go."

"Are you going to attack again?"

"If I say yes, are you going to kiss me again?"

He opened his embrace and stepped back. "Just say no."

Her lips tingled. Her whole body tingled. But that was the hard part about temptation, wasn't it? Saying no.

Also by Jessa Slade

Seduced by Shadows

FORGED
OF
SHADOWS

A NOVEL OF THE MARKED SOULS

JESSA SLADE

A SIGNET ECLIPSE BOOK

SIGNET ECLIPSE
Published by New American Library, a division of
Penguin Group (USA) Inc., 375 Hudson Street,
New York, New York 10014, USA
Penguin Group (Canada), 90 Eglinton Avenue East, Suite 700, Toronto,
Ontario M4P 2Y3, Canada (a division of Pearson Penguin Canada Inc.)
Penguin Books Ltd., 80 Strand, London WC2R 0RL, England
Penguin Ireland, 25 St. Stephen's Green, Dublin 2,
Ireland (a division of Penguin Books Ltd.)
Penguin Group (Australia), 250 Camberwell Road, Camberwell, Victoria 3124,
Australia (a division of Pearson Australia Group Pty. Ltd.)
Penguin Books India Pvt. Ltd., 11 Community Centre, Panchsheel Park,
New Delhi - 110 017, India
Penguin Group (NZ), 67 Apollo Drive, Rosedale, North Shore 0632,
New Zealand (a division of Pearson New Zealand Ltd.)
Penguin Books (South Africa) (Pty.) Ltd., 24 Sturdee Avenue,
Rosebank, Johannesburg 2196, South Africa

Penguin Books Ltd., Registered Offices:
80 Strand, London WC2R 0RL, England

First published by Signet Eclipse, an imprint of New American Library,
a division of Penguin Group (USA) Inc.

First Printing, June 2010
10 9 8 7 6 5 4 3 2 1

*To the Rose City Romance Writers
(is there room here for a hundred-plus names?) for
the cheering, the commiserating, and the whip cracking,
as needed. Write on!*

Acknowledgments

Much love to my family for their enthusiastic support during the "Year of the Book."

Deep appreciation for all the great folks at NAL for "Year of the Book: Part 2," especially Adam Auerbach and Anthony Ramondo for this cool, sexy cover, and copy editor Michele Alpern for reminding me about antecedents.

Deeper bows yet to editor Kerry Donovan and agent Becca Stumpf, who answered all my curious (sometimes anxious) e-mails during the wood ducklingesque transition from writer to author.

Big, big thanks to my mentors (who don't really know they're my mentors), including Michelle Buonfiglio and Sue Grimshaw, for making books smart and superfun, and the PASIC authors for their knowledge and generosity.

Credit (and kisses) to Rainstick Cowbell for the *Seduced by Shadows* theme song.

And to all the readers, thanks for giving the words a place to go.

Prologue

Gray dust clogged the frigid air. Filthy snow lay all around, streaked with ash and blood and some odd fibrous, gelatinous mess.

He put his hand to his aching head. Bone pulped under the tentative touch and he winced. His fingers came away slimed with crimson and gray matter.

That couldn't be good.

Stones rained around him, and he choked on the acrid stink of demon-realm winds. Dimly, he remembered. He'd been trapped there, his soul bound into the Veil by that bitch talya and her lover.

But here he was, back in the human realm. His pores beaded with sulfur as his demon ascended, struggling to protect his all-too-human flesh from the stoning.

It coiled through him, the demon, and tightened its grasp.

He'd fleetingly—so fleetingly—hoped to be freed from it after all the long centuries of slavery. Now a slave again.

He tried to weep, but the acid sting of birnenston tears only burned furrows in his cheeks.

He wanted to succumb to the pounding stones, be buried forever. But the demon yanked him upright, shedding dust and ice and blood like some terrible birth cowl. He clenched his teeth, resisting the demon's intangible grip, but his head ached all the worse and he could summon neither wit nor will. The demon awkwardly coordinated his limbs into a shambling gait.

Worse than a slave.

As the demon rode him like a dumb animal away from the collapsing building—the site of his desperate bid to free the world from the chains of helpless good and hopeless evil that bound it—Corvus Valerius could not decide whom he hated more: the malevolent djinni that had brought him back from the dead, or the bastard league of the teshuva who'd had the chance to kill him once and for all and had failed.

Chapter I

Four months later

What would Jackie Chan do?

Not for the first time, Jilly Chan wished she'd been born with the ass-kicking aptitude of her Hong Kong movie-hero namesake. Lau-lau always said denying her heritage would get her in trouble. She just hadn't realized trouble meant dead. Duh. How many times did the universe need to hit her in the head with a brick before she learned to duck as quickly as Jackie Chan?

"Dee, Iz, don't move." She edged in front of the two kids. As if her five-two self could hide them. Maybe the darkness of the Chicago alley at night would work in their favor.

"What is that?" Iz's teen voice cracked, which lately made him swear. But he obviously realized they had bigger problems than his impending manhood. Such as their aforementioned impending deaths.

"Did it escape from the zoo?" Dee clutched Jilly's shoulder.

Jilly elbowed them both backward. She hated retreating, but the thing at the mouth of the alley had them blocked. "I don't know what it is. But it isn't friendly."

"You can tell by the way it drools," Dee agreed. "Eesh. Is it burning holes in the pavement?"

"Nothing that big has mandibles," Iz squeaked, stuck on panicked puberty. "Only insects have mandibles like that."

"Tell that to Supersize-Me Drool Boy over there," Dee said. "I bet it eats know-it-all nerds for its midnight snack. Which would be, oh, right about now."

"Fly vomit could, in sufficient volume, theoretically dissolve concrete."

"Oh, gross, Iz-kid."

"Quiet." Jilly took another step back, shooing the kids along behind her.

The creature didn't move, but a flash of orange eye-shine gave her the sinking feeling it could see in the dark. And it was looking right at her.

A chill that had nothing to do with the rude March wind traced her spine and wrapped around her chest. "Dee," she said softly, "my cell is in my right pocket."

With her gaze locked on the thing, she never felt the teen's nimble fingers in the puffy material of her coat. Hmm. She'd better have another talk with the girl, make sure she wasn't keeping up her old skills. Assuming a not-worst-case-scenario outcome to tonight's adventure, of course.

"No sudden moves. No loud noises," Jilly said. "It doesn't seem ready to attack."

"Yet." Iz's voice dropped an octave.

Behind her, Dee muttered, "Hello? Why won't this thing— *Help?* Jilly, I think the battery—"

A hideous screech blared through the alley, and they all flinched. But it was only the cell phone, feeding back. The signal spit and gibbered, far too loud for the tiny speaker.

The thing in their path took a shambling step forward. It paused in the narrow cone of light cast by the neon sign on the corner of the building.

"Turn the phone off," Jilly and Iz hissed in unison.

Jilly claimed no particular knowledge of entomology. She knew two kinds of city bugs: the fast ones and the ones she scraped off the bottom of her Wescos. But Iz was right. The thing coming toward them had the basic look of something caught between her treads.

"I bet this is what got Andre." Iz's voice broke off. "Now do you believe me something weird's been going on? Now you see why we had to come out here?"

"Iz-kid, I'm seeing it, and I still don't believe it." Jilly stretched her arms. At least she could make herself wider, if not taller. "I want you two to make a run for it the second I yell 'go,' okay?"

"Run for it?" Dee asked. "You're kidding me."

It wasn't interested in the kids, Jilly told herself. It had never once looked away from her. How flattering. "I'll scare it. You guys get clear of the interference and call 911."

"Scare it?" Iz sounded even more doubtful than Dee. "How?"

Dee squeezed Jilly's arm. "Just say 'go.' "

For once, Jilly was grateful for the years on the street that had sharpened the teen's self-preservation instincts. "Dee," she warned, "take Iz too."

"As long as he's fast."

"Andre could outrun any cop in the precinct," Iz said gloomily. "Bet it didn't help him none."

"Ready?" Jilly stiffened, preparing to . . . She hadn't quite worked out that part yet, but it had something to do with kung fu. Or maybe tai chi. Whichever. "One. Two . . ."

And before she could say "three—go," two more of the humanoid insect things loped into the mouth of the alley.

"Uh, Jilly?" Iz tugged her sleeve. "I don't think you're going to be able to scare them now."

She could distract one with the half-assed assault she had in mind. Three, no way. "Change of plan. Head to the back of the alley, to the fire escape. There'll be an access door on the roof that leads into the building."

"It'll be locked," Dee said. "We'll be stuck on the roof."

"Iz has his picks. Don't you, Iz-kid?"

"What? And violate my parole?"

"We'll discuss your punishment later." And there *would* be a later. "Keep trying the cell."

"We're going," Dee said over Iz's plaintive, "But what about you, Jilly? You can't run."

True. She knew better than to stress her lung. Good thing she preferred to stand her ground.

She kept her ear cocked to the scuffle of the teens' retreating footsteps. At the mouth of the alley, the hungry eyeshine of the monstrosities never flickered.

Monstrosities? She meant monsters. Unease roughened her breath to sandstone in her throat.

She winced at the rumble of a Dumpster across the concrete behind her. Apparently the kids hadn't been able to reach the fire escape without a makeshift ladder. Despite the commotion, the trio ahead of her didn't twitch.

Okay, a plan. She couldn't ward them off forever with her don't-fuck-with-me stare. Jackie Chan routinely took on dozens of opponents. Of course, he had a more optimistic sound track than the "Ride of Valkyries" doom tune that was now going through her head.

She cut a quick glance right and left. Damn, where was a ditched murder weapon when she needed one? There wasn't even a loose bag of trash—just a pile of recyclables. Could she guilt them to death with packing peanuts?

Behind her, the rattle of the kids on the fire escape grew fainter. They must be near the top, out of the fray.

In her calmest, pre-saloon-brawl voice, she said, "I don't want any trouble."

Didn't want, yet always seemed to find. The three monsters took a step in unison toward her.

Yeah, that line never worked in the movies either.

She should have been terrified, considering what had

happened the last time she faced a monster like these. Well, not quite like these. Rico had been a plain old human monster with one gold tooth, not mandibles. Somehow, these actually seemed less scary. Her heartbeat ramped up, not with fear—or not only with fear—but with a savage glee so that the catch in her compromised breathing sounded as if it were eagerness. How sick was that?

She couldn't hear the kids at all now. She was alone. Her pulse went semiautomatic fire in her ears, and her muscles burned as if a dozen police flares had been struck in her joints.

"Okay, then. Red rover, red rover, let Jilly come over." She took three steps forward. Her bootheels rang hard on the pavement.

Then a fourth figure appeared, not so hulkingly broad as the first three, but every bit as tall.

The newcomer's wings flared low—no, not wings; a duster. The monster Jilly's eyes had conjured became just a man.

He paused there, bareheaded against the gusting wind that ran eager fingers through his shoulder-length dark hair. Some glint of neon caught in his eye, flaring violet as he turned toward them.

The newcomer twitched open his duster and withdrew a . . . a what-the-hell hammer. The haft extended almost too long to be hidden under his coat, even as tall as he was. The blunt business end was as big as her head.

"Now, that's the murder weapon I was looking for," she muttered. Too bad it was going to be used to murder her.

The man whirled the hammer in a broad arc. Above the hollow whistle, he shouted, "Jilly, get out of here."

As the monster trio whirled to face him, he lowered his head and charged.

For a heartbeat, she froze. How had he known her name? Did she know him? She almost recognized the feral grace of him, as if the old comic books she'd once devoured had come to life. Thanks to the crappy alley light, he was cast in black and white and shades of gray—but he was every bit as strong and fearless and take-charge as the heroes of her fantasies.

Right, as if she were going to rely on anyone else to fight her battles ever again.

She dodged to one side of the alley. She'd seen a glint beside the neatly stacked boxes—right there. Yes! Someone had forgotten a box cutter.

She scrabbled at the cardboard, fingers closing around the narrow metal, sliding the tiny razor tooth out in the same motion. She spun back to the fight.

Despite her speedy weapon procurement, Thor already stood, legs braced, over one carcass. With another swing of his hammer he dispatched the second creature. He knocked its mandibled head right off its shoulders as if it were a meaty croquet ball. Jilly's stomach heaved at the wet thud of the head thwacking into the brick wall.

The last monster—obviously smarter than Jilly herself—ran.

The man whirled, every line of his body poised to pursue. Jilly's breath caught hard, this time in pure pleasure at the taut, precise flow of his moves. He seemed so familiar, like something she'd dreamed. Maybe as she'd fallen asleep in the middle of one of those gawd-awful CGIed action movies.

The monster-head stump oozed black scum, and she swallowed hard at the blunt reminder; this hammer-wielding superhero was no faker.

Since when had she forgotten she wasn't impressed by superheroes anymore? They were all fakers, by their nature. She scoffed to herself. As if he'd heard her, the man wheeled back around. The heavy oiled-canvas hem of the duster swirled above the pull straps of his boots. Her bravado withered at the stark expression that drew down the otherwise sensuous lines of his full mouth.

"Just what the hell were you going to do with that little thing?"

The lilt of his Irish accent captivated her for a moment, so she didn't pay attention to the words. Then she was insulted. She wasn't *that* short.

Finally she noted his focus on the box cutter in her hand. "Defend your honor?"

The grim set of his mouth softened, just barely. "Defend me?" He let the hammer swing down into a slow, mesmerizing ticktock. "Did I look like I needed defending?"

The hint of amused arrogance in his voice made her lift her chin in defiance. "Maybe a little. It's a very small knife anyway." She clutched it tight as he strode toward her.

Her gaze locked on the bold tattoo that rayed across his left temple to brush the corner of his blue eye. God, that must've hurt—needles nicking that rugged cheekbone for hours.

She snapped upright. "Now I remember. You were at that homeless outreach we did in the park last weekend." She stiffened even more as realization crept over her. "You know my name. You've been following me."

The final tock of the hammer pointed at the headless corpse. "Good thing, huh?"

She didn't want to think about it. "I have to make sure Iz and Dee are okay."

"They made it to the roof. I'll have someone escort them down."

Jilly narrowed her eyes. "Someone, who?"

"One of my people."

"Your people, who? Never mind. Dee was supposed to call 911."

"The call couldn't get through the interference. That's typical with these attacks lately. Besides, what are you going to tell the authorities?"

Yeah, she knew how the authorities dealt with monstrosities, even the purely human kind. "I want to see the kids."

"My people will take them back to the halfway

house. They'll be fine without you." His voice dropped, the brogue's cadences waxing again. "They'll have to be from now on."

Jilly gripped the box cutter. "What's that supposed to mean?"

"You know, don't you, that it's too late?"

"Too late for what?"

"I didn't understand the restlessness, or I didn't want to listen. It's too late to give you a chance."

Her voice rose with annoyance. And the first touch of unadulterated fear. "Too late for what?"

"To say no to the demon."

CHAPTER 2

Liam Niall had regrets. Many regrets. Any 180-year-old man could expect to fuck up now and then. An immortal man could expect to survive the fuckups with the burden of guilt weighing ever heavier.

As the word "demon" reverberated between them, he contemplated the incredulous woman before him. His delay finding Jilly Chan, his failure to warn her that she'd been chosen by an unbound demon that would possess her soul and doom her to an eternity fighting the endless battle between good and evil . . . Yeah, this particular fuckup was going to haunt him for a very long time.

But as the leader of the Chicago league of talyan—soul-damaged warriors possessed by repentant demons called teshuva seeking salvation—he'd long ago stopped listening to the little voice inside that warned of danger and destruction and doom. Damn it, he was possessed by a demon hell-bent on obliterating every lesser demonic emanation from the other-realm that had the bad luck to cross his path. The little voice inside him was always freaking out.

And so he had squelched the restlessness that had kept him wandering the streets long after the rest of the league retreated for the day to sleep off their wounds.

But as the nights passed, the little voice had gone from a whisper to a scream, until he was frantic with the need to silence it. Roaming the neighborhoods, he'd felt like he was missing something, and the sensation had been unnerving.

As the league's leader, missing something was tantamount to betrayal. He'd looked for a ferales' lair or malice flock, or another potentially disastrous tear in the Veil like the one that had nearly spelled their end just a few months ago. Even a disturbance in the other-realm ethers could mean yet more peril for his possessed fighters.

And then he'd found it.

Found *her*.

Trailing her unbound demon like a silk scarf, the pixie with the triple-X-rated curves had instantly caught his eye, as both a demon slayer and a male. Her black hair, spiked with propane-flame blue, matched the titanium loop piercing the nostril of her flat-bridged nose. Both affectations faded beside the golden honey and cinnamon of her eyes.

That exotic regard had passed over him without interest, focused as she was on handing out socks and sandwiches to the homeless who'd gathered in the park that day. But even that glancing heat had turned his watery bones to steam.

It shamed him now—without changing his belief that he'd do exactly the same again—that he'd run back to the familiar cold comforts of the league.

But one of his best fighters, Ferris Archer, had looked him over and said, "You found her."

For the first time in a long time, Liam rejected necessity and played blissfully ignorant. "Found who?"

"You can't just blow off the mated-talyan bond. I should know." Archer lifted one eyebrow in a self-deprecating gesture. Winning that recent battle to save the city had proved easier than winning Sera, the first female talya in living history, though in the end, she'd only asked Archer to give up his death wish, his bloody arrogance, and his heart.

"We don't know anything about joined talyan," Liam objected. "Thanks to Bookie absconding with the only extant reference." He peered at Archer. "Unless Sera has found something you haven't told the rest of us bachelors."

Archer schooled his expression, but a glint of sinful pleasure—and a touch of that arrogance—brightened his eyes. "She's been working her way through the archives, trying to find any references to female talyan, the mated bond, soulless armies, and all the other crazy shit we've been facing lately. But there's a lot to go through, especially with no trained Bookkeeper."

"Then if you don't know anything—"

"I know that even with demon-amped strength, you can't run from this."

"Since when do you believe in destiny?"

"Who said anything about destiny? I mean you can't run from this fight."

Bowing to the inevitable, Liam had sent the league's best tracker to find the new female possessed. Haji had learned that Jilly Chan spent more time on the street than at her desk for her job with Reach Out, a halfway house for homeless teens, but she'd been absent from her usual haunts, no doubt subliminally unsettled by the other-realm forces focused on her. The tracker had chased the intermittent energies of the unbound demon with no luck. They'd missed picking her up before she got to her apartment one night, and then a surge in demonic activity had distracted them.

Finally, following the relentless echo in his chest, like an indefinable hunger determined to assuage itself, Liam had found the source of his unease facing down not one but three ferales, with their demonic emanations clothed in menacing corporeal husks.

The recent pack behavior of the previously solitary ferales was worrisome enough; to think that they'd had

Jilly cornered, her demon's powers latent and inaccessible until the final ascension, made his blood curdle.

Now, staring at the pint-sized woman with the hot-toddy eyes, he wondered which lucky bastard would help escort her through the terrifying new life that awaited. For the merest heartbeat, he wished . . . But no, overseeing the league itself and the repentant teshuva's eternal mission to atone was his calling.

He glanced down at her shit-kicker boots. He didn't necessarily envy the man chosen to guide her next steps.

She narrowed those heated eyes at him. "Demon?"

He stifled a sigh. If the league kept adding new fighters at the current rate, he'd have to come up with a welcome kit, a handbook, and probably name tags. Since when had fighting evil included management issues?

"This sounds insane, of course," he started.

"Yeah, why stop the reality thrill ride now?"

"These . . ." He toed the butchered feralis. "These are lesser demons, drawn to the demon that has possessed you."

She straightened, though the extra inches barely lifted the blue spikes of her hair up to his chin. "Is my head coming off next?"

Ignoring the ichor staining the hammer, he slipped the weapon back into the sheath in his coat. The move didn't seem to particularly reassure her. He couldn't blame her. "The teshuva demon in you is repentant, seeking to atone for its sins. Like the one in me."

She stared at him. "You're possessed. By a demon."

"You're finding it hard to believe, I know. But soon your demon will make its virgin ascension. Its influence will spread completely through you. Then you'll understand what I'm saying. For now, I just need you to believe that you could've been killed tonight by these monsters. And more of these will be drawn to you until you've fully integrated the teshuva. So you'll take the guard I give you."

Her glare struck him like a match head.

He shrugged. "Think you can stop me?"

She looked down at the tiny blade in her hand and echoed his shrug.

"I'm not crazy," he said. "And you're not crazy, seeing these entities or listening to me. I know you've gone through some rough times lately, that you've been feeling isolated and alone, as if you've drifted away from your life."

"I suppose you stalkers prefer isolated victims." She flicked the blade in the box cutter another notch longer. "I should warn you, lonely or not, I won't go easy."

"No doubt." He refrained from explaining that a demon-ridden warrior who went easy wouldn't be much use in the never-ending battle against evil. "I'm just telling you what we know of possession. The other-realm entities that possess humans always mark people already trapped between hammer and anvil, with fire all around."

"That doesn't seem particularly fair."

"Resisting temptation is easy when you're feeling strong."

The restless flick of the box cutter in her hands stilled, and a shadow darkened her eyes. "What do you know about temptation?"

A curl of awareness made him stiffen against his teshuva's sudden predatory interest. "I can tell, based on the trailing ethers around you, that the demon came to you—what?—last night? Or maybe the night before." Guilt pricked him. "I had people looking, but they couldn't find you."

"Until too late," she murmured, echoing him. "Nothing like these things . . . these demons came for me before tonight." She pinned him with a needle-sharp gaze. "Before you." Then her eyes widened.

"What?" He stared into the black rounds of her shock-expanded pupils, seeking that first hint of violet.

"Before you," she said again to herself. "I thought it was a dream." Her gaze tripped over him, and his skin prickled as if she'd physically swept her hand across his body. She lingered on the mark at his temple, avoiding his eyes. "Never mind. This *is* crazy. I have to go."

He didn't want to let her go. Because, he convinced himself, the league needed all the fighters that came its way. Not to mention the world didn't need any rogue talyan, confused by their demons, wandering the streets without purpose. At least the battle between good and evil offered job security.

"Take the escort I'm giving you," he urged. "For the kids' sake, if not for your own."

That brought her gaze back to him. "Don't try to manipulate me." Despite the exotic cast of her features, her tone was raw icy Chicago street. "Especially not with the kids."

"Noted."

After a moment, she blew out a breath. "Fine, somebody can walk me to the halfway house. And don't bother telling me not to go."

He stepped back, out into the street, giving her room to come out of the alley. She kept the box cutter in hand.

She skirted the carcasses warily, her lip curled in disgust. "I don't want one of those inside me."

"You've been possessed by a teshuva, a repentant demon," he reminded her. "These are ferales. Lesser emanations from the tenebraeternum—the demon realm—that merge and mutate human-realm matter into corporeal husks like these."

She eyed him with only somewhat less disgust. "Maybe I don't want a . . . a teshuva in me either."

If only his advance team had had more time to build up a dossier on Jilly Chan. Maybe some of her secrets would give him an insight to her personality, a clue, a weakness that would bring her around more easily. Though he had a sneaking suspicion that her weaknesses were even better guarded than the rest of her.

"It chose you for a reason," he said. "Something made

you vulnerable. You let it in, and if you reject it now, it will tear open that vulnerability on its way out. You'd never be whole again, in body, mind, or spirit."

She flattened one hand against her ribs, under her breast, as if she had a stitch in her side. "If there's something inside me, then I'm not whole anyway, am I?"

"Better than the alternatives."

"Which are?"

"Death and damnation now."

"Instead of?"

"Death and damnation later."

She huffed back something that sounded like laughter. "As a killer, you're pretty impressive. As a welcoming committee, you suck."

"Thank you," he said drily. He glanced across the street, signaled with two fingers to the alley, then with another finger pointed out the path the third feralis had taken. He gave the roundup sign to have the talyan finish sweeping the area, and he fell into step beside Jilly.

She watched him. "What was that?"

"Giving the crew their orders."

"The crew. Of other demon-possessed killers."

He ignored the incredulity laced with mockery in her voice.

"So you're their boss?"

He lifted one shoulder in a reluctant shrug. It felt as if the weight of the world pressed down on him there, but that was just the heft of the hammer.

She kept the width of the empty sidewalk between them. "How many demons are there?"

"Not as many repentant teshuva as quite unrepentant tenebrae. You'll meet the rest of our league eventually."

He watched her study the night, eyes narrowed and nostrils flared so that the ring piercing winked. She couldn't know it, but the demon was already changing the way she looked into the shadows. Although something about her told him she'd always faced the darkness with defiance.

Who would make a good partner for her, with her

prickly punk attitude? Haji was too quiet. Jonah was too straitlaced. Maybe Ecco, with his crude humor. No, she'd eviscerate even that powerful fighter and ask no quarter.

The final stages of possession could get ugly as the human and demonic elements struggled to find a new balance. Archer and Sera had been reluctant to explain the details of how they'd gotten through that last dangerous night. He'd have to bully past their shared silence so he could make the right choice for Jilly.

God knew, possession was hard enough already.

To distract himself from the memories that threatened, he asked, "What were you doing poking around this part of town so late?"

"It's part of my job, keeping an eye on the kids."

"Wouldn't it be safer to keep an eye on them at the halfway house instead of roaming crap neighborhoods after midnight?"

Her lips twisted in wry agreement. "Iz got it into his head to investigate the disappearance of a friend of his."

"What do the police—" Liam stopped himself. "I suppose the authorities don't have a lot of time to spend on a missing street kid."

Her lifted eyebrow implied he'd get no cookie for that brilliant deduction. "Luckily, Dee ratted him out and brought me here. And if you hadn't come . . ." Her smile upended and vanished.

He didn't try to reassure her. Better that she was frightened.

After a moment, she composed herself. "The kids have been talking strange lately, and Iz blamed Andre's disappearance on things I couldn't believe. I tried to tell him Andre had been getting into some nasty stuff. Not strange, just nasty, like dealing solvo."

Dismay stiffened Liam's spine. "Solvo and strange are more closely linked than you know. If Andre was using, you should write him off."

One hard shake of her head rattled her blue spikes. "I don't write anyone off."

"You don't get a choice with solvo addicts."

"There's a way back from everything—"

"Not from being soulless."

"Soulless? But that's crazy. . . ." She fell silent.

"Solvo is the chemical distillation of a demon weapon called *desolator numinis*. The soul cleaver." He let her walk most of a block without speaking. "You're thinking about what you've seen tonight, and that maybe it's not so crazy after all."

"No," she said softly. "It's still crazy."

"But true."

She hesitated. "It would explain some things."

He put his hand on her arm to stop her. At the feel of her, the shock that went through him had nothing to do with demons and everything to do with temptation. God, when was the last time he had touched a woman? The lack of a ready answer halted him in his tracks.

When she faced him, her widened eyes exposed the darker ring around her golden irises.

He shook off the potent jolt. If it didn't rouse his demon's warning, then it didn't matter. Never mind what else might rouse in him.

"Look over there, by the fast-food place," he told her.

After a long moment, she dragged her startled gaze off him and followed his directions. "What am I—Jesus, what is that?"

The substance oozing around the entrance looked vaguely like a ghostly rat covered in burned fryer oil gone bad. Gone very, very bad. "It's a malice. Another sort of lesser tenebrae, but it stays incorporeal, unlike the ferales in the alley. They skulk around in small flocks, drawn to chaotic negative emotions." He glanced at her. "Like yours."

She recoiled. "It's coming this way."

"There are more coming. So get a grip."

Her fingers tightened whitely on the box cutter.

"Control your emotions," he clarified.

"How am I supposed to do that?"

"Like me." He turned her away from the malice, to face him again. He stared into her eyes. "You can't let it get to you."

He made it sound so easy, he almost convinced himself.

"You said it already got to me, or something like it." Her chest heaved with an uneven breath.

He tightened his grip on her arm to draw her back from the edge of bolting. Would she be fleeing the malice? Or him? "Now you have to control it, dominate it."

"The demon . . ."

"Your fear."

She scowled as the word tripped a visible switch in her from dread to annoyance. "I've faced worse than monster blobs." She narrowed her eyes, cutting him off. "Worse than you."

"Undoubtedly." Why else would a demon choose her? "You have new weapons now."

She slowly drew in a breath that caught in her throat once, as if it hurt. When she let it out, the tension drained from her face. She pocketed the box cutter and let her arms fall loose and ready to her sides. Those hot eyes still glinted at him, half veiled behind short black lashes. "I don't want a hammer. Doesn't accessorize well with my ass-kicking boots."

He let her go. Guessing by the hard curl to her lips, he'd lay odds she'd mentally lined up his ass for that kicking too.

Chapter 3

Jilly had years of experience with people making up shit. The kids were masters at reinterpreting reality to suit their unmet needs. And the many "uncles" her mother had brought home had all sorts of explanations for why they couldn't work, couldn't cook, couldn't help themselves.

But nobody had faced her with wilder stories than this guy with his whack-a-demon hammer and his anti-social tattoo.

Except maybe the comic books she'd once loved, but those never drooled holes in concrete like that dead monster had. Though there might have been a bit of preteen panting over a man in a mask....

She strode down the street, forcing him to keep up with each strike of her bootheels. She told herself she wasn't running away. Good thing, since he had no trouble keeping up. Those long legs moved so smooth beneath his duster he practically floated beside her.

Compared with his steely grace, she felt grubby, not to mention shorter than usual. "You know my name. You even know what I dreamed about last night." Speaking of panting, thank God he didn't know the details. Did he? "But you haven't bothered to tell me your name." She almost winced at the aggrieved tone—not to mention fairly irrelevant nature—of the question. It had been a bad night.

Plus, apparently, now she was possessed by evil spirits. Certainly that excused a reasonable amount of bitching.

"Liam," he said. "Liam Niall."

She mouthed it to herself, and the name danced over her tongue. "I thought Irish people had red hair."

"And here I thought only old people had blue hair."

She wrinkled her nose at him, just in case he hadn't noticed the ring through her nostril. "I've never been to Ireland. I've never been outside the burbs."

"And I haven't been back in ages." His lips quirked without much humor. "Truly, ages. So we have something else in common."

"No, really, we don't."

"Our demons, then."

She shot him a look intended to make him acknowledge how ridiculous that sounded.

He continued. "Your breathing is better. As the demon settles deeper, it erases evidence of your past life. On the plus side, that means your old aches and pains are healed."

She slammed on the brakes. His long strides carried him a few steps past before he turned to face her.

She forced the words out past gritted teeth. "What do you know about that?"

"You were injured somehow. That is always part of the vulnerability the demon marks in you."

He might have been able to guess at her old injury from the way her breath rattled, and maybe he'd noticed that she hadn't been able to move too fast for too long. But he couldn't have known when it stopped bothering her. Because she hadn't noticed herself until he mentioned it.

She took a breath, deep, all the way to the bottom of her lung, past the gnarl of scar tissue she'd seen in X-rays. Nothing. No wheeze, no rasp. She huffed out the breath. "What is happening to me?"

"The demon."

"Damn it. Stop saying that!"

"Will not saying it make it less true?"

She pushed by him—skin prickling with the awareness that he could stop her without even pulling out that hammer. He was so tall, but he'd moved like a dancer. A murderous dancer, sure. He was rangy too, the duster hanging from his broad shoulders as if he didn't eat quite enough. Lau-lau would tell her to make him sweet dumplings with duck and plum sauce. If the way to a man's heart was through his stomach, then he'd apparently closed off his heart a long time ago.

She yanked up her hood and kept walking, faster now. Because she could. And because, maybe, she was running away a little. She hadn't wanted to explain the strange dreams that had haunted her for most of a week now. Or she'd thought they were dreams—vague, edgy desires ignited by the briefest glimpse of a hot guy in the park while she'd been distracted with her job.

She knew better than to hook up with big, tough-looking males with the smell of iron and concrete and danger clinging close about them. Thanks to her family life, she'd learned how stupid *that* was before she was half Dee's age. Which didn't mean she hadn't indulged the occasional ridiculously trashy fantasy.

Who knew fantasies could come so violently to life? But now after what she'd seen, what she was feeling, to continue to deny that *something* was strange would be even crazier.

Ten minutes of silence brought them to the halfway house. A wire-caged porch light blazed above the front step of the narrow apartment building. Tonight, though, the bright lamp glowed with an odd nimbus, as if some oily smoke hung in the air. She sniffed suspiciously. But the lingering stench wasn't pot or even cigarettes.

"Sulfur," Liam said. "Leftover stains from the malice that have been hanging around here."

She recoiled. "More demons? Here?"

He held up one hand, meaning to be reassuring, she

knew. But the gesture revealed the haft of the hammer under his coat. "Your unbound demon has been trailing etheric energies that attract them. But don't feel too guilty. Some of them were probably already regulars. The kids might as well be tagged 'Malice eat for free.' I can feel the negative emotions leaking out of the bricks."

She bristled. "I'm surprised you feel anything through that superiority complex."

He gazed over the top of her head, unruffled. "Don't snarl at me. It's just the truth."

"How are they supposed to feel? Some of them have been abused or neglected. The ones that lie about it are just confused, trying to get their feet under them, trying to spread their wings. They don't need people like you judging them."

His calm expression smoothed into utter nothingness. "I only care about the consequences. And all these roiling emotions are prime breeding and feeding ground for the tenebraeternum—the eternal darkness. Doesn't matter if you don't want to hear it."

Jilly ground her teeth together. While she never thought she could keep the kids safe from every threat that faced them, she'd always believed she at least knew what the threats were. Gangs and drugs. Homelessness, lack of education, and early parenthood. Missed opportunities and bad choices.

But demons?

How could she protect them from *demons*? Real demons, not the metaphorical kind. Apparently, she hadn't even been able to protect herself.

She flexed her chilled fingers, wanting to reach into her pocket for the box cutter, knowing it was pointless. She glared up at the man beside her. "Okay, what do I do? How do I kill the ... the malice? How do you knock the head off an incorporeal being?"

That brought his aloof gaze back down to her. His lips twitched, finally giving his chiseled features a sign of life. "You can't. But don't worry about the house tonight. That whiff you're catching is the smell of drained malice.

My people have been keeping the block clean since we started looking for you. All that's left is the stink."

She nodded once stiffly. "Well, thanks, then."

He cocked his head. "That's hard for you to say, isn't it? I thought that's one of the first things you should teach a kid, how to say 'thank you.' And 'please.'"

The way his tone dropped half an octave sent a flush through her. She glowered. Dee would have pegged that as a come-on. But come-on or criticism, she wasn't interested. Never mind the eerie sense of familiarity that kept her measuring his body against hers.

She cared only about the kids. If Andre had faced those real demons, they needed her more than ever. "Will the monsters come back here?" She bit at her lip. "Will they follow me?"

"Maybe. If they do, we'll take care of it. There's a device we can install—an energy sink—that will lessen the negative vibes in the future."

She nodded, didn't even bother saying thanks again. He didn't seem influenced by her gratitude or lack thereof. He didn't seem affected by much of anything— a real tough guy. Remote and composed. The worry nibbled at her that she was going to owe him. Big-time.

She studied the building a moment, the front facade a checkerboard of small windows, some of them lit even this late. Or early, depending on which side of sleep she considered herself. Teens kept strange hours.

"You said your people brought Dee and Iz back here safely?"

"Yes."

She spun on her heel and stalked away.

After a few steps, he caught up with her. "You're not going in? You're just going to believe me?"

She grinned at the note of shock in his voice, glad to have thrown him off at least half a step. "Dee's room light is on. She's fanatical about her privacy, so I'm going to assume it's her and that Iz made it back with her." She cut a glance his way. "Unless I should think you're lying to me."

"We try not to lie. We have enough dings against our souls."

She stuffed her hands in her pockets. "Then there's nothing more I can do for them tonight. Except maybe bring down more monsters. I'm going home."

"It's a long walk. I'll call a ride."

She rocked to a halt. "You know where I live?"

"I did save you from certain death," he reminded her. As if that was an excuse for stalking.

Her indignation soon bled away. She supposed it *was* a damn good excuse.

She said nothing as he called from his cell. Within a minute, a dark sedan pulled up. Not a cab. "Your people again?"

He nodded and held open the door for her. She hesitated, but what was the point? She felt wrung out by the night's oddities and the sneaking realization that there were more dangers facing her than climbing into such a carefully nondescript car with such a strange man.

"You could have murdered me already, right, and left my body in the alley? I mean, if you'd wanted to. No one could have stopped you."

"Yes, I'm an unholy powerful fighter. No, I wouldn't have left your body anywhere. I'm unholy powerful but also surprisingly tidy."

She noticed he didn't disavow the murder part. She huffed out a long sigh and climbed into the backseat.

Liam settled beside Jilly, conscious of her heat near him in the closed space. And her scent. No perfume for the punette pixie, just the wet leather of her boots and the waft of some fruity hair gel when she pushed back her hood. And the faintest hint of something else, something wild. Something just her.

Too bad his teshuva protected him against even the simplest head cold. He didn't need to be distracted by sniffing after a temptation he knew he couldn't indulge.

He kept his knees tucked in, careful not to brush against her as he reached into his back pocket for his wallet. He pulled out a business card and handed it to her.

She looked down at the simple black card with its two lines of white text: a phone number and the symbol @1. "At one?"

"Atone," he corrected, running the implied letters into a single word. "Possessed humor."

"Dial the devil at 666-6666?"

He started to correct her because the number on the card was quite ordinary. Then he realized she was joking. As if he'd forgotten where he put it, he dredged up his sense of humor. "That phone number was taken already. I guess evil has a better business manager and marketing department than repentance."

Her piercing winked at him when she snorted.

On the quiet early-morning streets, the ride to her apartment didn't take long. They idled, double-parked in front of her building. He wished they could circle the block, keep her beside him. To keep her safe, he told himself.

"What does Andre look like?" he asked abruptly when she reached for the door handle.

She paused. "He's sixteen. About five-eight, one seventy. Black Latino. Shaved head. Homemade tattoo of a skull on his left calf. Last seen in a dark blue hoodie and jeans. I can get you a recent photo."

He wondered whether she kept an updated description of every kid in her charge so close to the tip of her tongue. How many did she lose? And how could she be willing to suffer the heartache of not saving them? "If I promise to have my people keep an eye out for him, will you not go looking again?"

She considered long enough that he figured she was going to tell him the truth. "Not tonight."

"Fair enough." The demon would ascend soon and she'd be too busy to worry about one missing teen.

Soon she'd be lost herself.

He studied her. "You know we're not likely to find anything good."

"If you find anything at all, at least we'll know. Which is more than we often get." Her expression was shuttered as she stared out the window at her door.

"You're already getting better at controlling your emotions." He tried to sound approving. "You'll need it."

She slanted a glance at him, so full of rage his breath caught. A hint of violet flickered in her eyes, as if the aurora borealis had drifted too far south. The demon, coming out to play. "Yay, me."

"I'll let you know what we learn. And if you need anything, anything at all, call that number," he added, knowing she wouldn't.

She crumpled the business card in her fist. "Sure." She jolted out of the car and stomped to the door.

Liam watched her go. "She couldn't be sweet and easy, like Sera?"

Archer slung his arm over the front seat. "You must be talking about a different Sera."

They both winced as Jilly let herself inside and slammed the door, never looking back.

"I suppose it's unreasonable to expect a demon to possess a nice person," Archer continued. "Even angelic forces aren't really interested in nice people."

"The battle between good and evil does seem to call for a certain fortitude of spirit," Liam agreed.

"You think?"

They waited in silence a moment.

"Did Ecco get surveillance set up in her apartment?" Liam asked.

"Energy sink. ESF recorder. Audio. He wanted video. Sera nixed it. Said the bad ol' boys' club would have to rent their porn just like regular nonpossessed assholes."

Liam sighed. "Why do I get the feeling that adding another female possessed is like peeking through the underwater view port on the *Titanic*?"

"Ice is all you'll be peeking at." Archer smirked at him. "So you're ready to acknowledge that you want her?"

Want. That one word zinged through Liam like a bullet off bone, leaving a jagged wake. "What does want have to do with being talyan?" His voice sounded harsher than he intended. The teshuva couldn't risk wanting—not when wanting dovetailed so closely with sin. With an effort that tightened his throat, he modulated his tone. "She's another fighter. We need those. Desperately. I'll find someone to help her through possession."

He believed in all his men, valued each of them for their unique abilities. But this job . . . He folded his hands together, interlaced fingers over tautly strung tendons. "You could do it."

Archer recoiled. "No. I found the other half that fits my broken pieces. And she'd break me into dust if I let anything come between us."

"For the good of the league—"

Archer's eyes flashed violet and his voice thrummed with the double-octave lows of demon harmonics. "Not for the world itself."

"Ah, right. How could I forget?" Liam subsided. His grip eased. "I'll find someone."

"Idiot," Archer muttered.

Liam let himself out of the car. The instinctive violence of Archer's reaction just went to show why the league's leader couldn't get so involved. A leader had to keep perspective, which would be impossible if he got too close. Too close to anything, or anyone.

"Where are you going?" Archer rolled down the window and leaned out. "I thought you'd stay through the night, pining hopelessly outside her window, too self-sacrificing to make your move, too entangled to walk away."

Liam shot him a withering glance. "It's not a romance, jackass. It's death and damnation and doom, remember?"

Archer slapped the flat of his hand on the steering wheel. "Exactly."

They stared at each other for a minute.

"I'm going to find a feralis and tear it apart," Liam offered conversationally.

"Have a lovely evening." Archer settled back in his seat. "Bring me a nice cup of tea when you can't stay away any longer."

Liam stalked away, neck stiff to stop his gaze from lingering where Jilly had gone. There was no one he trusted more than Archer to keep anything dangerous from making its way through her door.

Anything dangerous. Like Liam himself.

Chapter 4

In the bright light of the new day, everything looked . . . strange. The breath-stealing low temps hardened the outlines of the buildings against the sky until the city gleamed like a razor stropped to a killing edge. Over the rims of her sunglasses, Jilly studied the street for signs of idling dark sedans, lurking monsters, and tall duster-clad men bearing war hammers. So far, nada, which actually made the day even more surreal.

After one last glance around, she let herself into the halfway house. She spiked her windblown hair into place as she came to attention just inside the office door stenciled DAN ENVERS, ADMINISTRATOR.

The man behind the desk leaned back in his chair. "Jilly." He drew the two syllables out slowly. "You shouldn't come back here. It's confusing for the children."

Flatly, she said, "It's confusing because there was no reason to fire me."

"Budget cuts—"

"Oh, please. I didn't make shit for wages." She rolled her eyes when he frowned at her cursing. "I don't do this for the money."

"Now you don't do it at all." He tapped the eraser of his pencil against the desk, as if to rub her out. "I let you do the park outreach as a volunteer, but I can't have you traipsing in here—"

"I came to make sure Dee and Iz are all right."

The pencil stilled in his hand. "Why wouldn't they be?"

"If you don't know, maybe you shouldn't have fired me."

He rummaged across his desk and freed a sheet of paper. "Roll call says they're both at breakfast."

A filament of the steel in her spine softened. Liam had kept his word about getting the kids back safe.

So what else had he been truthful about last night?

She shot a reinforcing burst of concrete around the spine steel. "Iz was right. Andre got into some bad trouble." She hesitated, trying not to remember the burgeoning helplessness she'd felt in the alley, worse even than when Envers had handed over her walking papers. "I saw something last night—something weird I can't explain."

Envers lowered his head into his hands, the pencil stuck up between his fingers like a rude gesture. "You aren't supposed to encourage the children in their mass delusions. *Look* at you. You're as bad as they are."

She gripped the doorframe, anger driving her blue-polished nails into the wood. "Is that why you got rid of me?"

Staring down, he seemed to be addressing the papers more than her. "Do you know how many kids we lose? And don't count Andre, since he'd already gotten himself kicked out."

The question rocked her back on her heels. "Too many."

He tossed the pencil at her, glowering when she didn't duck and he missed anyway. "You don't even know actual numbers, because you just deal with the next one, and the next one. You have no idea what it takes to keep this facility operational."

"It's not a facility. It's a home, the only home these kids have, and it may not be safe anymore."

"Safer than the streets, that's for damn sure. Ask Andre. If you ever find him."

He tugged at his shirtsleeves, collecting himself. "This isn't your job anymore, Jilly. Go find some other oppressed people to save."

She could follow the sweet tang of pancakes and fake maple syrup to the dining room, get her cell phone back from Dee. But they'd have questions she couldn't answer.

"Security knows the situation," Envers said. "Don't make me call them."

"I don't make anybody do anything. That's your trip, not mine."

"The children need someone willing to use her authority, somebody who doesn't get in even more trouble than they do, not another rebel without a chance. We're done here, Jilly." He made a note on the paper in front of him, dismissing her like she was just another item to be checked off his list.

As if pretending something didn't exist made it go away. God, she'd always hated that sort of bullshit. She took another deliberate step forward. His head snapped up at the thunk of her boots.

"Maybe I don't keep all the stats like you do." She remembered Liam's promise and echoed it with her voice pitched low. "But since I have all this free time, I'll find out what happened to Andre, and I'll be sure to let you know if he would've had a chance."

The weight of his stare followed her out.

She stalked down the street, fists thrust into her pockets. Just as well she hadn't tried to go in last night with Liam watching if Envers had told the night crew to toss her out on her ass. What a coward to assign the task to someone else.

"A real man does his own dirty work," she muttered.

"Yet the women still get to clean up after."

Jilly whirled to face a slender blond woman in a scarlet trench coat. Her squared stance, light on the balls of her feet, screamed confidence louder than the coat.

She held up her hands, palms out. "Hi, Jilly. I'm Sera. Not too long ago, I was like you. Feeling cut off from everyone, just lost my job, didn't think I'd ever recover from that wound." Her hazel eyes darkened. "Or the ones that had come before. And now I'm possessed by a demon. Like you. Liam sent me to reassure you that you're not crazy."

Jilly tried to absorb the awkward introduction, then decided to just skip it. "I knew I was being tailed."

The woman—Sera—tilted her head. "Following the boss's orders."

"Your boss. Since you're possessed by a demon, that would be the devil?"

"Ah, no. That would be Liam."

"Who is apparently not one of those real men who does his own dirty work."

Sera sucked a breath of air between her teeth. "He seemed to think another woman would be better able to answer your questions. As if there's a gentle way to tell you your soul is forfeit to the never-ending battle against evil."

Jilly pulled off her sunglasses to squint at the woman. "Battle *against* evil? I thought having a demon would make me evil."

Sera planted her hands on her hips. "Didn't Liam at least explain the repentant part?"

Jilly snorted. "The goo dripping off his hammer must've distracted me."

"Okay, then, do you *feel* evil?"

Jilly pictured Envers standing up to the monsters in the alley last night. "A little."

Sera grinned, a bright flash that edged her from confident to confidante. "Oh well, that's why you're repenting. C'mon. We need doughnuts. It's my treat."

Jilly dug in her heels. "It's my ass. And I don't need more of it."

Sera shook her head. "Since Liam didn't get to any of the good stuff, I'll enlighten you. A demon-revved metabolism means you can eat all the doughnuts you like. And, anyway, your ass belongs to the league now."

"I hate being railroaded," Jilly said.

Despite the chill, they sat outside the doughnut shop, clutching their coffee cups. A dozen pigeons strutted around the table.

"Shanghaied would be more accurate," Sera said.

Jilly had put her sunglasses back on, but she hoped the other woman could feel her glare. "Was that a cultural slur?"

"'Railroad' implies a nice straight track going from point A to point B in a timely manner. Joining the fight of repentant demons against the darkness—the tenebraeternum—is more like being shanghaied. You're blindsided one night and wake up on a ship where no one knows your language, bound for God knows where." Sera waved one hand. "The analogy works pretty well." She looked at Jilly. "Except now *you're* here."

Jilly swallowed her bite of doughnut so she wouldn't choke on the powdered sugar, then let out a long-suffering sigh. "Explain. You know you want to."

"Shanghaied sailors were all male. They were stronger, of course, more resistant to the horrors of shipboard slavery. Plus, there was that whole 'women on board are a curse' wankery. I was the first female talya in the league's memory. And since the talyan are immortal, living memory is a long time. My appearance marked a change in the teshuva battle plan. Your possession marks an acceleration in that change."

"I don't have time to save the world." Jilly knew how absurd that sounded even as the words popped out.

"You're immortal now, remember?" Sera's hazel gaze softened. "What else is there?"

Jilly tried to forget Envers's mockery. But he was right. "I was busting my butt just to keep a few dozen kids from falling prey to everyday evils like getting caught rolling a joint in the school bathroom. Yet, half the time, they'd disappear from the system and I'd never find out what happened to them."

"And now you're not even doing that." Though Sera's voice was gentle, the blow of her words knocked Jilly's breath back down her throat in a hard knot. "Our world falls away, bit by bit. I haven't figured out if the presence of the unbound demon stalking us makes that happen, or if that's what makes us vulnerable to possession."

Vulnerable. How she hated that word. Jilly washed it down with a pull off the bitter chicory coffee.

Sera threw a few pieces of doughnut toward the pigeons. But a blur of black wings descended from the wind-torn awning and they scattered. The crow gobbled up the treat and cocked its head to eye them.

"You shouldn't feed wild animals," Jilly said. "Gives them ideas."

"So very true." Sera tossed the crow another piece with a smile. "But it's good to make friends where you find them."

If the crow was a friend, Jilly thought, this league of theirs needed better networking skills. "If you people . . . you demons . . . What are you?"

"We are called talyan," Sera said patiently. "Human, but possessed by teshuva demons which lend us their immortality and their unworldly powers to fight. And survive the fighting."

"Immortality," Jilly mused. "Here I was, always telling the kids not to think they were immortal."

"You told them that because thinking otherwise would get them into bad trouble. Which, turns out, was even more true than you knew. The immortality, the speed and strength of inhuman fighting skills, the recovery from heinous injury, all that is just a consolation prize the demon offers while we fight eternally for redemption."

"Right." Jilly drew out the word to emphasize her skepticism. "If you win this never-ending battle against evil, does that mean no more monsters?"

Sera tilted her head thoughtfully. "That's the hope."

"Hope." That sounded a little too much like vulnerable to Jilly.

Sera must have heard the note of reservation. "It'll get you through the next few days."

"I thought the battle was never-ending-ish."

"But in the next few days, your demon will make its virgin ascension. It's a particularly hazardous time for the newly possessed. Until you balance the demonic emanations within you, you could be pulled to the other side."

"To hell."

Sera's open face settled into a stillness that would've done Mona Lisa proud. "It has a strange attraction, but you wouldn't want to live there."

Jilly stared at her.

"Long story. But speaking of places to live, I'd really like to bring you to the league HQ, introduce you to some of the guys, let you pick out a . . . room." An incongruous touch of red brightened Sera's pale cheeks.

Jilly frowned. "What do I need a room for?"

Sera cleared her throat. "Since you're one of us now—"

"Whoa. Just because I'm intrigued by the idea of ending the threat to my kids doesn't mean I'm enlisting with any demon army or whatever."

"You may not survive without the league." Sera spun her coffee cup in her hands, gaze fixed on the dark slosh. "Not without a talya lover as escort." She raised her head, and under the hazy sky, her eyes sparked with a faint violet light. "Not without Liam."

The name and that uncanny glow made Jilly feel sheathed in strangeness. She pushed to her feet, slowly. The gust of blood through her muscles worried her that if she moved too fast, she might inadvertently upend the table, dumping doughnuts, steaming coffee, and a heaping pile of invective over the other woman.

She tried to tamp down the wild rush, unnerved by the reckless thrill triggered by that one word. "He is not my lover."

"Not yet, but that's how you'll balance the ascension."

"Not ever, if that's why he came after me." The unexpected—unwanted—wave of longing knotted within her. But the pain was preferable to surrender. "I've had enough of pimps."

Sera tsked. "Unfair. But I've read your dossier, and that pimp stopped after merely sticking a knife between your ribs. What's coming is far worse, far more intimate, and will leave you with your soul—not just your lung—in tatters."

Jilly fisted her hands, as if Sera had feinted at her, though the other woman made no effort to rise. "You don't know anything about me." Despite the tension in her body from frustrated desire, her fuming breath moved easily through her for the first time in more than a year, and she wondered, did she even know herself anymore?

Sera fanned her fingertips along the edge of the table, the only betrayal of her own tension. "The league has entirely too many tough guys, Jilly. If you have to lower those impressive defenses of yours long enough to let one of our fighters save you, then by God—should I say, by the demon possessing you—that's what you are going to do."

If Liam thought he'd sent Sera to be sympathetic, Jilly decided she'd have to disabuse him of that notion. "Whatever info you've been collecting on me, at the very least you should know I don't back down from vague threats."

"Sometimes vague is all we get. But I do know that one of those talyan saved me from something awful. And I'm not just talking about demons."

"What could be worse?" Jilly muttered. But she already knew some of the answers, though she couldn't picture tall, blond, self-confident Sera ever making the sorts of bad decisions where demonic possession looked like a self-improvement project. The uncertainty kept Jilly on her feet, but she didn't walk away.

Sera must have sensed her victory, but she didn't gloat. She stood in a rush of red, startling the crow into the sky. "It's not all bad. Repenting, I mean. You get a place to stay. A mission to last the rest of your potentially very long life. And there are other perks." She ducked her head and gave Jilly a sidelong glance.

"Nothing else about lovers," Jilly warned. Bad enough that her breath caught with the vague claustrophobia of sharing her skin with a demon. Sharing it with a daunting male like Liam Niall . . .

"No, no." Sera's gaze wavered. "I was just thinking, maybe I get a sister in a houseful of men."

The genuine wistfulness snagged at Jilly's resistance, though pain flared as quickly behind it. "I make a terrible sister." She ignored the flicker of disappointment over Sera's face; if the other woman had read her file, she'd understand. "I only want to find out what happened to Andre. So show me this league of evil-undoers."

They fell into step and headed uptown. The crow wheeled once against the white clouds and was gone.

The lantern tipped. Flames raced across the straw. A glint of steel, and his temple exploded with a flash of light across his eye. Then darkness. Endless darkness.

And pounding.

Liam jackknifed up and shoved away the entangling bedcovers. The darkness and pounding endured, but at least he was awake. He touched his temple and winced at the flicker of demon violet that illuminated his shaking fingers.

"What?" He winced again when the word came out as a roar.

The pounding at the door stopped. "Sera called. She found Jilly and is bringing her in."

Liam rolled out of bed and pushed aside the blackout curtains over the windows. The stark sunlight narrowed his eyes but brought no warmth to his naked flesh. "I'll be out in a minute."

"You've got ten." Archer's voice was brisk. "Use it. I

can smell your nightmare through the door. You'll scare her off before she's even gone through the teshuva's ascension."

"Insolent bastard," Liam muttered.

"I can hear through doors too."

Liam waved his upright middle finger vigorously, though Archer was stomping away. Liam dropped back to the bed. He'd avoided going back to Jilly's apartment last night, knowing Archer was keeping watch. So he had no excuse not to have managed a good night's sleep.

No excuse except those dreams that always ended in flames and darkness.

He pounded his head once into the pillow and stared up at the ornate headboard above him. Entire graveyards boasted fewer chubby, cavorting cherubs than this oak behemoth. He couldn't imagine what the woodworker had been thinking. It would be impossible to have sex in this bed.

Yeah, that could be the other excuse for no good night's sleep.

In five minutes, he'd run a cold shower, downed a cup of burned coffee, and ensconced himself behind his desk.

After the league's last refuge had been poisoned in the tenebrae attack, they'd retreated to one of their holdings fronted by an architectural-salvage warehouse. The warehouse lacked the style of their previous retro hotel, but it had a kitchen, a few apartments, a dormitory, and an armory. If there was one thing the league did well, it was break things and pick up the pieces. The three-legged walnut desk he'd propped up on a knock-off Grecian urn at least had a certain presence. Anyway, it was big.

He gripped the thick edge and waited for Sera's knock. She entered and stopped just inside the door, while Jilly marched up to the other side of his desk and tossed her puffy silver coat on the guest chair.

She planted her hands on her hips, which puffed up other parts of her. Under her snug short-sleeved T-shirt, the roundness of her breasts seemed counterintuitively soft. He found himself distracted by the butterfly tattoo that rode the upper curve revealed by the V neckline, the navy cotton setting off her anger-flushed tawny skin.

"What the fuck?" she snapped.

Good thing it was a big desk. He slanted a glance at Sera, who grinned and sidled out.

He returned his attention to Jilly and wondered if the oak headboard would have blocked more of the fury that vibrated off her. No. No thinking of Jilly in his bed. "Which part is fucked?"

She glared at him, and for a moment he was mesmerized by the golden snap in her eyes, the tint of flames in straw.

"If you wanted to recruit me, sell me yourself." She faltered, as if that hadn't come out as she intended. "You knew I'd come, given the chance to find out what's happening to the kids on the street. You didn't have to send Sera."

"She had the best chance of convincing you."

"And do you always use people for what they can do for you?"

He steeled himself against the sting of her words. He was spread too thin to regret delegating when necessary. Not when he knew that strain would bring him one step closer to a break the league might not survive.

Not when her burning eyes were the straw to break the beast of burden.

"I save myself for the fun parts," he said coolly. "I'm sure Sera explained what we're up against."

"She explained a lot." Jilly set her chin off-kilter, as if she was holding back words. "What are we doing to chase these monsters—what did you call them?—these tenebraeternum off the streets?"

" 'We'?" Liam leaned back in his chair and templed his fingers. He waited for the flare of triumph at bringing another tyro aboard. God knew, he needed this ardent young fighter in front of him. Instead, her fierce zeal

made him feel older than the dirt that crept into every
nook of the league's salvaged stronghold.

And his need would never be assuaged.

"The tenebraeternum is the place where the demons
come from," he said. As if reciting the chronicles of league
history would relieve the ache that arrowed through
him. "The lesser demons en masse we call the horde-
tenebrae."

She wrinkled her nose at the impromptu lesson. "Sera
already made it clear I might not even survive my demon's ascension. If I only have another hour or another
day, then I want to find out what happened to Andre and
make sure the things and the place never bother any of
the kids again."

She paced in front of his desk, all impetuous curves
and spiky nerves. He tightened his jaw against the clomp
of her impatient boots. She wasn't much more disci-
plined than the kids—streetwise teen hooligans, more
like—she claimed as her own. But he'd bent wilder spirits to this unending task. "I can't promise that."

"I don't believe in promises anyway. Give me something real I can sink my teeth into." She swung to face
him, her hand cocked on the hip of her low-riding jeans.
"Give me something bigger than that stupid box cutter
and I'm your warrior woman. For tonight anyway."

He felt the tightening in his muscles, the prickle of
his skin, as the demon in him stirred at the unruly battle cry in her words. He wrestled down its ready and
willing mayhem, so in tune with the young woman before him. The demon possessing him might take hungry
leaps toward repentance, but every swing of his war
hammer thrust him away from the desperate detach-
ment keeping what was left of his soul—what was
him—intact.

Once, he'd worked with his hands to create; now he
was half ravager. And the molten gold of Jilly's eyes
only lured him closer to his doom, like a stupid moth to
singeing flame.

"Come on, then." He thrust to his feet and strode past her.

"Where are we going?"

"I'm giving you what you want." Avoiding the jumble of iron railings, reclaimed brick, and unique old tile, he led her through the halls. The stairs down to the basement were hung with empty picture frames, too opulent to hang above any couch and too battered for a museum. At the bottom of the stairs, he slapped his palm over a pale green lit square. When it beeped at him, he threw open the double doors. The lights brightened automatically.

Axes, double-edged swords, daggers, razor-tipped gauntlets, and more lined the sterile white walls. Even under the buzzing fluorescent fixture, the blades shone with brutal, honed beauty.

Jilly cleared her throat. "At least I know where to arm myself if World War Three breaks out."

"It already has." Liam strode into the room, then turned to survey her. He tried to keep his gaze critical as he swept her once from blue-streaked locks to heavy black shit-kicker boots. "Good weight on the bottom, at least."

She stiffened at his perusal. "You saying my ass is big?"

It took all his unholy strength to move his gaze onward. "I'm saying, no sense throwing off your balance with an oversized weapon."

"I've handled bigger weapons than yours."

Her bold words rebounded between them. The first hint of uncertainty he'd seen in her—even when she faced the ferales in the alley with nothing more than a dull razor blade—flushed her cheeks with color, and she bit her lip.

The hunger that stirred in him at the slight vulnerability had nothing to do with the demon. He swallowed hard against it, and leveled his tone coolly. "No doubt your bravado has served you well. Did the demon come to you with the promise that now you'd finally be able to carry through with all that bluster?"

She stiffened at the question; her cinnamon-honey eyes narrowed.

"The demon always makes an offer we haven't the strength to refuse," he explained. "It knows us better than we know ourselves. I suppose that is the nature of temptation." How fortunate for him that he'd been around long enough to amass scars of resistance.

"I'm tempted," she said, "to grab that spiked mace and take a swing."

He forced himself to focus on work. Pairing an un-proven talya with the right weapon was vital. "If you want to try it out—"

"Just on you."

Ah. He balanced on the balls of his feet as the demon shifted eagerly within him. "Always happy to help my tyros, my new fighters."

"Yours?" When she wrinkled her nose, the piercing there glimmered.

Oh, so the ancient military term didn't bother her, just the implicit hierarchy. He crossed his arms over his chest. "I am the boss."

Her hands clenched as if longing to wrap around that mace handle. Or maybe just his neck. "If you're the boss, you should know human resources regulations don't al-low you to ask how people were lured to the dark side."

"You're not a human resource anymore, and techni-cally, we're the repenting side, which is at least a half dozen steps from the dark side." Thinking of her hands on his skin wasn't helping his focus at all. But how had the demon cozened her if not through her boldness?

He took a long step back—physically and mentally—and swept out one hand. "Choose."

In his many years commanding the league, he'd learned a new talya's choice of weapon indicated some-thing about the man and the teshuva inside him. He was getting ahead of himself, putting Jilly through his tests so soon, but the urgency that had ridden him since the appearance of her unbound demon strengthened when she was near.

And with her hell-bent attitude, he suspected she might need all the weapons she could get.

He held himself silent and still though every muscle twitched to follow as she stalked past him to circle the room. She paused near the mace, slanted a molten glance at him, and kept moving.

She passed the white-men-can't-jump wall of massive, double-handed swords representing a wide, bloody swath of European history. The aesthetically organized Asian collection of katanas and throwing stars earned not even a second look. Instead she came around again to the blunt-force-trauma corner. "No guns? No rocket launchers?"

"Rocket launchers tend to get noticed. We try not to be. More important, our teshuva need to get up close and personal with the tenebrae to destroy them."

"I tracked down my sister's pimp about a year ago, trying to find out where she'd gone. He stabbed me." She put her hand against her left side, just under her breast. "Punctured a lung. Nicked my heart. But you already knew that—didn't you?—from the dossier your people put together. Did it tell you that, even coughing up blood, I managed to knock out a few of his teeth?"

Liam pursed his lips. "So you're saying you don't need a mace."

The protective cup of her hand slid around to settle on her hip again. "I'm saying I don't need a mace."

He wanted to argue in favor of the mace, full Kevlar—never mind that body armor interfered with the draining of demonic emanations, which was the sole reason for their immortal existence—hell, throw in a popemobile too. After all, the ferales had sniffed her out for some nefarious reason. And she was the one who'd asked for a weapon.

Ah, of course. He'd dealt with some angry, violent men in his time with the league, but nary a one as prickly as Jilly. She needed a weapon—she might even want one—but she wouldn't want to need his. Or *him*.

Understanding didn't blunt the poke of annoyance at her rejection. Just what he needed: yet another fiercely temperamental, insubordinate diva to go with the others—female and male—he already had. The teshuva seemed inexplicably drawn to the type, himself excluded, which often made him wonder how he had ever become their leader. Despite her rebellious independence, she'd come back to him. He would make her see she needed his protection.

And yet, he couldn't quite curtail a pang of reluctant respect. Like all incoming talyan, she had to be confused and scared, but unlike some tyros he'd dealt with, she hadn't collapsed in a catatonic trance, overwhelmed by the teshuva's energies. Instead, he suspected her teshuva was going to have its hands full reining her in. Much as he himself would.

Refusing to indulge the image of his hands full of her, he gave a deliberately casual shrug. "When you change your mind about the weapon . . ."

"I'll be sure to let you know."

He withheld a snort. She'd voluntarily admit to anything that smacked of weakness only after a snowball survived August in Chicago. Which was even less promising than its chances in hell.

She marched out of the weapons room but paused as he closed the door. "Sera said I'd meet the rest of the crew."

He hesitated, picturing the predatory interest of his wayward, womanless fighters. "Later. They're recovering from last night's battles." When she opened her mouth to protest, he added sharply, "You'll be one of them soon enough."

From the defiant flicker of violet in her eyes—obvious in the basement gloom—he thought soon might come even sooner. Instead of stopping at the main floor, he continued up, their steps clanging on the steel treads, until they reached the roof. He shoved open the access door to a swirl of frigid March air.

Thin clouds blanked the sun into a matte white disk that leached the dimensions from the surrounding industrial district. The gray-walled buildings looked flat as cardboard cutouts. Even the graffiti, unreadable at this distance, assuming it was ever readable, had dulled.

The wind rattled Jilly's blue-spiked hair but couldn't bend it. "King of all you survey, hmm?"

"Not even a knight," he demurred. "I want you to see what we're fighting for."

"We'll be hailed as conquering heroes, no doubt."

He shook his head. This part of the test was always hard for the tyros to swallow. "No one besides us will ever know. Demons stalk the Magnificent Mile as often as the South Side, but the battleground doesn't matter."

"Not so different from my day job. I did three-quarters of my work on the street anyway. And just like those horde-tenebrae, the kids are half invisible to most people. Hell, most people didn't even see *me*."

Did she truly understand, or was this more of her bravado? Against the bleak landscape, her bright hair and warm skin tones gleamed. "They'd see plenty more hell if not for us." He curled his fingers into fists to stop himself from reaching out to her and tilted his face to the sky. "Unfortunately, this is as close as you'll get to heaven."

She pivoted to face him. The wind bit through his shirt and he knew she must be equally chilled, but she stood without shivering. Though the top of her head didn't even reach his shoulder, she sized herself against him with a long, slow look even more deliberate than the one he'd given her. Was it his imagination, or did she linger over places a good repentant demon should make him forget?

She breathed out a soft noise that left him no indication which way she had judged him. "This close, huh? And I haven't even been properly damned yet."

She took a step forward, tilting her head as if to get another perspective.

He tightened his hands into fists at his side, not against the cold, but against a rising heat that seemed to spark off those spiced eyes. "You will be. Soon." Obviously some demon was at work that she would tease him so.

"We have hours before nightfall," she said. "Hours before I can meet your fighters. Or my demon. So let's go. Show me something to make me believe I have a better chance if I join you."

And that latent demon in her apparently still had power to call to him, because he—who of all the talyan should know better than to give in to temptation—followed her.

CHAPTER 5

Jilly tried not to feel him like a shadow at her back, dark and silent, down the stairs. She wasn't ready for whatever he had to show her, even if, as Sera implied, she now had supernatural fighting skills to rival her old superfriends', but she'd be damned—again, apparently—if she let him know that. They retrieved their coats from his office and headed out to the street.

Despite her purposeful stride, in one long step he moved up to pace her. "I told you we'd look into Andre's disappearance. We discovered his last general whereabouts." Liam steered her down the sidewalk. His big hand cradled her elbow, the old-fashioned gesture so instinctive she wondered if the women he favored had trouble walking on their own. "He had a favorite corner. You already knew he was dealing solvo."

She lifted her arm out of his reach. "He was kicked out of the halfway house because of it. You said solvo has been connected to some bad shit."

"Soullessness," he reminded her. "Yeah, that's about the worst." He ran his fingers through his hair, then drew one lock forward around the tattoo that spread from his temple, not quite hiding it, but enough that a passerby wouldn't notice anything strange. Just a tall, lean man with eyes that had seen too much.

She recognized that look. She stuffed her hands in her pockets, although it was harder to bury the unwelcome rush of sympathy. "How can a drug steal your soul? I mean, other than the metaphorical soul stealing."

"Not steal, in this case. Dissolve. Gone forever." When they crossed the street, he passed behind her, edging her with the bulk of his body to the inner part of the sidewalk. "It's a djinni weapon."

"Djinni?"

"In the hierarchy of malevolent forces, the djinn rank among the most treacherous. The malice are clever but weak; the ferales strong but dim. Djinn are smart, strong, and unstoppable. And they possess humans just like the repentant teshuva. Only the djinn aren't sorry for any of it."

"Humans possessed by evil incarnate?" She shook her head. "That's no more shocking than repentance incarnate, I suppose."

His gaze weighed on her, heavier than his hand. "You don't have to pretend this is easy."

What were her other choices again? "Would ignoring what's right before my eyes be easier?"

The faintest dimple appeared in one cheek as he gave her a lopsided smile. "That's what most people believe. Of course, if you were most people, you wouldn't be here with me now."

She couldn't decipher from his tone if he was pleased or pained at her presence.

Once clear of the sparsely traveled warehouses, they caught a cab across town. The backseat of a sedan had never seemed so confining. As he maneuvered the long length of his thighs, he took up his legroom and half of hers. Pressed against her door, she avoided the open flap of his duster, but she couldn't escape her awareness of him. Even in stillness, big hands resting on his knees, he radiated a compelling force. More than the heat of his rangy body that seemed to lull the tension in her muscles, beyond the unique male scent of him that teased her with a hint of woodsmoke and heather, his aura of effortless dominion captured her focus despite her very best intentions not to be awed. The demon, or the man? She hoped it was the demon, as unwise as that sounded, because entrapment by a demon seemed more forgivable than being drawn to a man who broke all her private rules: too big to throw out, too tough to care, or too hard to forget.

Determinedly, she turned her gaze out the window to the mounting evidence of gang tags, broken windows, and junker cars. "What are we doing this far out? None of the kids come here."

"You wanted to know what happened to Andre. Well, he wasn't dealing in that alley anymore. He lost it a while ago."

The news stabbed her, deeper than Rico's knife had ever gone. "Lost it?"

Liam lowered his voice. "His soul. A lot of them from this side of town end up here. There are a half dozen places around the city where they congregate."

She tried to picture herself turning to steel, hard as a knife. Hard as Liam seemed to her. "Have you actually found Andre?"

"No, but we've been keeping track of these soulless clusters. We've had some trouble with them recently." He snorted softly to himself. "The kind of trouble where they almost destroyed the world."

Probably too much to hope that he was exaggerating.

He directed the cabdriver down a street of brick bungalows with identical short walkways leading up to identical small stoops. Decades ago, Jilly knew, the homes had been respectably working-class. Maybe in another decade, gentrification would creep in. For now, the black security bars over the picture-frame windows dulled the daylight like half-shuttered eyes.

"Stop here." Liam handed money over the seat. "I don't suppose you'd wait." When the driver merely looked at him, Liam shrugged.

Jilly stepped out onto the sidewalk and glanced both

ways as the cab pulled away. With the trees bare and the grass dormant—as if the first hints of spring had zero luck making the faintest inroads here—even the fretful wind made no impression on the empty street. "It's dead."

"The soulless don't die, as far as we can tell. It's quite the spiritual quandary. Not to mention a logistical nightmare for the league."

"I can tell you're really broken up about it." She crossed her arms against her chest. Pissed, she told herself, not nervous.

He lifted his head to stare past her, and the lock of hair pulled toward his temple shifted to reveal the stark swirls of the tattoo. "I don't have the luxury to feel bad, Jilly."

"Then you might as well be sucking down solvo yourself."

"Sometimes I feel like I am."

He squared his shoulders. The duster around his lean body hung as motionless as the rest of the dead street, as if the wind itself couldn't touch him, he was so alone. A twinge of regret at her sharpness had her reaching out to touch his arm, to distract him from his introspection. Sure, she made it a point to flout authority figures, but she had to admit, as far as overbearing petty dictators went, he had a hell of an excuse. Literally.

Which reminded her abruptly that his long coat remained unmoved by the wind because of the weight of the hammer in his freaking pocket. The hammer he used to bash off the heads of monsters. Without flinching. Monsters of the same sort as himself—and her.

She should probably keep her weak, pointless—oh, and not to mention *false*—reassurances to herself.

So she let her hand drop.

He moved on, unaware of her almost blunder. "This way."

Around the corner was another short stretch of bungalows. As they walked, he said, "Here's the short, boring version. For millennia, the tenebrae have been satisfied with wreaking their petty, and sometimes not so petty, havoc on the world. But four months ago, a djinni broke ranks and decided to tear open the barrier that divides the human realm from the demon realm. It would have been hell on earth.

"But the djinni's machinations freed a powerful demon that then possessed Sera. With its unusual powers, she and Archer were able to kill the djinn-man and close the rift in the Veil. But we paid a high price."

He gestured for her to walk ahead to a line of stubby concrete pillars that marked the entrance to a park.

Jilly paused between the pillars. "I don't see what— Oh."

A small crowd of people had gathered in the park, but they stood so motionless, they almost vanished against the background of barren trees.

Liam's hands flexed at his sides, though he didn't reach for the hammer. "The surviving remnants of a djinni army. Archer calls them haints, says they remind him of stories from his Southern childhood."

An army of young and old, male and female, all in a variety of skin tones and clothing styles. For the most part they stood, although a few sat at the picnic tables and benches and one perched on a swing, all of them facing in different directions.

"They're waiting," Jilly blurted out. "I can almost . . . hear it—no, feel it—on my skin."

Liam slanted a glance at her. "Yes. The question is, waiting for what?"

"Whatever will make them whole again." She shuddered at the waves of pining that flooded the park like an inaudible rock power ballad for zombies. "God, it's worse than the kids at *their* worst."

"Then there's that whole destroying-the-world thing I mentioned." Liam propped his hip against the concrete blocks. Despite the casual stance, his taut wariness prickled at her nerves. "They've lost their focus along with their djinni controller, but we haven't found the source of the solvo, so more and more of these are forming. It's only been a few months, and in their passivity they tend not to accumulate too much damage. I dread the day one of them takes a fatal wound, ends up in an ER . . . and continues to live, bloodless and rotting."

She wrapped her arms around herself. "Can't you do anything for them?"

He lifted one eyebrow. "Because in your line of work you know how easy it is to get help for the dispossessed." When she scowled, he rubbed his temple and sighed. "I'm *possessed*, Jilly, not a miracle worker. The league destroys. We have no doctors or priests, and we can't go outside our ranks. The world can't help us. It never could, even before we were possessed."

She stiffened. "Speak for yourself. I was helping."

"Ask Andre," he shot back. Then he closed his eyes. "That was unnecessary."

"That was asshole," she snapped. "Just because I couldn't save them all doesn't mean I wouldn't try to save one." Never mind that most of them passed through her hands without leaving a mark. At least not one that anyone could see.

"You can't help these," Liam said. "There's nothing left to save."

She knew he was right. The emptiness in the crowded park threatened to swallow her. And she would never let that sort of collective despair consume her again. She'd worked too hard to fight her way free from her family's dysfunction to fall in with a tough guy from a bad crowd. The ring in her nostril had been a sharp-pointed reminder to herself—one she looked at every day—not to be led again.

She took a shuddering breath, the old knife wound gone seemingly only to make way for fresh pain. "So why are we here?"

"To show you."

"You're doing a lot of that." She glared at him. "You're not showing me. You're testing me."

"If you're going to collapse on me, I'd as soon know it now."

She challenged him. "Do I look like I'm going to collapse on you?"

He inclined his head in silence.

She stalked out into the crowd. He followed without protesting, although he opened his coat, leaving easy access to the hammer.

Nothing moved besides the two of them. At the far end of the park, she came to the chain-link fence that marked the boundaries. On the other side, traffic whisked past, oblivious. "I didn't see Andre. Maybe . . ." She couldn't continue.

Liam's tone was neutral. "He might not be here, not yet, but all solvo addicts come to this in the end. The haints are lost to everyone, even themselves. Jilly, you can't save this one."

She curled her fingers through the chain link. "Then what's the point of these demons inside us? Why did it tell me I could finally . . . ?" The wire bit deep as she tightened her fists.

He went still beside her. "You could what?"

She slanted a glance at him. The deep blue of his eyes was all the more intense for his stillness, though the restless wind had finally reached him. It ruffled his shaggy hair, covering and uncovering the stark black lines around his temple. "Nothing. Never mind. Who listens to the promises of a devil?"

Besides the obvious—them—of course.

She slammed away from the fence. "You'd think I'd know better than to listen to sweet lies. Even if—especially if—the lie comes along with a bribe."

From stillness to a blur of motion, he spun on his heel and grabbed her arm. "The teshuva gave you a gift?"

She tried to wrench free, but his grip was unbreakable. "Now don't you feel bad about not offering at least paid sick days?"

"You won't get sick," he growled. "You'll just get dead. What was the bribe? A stone? In a pendant?"

His intensity unnerved her, so unlike the habitual reserve that carried him above her even more than his height did. She shook her head. "A bracelet. Woven metallic."

He pushed back her jacket sleeve. "Where is it? You didn't lose it, did you? Are you wearing it?" His grasp scalded her flesh.

As if he had the right to handle her. Oh, she knew how that went. She'd watched her mother submit, over and over, until cowering looked more natural than standing upright. She'd made the same mistake once—only once. This time, she summoned a furious strength and shoved him hard enough to make him stagger. "Get your hands off me. Don't you ever . . ." To her horror, her eyes prickled with hot tears.

He took a long step back. With his height, that step carried him a ways. He raked his fingers through his hair. "My fault. Don't reach for your demon." The tattoo beside his eye seemed blacker than black. "I'm sorry."

She gathered herself, wrapping layers of anger around the hurt as she'd learned to long ago. "Sorry because I won't let you push me around." She hardly recognized her own voice, harsh with the anger and still trembling with the hurt. The twist of the two made her chest ache more than the negligible twinge of her wrist from having yanked away.

"That push is the demon," he said.

"Mine? Or yours?" She refused to look away when his gaze snapped up to her. "You are not so in command as I thought."

He straightened. Not in threat, she realized, but as if she'd caught him out. His fists clenched, then fell open, empty. "And that was little enough indeed." The Irish lilt was stronger for just those words.

They stared at each other a moment. Finally, he added, "The battle isn't what it was, Jilly, and I am struggling to keep ahead of the changing tide, lest we all be washed away. The bracelet may be a relic from the tenebraeternum. It may be a weapon we can use."

"You said the solvo was a demon weapon too. Seems like demon weapons are a bad thing."

He hesitated. "Could be. But as you've noted, we're not entirely good ourselves."

"My demon might've mentioned the weapon part if it wanted to be helpful." She manacled her wrist over the memory of cool metal and Liam's urgent grasp. She didn't have to forgive him; she was possessed by a demon, not an angel, after all. And even before he told her about demonic energy sinks, she'd known how to lock away her feelings.

Keeping her voice level, she said, "I found the bracelet after the . . . after the demon came to me. I thought it was just a weird dream. I hadn't been sleeping well, and I thought maybe one of the kids had hidden it in my bag as a going-away present after I got fired. Or . . . I don't know what I thought. Lau-lau said it was a good-luck charm. I just put it in my jewelry box before I went to meet up with Iz and Dee and forgot about it."

He settled back on his heels. "Who is Lau-lau?"

"My landlady. She lives downstairs from me." She shot him an arch glance. "When I moved in, she asked me to call her grandmother in Chinese. She can't possibly be a demon."

He didn't respond. "We need that bracelet."

"We?"

"You. The league. It's all one now, Jilly."

She stiffened. "Is it?" So much for their little détente.

A violet light glimmered in his eyes. "That's what the demon promised you, isn't it? You'd finally get the chance to save those little hooligans, get to be the hero no one else wanted to be. That's why you let it into you."

The words knifed through her, so similar to her old boss's taunt. *Rebel without a chance*, Envers had called her. "Do not mock me." To her shock, her voice held a strange timbre, low and menacing, as if someone behind her—someone way bigger—repeated her warning.

Liam held up both hands. "We're getting carried away. Stand down your demon. And stop riling mine."

Her skin prickled like static electricity, and she wondered if her hair was standing on end. "I don't even know what the hell I'm doing."

"Yes, yes, hell. And thank you for actually admitting you don't know. You'd be very proud of one of your kids for saying that."

"Are you trying to start a fight?"

"Part of me is, apparently. Damn it."

"Yes, yes, damn you," she parroted snidely.

Abruptly, he smiled. The flash of white teeth startled her. "If I do or if I don't. So I might as well."

Hands clasped behind his back, he leaned over and kissed her.

Jilly sensed the incoming kiss, felt the pressure wave of the electric current spike the moment before he moved, so her skin flushed with warning heat. And she didn't step back.

She'd wondered, of course, how his kiss would be. No woman with breath wouldn't wonder. She hadn't thought she'd indulge her curiosity, though, since she was a woman who knew stupid as well as sexy, and while Liam Niall was definitely sexy, kissing him was definitely stupid—especially since he was far too calculating for his own good, or for her own bad, as the case might be.

And then he slanted his mouth over hers and the wild circle of her thoughts flew apart.

Warm. Soft. And as fleeting as his smile.

The sigh of his breath was gone before she caught more than a whiff of that elusive scent, heather and woodsmoke. Her own breath hitched in her chest, as if he'd taken something from her, more frightening than the knife that had pierced and slid from her body with such ease.

He lifted his head and gazed down at her. She realized her hands were fisted in the front of his coat, not flattened to push him away, but tangled tight to draw him closer. In the dark blue of his eyes, she caught a glimpse of bewilderment as profound as her own. Where had the steady, reserved leader gone?

She drew in a deep lungful of bracing chill. "What was that?"

"A kiss, last I checked." He paused. "Although I admit it has been a while." With one finger, he touched his lower lip, just a glancing caress, as if he was double- and triple-checking.

That hinted uncertainty sent another wave of heat coursing through her. "Why?"

"Leading a gang of immortal demon slayers doesn't leave a lot of time for deep, meaningful relationships."

She glared at him for his purposeful obtuseness. "Why did you kiss me?"

"Because you are a beautiful, startling woman."

She clenched her fist.

She didn't swing, but he reached out and caught her hand. He pressed her white knuckles against the rough canvas of his coat. "And right there would be the more pragmatic reason. Your rising demon was making you unmanageable."

"And you managed me." She kept her voice level. "With a kiss."

His gaze narrowed warily. "Yes?"

So the practical leader had done the expedient thing. She gritted her teeth until her jaw popped. "Is that how you always inspire your troops?"

He shifted his grip higher, so the callused pad of his thumb brushed the pulse in her wrist. "Only the ones that kiss me back."

With all her strength and some that didn't belong to her, she powered through his gently imprisoning fist and knocked him back a step.

His eyes widened with surprise. But he recovered quickly and pivoted behind her. His duster wrapped around her when he drew her close.

"Don't summon it again," he murmured in her ear. "Who knows what we'd have to do next time?"

She held herself taut against the hard plane of his chest. "Is that a hammer in your pocket, or are you just glad to see me?"

His soft laughter warmed her cheek and still made her shiver. "Yes."

Something coiled deep in her, and it wasn't any demon. A demon would be easy to banish in comparison. "Let me go."

"Are you going to attack again?"

"If I say yes, are you going to kiss me again?"

He opened his embrace and stepped back. "Just say no."

Her lips tingled. Her whole body tingled. But that was the hard part about temptation, wasn't it? Saying no.

Still, he was right that the sudden attraction had been a distraction. She looked away from him and froze. They'd distracted everyone, apparently.

"Uh, Liam? We seem to have an audience."

He whirled, putting her against the fence behind him. After a heartbeat, he relaxed marginally. "They don't seem inclined to attack. Unlike some others I could mention."

The haints hadn't moved from their positions around the park, but their heads had swiveled, several looking so hard over their shoulders that their necks appeared broken, to face Liam and Jilly. Despite their new alignment, their expressions were still uniformly slack, eyes as blank as the windows in the neighborhood.

Jilly huffed out a breath and stepped away from Liam. "Okay, that's just creepy."

As if an unheard voice had moved among them, whispering, "Nothing to see here," the watchers slowly returned to their neutral stances facing in random directions.

"Like somebody cut their strings again," Liam murmured. "But what plucked at them to begin with?"

He glanced speculatively at Jilly, but she backed farther away. "Nuh-uh. I told you, no more testing."

"Something about you tweaked them."

"Me?" She wished she hadn't squeaked the word.

"I've been through this crowd a half dozen times and they never twitched."

"Well, aren't you special?"

"No, but you must be."

"My mama would be so proud." She'd meant it as a joke, but she choked on the bitterness that welled up instead. "I want to get out of here."

He nodded. "We need to retrieve that bracelet."

For all the distractions flying around, he hadn't forgotten what he'd really wanted. Of course not. She wasn't *that* much of a distraction, after all. The realization needled her. "Fine. I don't want a demon weapon laying around my apartment anyway." Other than herself, of course.

And from the unabated shiver of her skin, she wondered if she'd mind having the unfathomable demon weapon that was Liam Niall lying in her bed.

They crossed out of the park to the other side of the fence, where traffic and life continued, unwitting of the army in stasis among the trees.

Jilly glanced back as Liam waved down a taxi. She tugged her coat closer around her. "They're like Emperor Qin's thousands of terra-cotta warriors, waiting for the afterlife."

"Considering that more than one tyrant liked to take living victims as funerary accompaniments, I doubt what waited for them was heaven." When the taxi pulled over, Liam opened the door for her. "Dictators have a bad habit of draining resources to build their clay armies. The djinn-man who drained these haints came to the same bad end. Now we're left with the dust and debris."

Jilly deftly avoided his helping hand and slid in to the backseat. "Chinatown," she told the driver before scowling at Liam as he climbed in beside her. "How can you talk like that? They are people."

"Are they? Without souls?"

Jilly hushed him, inclining her head toward the front seat.

Liam shrugged. "No one believes all the crazy talk about souls. Right?"

The driver glanced in the rearview mirror. "I'm as infidel as they come."

Liam grinned at Jilly. "See?"

Jilly settled back. "You're very cavalier with other people's souls, lives, whatever."

"I've gotten used to it." But his grin faded, and he looked down at his hands, folded in his lap. She didn't think he was resigned at all.

Still, his regret didn't change the fact that—more brutal than any ancient emperor—he'd lead them all to destruction to achieve his ends.

They rode the rest of the way to her apartment in silence.

The old Sears Tower was a dramatic charcoal spike at the end of Wentworth Avenue, but Chinatown was oddly quiet, stuck between the business-lunch crowds and the evening go players, sipping tea while they flipped their black-and-white stones. No one stopped to peer into the import and herb shop on the ground floor under her apartment, despite the OPEN sign spelled out in orange neon in English and Mandarin.

Jilly lingered on the sidewalk. "Play it cool, okay? Better yet, just stand there and keep your mouth shut."

Liam finished paying and glanced back at her with a frown. "What do you—?"

"*Xiao*-Jilly!"

She turned, blocking Liam. "Hi, Lau-lau. How's business today?"

"Better, if you have brought me a shopper." The old woman sidestepped Jilly, keen black gaze roaming the length and breadth of him. "You don't feed him enough. Haven't I told you—"

Jilly closed her eyes and took a calming breath. "Duck and plum sauce. I know."

"It *is* almost suppertime," Liam pointed out, not helpfully.

Jilly tsked. "Too bad about those darn MSG headaches."

"No MSG in my cooking," Lau-lau broke in. "And I have soup on the stove. With dumplings."

Liam tagged behind her. "Dumplings sound good."

Jilly brought up the rear, staring daggers that no one noticed.

Or so she thought. When Lau-lau slipped behind the beaded bamboo curtain separating the back room, Liam pulled her close. "Your neighbor recognized something about the bracelet. I just want to hear what she knows and then we're gone."

Unreasonably, she was offended on her elderly neighbor's behalf. "Taste and run, huh? Nice. You really know how to treat the ladies." Not that she meant herself and that kiss.

Liam's expression was as smooth as the jade Buddha's belly next to her. "I just want to make sure she's not in any danger from whatever your demon brought along for the ride."

"And make sure that she's not a demon in disguise."

His lips quirked. "Oh, she's more frightening than any demon. She's a matchmaker." His gaze slipped past her and his smile widened as he stepped forward to take the laden tray from Lau-lau. He took a deep breath. "Ah. Egg flower soup and green tea. With lotus blossom?"

Lau-lau beamed. "Your senses are exquisite."

Jilly rolled her eyes at their flirting and pushed aside a display of corkscrew bamboo shoots on the counter to make room for the tray. She took her soup and a teacup and went to perch on a ceramic plant stool.

Liam cradled the small cup in his big hands. "I find I have a deepening appreciation for Far Eastern exotics." When Jilly choked on her scalding tea, he went on blandly, "Jilly tells me you liked the bracelet I gave her."

She set down her cup with a clatter. "You didn't—"

Liam glanced at her. His eyes were half lidded, but the warning clouds in the dark blue stopped her. "I didn't appreciate the nuances before, but I always knew it was perfect for you, sweetheart."

Lau-lau's glance shuffled between the two of them.

Jilly knew the only gossip to beat a charming romance was a bitter breakup. She eased back on her hard seat. "Well, *xiao-long*, at least you know when you need to make amends." She hoped her sideways glower told him the reparations would be steep indeed.

Lau-lau chuckled. "*Xiao-long?* Have you forgotten your Mandarin? Haven't I told you not to ignore your past?" She lowered her voice, as if Liam weren't right there. "I very much doubt he has a little dragon."

Jilly smiled sweetly and sipped her tea.

Liam cleared his throat. "Of course not. After all, you did tell Jilly the bracelet is good luck. And she sure needed it."

Lau-lau nodded. "True, true. And good luck for you too that she brought you to me for your little ... ailment. I have an infusion for that." She rose to poke through her herb cabinet. With each drawer she opened, another scent wafted into an invisible whirlwind of florid and dank that puckered Jilly's sinuses.

Over the scuttle of dried leaves and paper packets, Liam whispered, "This won't kill me, will it?"

"If not, maybe I will. 'Sweetheart'?"

"'Little dragon'?" he shot back.

She shrugged.

"Chinese knot work does more than bring good luck," Lau-lau said over her shoulder. "But confusing demons won't help your problem either."

Jilly and Liam locked glances.

"What kind of demons?" Jilly kept her voice as casual as when she asked one of her kids if they really thought getting double-digit piercings would help with their job hunts. And speaking of hunts, the stark pattern of Liam's marking blazed as he fixed the old woman with an intent stare. "Just bad demons?"

"All demons are bad." Lau-lau dumped the ingredients she'd collected into the hollow of a marble mortar. She tapped the matching pestle briskly against the bowl.

"But little-dragon syndrome is caused by poor circulation, not demons." She chuckled.

Jilly managed a weak echo. "Confusing demons. How quaint."

"In the old stories, demons get lost in the intertwined patterns of the knot and bother you no more." Lau-lau crushed the herbs, releasing a scent unlike any that had gone into the bowl. The faint musk evoked moonlight on rumpled bedsheets.

Jilly shook her head. She certainly didn't believe in that herbal crap.

Of course, she had to believe in demons now too. She held her breath until the leaf dust had settled. Or until her hormones had.

Lau-lau whisked around the counter and dumped the contents of the mortar into the remains of Liam's tea. "There. That'll put the snap back in your New Year dragon firecracker."

"Why, thank you, ma'am." He smiled, looking only slightly less green than the contents of the cup.

As Lau-lau cleared away the soup, Jilly smirked at Liam. "What are you waiting for? I thought talya fighters were immortal."

He peered doubtfully into his tea. "We don't die, but we can be killed."

She snorted. "Lau-lau has only been a person of interest in one poisoning."

"Oh. Well, then." He downed the tea in a gulp, then set down the cup.

A droplet lingered on the center of his bottom lip, and Jilly realized she was staring. Worse, she wanted to brush away that drop. She dropped her gaze guiltily and tucked her hands under her seat.

He huffed out a breath. "Not bad. Tastes like . . ."

She glanced up and caught the flicker of his smile. If he did that more often, smiled like he had a secret he wanted to share, she might actually be in some trouble here. "Tastes like what?"

"I'm not sure. Maybe you should take a sip."

"You finished it all."

He just looked at her.

Heat flashed through her, sudden and overpowering. Only Lau-lau's return kept her from leaping to her feet and . . . she wasn't sure. Even if the knot-work bracelet was capable of leading demons like hers astray, that still didn't explain the waywardness of her purely human response to the man sitting just out·of arm's reach.

Lau-lau glanced at his cup. "Good man. You don't fuck around."

Jilly swiveled on her seat to goggle at the old woman.

Liam inclined his head solemnly. "Ma'am, indeed I don't."

"Up you go, then." Lau-lau grinned at Jilly. "You can pay me later."

CHAPTER 6

They left the shop and climbed the steep, narrow stairs past Lau-lau's second-floor apartment to Jilly's garret loft on the third floor.

Liam hummed to himself as she unlocked the door. "A knot-work labyrinth. The Celts had similar stories in their mythology."

So the calm, cool, and collected commander wanted to ignore all the irrelevant stuff that had happened downstairs. How very calm, cool, and collected of him.

"Sacred path or trap," he continued, all professorial, "depends on what you find in the center."

God knew what happened in her center every time he turned that deep gaze on her. Butterflies, felt like. Butterflies couldn't be evil, could they?

She opened the door and stripped off her jacket. She paused, looking down the entry hall, past the cheap pine table with its collection of random papers and knick-knacks to the kitchen doorway and the living room visible at the far end. Lately, whenever she stood here, it seemed that the place should be different. She had changed so much over the last year.

The attack. Rico's subsequent trial and conviction. More recently, her firing. And now the demon.

"What's wrong?" Liam's hand was a solid, warm pressure between her shoulder blades. "Is something out of place?"

Besides her? For a weak moment, she was glad he stood there, a convenient focus for her confusion.

"I found the bracelet on the floor here. After I . . ." She turned back to the hallway table. She rummaged through the catchall bowl. The etched glass chimed with the discordant music of spare keys and loose change. "I tossed it in here somewhere. Ah."

She lifted the bracelet. The matte silvery metal was an intricate design of finer strands woven over and under each other, coming together and separating again, doubling back to form a flat cuff just wider than her two fingers when she held it aloft. The convoluted weave, glimmering between the strands, made her eyes ache.

"It needs polishing," she said.

"Nothing in this realm would touch it." He showed no inclination to, peering at it from a short distance. A flicker of violet deepened his blue eyes to a midnight storm. "Gangue—that's the waste rock around a mineral deposit—and fluorspar. See the shine? But it's a demon artifact, all right. The etheric mutation is strong enough that the base matter of it isn't even rooted in this world anymore."

She clenched her fist, and the edges of the bracelet bit into her palm. She wanted to drop it, punt kick it back to whence it came, along with the demon who'd presented it.

"I came home late after the homeless outreach at the park. That was the first time I saw you, wasn't it? I didn't remember until I saw you in the alley last night." She wasn't sure why she was telling him. Except who else could explain the beginning of this end she had come to?

He lifted one shoulder in a shrug. "We talyan have a knack for blending into the shadows. Occupational hazard."

"I think I was still furious that Envers had fired me and then been so kind as to 'let' me work the event.

Anyway, I went out for a drink after." She hesitated, then met his gaze levelly. "Maybe it was more than one drink. When I came home, you were here."

The violet flare in his eyes was unmistakable this time. "I wasn't."

"Yeah, I figured that out already. At the time, though, I wasn't thinking quite right. I wanted a fight. Or something. And then here was this guy, too skinny and sad looking to be scary."

He pursed his lips. "Definitely not me."

The violet highlights of the demon overlay in his eyes almost distracted her, but underneath, she caught a glimpse of the imaginary man in her apartment whose ass she'd hesitated to kick that night. What had the demon teased her with? A lie? Or some deeper truth?

She shook her head, not agreeing with him, but banishing the distracting thought. Whatever—whoever— was hiding under his duster and feral tattoo didn't matter; the clan chieftain he'd become would never let it out.

Probably best. For both of them.

She continued. "The thing pretending to be you gave me the bracelet."

Liam studied her as if he heard the reticence in her tone. "Just gave it to you."

"Sort of dropped it. After I punched you. It."

"Punched it. What happened to sad and skinny?"

"Well, there *was* a strange man in my apartment. And it was standing too close. And then its eyes turned creepy."

"Creepy?" Liam cut himself off and said between gritted teeth, "Can you just tell me what happened? In order?"

She huffed out a breath. "I came home from the bar. You—it was waiting for me. For some reason, I wasn't afraid."

"Back to the skinny and sad thing." He sounded irked.

"Am I telling this story? We talked for just a minute

about . . . nothing, really. Then it tried to kiss me. But its eyes turned all solid white with little black slashes." The remembered horror made her voice shake, and she cleared her throat. "Anyway, I took my comic books seriously as a kid and I know *that's* never going to end well. So I decked it. It dropped the bracelet, and the sound of metal hitting the floor woke me up."

"Or sobered you up, since you said you were drunk."

She tapped the bracelet against her leg in annoyance. "I said I had a few drinks. I wasn't drunk enough to black out or hallucinate."

"Just drunk enough to let it touch you."

Her thigh, where she'd flicked the bracelet, tingled. "That's how I was possessed? Because I wanted . . ." She swallowed the rest of the words. After all, it didn't matter what she'd wanted. *Whom* she'd wanted.

After a moment, he shook his head, his expression shuttered. "The demon had chosen you. Your possession was inescapable." His blue gaze pierced her, so unlike the eerie white of the demon's eyes that had finally snapped her from her daze. "What did you want, Jilly?"

She felt she could fall endlessly into that deep blue. Except he was a trap worse than any other, the kind where a girl could forget to fight her way free. "You said it didn't matter what I wanted. Maybe I'll give the parting gift back."

"Impossible. The only thing worse than your having it would be leaving it for something more evil to find."

"More evil than me. You sure know how to charm a girl." She slipped the bracelet over her wrist and backed away from him.

"The demon had time for that. I don't." He stalked after her, and the prickle that had started in her spread at the predatory intentness of his gaze, until every nerve seemed to stand at attention. She wondered if she'd have to attack him as she had his demon double. And if she'd have any better luck this time around.

He made no move to touch her, only circled around her to cast sidelong glances into the tiny galley kitchen, then the living room with its mass-produced Scandinavian furnishings.

She watched him narrowly. "Nothing so cool as your warehouse. And I only got the one piece of weird jewelry."

"I was just checking to see if the surveillance equipment was in place as I ordered."

She froze. "Excuse me?"

"You're obviously on the verge of your virgin ascension, and it will be enlightening to have the event on tape."

The short hairs on the back of her neck rippled. Fury, she recognized idly. Even the demon—an entity of pure, if repentant, evil—hadn't pissed her off so bad. "I am not a guinea pig."

"No. Presumably a demon wouldn't find much use for a guinea pig." He poked at the phone on the table beside the couch, then peered under the fringe of the lampshade. "Ah, there it is. Good." He swiveled on his heel and settled onto the couch. He flicked aside the hem of his duster and splayed the dark canvas across her generic but easy-to-clean upholstered cushions.

She narrowed her eyes. How easy to clean—now, *that* would be worth analyzing as she scrubbed his blood out. "I'm not going to transform before your eyes."

"You are already." Violet gleamed as he swept her with a glance. "I can see the dilation in your eyes, the capillary expansion flushing your skin." He took a long breath.

She shot up a hand before he told her what she smelled like. "That's annoyance you're seeing. Because I'm thinking about killing you."

"That would be the demon," he said patiently. "Jilly, we've all been through it, we talyan. Unlike Andre, you may still be saved. In that, at least, your demon didn't lie."

She walked slowly toward him. "And you're going to give me that chance, lead me out of danger?" Eyes half lidded, he watched her as she edged between his knees to stand over him. "You going to be my hero tonight?"

He angled his face up. She bent just a little at the knees.

And reached sideways to grab the lamp by its base. She hefted the ceramic over her head, and brought it smashing down on the table. The cheap lamp exploded, and the cheaper table crumpled under the blow. Impossibly, in the indirect light from the kitchen, she glimpsed the arcing flight of the tiny black transmitter.

Liam watched her with one eyebrow raised as she snagged it midair.

She crushed the transmitter. The sting of crystallized components biting into her palm stirred a sharp delight. "Well. Now we are alone."

Liam pursed his lips. "What will Lau-lau think?"

"That we're having mind-blowing sex. That is what we're going to do next, right?"

He stiffened. Not the part of him she was leering at, but the rest of him. "We were just getting information from her, not actual marital aids."

"You haven't kept pace with the times. You don't have to be married anymore to have sex. And you obviously haven't talked to Sera about the birds and the bees and the demons." She tossed the transmitter over her shoulder and started to turn away, bumping his knee aside.

He grabbed her wrist and—in a move she couldn't quite reconstruct in her head, although it had something to do with putting her over his knee—had her flat on her back on the couch. He loomed, pinning her arms above her head. "What do you mean? What haven't I been told?"

Oh sure, threaten to beat him to a pulp and he yawned. Imply that his troops weren't marching neatly in order and he snapped. She strained against his hold until her joints creaked. To no avail. Possibly that's why he yawned when threatened.

The bracelet pressed hard against her flesh. She relaxed, the better to lure him into a false sense of security. "I figured Sera hadn't actually told you how she and Archer made sure she survived the ascension of her demon. She seemed a little embarrassed to be pimping for the big daddy."

Liam scowled down at her, a deep V between his brows. "The veteran talya has to make sure the tyro isn't ripped apart in the tangle of intertwined demon and human energies. Ancient league texts detail a prescribed formula of meditations and purifications to mark the first ascension. But usually the two talyan go out drinking and fighting and that keeps the novice nailed down in this realm." He trailed off.

Jilly knew she shouldn't be enjoying his fumbling so much. "Yeah, go back and think about that nailed part."

He reared back, glaring at her.

She caught her breath, not at the fierce look, but at the grind of his thighs against hers. She wasn't in the best position to tease him.

Or, actually, she was in the perfect position to tease him, but she wasn't sure it was a good idea.

Or, more actually, she was perfectly sure it was a terrible idea, and yet . . .

She stared up at his aghast expression and started to wonder whom the joke was on. "Is it so hard to believe that a man and a woman facing possible destruction, not to mention evil at its core, would join up against it in the most intimate way? Or is it just that it wasn't your idea first?"

"I'd do whatever it takes to keep my men—my people—safe." He made it sound like a desperate prayer.

"Including step out of the way?" She lifted her hips, denim against denim hissing. "Or including this?"

He jumped off the couch so fast the breath whooshed back into her lung almost painfully. Maybe it was just the speed of his dismount that stung.

"I guess not that," she murmured to herself. So much for praying.

"This is demonic work indeed," he muttered darkly, even more to himself.

"Gee, thanks."

He stood staring at her, hands fisted at his sides. "I cannot—"

She refused to drop her gaze halfway and snicker like a silly teen, but thanks to the snug fit of his jeans, the problem was quite obviously not that he *couldn't*. "I don't mind drinking and fighting. Although I hear dying is out of my hands now."

The twist of agony on his face only made her more furious.

"Maybe we never had a chance after all." Her voice came out harsh, cracking into a second octave not her own.

Despite the implied violence—or maybe because of it—his expression finally calmed. "Perhaps not, but if I can save you, then I will."

She backpedaled on the couch. "Never mind. I wouldn't want to be a burden."

"No. You will be a league fighter. If you live." His jaw flexed. "So you will live."

Okay, knowing that he saw her as merely another tally on his checklist was even more insulting than being a big flapping albatross around her neck.

He advanced on her, gaze intent, and she scooted up against the arm of the couch. Her back rammed against the insufficient stuffing, wood hard against her spine. Every nerve ending tingled in anticipation.

He kept coming. She held up her hand, straight-arming him with her palm centered on his chest. The bracelet glinted dully in what light shone from the kitchen.

"I won't be letting this change take you from me." His voice rumbled through her hand, the touch of Irish brogue deepening.

"Maybe you won't have a chance to do anything else."

"Oh, I'll take it."

His heart thudded under her fingers until her pulse

sought to match itself to his, as if he would take her over
in place of the demon's ascension. Which was more of
a threat? Some crazy demonic possession when she'd
never particularly believed that hell was anything besides a human construction of bad choices? Or the
glimpse of heaven on earth she must be imagining in his
blue eyes?

And when exactly had her admittedly hazy concept
of heaven included a bad boy like this? Oh, right, when
her only chance at salvation lay in his big hands.

She curled her fingers into his shirt. The fine material
parted under her grasp, though she hadn't meant to be
rough. This wasn't her, playing power games with a man
who didn't know the meaning of play, unless it was play
for keeps.

Or playing with fire. Heat radiated through her, tracing down her arm. But it stopped at the bracelet, as if
she couldn't quite break through to him.

A chill washed back along her skin, creeping inward
until her vision dimmed.

"Jilly?"

His voice barely reached her, the tone warped as if
across a vast expanse. She tightened her numb fingers,
but the edges of herself seemed to blur. Like when the
knife had slipped free of her flesh, the blood had poured
out, and with it her life.

Like she was dying again.

"Jilly."

Liam pulled her close. The shock of his chest hard
against hers, with only her manacled wrist between
them, jolted her free of the threatening oblivion. Whatever distance she'd imagined was gone now.

"It's coming," he murmured.

One slow breath pressed her breasts against him. Her
desire swelled at the intimate contact. "Takes me more
than ten minutes." Maybe not, this time.

He frowned. "The demon."

"Oh. Right." She swallowed. "Is it too late to go
drinking?"

His gaze dipped to her mouth, so intense she felt it like a touch. "Much too late."

"Well, then." She wrapped her free arm around the back of his neck and pulled him down to her kiss.

Lips fused, hot and damp. She tasted Lau-lau's potion on his tongue, but her gasp brought her the richer, more subtle brew of aroused male.

Even as the blood rushed to his head, Liam told himself to keep his mind on the task at hand. So close to his hand. Where he gripped her upper arm, the curve of her breast brushed the backs of his fingers.

He struggled to rein in the flare of excitement. No, the only task was to shepherd her through the demon's ascension. If the task was achieved through more pleasurable means than was usual in his deadly line of work, that didn't change the urgency.

God, whom was he fooling? If anything, the urgency here was *more* deadly. His body tightened from the inside out—not the demon coiling, but just plain old human sin of the more primal sort—and he groaned against her mouth.

Though he closed his eyes, still she shimmered in front of him. Waves of ether pulsed in a chaotic pattern that set his heart hammering. He wanted to spread her beneath him and coax that trembling over the edge. He willed himself to go slowly, not rising to the lure of her need, though her fingers twining through his hair was goad enough to shatter him.

How long had it been? Did he trust himself to this task?

He lifted himself just enough to clear her lush lips. Her dusky skin was flushed from the force of the kiss, her golden eyes half lidded. He touched the corner of her swollen mouth. "I should not be the one for you."

"And yet you came up with no one else." She strained back as if to escape him.

The exposed column of her throat drew him down again to set his teeth none too gently against her pulse. He growled when she speared her fingers through his

hair and guided his head down. Down past the V neckline of her T-shirt.

The invitation was more irresistible than any temptation ever laid before him. He lifted the bottom of her
shirt even as she shoved back the lapels of his coat.
Their arms tangled briefly, and she gave him a flirty
upward glance and a breathy laugh that snagged his
heart.

When he paused, she tugged what was left of his shirt.
The fabric sighed apart, and then her palm was scalding
against his bare chest.

"Don't stop," she whispered. "It's all around us now.
Do you see it too? It's the end."

He saw nothing but her, the dip of her waist, the generous flare of her hips under stretch black denim and a
rivet-studded belt. "It's beginning."

He nudged her shirt up and groaned again at the ripe
flesh displayed in orange lace and wire. She arched her
back, not to escape this time, but to tempt, and draped
her arm over the back of the couch. The demon bracelet clunked against wood, a sullen reminder of why they
were there.

"Fuck that," he whispered harshly.

"Please do." Her smile was wicked and welcoming.

He pressed a kiss to the center of her cleavage, where
the fleeting wild scent of her hid like a secret only he'd
uncovered. Sweet skin and lotus and excitement. "God,
I love these new corsets." He skimmed his fingers along
the wire underneath each breast, the texture of the lace
tantalizing his fingertips. "All the beauty." His thumb
found the catch. "None of the laces."

With a single flick, her bounty was his.

The butterfly tattoo no bigger than a postage stamp
rode the upper curve of her left breast. A delicate thing,
its trailing wings outlined in the thinnest black lines,
the tattoo brought him up short. "Not a tiger," he murmured. "Or a dragon."

He brushed his thumb over the pale swell and she
shuddered. "It's just art, not a spirit guide."

"Actually, moths have often been associated with the spirits of the dead."

"What with me maybe dying and all, can we not talk about this now?"

He cupped the high handful of her, and his ring finger found the remnants of scar where the knife had gone. Rage flashed through him, a deep hatred that summoned the ravager demon within. The room blackened except for the point of his focus, and he realized he did not have anywhere near the control he fancied. "You could've died."

"If I had, we wouldn't be here." The tremble in her voice made him pause.

She didn't mean to state the obvious, he understood. She was asking him whether it would have been better to die. In the face of her vulnerability, having nothing to do with her nakedness, his demon quieted, and he foundered in the sudden loss of its bracing fury. "You couldn't save your sister, or yourself at that moment, but what you will become now may help us save the world."

From the flicker across her face, he knew he had not said the right thing. But it was only the truth, or the only truth he had anyway.

"That is all I can offer," he said softly to the unspoken disillusionment in her eyes.

"I guess that's more than I had before."

A gray shadow like encroaching ice rimed her gaze. He felt the chill on her skin. "No. Whatever sorrow started you down this path, you cannot return there. You strive forward or your soul is forfeit."

He flattened his hand in the small of her back and raised her up against him. Her dark nipples were a lure he could not resist. He skimmed off her shirt and loose bra in the same motion as he dipped his head so that her gasp of surprise filled his mouth with her warm flesh.

But she was no quiet lover to let him feast in peace. Her hands roamed from his shoulders to his flanks, her nails raising shivers from his bones.

When she fumbled down his fly, a chill of caution

swept in along with the breath of air on his cock. He lifted himself awkwardly on the angles of the couch to stare down at her.

She must have seen the hesitation in his eyes because she clamped her hands on his hips. "I won't let this thing take me to the dark place. I told myself I'd never let anyone do that to me again."

He wanted to smash all those unnamed anyones whose inflicted hurts had so toughened her. Regret that he was her only choice—her only chance—swept him. As league leader, he had failed her already. But he'd told her their only way out led forward. Outside, the day had faded, and in the gloom, her skin flushed with restless demon ethers he sensed more than saw. He had to channel that confusion of power until she could control it herself. He could give her that, at least. Then she'd be free of him, if not of her demon.

Deliberately echoing the pattern of her hands over his body, as if he could re-create the ancient meditations that had once guided the league possessed through ascension, he unbuckled her belt and slid the denim down the width of her hips, the generous arch of her backside.

Even the light dance of her hands threatened to unbalance him, so he slid free of her touch, dropping kisses along each inch he uncovered, from her navel, across the matching red and orange panties, down her thigh to her raised knee. She had barely finished fumbling with the laces on her big black boots when he yanked away the whole tangle of denim and lacy underwear and leather and fell back on her, afraid to let her go.

Because now he sensed it too, the yawning of the abyss, hell as close as it ever came, as her demon ascended and other-realm mists breathed around them.

He said it aloud, for anything listening. "I won't let you go."

"How will you get your pants off?"

"You started this."

Then his jeans were somewhere in the pile with hers.

His knees drove into the couch cushions, rocking her toward him as he centered himself between her thighs.

"Now," she said.

"No." He anchored her hips by the double handful. "Take it slow."

"Why?"

What to say? Because he needed a moment to remember how this went? He didn't want her to laugh. Because he feared no such chance would come to him again, and he wanted to savor every feeling? That thought revealed even more vulnerability than the first.

Rather than speak, he smoothed his erection over her cleft. That silenced her, and widened her eyes so the cinnamon-honey gleam eclipsed the creeping icy gray. When she gripped his shoulders, the force of her fingers drove muscle almost painfully against bone. He didn't mind. If only she could leave bruises to mark him forever.

He slid against her, down to cover her mouth with his. He tasted the lotus, sweet and innocuous, not the dream-inducing drug of legend. And yet somehow . . . He slid lower yet, his lips finding the puckered flesh of her nipple, then the taut quiver of her belly as she caught her breath, and then . . . Ah, there was the bloom he sought.

The dark flowering between her thighs was no sweet dream but a wild fantasy of silk curls and musk. She opened to him with a sigh that started as his name and ended as a hum of passion, and his entire body zinged with the force of shared pleasure between them, a ratcheting tension that threatened to destroy his hard-won equilibrium.

The hunger in him grew despite the attention he lavished on the core of her. This time, when her fingers raked his shoulders, urging him up, he did not resist but surged over her.

He paused with his cock at the ready. If Sera had explained about talya sex, Jilly already knew he carried no disease and could never give her children. She'd bear no consequences from this liaison.

Would he be able to say the same about himself?

Poised on the desperate, heedless edge of his oblivion, he struggled to remind himself of his mission. If he couldn't keep himself in hand, how could he hope to control the fierce and brutal talyan? If he found solace in her touch, how could he still expect those wounded souls under his command to fight on, eternally, without release?

The bone-dust winds of the demon realm coursed around them. Right. Death and damnation, just as he'd warned Archer.

He could not leave her to face that alone. For her sake, for the league, for the world itself. Ah, the sacrifice.

He buried himself in her with a hiss at the exquisite hot grasp of her flesh around him.

When he would have gathered her close, she held him at arm's length, palm braced against his chest. The bracelet fell to her elbow, and the dull metal gleamed at him. He took her hand and lifted it to his lips, pressing a kiss to the inside of her wrist where her pulse surged with frantic power.

Another kiss, then tongue, then his teeth nipping lightly at her flesh until, with a moan, she loosened her locked arm and let him closer.

Teasing, he withdrew, plunged himself in the heat of her again, and then again. She stared up at him, eyes wide open. He could not escape the coruscating whirl of violet and glazed gold as the demon and her climax rose within her.

He gritted his teeth against the urge to come. He was fucking immortal; he would wait. He would wait.

He flattened her hand against his chest again. Maybe better if she held him away. His pulse was a deafening hammer, and her fingers curled into his chest as if to hold it tight.

For a heartbeat, gold eclipsed the violet in her eyes. Then, in utter silence, she arched her back and came. The convulsion drew a gasping shout from him as he found his own release with a shuddering violence.

His vision grayed. Not the demon realm, just *la petite mort*. His strength failed him and he collapsed, half on her and half teetering off the edge of the couch.

Gradually, his breath evened.

"Erk," she said.

He grunted, his cheek nestled against her shoulder. From this angle, the shadows elongated the wings of the butterfly alighted on her breast, like the afterburner contrail of a fighter jet across the sky, but black instead of white.

Then he realized there was nothing to cast those curling shadows.

He sat up.

She dragged in a deep breath. "Thanks for the air."

He turned her gently to her side.

"Hey, air good, yes, but I'm not an inflatable toy here."

"No," he murmured. "Not a toy. A weapon."

The *reven* unfurled from below her left breast down across her rib cage to the point of her hip, and rose up to the butterfly tattoo. The lines spiraled off, confusing his eye, though he traced a fingertip along one path.

He tried to ignore the pain that unfolded through his chest as if in echo. "Welcome to the league of demon-possessed warriors, Jilly Chan."

CHAPTER 7

Jilly craned her neck to follow the course of his finger down the side of her breast where the knot of the knife scar had faded to a mere memory on her skin. "Insta-tattoo. Not temporary, I'm guessing." She shivered at the tangled memories of trickling blood and now her new boss's erotic touch. God, it was all fading. Her scars that reminded her of bad choices, her courage, and—oh yeah—her very *life*. She scooted away and snatched up the T-shirt flung over the back of the couch.

Liam wiped a hand down his face. "The *reven* is the teshuva's mark on you. Once, the patterns told the league how strong and what sort of demon had crossed into our realm. I've read accounts from previous leaders who organized their ranks by teshuva class and power." A tick beside his eye jerked once. "I don't have enough talyan to give me choices."

She studied the mark at his temple. "What's yours? How strong is it?"

"Ravager class. And strong enough." He returned her narrowed, assessing gaze. "I don't need to check the archives on yours. Discord class, undoubtedly." She opened her mouth to protest, but he continued. "The *reven* shows you passed the first ascension, and the con-flicting emanations are balanced enough that you won't be pulled into the demon realm. Against your will anyway."

She frowned. "Why would I go willingly? As if this hasn't been bad enough." When his expression went blank, she winced inwardly. She hadn't meant that quite the way it sounded. But she didn't correct herself. Not like they were going anywhere with that anyway. Discord, right?

All these negative thoughts—blood, demons, the sad lack of long-term relationship potential despite her new immortality—were really taking the shine off her afterglow.

He pushed to his feet. "There is much about being talya that you don't know, that none of us know. Despite all Sera has apparently shared with you."

"You could share more," she pointed out. "Or have we shared enough for tonight?"

He gave her another unreadable look, then bent to collect his clothes.

She indulged a wistful mental sigh at the sight. Too lean by half, though the sensuous play of muscle under his skin made her fingers tingle. But she knew better now than to be tempted. Twice anyway.

Not only was he her new boss; he was her eternal boss. Meetings around the watercooler could get way complicated after a few hundred years of clandestine sex.

Or, considering the lamp, table, and transmitter she'd smashed, even more awkward after not-so-clandestine sex.

"What have I done?" she whispered as she tugged her shirt over her head.

In the dim lighting, Liam's gaze flickered toward violet. "What we had to do." He zipped his jeans with a touch more force than necessary. "It's how we survive long enough to erase some of the stain on our souls."

Here she was worrying about the mark on her skin when the fatal stain was on her soul. Silly her.

She wiggled into her jeans while Liam searched for

the scraps of his shirt. Sera had promised her a metabolic boost, but the jeans seemed snug as ever.

Letting the demon in her soul, then the demon-killer into her body. She was becoming quite the slut. She tried to dredge up a silver lining. At least she could kick some of the ass that so seriously needed kicking, now that she'd finally identified an appropriate target. That target being all of evil. And she was always telling the kids to set specific, realistic, and achievable goals.

She was fiercely glad they couldn't see her now. She'd always considered herself an outsider, and now continuing the fight from the shadows would have to satisfy her forever.

As for the satisfaction glowing through her body tonight . . . She steeled herself against the faint after-sex pang and pleasure. If Liam could stand there and glower in his shirt with a handful ripped out of the front, then she could cultivate a demon-slaying 'tude.

She cocked her hip to kick off her new look. "So now what?"

His hand scraped through his hair to reveal the mark at his temple. "Hell if I know." Then he seemed to realize he was losing his composure. "You survived the transformation, so we add you to the league register with your demon's subclass. Then I'd like to see what we can learn about that bracelet, so don't let it out of your sight. And you still haven't picked out a weapon."

She eyed him disbelievingly. "I'm possessed by a demon, and we're going to do paperwork?"

"Paper, rock, or scissors, I don't care what you use against the horde-tenebrae," he grumbled.

She blinked. "Ooh-kay. I gotta pee."

As she walked away, she swore she heard, "Well, that won't work against them."

The bracelet clanked against the porcelain when she gripped the sink and stared into the mirror. Did she see a glimmer of the demon in her own eyes? Nope, just a wink of light off her nose ring. She switched it out for a tiny sapphire stud to match her hair color. No sense getting her nostril ripped in some demon scuffle.

She slicked on some cherry lip balm and worked more gel into her hair. She doubted the spikes were much defense against anything either, but at least she felt a little taller. She needed to get her boots back on too.

When she returned to the living room, Liam stood staring out the window, a tumbler of water in his hand. The streetlamp outside, shining through raindrops on the glass, added spangles of light to his pensive face.

For God's sake, the man killed monsters for a living. Was being with her so terrible?

And why did she care what he thought?

Anger prickled through her, adding sharp edges to the room despite the low light. The lingering scent of sex prodded her temper even higher. This must be what Liam meant when he talked about the demon rising.

He glanced back at her. From the glint of violet in his eye, she knew he was responding to her simmering violence.

"Let's go, then," she prodded. Anything to get away from the scene of the crime.

He took a long drink of the water. She couldn't help but trace the line of his throat with her eyes. With the rain behind him, her overwrought senses tricked her with the feel of cool water in her own mouth. She swallowed hard to clear the sensation. She wasn't interested in living in his skin, no matter how good he had felt moving against her.

She'd seen how being wrapped in another person only led to both souls smothering. She could only imagine how much worse it was when the demon-pocked souls in question had all the structural integrity of a *Star Trek* spaceship at the forty-eight-minute commercial break.

In two separate bubbles of silence, they descended to the street.

To Jilly's relief, the herb shop was closed, and Lau-lau was nowhere in sight.

Liam stalked across the street toward a dark town

car. Jilly hung back as the window went down, but Liam seemed unsurprised.

The man inside studied them. "Lost the audio."

"Technical glitch," Liam said.

"ESF readings caught the spike. So she made the transition."

Jilly angled closer. "'She' is a badass demon-exterminating mama now, heading for another shopping spree in your weapons room, who hates being talked about like she's not here."

The man lifted one eyebrow. "But doesn't mind referring to herself in the third person."

After a moment, she grinned. "Presumptuousness is okay when I'm doing it. I'm Jilly."

His dark brown eyes glinted with amusement. "Archer. Sera's mate."

It was her turn to lift an eyebrow. "Mate."

"She's still working on a scientific term that doesn't make me want to smash something."

"I've heard compromise is the heart of any good relationship." She tried to sound encouraging.

He just shrugged. "She is my heart."

The flat finality of his voice—leaving no room for argument—set her back a step. To proclaim himself with such irrevocable simplicity . . . For a heartbeat, she thought she could hate Sera, and not just for her size-four ass.

Liam growled under his breath and opened the car door. "Come on."

She slid in and was relieved when he closed the door gently and went around to the front passenger seat. The town car was big, but not big enough. She wanted her space.

Liam hadn't said anything to her about mating.

She caught Archer's glance in the rearview mirror and focused her attention out the window. But she eavesdropped shamelessly as Liam made a half dozen calls organizing what sounded like a covert tactical sweep of the city's least loved neighborhoods.

"I'm not coming back before everyone heads out tonight," he was saying. "Send Jonah to check the data recorders at the haint clusters. The mass at Pickers Park had an odd moment this afternoon and I want to catch if they're tweaking on something we've missed." He paused, listening. "Just odd. If I knew why it was odd, I wouldn't have to send Jonah, now, would I?"

She snorted to herself. There was more to that story, but if he didn't want to explain the kiss, she'd never tell.

He closed the phone with a snap. "Drop us off at the Coil."

Archer's gaze snapped between them. "Little late to go the drinking route."

Archer knew, of course, Jilly realized. He'd gone through the same experience with Sera.

Fury pulsed off Liam in palpable waves. "It's never too late for a drink or a fight, and the Coil is always good for both."

His unfocused anger seemed to spill into Jilly's space, begging to be picked up and stoked high. She'd worked with enough wayward teens to recognize that pointless spiral, where no one could reach outside the shattered expectations and hurt. She wouldn't get trapped with him.

But she wondered how a man as strong and dedicated as the league's leader could subtly remind her of a lost and frightened child.

Then she steeled herself against the yearning to soothe his ire. Her mother had catered to a string of men like that; not a heritage Jilly was interested in perpetuating, especially with the eternity angle. He wasn't one of her unofficial wards; if anything, she was one of his. When Liam glanced over the seat back at her, she studied her nails as if the slightly ragged blue paint held the secrets of the universe.

He straightened in his seat with a muttered curse.

As she'd surmised, the Mortal Coil was a bar, but she hadn't thought it would be so trendy. Liam seemed more a pint-at-a-pub man than a vodka-martini-by-the-dance-floor boy.

The neighborhood around them was in flux, torn halfway between art gallery and pawnshop—one loft balcony was strung in delicate paper lanterns, while the one below had been tagged with an illegible scrawl of gang sign. The place seemed poised to pull itself out of the muck. Or collapse again and die.

Despite the sketchy surroundings and early hour, a line of shivering hipsters snaked halfway down the block. Archer stopped the car at the front of the line.

Liam stepped out and opened the door for her. She got out, felt the weight of stares on her less-than-red-carpet-ready self. Liam nodded to the bouncer, who returned the nod, and they slipped inside.

She glanced back as the neon and heat of the club enveloped them. "Does he know what you are? He can't have guessed you're anyone, not with the crappy cars you drive."

"The league's investments have seen better days," Liam admitted. "But his boss still likes to see me."

She persisted. "Does the boss know what you are?"

Liam hesitated. "She knows more than she lets on. About many things. Which is why I want to talk to her."

Though the stuffy darkness of the club was utterly different from the open chill of the park, Jilly was uncomfortably reminded of the soulless cluster by the way this crowd also stood in random array, absorbed in their drinks and the blue-green glow of their cell phones. She sheltered behind Liam's height and let the flare of his duster clear a path to the bar.

He wedged a hip between two patrons and made a place for her under his arm. She gritted her teeth at the casually possessive gesture and slipped in, since she wanted to hear the conversation.

Her gaze skipped over the two bullet-headed bartenders and went directly to the curvaceous woman whose red beehive was just a few shades off her red baby-doll tee, so that she seemed to vibrate at that end of the spectrum. Her eyes behind the cat's-eye glasses, however, were almost eerily devoid of color.

"She's blind," Liam murmured. "Don't let that fool you." He raised his voice. "Bella."

The woman took a few steps down the bar, overshot them, then edged back again. "Liam, darling. How good to see you." Her smile was sharp, bordering on cruel. "And who is this charming little thing with you tonight?"

Jilly shifted, wishing there was room to move out from under Liam's arm. She hated feeling petite. Almost as much as she hated feeling laughed at. "Hello, Bella." She resisted the urge to add "Lugosi." No self-respecting vampire would keep that hairdo. Maybe the woman couldn't see, but she was as blind as a vampire was vegan.

Liam dropped his hand to her shoulder as if he sensed the snark-attack coming on. "This is Jilly. I was hoping you'd have a minute to talk."

"Have you brought her for my blessing?" On the word "blessing," Bella's smile widened. "Or will you be busting up my bar like you do with your boys?"

"Just talk," Liam said.

Bella lifted her face as if to scan the room. "It's quiet for now. Let's go in back."

Considering the techno beat coming from the dance floor, it wasn't quiet at all even in the cramped storeroom. A spindly chair next to an overflowing ashtray was the only seat beside the cases of liquor bottles, and Bella settled herself there with a sigh.

She kicked off her Mary Janes. "Sorry for the stink, darlings, but my feet are killing me." She smiled at Liam, more coy this time. "Or are you here to tell me something even worse is coming?"

"I try to keep you in the loop. You've been good about the men blowing off steam here."

She reached unerringly for a pack of cigarettes and a lighter on the shelf behind her. "You always pay the damages, and your boys—even at *their* worst—tend to keep those even-worse things at bay." She tapped up a cigarette. "So what is it this time?"

"I'm hoping you can tell me. When I warned you to keep the solvo out of here, you'd already noticed there were . . ." He hesitated. "Untoward effects."

Her expression was shuttered. "You don't stay in this business long if you can't tell the difference between a drunk and a real danger. I knew solvo was no good-time club drug."

"You've been keeping track of the addicts. Jonah saw you at one of the clusters. Why?"

She pursed her lips, rouged yet another shade of red. "They interested me." When he waited, she shrugged. "I find them very peaceful. Like watching fish."

Jilly jerked once.

Bella angled toward her, the upswept corner of her glasses catching the light from the bare bulb hanging overhead. "You think that's sick?"

"You could *do* something instead of just feeding off them." Jilly bit off the rest of the words.

Bella turned back to Liam. "She is very new on your crew, isn't she? What do your boys think of your fresh meat?"

"It's not like that. Besides, the shine wears off quickly." He rubbed the mark at his temple as if, Jilly thought, he could feel her dagger glare. "I want to know if you've seen anything odd in the clusters lately."

Neither he nor Bella seemed to think his choice of "seen" was inappropriate. Jilly realized he was willing to make use of any resource, however weird—or *more* weird, she supposed—to pursue his mission.

Bella tilted back in the chair. "I haven't been out lately."

"Fish get boring," Jilly growled.

"After a while, you get the sense they might be a little more like waiting piranha. Then they do not seem so peaceful."

Liam perked up. "Piranha? Did you see—?"

"Nothing," Bella said. "Just an impression. But I

can tell you there's more solvo on the street now than ever. James tosses out at least one pusher a night, and if I eighty-sixed everyone at the bar who shows signs of having indulged . . ." She shook her head. "But you've never told me why it's so bad."

"I didn't have to tell you," he reminded her. She made a moue of displeasure, but he went on. "Just keep an eye out, okay, and get word to me if you get the heebie-jeebies."

Bella's smile returned, more calculating than ever. She flicked the lighter. "I've got your number, darling."

On their way back past the bar, she poured three different drinks, her hands picking deftly among the bottles. "On the house this time," she said as she tipped back her own glass and returned to her work, the cigarette behind her ear.

Liam and Jilly took their drinks and continued to an empty spot along the railing overlooking the dance floor.

Jilly looked into her glass and snorted. "Absinthe. How chic."

"Speaking of which, now that you're immortal, don't you think you're too old for blue hair?"

"Even if you're immortal, don't you think you're still too young to be such a drag?"

He took a draft from the pint of dark beer Bella had drawn him. "I'd look terrible with blue hair." The tip of his tongue caught the faint shimmer of foam on his upper lip.

She froze at the pang of lust that arrowed through her. Damn, how could she blame that errant sexual escapade on saving her life if she wanted a repeat performance now with no excuse? She downed her evilly green glowing drink in one swallow. The herbal astringent puckered her throat and she made a face.

Liam was watching her. "How are you feeling?"

"Better." When he raised an eyebrow, she realized that might've been a little insulting. She let it stand. "Why's Bella so odd?"

He gave her another look. "She who is possessed probably shouldn't throw stones."

"I'm not stoning her." Although the thought held a certain appeal. "Is she human?"

"As far as I can tell. I've been wondering if she'd serve as our new Bookkeeper." At her questioning sound, he explained, "The league has always had an outsider, not talya, who acts as historian and researcher and sometimes our last connection to the worldly realm. We've been without a Bookkeeper for some time now."

At his suddenly forbidding tone, Jilly asked, "Did the last one die?"

"Unfortunately, no." He didn't elaborate. "Bella guesses that we are something more than we seem. And she has hinted at connections that could be useful to the league, underground resources that keep us out of the everyday eye." He returned his attention to Jilly. "I hoped having you along would make her more comfortable about joining the crew, knowing there are other women." He scowled. "When I make Sera come here, she makes me dance."

Jilly smiled, picturing his lean self in a white leisure suit, busting a Travolta. Then her amusement faltered. "I bet you'd have fine luck with Bella if you came by yourself and offered her a place in your . . . league."

"No need to insinuate," he said. "Bad enough having female talyan, which at least has precedent if I'm willing to go back a few thousand years. A female Bookkeeper goes against our entire history."

"Your history is not your future. I tell—told the kids that all the time."

"I am not one of your naive runaways."

"No." Jilly pushed her glass away.

Liam stared into his beer, as if he might find answers there instead. "Still, you're right that what has worked before isn't working now. I'll do whatever I must to lead the league into these new dangers."

Into danger, she noted. Not out of. But she supposed that part hadn't changed. "Even if that means accepting the inevitable woman or two. How open-minded of you."

Violet flared across his eyes, more intense than the strobe of the club's pulsing lasers. "Our last Bookkeeper betrayed us and lost his soul and his mind in a very bad bargain. A friend of Sera's found a place for him among the angelic host. But he's alive simply because, without his soul, he can't die."

She let his anger wash over her. From experience, she knew better than to cut short the words now that he'd started.

Sure enough, he went on. "Sickeningly, I take some consolation in his predicament because at least he brought it on himself. The others, the talyan, *I* send out to their pain and destruction." His voice dropped, which only underscored the anguish rather than fed the anger. "They go out and suffer and die on *my* word."

She sat in silence with him for a minute. "As I understood it, they go out because it is their destiny, one they absorbed with the demon. Unless your demon double was there for all their possessions too?" She gave him a wry look.

After a moment, his lips quirked. "None of the men mentioned it."

"Then maybe you're assuming a little more guilt than is due you." She kept her tone neutral. "I'm sure you can lay claim to enough wickedness without that."

He finished the beer in a long gulp and thumped the glass down with extra force. "You are teasing me."

"I don't tease."

He swept her with a glance that shifted from violet to a smoldering blue. "No. I guess you didn't."

He was trying to distract her. The heat that traced over her skin sank deeper, into her bones, like a hook that drew her helplessly to him.

But she was not helpless. Hadn't been for a very long time. She refused to contemplate how the demon playing on that fear had gotten her here. Could a discord demon play at all, or would it be out of tune? The fleeting, irreverent thought gave her the impetus to lean along the railing and put her hand on his arm. The shock doubled back along her nerves, but his eyes widened. Good.

She met his gaze, dark not with the rising demon but with desire. The sparks between them snapped a little higher. Then she deliberately removed her hand, letting her fingers trail up his arm for a heartbeat. "I just wanted to remind you, Liam, sometimes it's not all about you charging in and taking command."

His eyes crinkled with sudden amusement. "I can hold back, let someone else go first." He wrapped his long fingers loosely around her elbow and reeled her closer. "Didn't I?"

The darkness of his long coat around his wide shoulders made a private space at the crowded rail. While she struggled to decide whether she was more annoyed by his male arrogance, insolent manhandling, or the fresh jolt of lust that shot through her, he said, "Now let's see what you can do."

She stared up at his mouth, remembering the graze of his lips on her skin. "Here?" The boss man was kinkier than she'd guessed.

"No horde-tenebrae here," he said. "We're done with our drinks. Next stop, draining a malice."

She jerked her gaze up to his eyes. He hadn't grabbed her arm just to continue their touchy-feely moment. He was studying the bracelet peeking out beneath the cuff of her jacket. The silvery metal seemed to absorb the light around it, deadening the air.

Yeah, it sucked all right. "The horde. Of course." The reason they were here. The reason he was here with her.

The memory of the headless feralis in the alley snuffed the embarrassed heat lingering in her cheeks as they left the club, Liam cutting a swath through the crowd. It would never occur to him to think of leading her on. He'd simply lead and expect her to follow.

And it was one thing to think about taking on a trio of ferales with a box cutter when she was in crisis-hero mode. It was something else to head out, stone-cold sober despite the wimpy absinthe, with the intent to slay demons.

They passed the bouncer with another man-to-man nod from Liam. Would she ever master that distant coolness? Or did one have to have a big, dangling . . . hammer to pull it off?

She stopped and turned on her heel to face the bouncer, her jacket only half zipped. "Bella mentioned you've had to toss some solvo dealers lately. You confiscate any fake IDs? I'm missing one of my halfway-homeboys."

The bouncer looked her over as he passed another couple into the bar. His gaze lingered a moment on the neckline of her T-shirt. Then he dug through his back pocket and brought out a fistful of IDs. "We hand 'em over to the police once a week."

She shuffled through the cards. "I don't see him. It was a long shot, but thanks." She handed back the plastic stack with a smile.

Liam fell into step beside her. "What was that about?"

"Those were some pretty half-assed fakes. Not a competent lamination in the bunch." When he lifted an eyebrow, she shrugged. "I worked with budding juvenile delinquents, remember? I know my fake IDs. I'm guessing bouncer boy tosses the wannabes and passes at least a few of the pros for a cut of their profits." She slanted a glance at Liam. "I wonder if Bella knows."

His brows drew together. "She knows how dangerous the *desolator numinis* chemical is."

Jilly gave him a look. "Anyway, now we have a line on the dealers we can follow."

"Follow to what?"

"To what got Andre, to the source of solvo. Or at least a step closer." At his deepening frown, she continued. "To get solvo off the streets."

"That's not our primary goal."

"To end evil—"

"We battle demons." He strode ahead, forcing her to hustle to keep up with his long stride.

"Solvo dealers *are* demons," she pointed out.

"Of the human kind. We're more literal minded."

"The definition of insanity is hoping for something different when you've been doing the same thing over and over for—"

"For eons. Since the dawn of man."

They passed below a broken streetlight. In the shadows, the edge of his jaw and cheekbone seemed harsher.

"Of man," she reiterated. "Not woman. You said female talyan just appeared on the scene."

"Reappeared," he said reluctantly. "We have old texts mentioning them. Just nothing recent. And by recent, I mean eons."

"You said you were willing to do anything. You even did me—"

He slammed to a halt. "You have no idea what you're talking about, what we're up against. Just like you never really knew what those kids were facing, even though you were out on the street every day. At least Sera had a degree, and she was just helping people die. What makes you think you're ready to fight the power if you don't know how to wield it?"

Each accusation snapped her like a whip, cutting deeper. She stumbled a step back, as if she could avoid his words. "If you think I'm so useless, why am I here at all?"

"Ask your demon. Oh, wait. You can't, since it's trapped inside you. You have no one to ask except me." He straightened to glare down at her. "And I'm telling you, all that fury you're beaming at me is about to bring down a world of hurt on both of us."

"What do you—?"

A malice boiled out of the alley, another up from the sewer grating in the gutter, still another down from the shattered light. A flood of oily black smoke swept around them at knee level. At the stench of rotting egg, tears poured from her eyes.

With a strangled curse, Liam grabbed her hand and leapt onto the roof of a battered sedan parked at the curb. They landed with a thump, and the peeling vinyl of the rooftop shifted under her boots. She kept hold of his coat and scrambled to right herself.

The malice milled for a moment, as if they'd lost the scent.

"I hate it when I'm so right," Liam murmured.

The malice swirled into a horizontal funnel cloud of blackness. The open maw stretched wide enough to encompass the car itself.

She clutched his coat tighter. "You said malice traveled in small flocks."

"And you said you wanted new." He shrugged under her grip. "Since when are you so clingy?"

"I'm looking for your hammer."

"*Xiao*-Jilly, now is really not the time."

She would gladly have knocked his head off. "A swing and a miss, you jerk. We're about to get massacred."

"No material weapon can stop them. We have to match our demonic emanations to theirs and siphon them off etherically, but I have never seen a mass formation like this. One by one, my ravager could overwhelm this lot in a night, maybe two, but all of them together . . ."

"There's something you can't do? Any other time, I'd be fascinated, really. But about plan B?"

"I'm hoping that will come to me in the next few seconds."

Then the maw, all obsidian razor claws and sparking crimson eyes, closed over them.

CHAPTER 8

Liam stared up through the inverted cone of whirling etheric dissonance. At the apex, the tiny circle of night sky seemed almost bright in comparison. And then it disappeared as the malice tornado tightened, with Jilly and himself at its center.

He let it all go. Anger. Fear. All feeling. Only danger remained.

And *he* was that danger.

He pulled Jilly close, away from the bristling smears of black smoke. She nestled into him, her hand fisted in the front of his shirt, but her eyes shone violet, and he knew she would not back down, no matter what.

That feeling—the feel of *her*, so heady and terrifying—he could not banish it even as he called his demon to the fore. "The malice are drawn to evil. So let's show them what demons can do."

Keeping Jilly against his chest, he reached out toward the funnel. After a moment, she followed suit, stretching her fingers to the other side. The woven metal strands of her bracelet shone with opalescent fire to his teshuva-altered vision.

Her fingers touched the spinning wall just as his did. The surge wrenched through his shoulder and rocked them both, but she steadied him, with her free arm tight around his waist, his knee braced between her thighs.

Their touch brought the engulfing tornado to a screeching halt. The shriek echoed through the immobile ranks of malice, the hint of dark wings, forked tails, and glittering points of eyes like a worn frieze of ancient evil.

Where the points of their fingers speared into opposite sides of the wall, black ooze dripped, as if they'd pierced a hole through to something much uglier than the vaguely animalistic malice.

Jilly slanted a glance up at him. "Now what?"

Despite the unusual pattern of their attack, the familiar malice chill spread up his arm and he clenched his teeth. "We drain what we can. The teshuva's stronger emanations will align and devour."

"You said there are too many. Or were you being modest?" The strain in her voice tugged at his heart despite her attempt at a light tone. "I think my demon will puke."

Rage and fear nibbled around the edges of his control, more chilling than malice teeth. Not that he feared for himself. He would go down fighting in a swirl of etheric dissonance if it came to that. But he would not lose his tyro on her first night.

His arm trembled with the effort of holding that seething wall in place. He couldn't believe Jilly withstood the mounting pressure. Of course, his admiration wouldn't mean much if they were swamped by the black tidal wave.

Too many. His demon was ancient and strong, and its energy patterns had subsumed thousands of the horde-tenebrae, overshadowing those lesser patterns and reweaving them into itself. But with so many malice, the mass was too chaotic for the teshuva's energy to overwhelm.

At least, for his teshuva alone.

He tightened his grip on the woman beside him. Despite the peril that had his ravager locked in destruction mode—or maybe because of that distraction—he was keenly aware of her on a visceral male level. The softness of her curves. Her scent, sweet and unruly like a wild spring wind tearing through cherry blossoms. Insanity, but he could not stop thinking of the scant hour lost in her body. It should have been all night. No, *nights*.

Now they'd be lucky to see the dawn.

"Only one thing left to do before we die," he murmured.

She glanced up at him in question, and he kissed her.

He had not quite understood how Archer could risk his heart, his very soul, even the world itself, just for his talya mate. They had a duty, damn it, a mission—all of them.

But duty, mission, heart, soul, and world were mere tinder to the conflagration that swept him on Jilly's soft moan as his lips passed over hers.

He loosed his grip on the blackness around them, the better to enfold her in his embrace. She molded herself to him, the slick, soft fabric of her unzipped puffy jacket crushed against his chest. Half hidden by the neckline of her T-shirt, the *reven*-sparked wings of her butterfly tattoo fanned his desire. The black wall of malice swirled into sickening motion, faster and faster. And they mattered less than scattered leaves in the flames that consumed him. All was madness. And he didn't care in the least.

On some level, he realized that didn't bode well for the world.

The cyclonic wind tugged his coat and whipped his hair to tangle with Jilly's blue spiked locks. When she cupped his face, angling her jaw to deepen the kiss, her fingertips brushed the *reven* at his temple. At her touch, the bracelet around her wrist glimmered as if coming to life. The lunatic malice swarm was like a negative of the silvery interweaving, the strands that looped around and back, lost in themselves, trapped. . . .

He drew back suddenly. "We don't have to drain them. We just have to trap them."

He struggled to focus past the chaos of the malice, of the bracelet, of his lust. Underneath was . . . stillness, at least. If he could reach it. "Lau-lau said the knot work was a demon trap. We use that pattern."

She swayed against him. "I don't want to be trapped."

"Not us. The malice." After that kiss, he refused to think how trapped he might be.

She took a step back from him. The whirling malice had tightened their circle, and the oily black smeared past them. He also didn't want to think what would happen if he was wrong.

To be eaten in a single gulp by a monstrous feralis would suck, but death by a thousand malice mouths was just no way for a talya to die. His demon would never forgive him.

He held her hand tight. The bracelet glinted between them. He raised her fist. "Bend the malice to this pattern. Back upon themselves. Evil consuming evil." His voice fell into a rhythm, almost a chant. He held her gaze every bit as tight. "Locked into eternity. Trapped. Leaving us free."

Did he want to be free? He forced the thought away.

"We're all trapped," Jilly murmured. "Always have been. Which is worse? When we try to lock someone else in with us? Or lock everyone else out?"

Within the thickening blackness, glitter appeared like a hint of hoar frost, a chill gleam matching Jilly's bracelet. Over the sulfurous stench of malice, a desiccating cold burned in Liam's lungs as the tenebraeternum leaked into the world. A few whirling malice snagged on the points of eerie light. The ether that swirled behind them in translucent oily ribbons looped and coiled. And knotted together.

More malice blundered into the knots, and the tangle expanded, capturing more of the seething tenebrae in a laced matrix of shadow and demon light, as finely woven as the fluorspar and waste metal of the bracelet. The smoky tornado turned to sludge and began to crystallize. One by one, the crimson stars of malice eyes winked out, leaving only needle pricks of oblivion behind.

Leaving Liam and Jilly enclosed in a cone of shining black ice.

In the stillness, the sound of their matched breath was preternaturally loud. She tugged her hand out of his grasp.

"Jilly," he said. "Wait."

She didn't. She slammed her fist through the malice. He grabbed her and yanked her under the shelter of his coat as the shimmering blackness crumbled and the latticework of interlocked malice flaked like charred dust on the Chicago wind.

She peeked out. "Good thing that didn't bring them back to life."

He coughed and jumped down off the car roof. The malice storm had scoured the paint and etched the bare steel like scrimshaw on whalebone.

He scowled, thinking of the car's owner scratching his head in the morning.

Jilly jumped down beside him. Her boots thudded like his heart. "What?"

"I hate when the tenebraeternum leaves its mark on this world."

Her gaze flicked up to the *reven* at his temple, which he knew must be blazing with the teshuva's amped energies. "You can only do so much."

"If by 'so much,' you mean fail again, you're right."

"We survived."

"That is not enough."

"But it's a start."

"After a century or two, you're ready to finish it."

"And with that attitude, you wanted to be leader?" She shook her head. "I guess leader is not the same as cheerleader."

"I never wanted this." He bit back the rest of the words that threatened to pour out of his exhaustion like so many unfrozen malice.

She rubbed her wrist where the bracelet had dulled

to matte gray again. He didn't think it was a good sign that the demon's gift came to life only when hell was rising . . . and when they touched. "Then why stay? Why do it?"

The cold concepts of duty and mission he had jettisoned so readily while in her arms spiraled up around him again, locking him in place. "It is all I have left."

That was too honest. The chill was settled so deep in his bones, it didn't even stop him from moving now. He crouched beside the wheel of the car where a drift of the black dust had collected. The license plate was polished to a featureless rectangle, and hairline fissures crazed the tires, as if the dust had parched and aged the rubber. After scraping a handful of the inert malice residue into his pocket, he rose. "If only the league had a veteran Bookkeeper, this might be interesting. Maybe even useful."

Her fingers flexed into fists, then opened again, as if she wanted to drag something more from him. "You can always do this again some other night. Since that's all you have left."

He studied her. "I didn't do that. Not alone."

She stared back. "What do you mean?"

"Didn't you feel it?" Disbelief surged through him when her gaze went as blank as the crystallized malice eyeballs. How could she deny that jolt of power? "Something bound us in that moment when we followed the fluorspar weave and trapped the malice together."

She took a step back, her fingers digging under the edge of the bracelet. "Hey, I'm already stuck with the demon. I'm not bound to anything else." *Anyone else.* The unvoiced words echoed like a malice cry.

Still the tough rebel, despite what they'd been through. Or maybe because of what they'd been through?

Not that the reason mattered. He'd walked a fine line with his bitter, wounded crew long enough to know that prying into their emotions and histories only overturned rocks and released lots of creepy-crawlies—and they had enough of those in their immortal lives.

They'd all been possessed for a reason. Their wounds resonated with the tenebraeternum, which brought the teshuva and the lesser demons down upon their heads. Or souls. After what happened tonight in the spillover of her anger and his lust, he should know better than to poke at her wounds and rouse those demons of the literal and metaphorical sort. And yet, he wanted to know *her*.

She, clearly, didn't return the interest. And maybe she was wiser than he, because thanks to Archer and Sera, he'd already seen what a mated-talyan pair could do—*would* do—if anything came between them. It seemed the only force more threatening to the world than evil was love.

Merely thinking the word rippled the hackles up his neck.

Damn it, he didn't have time for any of this, not the strange and perilous trick they'd pulled with the even more strangely behaving malice, not the unnerving reactivation of the soulless haints, definitely not the needful wish to touch her that made his fingers curl into fists.

This was exactly why he'd told Archer he couldn't get involved.

"Come on. We've had enough trouble for one night." He walked around to the car's driver side, tweaked his demon, and punched out the window.

Jilly slipped in beside him when he opened the passenger door. She lifted one eyebrow. "Grand theft auto doesn't count as more trouble for the night?"

"Less trouble than the owner calling his insurance company, or maybe filing a police report. Or worse yet, thinking some supernatural phenomenon like city crop circles scraped all the paint off his junker and posting a conspiracy theory on YouTube." He ripped open the steering column and hot-wired the ignition, grimacing at the spark that burned across his busted knuckles.

She watched as the car sputtered to life. "You know, if it's always such an issue, you should probably carry a screwdriver. When's your birthday?"

He held back a sudden grin. "Your young charges teach you as much as you teach them?"

"Nah. I learned that from uncle number four." She knotted her hands in her lap. "Anyway, kids these days just carjack. Nobody wants to put any effort into anything anymore."

When he'd read Jilly's file, he'd noted that her mother had raised three children by herself. Apparently none of the uncles—how many had there been?—had stuck around long enough to make a blip on the dossier. He knew well enough that the seismic forces that shaped a personality often occurred too far below the surface to be remarkable. At least, not until the whole facade came shuddering apart.

He wrapped his bloody fist around the wheel, the better to strangle memories of his own. "The league will reimburse the owner. You'd be surprised how many people take an envelope of cash with no questions asked."

"Not surprised at all, probably. I think the director at the halfway house was into something like that. I might be a pain in the ass, but he was just too glad to get rid of me. But what do a bunch of barely-off-the-street kids have worth taking?" She slumped in her seat. "God, is the whole city rotten?"

"Don't ask God." Liam pulled out his cell phone and hit speed dial. The phone crackled in his ear. "Archer, can't talk long. Ran into a few malice, and their stain is playing havoc with reception. I need you to dump a car. No scrubbing. Just muddy the waters. I'll meet you at Millennium Park."

Jilly focused on him as he disconnected. "You guys do this a lot?"

"More often. It's harder for us to hide these days."

"Maybe it's time to come out of the shadows."

"We are the shadows." He shook his head. "Our first and best disguise has always been that no one wants to know how close evil stalks."

"That could be *why* evil gets so close: because no one knows to look for it."

He cast her a wry look. "Considering your job, you already had a sense of how bad bad could be, and yet you still barely believe in the forces that have become part of you. How much harder for the rest of them?"

She was silent a moment, looking down at her hands where etheric stains darkened her nails around the blue polish. She twisted the bracelet on her wrist. "I do believe."

Not in him. Not enough to reach out to him, to the connection building between them. A primitive urge to force her to acknowledge that link ramped up his pulse. But even though she'd accused him of doing anything for the league, he was not a monster. Or not the sort of monster who forced a woman to want him. He wrestled the ancient alpha-male part of his brain much as one would any reptile. He jumped on it before it could grab him in its sharp teeth, threw it in a gunnysack, tied a rope around it, and got the hell out.

In the middle of the freezing night, Millennium Park was empty. He parked the car in a temporary zone across from the Art Institute, and he and Jilly got out.

"Archer will meet us at *Cloud Gate*."

She waited for him to come around to the sidewalk. "You mean the Bean."

He glowered. "I mean the stainless steel sculpture in the middle of the park, the essence of which is more perfectly evoked by its given name than that ridiculous nickname."

"But that's what everyone calls it."

As they made their way down the treelined promenade, he scoffed. "Since when do you do what everyone else does?"

This time, she glowered. "You're just showing off how superior you think you are by calling it *Cloud Gate*."

"If sticking with reality is superior, then so be it."

"Reality bites." She bared her teeth.

He smiled back. "That it does."

They climbed the shallow flight of steps to the sculpture. The bowed silver towered over their heads, reflecting the darkness and the city lights with equal distortion.

Jilly reached out to touch it, just as many were drawn to do, judging by the fingerprint smudges across the surface. The bracelet—matte where the sculpture was shiny, intricately woven instead of smooth—winked with a fierce opalescent fire in its reflection.

"Lovely." She pulled her hand away before she made contact. "Will the malice come hunting us again?"

"Not here. Something about art tends to hold them at bay."

She tilted her head. "Odd."

"Not if you think about how many artists talk about their work as free therapy to exorcise their demons."

"A way out of possession."

He shook his head. "Only the art seems immune. The artists are just as vulnerable. Maybe more so."

"Oh well. I can't even finger-paint."

"I used to work with metal." The revelation popped out of him like a spark from an overheated forge. He winced at the curiosity that brightened her face. "That was a long time ago. Anyway, Archer will be here soon—"

"You were a sculptor too? No wonder you like *Cloud Gate* better than 'the Bean.' "

He shook his head. "Not really a sculptor. I just didn't want you to think some artistic bent could have saved you. Plenty of artists fall prey to evil. It's only their work that may be spared."

"So not a sculptor," she prodded. "An armorer? You have enough in your basement."

"Nothing so violent. Or so useful. I was just a black-smith back home."

"Home, as in Ireland." She stilled. "How long ago was it exactly?"

"I left in the winter of 1850. I've not been back."

She let out a slow breath. "That's a long time. When you said 'immortal,' I didn't really appreciate what that meant."

He gave her a crooked smile. "Ah, to be so young and carefree again."

Her lips quirked up in answer, and she waggled a finger at him.

Despite the invitation to share, he hesitated. Had anyone ever asked him about those days? If so, it had been long enough ago that he didn't remember. That seemed ominous. "I was the smithy in my village. I repaired tools, shoed horses, made pots, nothing fancy."

Her gaze flitted across his face so that he wondered what was showing there. "I suppose the hammer makes a certain amount of sense, then."

"I was familiar with it." His fist tightened.

She studied him. "I would've pictured a blacksmith as heftier than you. Except for the shoulders, you're more Scarecrow than Tin Man." Then she paused, and he saw her calculating in her head. "The potato famine. That happened around your time."

As if she had summoned up one of those interminable public-television documentaries, the memories of his past threatened to bore him to tears. Or anyway, his eyes burned for some reason. "Like many others, that's why I left."

Her eyes narrowed, as if she knew he wasn't telling all, just as *Cloud Gate* reflected only the highlights and skyline, none of the alleys or gutters. No one wanted to see that ugliness anyway.

She bit at her lip. "You didn't—you aren't still starving? Are you?"

"The demon freezes us like a fly in amber, but I wasn't possessed until later." More questions welled up in her eyes, but he didn't want to get stuck again as if a bug in fresh tree sap. "Archer will be here soon. You need to practice getting your emotions under control."

She scowled at him. A price he was willing to pay if it stopped her questions.

But he shook his head. "See? Right away, you're annoyed. I'm just trying to lead you."

"You're telling me what to do."

He wondered how he had ever seen her as a pixie, when she was obviously more grumbling gremlin. "You're not a child, Jilly, who needs to be tricked into doing the right thing. I shouldn't have to coerce you to do what's needed to survive."

"As if you could."

Last straw. Her challenge, along with the old memories, and the knowledge that, for the moment at least, they were safe from outside attack, cracked his self-restraint.

He stepped into her, forcing her back against the stainless steel. "Oh, I could. In fact, I believe I already did. Once." He drew a breath tinged with the scent of cherry gloss on her lips, and the crack in his discipline splintered.

She tilted her head back to meet his glare. "You were hopped up on Lau-lau's long-joy juice."

"Hmm. Is that why I was on top?" In the sculpture's reflection, the harsh violet glow in his eyes gleamed back at him, mocking. He let the demon out another notch, revving up his senses so that his skin prickled with the auroral forces of her body near his.

Something about her—something beyond the obvious immature rebelliousness of her unruly hair and piercing—was like a million testing fingerprints trashing his well-polished control. Unlike any maddening talya he'd known, she unerringly targeted his secret flaw: that he'd never really wanted to be in command. Indulging his temper was as stupid as swinging his hammer blind. It felt wild, wrong. And so good.

Especially when she put the point of her finger in the center of his chest and took a step closer. He closed his eyes at the radiating pleasure. Why did the fate of the world matter again?

"Don't try to dominate me," she hissed. "It annoys me and then I can't back down."

Her voice lacked the double-octave lows of a rising demon. Which meant he pissed her off on a purely human level. Yay, him.

"I am not trying," he said. And he didn't want her to back down.

"Oh? That alpha-male bullshit doesn't require any rational effort? Of course it doesn't. Thinking is not the alpha-male forte."

He opened his eyes. "Unfair. I actually think quite a lot." About her lips softening under his. Her head tipping back to bare her throat. Her hands clutching his shoulders . . .

Her eyes narrowed. "Right. I can guess what you're thinking."

"Demonic possession confers no mind-reading ability," he said officiously.

"Yeah, well, I think I have a certain power of mind over matter." She zipped her finger down his chest and hooked the front of his jeans.

Predictably, his cock surged to undeniable attention.

She gave him a crooked grin that he answered.

"Stalemate," he murmured.

"None of that mate crap." Her fist closed on his fly. Not a prelude to the erotic, if exhibitionist, unveiling he might fantasize. No, she just wanted the upper hand, as usual.

His smile faded. "Who burned you, *xiao*-Jilly, that this energy between us scares you more than a tower of tenebrae?"

"I'm not scared." The denial burst out of her so hotly, even she winced. "I just don't like to be pushed around. And Mom's boyfriends really liked to push."

"Really." He didn't move, but his pulse changed as his demon uncoiled.

She must have felt it. She scowled at him and gave a sharp tug on his jeans. "Don't go all vigilante. I took care of it myself. Anyway, it wasn't any of them." She looked down and seemed to realize how intimately she had taken hold of him.

Her hand sprang open, but before she could step back, he laced his fingers through hers. Not in a confining gesture, but too entwined to easily pull away. He modulated his tone the same, not demanding, but not to be denied. "Who was it?"

She shrugged as if it hardly mattered, but her grasp tightened. "After I left home, I couldn't afford a place of my own, so I moved in with two other girls. They hung with a rough crowd, but that seemed normal. I didn't even notice until I hooked up with one of the guys. We'd been going out for a while, and one night he got drunk and he smacked me." She darted a look up at him.

The shamed flush on her cheeks slammed through him, and Liam locked every demon-powered muscle to stop himself from pulling her into his arms. "I can find the bastard and kill him," he offered casually. "The league has resources I just don't use enough."

She didn't laugh—smart girl, she believed him—and her grip on his hand eased. "In a sick way, he smacked sense into me. I looked around, realized I was reliving my mother's life, blindly falling into the same trap she'd endured, and I refused."

And she'd been refusing ever since. The insight into how hard she'd fought against a different sort of hell didn't exactly surprise him. But he was shocked at his twinge of envy that her teshuva—discord class though it was—had found a perfect resonance with the warrior she'd become.

He shifted his hold until his thumb rested on the blood beating below the skin of her wrist. "Jilly—" He hadn't meant for that note of yearning to color his voice.

The deliberate scuff of footsteps made them spring apart.

Archer crossed his arms. "Interrupting anything?"

"Yes," they said in unison.

Liam laughed softly when Jilly rolled her eyes at him.

Archer didn't smile. "We have to go. Ecco found another cluster of haints. But these aren't our old zombie friends. They have hostages."

All amusement and desire fled Liam, the void they

left jagged as a bomb blast. "Our people?" The last time he'd lost a man . . .

But Archer shook his head. "Human." His expression softened with pity as he glanced at Jilly.

She took a step closer to Liam, as if he could deflect that sympathetic sorrow. "Andre?"

"No. Your sister is one of them."

CHAPTER 9

Jilly wanted to pump Archer for more information, but he'd already said he didn't know any more, that Ecco had made the cryptic call from a pay phone before racing back to the entrenched cluster. A howl echoed in her head, louder than the junker car as Archer floored the crap engine. Liam had refused to abandon the malice-molested vehicle, protecting the league's mission even as her life swung toward disaster.

She stared her outrage at the back of his head, but he was flying through his speed dial, rallying the troops to this unknown threat.

Despite his calm voice as he relayed commands, tension glowed off him. The *reven* at his temple flushed violet, and the skin around it had gone almost translucent with a darkness she couldn't bear to look into, as if shadows ate him from the inside.

Which, she supposed, they did.

All this save-the-world shit had seemed very theoretical—and not so unnerving—until she was caroming through the midnight streets at sixty-five miles per hour in a car tagged with demon graffiti.

With her sister at the other end.

Liam finished his calls and sat in deep silence a moment. Then he glanced back at her. "The dossier we put together on you was rushed, but it included the basics on your family. Your sister's been an addict for a long time. The chances that she hasn't already started on solvo aren't good."

She gritted her teeth. "Let's just wait until we find her before we decide she's dead."

"Undead," Archer chimed in. "Mostly."

She resisted smacking him in the back of the head only because he had the car almost up on two wheels around the corner.

Liam ignored the other man and the stunt driving. "Dory didn't even come around after you took that knife for her."

A toxic mix of guilt and rage churned in Jilly's gut. "I got her to leave her pimp."

"Not because she chose to leave him, but because your bloody DNA sprayed everywhere helped put him in prison. I don't want you to get your hopes up."

He'd taken away everything else. The car's tires squealed around another corner, shrill as a malice crying foul. She knew the unvoiced accusation was unreasonable. But considering how much she'd lost—not just because of the demon—she wasn't willing to lose another chance.

From his down-turned mouth, she knew he'd read her refusal without her saying another word.

They paralleled the L for a few blocks before Archer pulled over. "This is the address Ecco gave us." From just beyond one of the support columns for the elevated tracks, a man stepped out of the gloom. "Ah, there he is. And Jonah and Perrin are across the street."

"I called everyone in," Liam said.

Even if Archer hadn't pointed them out, the men would have caught Jilly's wary attention under any circumstances. Though varied in their police-blotter descriptions, they each exuded a dangerous stillness she associated with TV wildlife programs of big cats right before they pounced on something, all taut muscle and focused eyes.

Sheathed claws had been replaced, though, with unsheathed blades, cudgels, and other weapons of up-close
and-personal destruction. The headlights gleamed off
the razored gauntlets that embraced both Ecco's forearms. The second man, Jonah, stepped up beside him,
blond hair shining almost as brightly.

Jilly tightened her bare fists and wished she hadn't
been so cocky down in the weapons depot at the league
warehouse.

They parked and got out. As she glanced up at the
windows of the apartment building above them, the
smells of cold metal and trash reminded her too much
of that night outside Dory's apartment. Except for the L
train tracks, this vibe was almost exactly the same. Life
just a few steps off the street. Her chest ached, not where
Rico's knife had slipped between her ribs, but spreading
out along the dark threads of her *reven*, and she knew
her teshuva was coming online. She welcomed it, if it
drove away the fear.

She couldn't be afraid, not if she wanted to save Dory
again. Maybe for the last time.

The big man—Ecco—stalked up to them. He nodded
at her once, eyes assessing, but addressed his comment
to Liam. "You know how I love me some malice. I found
these while hunting tonight. They're crawling all over.
Seemed like too many for one place, so I poked around.
That's how I found the haints. And the others."

"This is not good." Archer shook his head. "I told
Sera to swing by the warehouse and grab some of the
ESF equipment before she came. Maybe we can pick
up some changes in the emanations to explain what's
going on."

Ecco snorted. "You trying to keep her out of the
fight? Good luck. She's onto you, man."

Archer pursed his lips. "Yeah, I know. But it sounded
legit."

Ecco snorted again. "You guys ready, then?" He
slanted another glance at Jilly.

"I called in reinforcements," Liam said. "Let's give them a minute. No sense getting dead for nothing."

Jilly shifted restlessly. "If Dory's in there now . . ."

Ecco crossed his gauntleted arms over his massive chest and stuck his jaw out. "She is. Now aren't you thankful you've been possessed by a demon and that we crawled all into your past so I'd recognize your sis? She looks just like you."

"She's my half sister—not that it matters—and she doesn't look like me at all. She's tall and blond."

"Same lost-little-girl look, though."

Jilly mirrored his crossed arms. She couldn't match his bulk, but she beat him on the glower. "Hardly."

Ecco lowered his arms with a *zhing* of stropping blades. "How long are we going to stand around without smashing something? I'm not going to live forever." He smiled, a flash of teeth as sharp as his gauntlets. "Oh, wait. . . ."

"Yeah, you can wait." Liam stared up at the building. "I don't like this. Another massing of malice so soon." He glanced at Jilly.

She huffed. "What? I didn't do it."

"Not you, no. But the conjunction of your emergent demon and the change in malice behavior is suspect." He lowered his voice. "Not to mention whatever we did that trapped them together." When she opened her mouth, he said, "And by 'not to mention,' I mean let's not mention that yet. Nothing gets this crowd more fired up than the possibility of unleashing an untried new weapon with unknown consequences."

"I'm with them," she muttered.

The edge of his jaw hardened. "No. You're with *me*."

In the next few moments, a half dozen men filtered out from the shadows. Jilly found herself pressed a little closer to Liam. Not out of nerves and the fact that she was topped by at least head and shoulders by each man, merely by the fact she didn't want to get sliced or bruised on their bristling armament.

She cleared her throat loudly. "You can't go in there flailing."

She realized she'd interrupted their plans when they all stared at her. Liam was the only one not returning her scowl.

"Why not?" Ecco propped his fists on his hips. "To flail is divine. Or damned. Whichever."

"There are innocents in there."

"There are no innocents," said one of the other men—Jonah, she remembered.

"Jilly's right," Liam broke in over the others' muttering.

Everyone—including Jilly—gaped at him.

He unsheathed the hammer. When he swung it down to his side, it hummed through the air as if in agreement. "Not about their innocence," he clarified. "That's irrelevant. But about flailing and failing. We need to know what this new cluster is, what these haints are up to. Flailing doesn't get us answers."

"It gets us closer to salvation," Jonah growled. "Which is why we're here."

Jilly bristled and moved to stand between the talyan and the door. "I'm here to save my sister. Where are they?"

"Most of the third floor," Ecco said. "And part of the fourth. They've busted out walls to make a hive. The place is spackled with etheric secretions."

"Creepy," Archer said.

"And maybe deadly." Liam put his hand on Jilly's shoulder. "Demonic secretions like birnenston—as in fire and brimstone—can interfere with your teshuva, especially if you aren't well integrated. Or just newly possessed."

She brushed off his hand. "If you're about to suggest I wait out here, forget it."

Ecco snickered. "She's no fool."

"Exactly," she snapped. "I won't be stupid, but I won't be left behind either."

Three more men had materialized from the night and

stood with the lights of the L gleaming on their drawn weapons, but even the combined weight of their impatience wouldn't shift Liam, she knew.

But she could crowbar his ass. "Just let me go with you, and I won't give you any more shit about being part of the league."

He studied her as if the morass of evil congregating in the building behind him meant nothing. "You still thought you could be anything but?"

"It's the not-giving-you-shit part I thought would appeal."

"You'll do as I say?"

That wasn't necessarily the same thing as being part of the league, was it? "Whatever. Let's go."

At her words, she sensed the sudden tension of the talyan yearning toward action, the preternatural crackle of energy as the teshuva inside them surged to the fore.

And yet Liam held them unmoving with the force of his stillness. His eyes, focused on her while he waited for an answer, stayed blue as Lake Michigan under cloudless skies, not a flicker of stormy violet. Reluctantly, she admitted he was not a man to be dismissed simply as a bully or a braggart.

He was much more dangerous than that.

"Yes," she said softly.

He took a step forward and the dozen talyan broke for the building.

In the controlled sweep forward, he tugged her into his wake. "Stay close to me. Get out of the way of anyone else with solid amethyst eyes. Don't go running off to find your sister. If she's here, we'll get her out."

A handful of the talyan peeled off, heading for the back of the building and the fire escapes, she guessed. She followed Liam through the front door. The tiny lobby was barren except for a few brown leaves crinkled into the corner beneath the mailboxes. The remaining talyan started up the stairs.

She smelled the lair before they arrived at the third floor. A biting sourness burned in her nose. She flashed back to one of her erstwhile uncles passed out against the bathroom door in a miasma of sweat and stale vomit.

She breathed shallowly against the smell, against the unexpected pain of the memory. Could her mother have possibly made any worse choices in her life? Could her sister?

Could she? And did the fact that this was her only choice make it any less terrible?

They hit the third-floor landing. An unlit hallway bent around the corner. The first talya drifted forward out of sight, footsteps inaudible even to her suddenly sharpened hearing. Her vision flickered, and veins of a strange calcified gray stretched down the hallway walls. She shrank closer to Liam to avoid touching them.

"Birnenston," he murmured. "It's a slow-acting poison to demonic energies. Don't get it on you. Not surprisingly, it burns."

The overhead lights were smashed, but the birnenston streaks gave off a sickly glow to her demon-spiked vision. Bits of glass twinkled in the debris of drywall and age-softened lathe strewn across the floor where walls had been torn apart, as if a giant rat had gone through the place in search of its cheese. The gray veins thickened around the damage. Whether the birnenston caused or had just taken advantage of the destruction, Jilly couldn't tell. The talyan moved down the hall, boots seeming to float above the trash; so smoothly did they move.

Jilly winced when her own feet stumbled, the crunch of her rubber soles across broken glass like a gunshot in her ears. But nothing hurtled out of the dark holes.

She held her breath against the thickening stink and noticed a faint rhythmic huffing sound all around them, punctuated by intermittent gasps. The hair at her nape rippled in atavistic unease.

Jonah, in the lead, halted in front of one of the anti-home-improvement renovations. He hoisted a giant Maglite—obviously he wasn't willing to rely solely on his demon sight—and flooded the hole with the high beam.

Thick ropes of birnenston bracketed the opening and laced the interior of the chamber. Gray stalactites hung from the ceiling. Yellow droplets oozed from the serrated tips and dropped to the mirrored stalagmites that grew up from the floor. Jilly figured she didn't need a childhood of comic book horror—or the teshuva recoiling within her—to know she should avoid the mess.

Several haints stood half embedded in the viscous gnarl, as if they'd lacked the initiative to take a single step out. The rest were arrayed between the tapering columns, equally gray. Where they happened to be aligned to face the hallway, their vacant eyes reflected the flashlight, but otherwise none moved. Jilly's flesh crawled, urging her to escape.

The huffing she'd heard was the haints' breath. She hadn't noticed it when she and Liam had visited the cluster in the park. Within the confines of the chamber that had once been the living room of one apartment and the kitchen and bathroom of another, the synchronized wheeze carried a tone of menace. She had the terrifying impression that despite their stillness and apparent unity, somewhere in their fugues they were trapped alone in sorrow and pain, their silence broken only by those soft hiccuping gasps, like a child in a closet crying itself to sleep.

"Who brought the flamethrower?" Ecco's voice rang in the quiet. "And the marshmallows?"

All the other talyan winced, whether at the coarseness of his tone or his joke, she wasn't sure.

A movement in one corner caught her eye and she swung around. And realized what Ecco had meant by the "others."

She was quite familiar with the classic junkie sprawl, arms slack, legs akimbo, head tipped, drool optional. She'd seen it often enough in her mother's boyfriends and in her own work. Pipes and needles littered the low table near this second group, an ugly mess compared with the pristine white tablets of solvo, which were no-where in evidence. She knew no one went back to the smack once they tried solvo. After its pure high, alleg-edly nothing else would work. So this group of addicts hadn't yet made the switch.

Which meant they still had their souls.

It seemed impossible these garden-variety addicts, surrounded by the haints, hadn't been converted, but she was almost ecstatic to see the agitated twitch of their muscles, the darting of their eyes behind half-closed lids. These people could still be saved.

Then she saw her sister.

"Dory," she gasped. Against all Liam's warnings, she found herself jumping forward. Stupid, she knew, but didn't stop herself. Some things mattered more than smart.

She was brought up short by a grip on the hood of her jacket.

"What did I tell you about running off?" Liam's voice was a growl. She half expected him to shake her like a dog with a bone.

"It's her."

"I got that. And we'll get her, along with the others. In a minute."

Jilly glanced around at him. Sera had come up be-hind them carrying what looked like an old portable-video-camera bag slung from one shoulder. She held a fat wand like a Geiger counter and raised it to the room. Archer loomed close. If the violet sparks in his eyes got loose, he wouldn't need Ecco's flamethrower; so fierce was his protective stance.

Jilly glared at Liam. "We could be getting them out of here and you're recording this for *America's Funniest Home Videos*?"

"It's something new. We don't understand it. We don't have a Bookkeeper to analyze it. Maybe we can find a Bookkeeper in another league in another city who may have encountered the same thing." He lowered his voice, but his grip on her jacket was unrelenting. "If I'm going to keep my men alive, I need to know what these things are doing."

"They're not things—not all of them, not my sister."

"She's not bound. She came here willingly. These haints have got to be the biggest buzz-kill around, and still she sat down with the others over there and shot up."

Jilly gritted her teeth. "I'm not going to argue morality and addiction-recovery theory with you. She's my sister."

"And you're my talya, my fighter. I won't lose you any more than I'd sacrifice my men."

"You sacrifice them every night," she hissed. "It's just that they're immortal, so they survive."

If her words penetrated his imperturbable armor, she couldn't see it. "Be that as it may, you'll wait."

She relaxed in his hold until he loosened his grip; then she tore free. The better to turn her glare on him. But she didn't bolt off again.

Sera walked past them, tracing the wand through the air in a slow-motion wave like some demented fairy godmother. "Emanation spike here." She studied them reprovingly, a glint of violet in her hazel eyes. "Get a grip, you two."

Jilly tamped down her wayward emotions. Liam's already perfectly composed face didn't change at all. Probably that spike was all her fault. Never mind the blue hair dye, she'd always been the hotheaded one. And look where it had gotten her.

She resisted the urge to look over at her sister.

Sera completed a circuit of the room, Archer never leaving her side. She frowned as she approached Liam. "Something odd just— Oh hell."

"What?"

"Hell," she said more urgently.

As one, the haints took a gasping breath. An etheric shock wave passed through the room at that moment. What was left of the walls seemed to bow inward, on the edge of collapse.

Jilly clamped her hand under her breast where the
flare of her teshuva's mark stole her breath worse than a
kick to the ribs. Though he must have suffered a similar
blow to his *reven* like an instant migraine, Liam never
flinched. He spun and pulled her under the edge of his
coat just as yellow poison suddenly gushed from the
birnenston stalactites, splashing across the floor in all
directions. As if the stones themselves wept in the presence of what had arrived.

Through the bilious fog, a deeper shadow moved.
Nothing corporeal, just a suggestion of a looming monstrosity given shape by the smoking birnenston. Something misshapen and ghastly, with a half-crescent
extrusion cutting up through the fog like an off-center
horn or enormous tooth or scythe. No, not one monstrosity, but a dozen.

The demons had returned to their lair.

CHAPTER 10

Liam whirled, putting Jilly behind him as he faced the attackers. His heart leapt into his throat, and a half step after, his demon leapt into his extremities and a word appeared on his tongue. "Salambes."

Shock and a taste bitter as dry ashes licked from a cold anvil made him grimace. The teshuva had surged past his humanity to give him that name. As if a name did them any good unless it had fairy-tale authority to command the demons, but he saw no hesitation in the attack at his outcry.

No, the only change was inside him. The unprecedented shift in the way the demon melded with him worried him as much as these unknown, unbound tenebrae. Change had never been in the league's favor.

The other talyan had already gone into fight mode. They fell into their old solitary-hunter stances instead of aligning themselves into a team as they'd been drilling. They'd been working the new patterns for only a few months, but he'd hate to have all that effort wasted. About as much as he'd hate seeing all of *them* wasted by the new demons.

As he called out for the talyan to regroup, frustration boiled through him. Just what the hell was a salambe? Big as a feralis, but only half materialized, like a malice.

League archives hinted at a vast array of demon subspecies in the tenebraeternum, but only a few kinds seemed disposed to slip through the Veil into the human realm. Had there been a breach? Such had never happened in his memory; would he even recognize one?

It was bad enough to fight in the shadows; the teshuva kept him fighting in the dark. If only he could know everything his demon knew. The taste of ashes choked him again. So maybe not.

The things came forward through the birnenston fog but never gained substance. A stink like rusting metal flooded the chamber.

With a battle cry, Ecco broke ranks and rushed forward, his gauntlets crossed for a fatal cut. But when he launched himself at the demon, he passed right through it and crashed to the floor on the other side.

The demon phased. Liam could think of no other word. It curled into a column of smoke and streamed into the nearest haint. The limp, pallid haint—a slender, sandy-haired man—suddenly flushed and straightened. His brown eyes clouded, then drained of color. For a moment, only bleached whiteness stared out.

Until a speck of red brightened the orb. Broken blood vessels spidered across the white, unbearably vivid. He turned on Ecco with inhuman quickness, at least one joint in his leg snapping with the strain.

Liam shouted a warning, but Ecco was already up, ready to face the threat. All around them, the salambes phased into the quiescent haints, and blank human eyes flared. But the connection was imperfect. Like a monster wearing an ill-fitting human suit, the salambes seemed to lurk over and behind the soulless human husks, as if they couldn't quite cram themselves in. Human flesh blushed feverishly. As one of the haint/salambe pairings jumped toward him, Liam felt the heat wave like a forge fired to the danger point.

He yanked Jilly out of the way, only to realize another doubled-up demon had sneaked up behind. Jilly used the momentum of his pull to fire off a gutter-punk kick that knocked the woman-wearing salambe backward.

"Tag teaming allowed," Jilly growled.

The thing toppled but sprang back so quickly the woman's head rocked. The crack of her spine made Liam's hairs stand on end. Her head flopped to one side, and the outline of the salambe's vaguely reptilian skull towered over her shoulders like a fiendish bobblehead.

The haint rushed Jilly.

"Down," he shouted.

Jilly dropped to her knees. The hammer was already swinging without his conscious thought. Its dull whistle howled through the air.

He knocked the haint clear across the chamber. Before the body hit the wall, the salambe had phased free and poured itself into the next nearest haint, which spun to face them, its exposed skin already starting to blister from the conflicting energies of human and demon realms.

"Keep them moving, people," Liam shouted. "They'll burn out."

From the corner of his eye, he saw Archer and Sera work in tandem to force the salambe to leap from one haint to next. The abandoned bodies collapsed, steaming faintly. Then he was too busy to oversee as Jilly pushed a salambe-ridden haint his way. He dispatched it with a mighty thunk.

It was just butchery.

Between the talyan's weapons and the salambes' caustic emanations, the haints were destroyed. When the last soulless husk collapsed, the smoke of incorporeal salambes swirled into a single thick column, then split, the half dozen streams escaping out into the hallway, through the ventilation grate, through a crack by the window to disperse on the midnight breeze.

Ecco let out a yell and raised his gauntleted fists as if the gore-smeared razors could stop the smoke.

The stink of rusting metal dissipated. The salambes were gone.

Bracing the hammerhead on the floor, Liam knelt beside the haint of the first woman he had flung across the chamber. The bloodied eyes were gone. Not back to human color. Just gone. The burned-out sockets stared up at him, empty except for the accusation that carved another divot in his already patchy soul.

Even as he watched, the soulless husk began to crumble. He touched its forehead and in another moment only dust remained.

Jilly stood beside him. "You wondered what would happen when the soulless died."

"Did they die?" He pulled himself upright with the hammer as support. "We can only hope."

She shuddered, and he dragged her close.

"Hey," she protested, but she didn't pull away.

"That's what happens when a poorly integrated human and her demon don't play nicely together." He forced himself not to wrap himself around her, shelter her from the horror. He wasn't coddling her, just trying to make sure she hadn't overdone the battle. She was so new to her own changes. "How are you? Hurt anywhere?"

Jilly stared down at the dust. "Not compared to that."

Liam glanced around at the other talyan. All of them were standing, except Jonah, who'd been thrown into a shattered pile of lathe.

Ecco smirked at Jonah. "Hey, missionary man. You don't actually have to crucify yourself. The demon'll take care of that for you."

Jonah heaved himself up, scrabbling through the trash as he reached for Ecco's throat. Perrin hauled him back to pick the bent nails out of his hide.

"Enough." Liam pitched his command soft and low to cut through the ruckus.

He felt Jilly shiver against him and knew the demon harmonics were in his voice. The men subsided, reluctantly, and edged away from each other. The energies of the risen demons always crackled uncomfortably against one another, probably one of the reasons talyan had historically been solitary hunters. But they could no longer stand alone against the forces hunting them back.

"What the fuck is a salambe?" Though the immediate threat had gone out the window, Archer was still standing guard over his woman, axe in hand, as Sera reassembled the scattered pieces of the ESF recorder. "I heard you yell."

Liam rubbed his temple where the *reven* still pulsed. "The teshuva just slipped the word into my head."

As one, the talyan lifted their eyebrows. Archer said slowly, "That's . . ."

"Fucked-up beyond all recognition," Ecco supplied.

Archer shifted his axe. "Odd. Since when do the teshuva give us anything besides what gets us into more trouble?"

"Let's not assume they've broken tradition," Liam said drily. "We'll have to find the reference in league archives."

"Never mind the history books," Ecco growled. "Even hardcovers don't do enough damage when you throw them."

Archer's scowl said he was inclined to agree. "With the discontinuity in our Bookkeeper line, we could be digging through old records for weeks and never find anything that will help us here and now. We already knew the soullessness of the haints can destabilize the weave of repenting souls that form the Veil. No surprise, considering the escalating number of solvo junkies, the weakness in the Veil let something like a salambe sneak through. The salambes filled the empty haints like they were coming home."

"Just long enough to burn the house down," Jilly murmured from where Liam still had her tucked under his arm. When he looked down at her, surprised she'd stayed so long, she touched his stomach and lowered her voice another half step. "Your demon mark is still glowing. Relax. The danger's over. For now."

He took a shallow breath, afraid to dislodge her hand. That was a danger too enticing to dismiss.

But he had to get the talyan back on track. "We might not care about the salambes' provenance, but we want to know how to destroy them. The malice are incorporeal too, but small enough to restrain while the teshuva matches their emanations and drains them. We can do the same with the ferales, once they are incapacitated in their corporeal husks. But the salambes have the advantages of both, and are stronger than malice and smarter than ferales."

"Not smart enough to keep weaponry in their lair," Ecco said. "Without the haints to maneuver, they had nothing."

"Good thing," Archer said. "Or they could have massacred us."

Ecco sniffed. "You maybe, forgetting yourself while watching your mate's ass."

"Watching my back, you mean," Sera said distractedly.

Archer and Ecco exchanged a glance. Archer shrugged.

Sera missed it all as she brought the recorder over to Liam. The screen was cracked, but when it whirred to life, the spike in etheric-spectral frequencies was unnervingly clear.

"That's where the . . . the salambes appeared," Sera said. "But you can see the background readings were already high, and not just from the birnenston. These demons have been camping out."

Liam glanced over at the decimated haints and the junkies sprawled obliviously against the far wall. "How long have the demons been cultivating these?"

"No way to tell," Sera said. "Human readings won't show on the recorder."

Jilly strained away from him. "Because why would the league care about humans anyway, right? Let me go."

He did, and she went straight to her sister.

Though there'd been a picture of Dory Chan in Jilly's

dossier, the emaciated, ragged blonde on the floor bore no resemblance at all to the curves and lush colors of his tyro talya. Only the roots of their hair were the same. Liam couldn't guess how Ecco had made the connection. He'd wondered before if there was more to the brutish fighter than flashing gauntlets, but had never had reason to pry.

Jilly knelt beside her sister and took the limp hand. She brushed back the stringy bleached hair. Even across the room, he heard Jilly's despondent sigh.

He realized Sera was watching him watch Jilly. "What?"

She didn't flinch, but as usual, questions churned in her hazel eyes. "Nothing."

"You female talyan are . . ." He bit back the rest, though gritting his teeth set off a fresh stab of pain through his skull. To match the pain in his ass.

She tilted her head. "Yes?"

"Never mind. Collect some of the detritus from these burned-out haints. We'll want it for comparison." He stalked across the room to Jilly's side.

She lifted her sister's arm. "The track marks are fresh."

"Then she's probably not using solvo." He didn't add "yet."

"The salambes only jumped into the soulless, did you notice? They didn't even try to possess these people, which means she still has her soul."

"So it seems."

She glared, not at him exactly. Maybe at the universe around him. "We got here in time. We got *her* in time."

Pity the universe if it let her down. Liam shook his head. "Come on. We need to go." He put a hand under Dory's armpit and levered her up. She weighed barely more than his coat. Without the hammer strapped into it.

Jilly slung her sister's arm over her shoulder. "You said the salambes were cultivating her. You mean turning her into a haint."

"When we get her sobered up, maybe we can ask her."

"That's the only reason you think she's worth saving." Minus the sharp sting of accusation, Jilly's tone broke with resignation.

"No." He didn't elaborate. Not with Sera across the room watching him with violet-tinged eyes that meant her demon senses were measuring his every capillary betrayal.

Dory most likely was beyond hope. And whatever she could tell them wouldn't change what he had to do. Yet for the sake of the grieving woman at his side, he wished cavalries really did ride to the rescue, that heroes really could save the day. The ravager twisted inside him, a rude reminder that heroes might have day jobs, but the talyan performed best at night.

He looked down at the twinkle of Jilly's nose stud, and his fingers yearned to thread through the blue spikes of her hair. The passion with which she threw herself into the fray terrified him. And enticed him. He'd almost be tempted to rebel too, but he wouldn't force someone else to step in to fill his vacancy. If he pierced a stud through his lips, it would be only to keep himself from telling them all he'd never wanted this hopeless task laid at his feet and he was tired of leading this painstaking charge to the end of the world, one foot in front of the other. He couldn't leave them foundering in the shadows, so he wouldn't indulge his desires and walk away, especially not from her.

So much for saving anyone. Including himself.

Jilly settled her sister under the covers in one of the apartments on the second floor of the warehouse. The mismatched furniture from the salvage offerings below created a sort of cheery, ugly hodgepodge semblance of a home. Against the garish bedspread, Dory looked even more pale and gaunt. Jilly stepped back, swallowing down useless tears.

Sera arranged the nightstand with a glass of water, a

puke bucket, a couple unmarked pill bottles. "She's going to wake up rough. These will help."

Jilly tried not to glare. "She doesn't need more damn drugs."

Sera's expression was calm. "She's an addict. Of course she'll need more drugs."

Now Jilly did glare, and let her temper call up a smidgen of the demon for the added light show she knew would appear in her eyes. Sera had been right about the demon's terrifying strength and speed coming out of nowhere. The memory of using Liam as a springboard to launch herself at those things seemed ludicrous in retrospect, even though her muscles and bones couldn't forget the turbulent pleasure of the attack. Or the feel of her talya boss's steadfast power.

Jilly crushed the recollection. At the very least, she didn't want the other woman to be right about Dory. "None of you care what happens to her."

"We want to stop this chemical version of *desolator numinis* from making more soulless blanks for the salambes to invade—you can believe that."

Jilly subsided. There was no sense being stupidly vicious as well as stupidly sad.

A knock at the door brought them around.

Liam stepped through. "We have the others down the hall. How is she?"

"Completely out of it," Sera said. "She won't remember a thing from tonight."

He sighed. "Same with the others, I'm guessing."

"I'll go take a look at them." Sera shook her head. "Who would've guessed my hospice training would be useful for the walking dead?" Then she slanted a glance at Jilly and bit her lip. "Sorry. I'm starting to sound like Archer." She slipped out of the room.

"We should take them to the hospital, to a detox center." Jilly could've bitten her tongue. Now she sounded stupidly optimistic. Who would unquestioningly take an unidentified baker's dozen of smacked-out bums, petty thieves, and one prostitute?

"After we talk to them, we will," Liam said. And he sounded as if he meant it. He crossed his arms over his chest as she plunked herself down in one of the mismatched chairs that flanked a table by the window. "How long since you've seen her?"

"Since before her pimp stabbed me. I'd gone to him looking for her." Jilly knotted her fingers in her lap. "I can't believe . . . She always wanted to be the rebel."

"Runs in the family, hmm?"

She shook her head. "I was never trying to run away from anything." She realized she sounded a little defensive. "She took off a year after my brother did. I tried to tell Mom that seventeen was too young, but she was too wrapped up in her own problems to listen."

"Those uncles you told me about."

After a moment, she nodded. "My brother had gotten mixed up with a guru one of Mom's boyfriends always talked about. Maybe it was safer for Dory to leave. I had my share of run-ins with Mom's guys too. Nothing I couldn't handle. But Dory was always more delicate." She clenched her fist. "Which is why I should have been there for her."

"You had school. If you hadn't finished, you wouldn't have been working with the kids. They needed you too."

Jilly grimaced. "And that's turned out so well." She scrubbed a hand down her face. "Don't listen to me. I'm being morose."

His lips quirked. "Yeah, because being Cuisinarted by malice shouldn't bum you out."

She smiled back reluctantly. "And then toasted by smoke demons."

"Throw in some cheese cubes and it was practically a party." He crossed the room toward her and parked himself in the second chair. He thunked his elbow on the table and propped his head in his hand, his eyes hidden from her, one thumb rubbing the demon's mark at his temple.

So close, she could reach out and touch the bold eddies, plain black now with the teshuva at rest. Not that she could stroke away the sign of his possession, but maybe some of the pain. And maybe some of her own.

The moment between them spiraled out. She felt the tipping point, when she should move, should tell him. . . .

"What set you on the path that brought you here today, Jilly Chan?" His voice was soft, muted by his raised hand. "What was your penance trigger?"

"Penance trigger?" The league-specific term jolted her back from the foolish romantic place she'd been headed. Because, really, what more bound them together than these shared scraps of hell?

"Every talya can trace their personal history back to a moment marking the point of weakness in his soul. Like a nail driven into ice that starts the crack and eventually allows the demon in."

She looked at her sister. "The hole Rico's knife made in my lung was big enough to drive a truck through, much less a demon." She shifted in her seat so the year-old scar didn't press against the arm of the chair. She didn't like wondering if that moment had been the beginning of her end.

But Liam shook his head, finally looking at her. "The penance trigger comes earlier, sometimes much earlier."

She raised her chin. "What was yours?"

He hesitated only a heartbeat. She could almost see him steeling himself for the leap. But of course he jumped. Because he'd do anything for his precious league. He'd already sold his soul; how could baring it to her be any worse?

"I was led astray once." He took a breath. "No. That's not quite true. I followed willingly, without question, when I should have walked away. Someone died because of it."

"You let that happen? I can't believe that."

He lifted one eyebrow with every sign of arrogance, but she sensed a vulnerability in him. "You saw me beat a woman across the room, and you think I can't kill?"

"She wasn't a woman, not anymore. But I meant I can't believe anyone led you anywhere."

"I was young."

"Hard to believe that too," she muttered.

He gave her a quelling glance. "Some lads of my village snuck out in the night to tear down English fences. They wanted me to bring my father's tools. His smithing was an act of creation, but we needed the chisels and snips to destroy. I knew it was dangerous, but I went along with nary a word. A patrol caught us. They rode over a boy—slow Dougal, too frightened to drop the heavy hammer that slowed him even more—and they killed him."

She closed her eyes, but that just made the image come clearer. She guessed from the deepening of his brogue that he was remembering too. "Here I thought the judges dealt harshly with tagging."

"Don't compare me to your wayward charges." He sat back in the chair, blue eyes half lidded. "I am not that boy now."

No, he certainly wasn't. "Because of the demon."

"Not immediately and by that time, it hardly mattered, but yes, that was the end."

She wondered what crappy events could make the progression from witnessing a murder to starvation to possession seem anticlimactic.

"And you?" His question was soft but insistent.

She hesitated longer than he had. Then she looked at Dory. Where had a lifetime of the desperate avoidance of their hurt gotten them? "I could have held them together."

"Your family."

She nodded. "Even as a kid, I knew it was up to me. Mom was basically a kid herself. Leroy, my brother, was oldest, but he didn't have the temperament. Dory was always the baby."

"What chance did you have to keep things together?"

"That's the point. I didn't try." As he'd described the

penance trigger, she pictured the nail poised above the brittle ice. "Leroy came home one night from the so-called church people he'd been hanging with, in a rage because he couldn't find his stash. I knew Dory had stolen it, and she'd taken some of his E even though we swore to each other we wouldn't go that route. Mom was crying and cowering when he raised his voice, because that's what she always did."

She glanced over at Liam and in his gaze saw the cloudy chill in the moment before the ice cracked. "Unlike you, I did walk away. I just left them." She straightened, refusing to drop his gaze.

But the break in the ice, when it came, did not reveal a bottomless pit of condemnation. Instead, a glimmer of warmth eased his expression. "But you didn't really stop trying, did you? That's why you went to work at the halfway house."

He didn't need a hammer; his gentle insight chipped a layer from her guarded heart. "I couldn't keep my own brother and sister from making the same rotten mistakes as my mother. I don't know why I thought I could help anybody else. And the only thing worse than losing track of them is finding out they ended up like Andre, or Dory."

"You tried," he repeated softly. "You tried to make amends."

"Nobody hands out gold ribbons for trying."

"Doesn't change the need to try. Ask the teshuva."

Repentant demons. Crazy. As crazy as her holding on to her concrete layers all these years. "You mean the demons come to us not because we're weak but because we're trying? Like they are?"

His brows drew together. "I don't know. I've never heard it put like that."

She snorted. "Talk about hopeless codependency."

A smile curved his lips. "Maybe in the striving there is hope."

She glanced back at Dory. "Maybe you're right."

At his silence, she looked back at him. The dimple

appeared in his cheek as his smile widened. "Me, right? And you said it without thumbscrews." He stood and held out his hand. "Let her sleep. You've done enough tonight."

"I have a lot to make up for." But the tremble in her limbs told her she didn't have much else to hold her up. She hesitated, then put her hand in his. The warmth of him made her sway as she stood.

His other hand under her elbow steadied her but brought him a little too close. Her breath caught.

His grip tightened, but when he spoke, his solicitous tone could have come straight from the demon-management handbook. "You're tired and worried, which is a dangerous place to be with a demon. You have a lot to learn about calling on your teshuva."

She wanted to learn, to stop what had almost happened to her sister, what had probably happened to Andre. She'd promised Liam she'd be a good little weapon for the league, so she wondered why it bothered her that he wanted her only for that purpose.

And she wondered at that same moment who was more dangerous—the demon inside her or the temptation of the man at her side?

CHAPTER 11

Liam felt the battering exhaustion of Jilly's grief and guilt as if they were his own. Yet he couldn't risk indulging those vulnerabilities he'd thought long banished.

He guided her down the hall to an empty room, careful to keep his touch impersonal, the way he would support any of his talyan. Before Sera came along, when Archer had fought nightly to the point of collapse, Liam had once or twice—which went to show how wrecked Archer had been—assisted the veteran talya to his room.

But he'd never lingered in Archer's doorway, making sure he stumbled to his bed. He'd never had to grip the frame, fighting the urge to turn down the damn covers.

And he certainly never watched any of the others the way he watched Jilly.

What had she done to him?

"Good night." His voice sounded more brusque than he'd intended.

She eyed him from the bed. "That's it?"

He didn't need his demon to sense the risky tension between them, like an invisible thread drawing him to her. And he knew well enough how easily—how willingly—he could lose himself there.

The cheap plywood doorframe dented under his fingers. "What else did you want?"

Want. The word reverberated, as if someone had plucked the thread binding them. He found himself leaning imperceptibly toward her and straightened.

"We'll work this out later," he said.

"'This'?" Her voice sounded threatening even in its simple human octave.

He waved one hand. "Between us."

The bracelet on her wrist gleamed as she made a fist in the covers. "Yeah. Later. Good thing we have lots of that."

He backed out and shut the door firmly. Because what other option did he have?

From the racing of his pulse, obviously danger of some sort had been narrowly avoided.

He stalked down the hall, refusing to stretch his senses to catch the sound of her lying back upon the bed. Most likely, he'd hear only a muttered curse. He had a few on the tip of his tongue too.

It was his own damn fault there wouldn't be anything else on his tongue tonight.

He slammed into the main warehouse on the ground floor. In an open area where they'd pushed back the dusty antiques, Sera hunched over a big dining room table fine enough to grace a Gold Coast mansion if not for the scarring scorch mark across the surface. She'd amassed a complicated tangle of beakers, wires, and computer monitors that gleamed unnaturally against the backdrop of reclaimed architecture.

"You need to find a real Bookkeeper," she said without looking up. "Organic chem in college does not make me a legit researcher in demonics."

"More legit than me." Archer leaned his hip against a counter nearby, arms over his chest. "We used actual horses for horsepower in my day."

"You just don't want haint dust under your fingernails, Civil War boy." She pushed a button and a faint miasma of sulfurous light pulsed from the test tube propped before her. "In a few hours, we can check again, but I'm guessing this haint sample will match leftovers that other Bookkeepers have saved of talyan whose teshuva are consumed in battle. Whether the soul is demon-marked or straight-up missing, once it's gone, all we have left is meat."

"Which is why we always give Bookies their own personal refrigerators," Archer muttered.

"Meanwhile," she continued, "I'm running a word search on 'salambe.' But you know the size of the database. And that doesn't count the records still on freaking goatskin and papyrus."

Liam bracketed his temples between spread fingers. The *reven* pulsed under his thumb. "I don't like this. Now we face demons that can phase from body to body."

"It's like we started working the team angle, and now they are too," Sera said.

Liam shot her a hard glance. "The league has been around for millennia."

"You had a clubhouse, but you weren't really a team." She studied his expression before continuing. "It wasn't any failing of yours, Liam. Keeping this crew from self-immolation can't have been an easy task." She scowled down at the dusty glass in front of her. "Even without the possession problems."

"We're not that bad," Archer objected. When Sera gave him a disbelieving look, he shrugged. "Anymore we're not. Much."

Liam squelched a twinge of jealousy at their teasing. "But what's behind this spread of demonic influence?"

In the silence, the whir of the haint dust in the centrifuge gave a mocking chuckle.

"Whatever it is," Archer said grimly, "we'll deal." He drew Sera up from her seat. When she resisted a moment, he reminded her, "It'll still be here tomorrow."

She sighed, and they left Liam in the big empty warehouse. Archer had the nerve to click off the lights on his way out.

Between the ambient glow of residual demonic emanations and Liam's own restless senses, the cavern wasn't pitch-black. But it was dark enough for him to see the cloud of faint pale shimmers hovering over the spinning test tube.

"Oh shit." So much for hoping the haints had died peacefully. Or, if not peacefully, at least completely.

While human hosts to angels and djinn-men could see soul matter, those possessed by the repentant te-shuva demons had lost the ability along with a few other useful skills. The downside of having the sanction of neither heaven nor hell. Or so he'd always been told. He shouldn't be able to see this—hell, he didn't *want* to see it.

Maybe the hovering light wasn't a soul. Just a ... a ghost. It wasn't even a coherent entity. More a disjointed collection, like a firefly convention. As if that made its lurking presence easier to stomach, considering he might've had a hand—or a hammer—in its demise.

The league had learned from its last Bookkeeper that solvo flayed apart soul matter even as it left the physical body intact. Apparently those scattered pieces had at least enough etheric power and instinct to wander back, looking for their old home.

"You can't go home again," he murmured. "Even shredded poisoned leftover soulflies should know that."

If the righteous angels and devilish djinn could see souls, he supposed it made a sick sort of sense that his te-shuva stood witness to the hopeless, homeless oddments that were all that remained of some sorry spirit. Like called to like. The awareness made no difference, of course; there was nothing he could do for the soulflies. His task was to keep the league's bodies and souls—and demons—together. Wasn't that enough?

Apparently not, if the teshuva had granted him the ability to see this. The knowledge only drove his failures to date all the deeper into his own battered soul. Considering the rampant spread of solvo over the past five months, how many tatters of soul essence fluttered around Chicago tonight, seeking their wayward haint bodies, never to be reunited and never to pass on? His stomach churned at the thought.

He turned off the centrifuge. As the test tube came to a halt, the faint fireflies sank into the glass. They'd wandered this far; at least he could give them some small peace in the little pieces that remained.

Weariness settled in his chest, heavy as the soulflies were light. He left the warehouse and walked the corridors. To his extended demon senses, the night was quiet. He'd sent out half the crew to check the other known haint gatherings to see if they could find the salambes. He didn't want an unidentified offshoot of the horde-tenebrae stalking the city on his watch.

Most of the other men had gone off to their own hunts. No doubt they'd seek deserving malice or ferales, matching the fury and anguish of their immortal lives against an evil that would never die.

His muscles tightened with the ravager's desire to head out into the darkness, to find his own relief in sanctified violence. His vision flickered into the black-light glow of a hunting teshuva.

A flare of purely human panic seared across his open senses. He spun around to see the woman frozen in her open doorway.

"Dory." His voice crackled with harmonic lows. He cleared his throat. "Dory, it's okay. You're safe."

Her expression, though still blurred with the drugs, screamed "Liar." He couldn't blame her.

"Jilly is just down the hall," he continued. "She's sleeping. You wouldn't want to sneak out before you see her." Although judging from the higher flare of panic visible in her expanding pupils at her sister's name, that was exactly what Dory wanted.

"I thought I dreamed her." Dory's words barely carried over the scant two feet separating them.

He took a step forward, backing her into the room. She lowered her head and gave way before him, as meek as her sister was belligerent.

He stopped, feeling like a bully. But he noticed the pill bottles Sera had left beside the table were gone.

Dory followed his glance. "I didn't consent to be

placed in some program." When she set her jaw, chin askew, he finally recognized a faint commonality with a certain other Chan.

He shrugged. "No, you didn't."

"Is this a locked ward?"

"No more so than the one you made for yourself."

She scowled at him. "You're as bad as Jilly."

He shrugged again.

Dory slumped through the room to sit on the bed. "How'd she find me?" Squirming, she freed the lump from her pocket and tossed the pill bottles on the rumpled bedspread. "Why'd she even look?"

"You were hanging out with some very bad people. Jilly didn't want you to be hurt."

Dory gave a coarse bark of laughter, more a cough. "She's the one got hurt last time."

"You knew about that?" Liam's hackles prickled, same as when he faced a malice, bloated on its night's antics.

"Who you think called the paramedics?"

"But you didn't stay with her." He kept the outrage out of his voice, but still she flinched.

"I couldn't."

"Wouldn't."

"Asshole." She glared at him.

"I can tell you and she are related."

Dory's taut jaw slackened, not quite a smile. "Barely. All we have in common is our mother." Her hand crept across the bed to the pill bottle. "Jilly should've saved herself."

"Too late for that." He watched her turn the bottle in her hands. "You already take one?" When she nodded, he said, "Don't take any more until tomorrow, when we all have a chance to talk."

She looked up warily, as if he'd snatch the bottle from her hands. Then she nodded again and held out the bottle to him. "Until tomorrow."

He pocketed it and left.

He walked down the hall and flattened his palm

against each doorway where they'd stashed the junkies they'd scavenged from the haint HQ. No one else was stirring. Maybe Dory wasn't as far gone as he'd feared.

But he wasn't sure if the dim sound of weeping from her room was a good thing or not.

The talyan trickled in with the first morning light. They reported ... nothing.

"Nothing," Ecco growled as he stalked past Liam. "Quiet as a grave. And I know damn well they ain't dead. Just damned. Damn sneaky bastards."

"Keep your demon primed for anything odd."

Ecco cocked his head. "Like?"

Liam pictured the drifting specks of soul matter. "Witches. Goblins. Ghosts. Whatever."

When Ecco swiped his hand across his forehead, chunks of demon ichor spattered from his gauntlets. "Yeah, of course. Ghosts. Got it."

Faint psychic screams of drained malice trailed in the teshuva's wakes as the men cleared the halls. Jilly stood at the far end, looking young and flustered, the laces of her boots untied.

Liam walked toward her. The remnants of tenebrae cries shivered over his face like cobwebs.

"How could you?"

Just out of arm's reach, he stopped. "I knew she needed to sleep, so I let her take one—"

Jilly choked on a short breath. "How could you send them out again after that fight with the haints?"

"You know why. You're not mad about that."

She glared at him. "Oh, I'm not?"

Considering her vigorous defense of anything in danger with any sort of tenuous hold on a soul, he guessed she probably was. But that wasn't the point. "You're mad because you know you're going to have to risk losing Dory again."

She stiffened. "You can't just throw her out there—"

"I meant by talking to her," he said gently. "You could scare her away, making her face what she's done."

"You just want to know what happened to her because that'll give you more ammunition against the tenebrae."

She must know that Dory had abandoned her, bleeding on that street corner. Yet she stuck up for those she loved without hesitation or restraint. Envy for those lucky souls nipped at him, even though the leader of immortal, demon-slaying warriors shouldn't need a defender.

He threw her accusation back at her. "You realize Dory put you in as much danger as I put the league. Don't you want all the ammunition you can get, on both counts?"

She subsided. "You're awfully in touch with your Oprah side for a demon-slaying monster man."

"Night job. Lots of daytime television."

She didn't crack a smile. "What do I tell her?" She tugged at the neck of her T-shirt, pulling it above the black curlings of the *reven*.

"Nothing. Demons are a metaphor as far as she's concerned. Just find out who got her high. How'd she make her way to the haints? Anything we can use."

"People have been using her all her life."

"Save the pity party. Dory wouldn't appreciate it any more than your halfway house hooligans did." Since she seemed unusually amenable to his character evaluation, he added, "You don't like it either."

For a second, he thought she would object just on principle. Then she nodded.

"How about you go down to the kitchen," he said. "I'll bring Dory."

She gave him a shrewd glance. "You don't think she'll want to talk to me."

"Just give her a second."

"Fine. I'll start breakfast."

He waited until she stomped away, bootlaces flapping.

He took a moment to clear his head of her irate vibes.

When he unlocked the door, Dory was waiting. "I heard part of that. She sounded mad."

"At me. And herself."

Dory scratched at her arm. "She'll be mad at me too."

"Maybe she should be." He started down the hall, leaving her to tag behind. The glare aimed at the back of his head didn't faze him. "You've made some terrible mistakes."

"I've had a hard life."

"We all have our demons."

"You're supposed to say tomorrow is a new day."

"Only if you survive this one."

When her footsteps stopped, he turned to face her. She studied him, hands on her hips. "Tough love?"

"Is there any other kind?"

He kept walking. But halfway into the utilitarian kitchenette that had come with the warehouse, he rocked to a halt, stopped by the almost visible wave of sautéing onion. Something inside him twisted: not his demon, his empty stomach.

"We used to have a very nice kitchen," he blurted, apropos of nothing. "It had copper pots. No one used them."

Jilly slapped a pan on the runty efficiency stove. "I guessed by the ingredients I found."

Talyan tended to be indifferent eaters, which had always saddened Liam. Immortality without cuisine seemed the ultimate ironic end to his journey. Without the end part, of course.

"Jilly was always an amazing cook," Dory volunteered from behind him. "She fed us when Mom forgot."

Jilly's shoulders hunched. "Just wanted to make sure the Family Services ladies saw fresh veggies in the house."

"No fresh veggies here." Liam sighed.

"You'd be surprised what you can do with oyster crackers, eggs, and canned chili."

And he was surprised when she slipped three plates of neatly folded omelets across the table a few minutes later. "Where are the oyster crackers?"

"I didn't say *you* had oyster crackers. Your pantry isn't just neglected. It's an embarrassment."

"I'm calling DCFS right now," Dory chimed.

The sisters shared identical smiles at his expense.

He dug into breakfast. He didn't mind their snickers if it got the ball—and Dory's story—rolling. Plus, the omelet was really good, even if he wasn't here for the food. "So, Dory, I'm guessing you haven't had a good breakfast in a while either. Who was luring you in with the drugs instead?"

Dory glanced up, a bite of omelet halfway to her mouth. "Lured?"

"It didn't seem like that to you?"

Her gaze slid away. "I was high. Nothing seemed like anything." She lowered her hand and pushed her plate away. "Anyway. What would they want with me?"

Jilly pushed the plate back. "We were hoping you could tell us." She tapped the fork against the ceramic and waited until Dory took another bite.

Dory ate, if reluctantly. Liam wondered if she was succumbing to Jilly's big-sister bullying . . . or delaying answering the question. But whom would she be covering for except herself?

Jilly laced her fingers on the tabletop. "We think they wanted to get you hooked on solvo."

Dory shook her head. "I told him I don't do that shit. Makes you stupid."

Jilly slanted a look at Liam, telegraphing her relief that she'd been right to tell him her sister could be saved.

He avoided meeting her gaze and just leaned back in his chair. " 'Him' who?"

Dory didn't seem to hear, muttering, "Can you call it luring if you go willingly?"

Jilly's knuckles whitened on her fork; then she tried

to copy his relaxed posture. "Who did you want to go with?"

Dory bit at her lip, eyes unfocused. "After you got rid of Rico, I had to look around, you know? I couldn't just take my chances out on the street. I needed a place."

Liam stiffened, as if sitting a little straighter could lift him above the rising bad feeling in his gut. Jilly would never forgive herself for tossing her sister out of the frying pan and into the fire if Dory had ditched her pimp for a soul-stealing pusher of the chemical *desolator numinis*.

Dory finally glanced up to scowl at them, as if she knew what they were thinking. "When I told him I don't do solvo, he said it was fine. He said freedom means everything, you know? That's why he calls himself that."

"Calls himself what?" Jilly's voice took on an edge, but Liam already knew what Dory was going to say.

"He calls himself Blackbird," Dory said.

"Corvus," Liam said flatly. "Corvus Valerius."

CHAPTER 12

Jilly had no idea why Liam stiffened up like the week-old bread she'd found in the half-empty kitchen cabinets.

"Blackbird found me," Dory was saying. "Stayed with me sometimes. He didn't have a crib of his own. Likes to be free. So I seen him around here, there, everywhere." She scratched at the inner crook of her arm, although Jilly doubted much remained of those veins. "He never made me do nothing I didn't want to do."

Jilly kept one eye on Liam's distant expression. A weather report including the chance of rain would've incited more reaction, and she'd already noticed the more he took himself in hand, the more the rest of the world should be freaking out.

In a tone so bland her heart rate trebled to make up for his nonchalance, he asked, "What *did* you do for Blackbird, Dory?"

With an insolent shrug, she shook back her bleached hair, but her face was pale when she glanced at Jilly. "I went on his rounds with him."

Jilly had thought nothing could hurt worse than a knife sliding between her ribs. She was wrong. "You were dealing solvo?"

"We didn't sell it." Dory looked at them as if it was a

point of pride. "He gave it away for free. He said he's all about freedom, and that's no lie."

"Funny how the devil doesn't have to lie," Liam murmured.

Jilly rubbed her forehead, not from any pain of her own but in sympathetic ache at the flare of Liam's *reven*. She didn't think Dory saw it. Which said more about her sister's lack of attention than any effort on Liam's part at camouflage. His recklessness made her gut clench with fear, a sick counterpoint to her horror at what Dory had done. How many haints had been created at her sister's hand?

"Oh, Dory," she whispered. She reached across the table to cup her fingers under her sister's clenched fist. Beneath her thumb, the tiny prick-mark scabs on the back of her sister's hand read like a Braille of lost chances. "Dory, do you know what you've done?"

Dory tugged her hand away. "We set them free, let their souls fly. Blackbird told me I mighta been a junkie whore—that's what you yelled at Rico, Jilly; do you remember, that he made me a junkie whore?—but at least I'd never sold my soul."

Jilly slumped back in her chair. She'd wanted to call Rico on his crimes, but she'd rather have taken two more knives to the ribs than discover her sister had heard that exchange. Knowing her vigilante attack on the pimp had only made Dory more vulnerable took away the last of her breath and pierced her heart straight through.

"Lost isn't the same as free." Her voice cracked.

Liam met her despairing gaze, but his words were directed to Dory, as lazily as any after-breakfast gossip. "How much is a soul worth these days?"

Dory glowered at him. "Mine in particular? To him, more than a do-gooder like you would pay."

He smiled crookedly. "Oh, Dory. I'm not good."

After a moment, she nodded. "Well, I'm not either. And Blackbird still wanted me around."

Jilly's empty hands clenched. Was it too late to grab Dory and run, as she should have years ago when they were both children? She'd been too frightened at the time, and she'd chosen a job trying to keep other kids from doing exactly that, but considering where they'd ended up, maybe they should've just taken their chances.

The memory of those early days strained her voice when she asked, "Do you know what happened to the other people who were hanging around in that apartment?"

Dory scratched again, at the back of her hand this time, to erase Jilly's touch or from memories of her own. "I remember shooting up. Then I remember the wall busting in." She pinned Jilly with a jaundiced eye. "I remember seeing you. And I remember hearing screaming. Just in my head. But I remember."

The blood pooled in Jilly's limbs, and her hands felt heavy. As if she held a hammer. A hammer drenched in blood.

In the end, there'd been no blood, of course. Every speck of the burned-out haints had morphed to ash.

"I'm sorry," Jilly whispered, not sure to whom she owed the apology—the sister she'd failed or the people Dory had doomed beyond death.

"About the screaming?" Dory shrugged. Lost in her own turmoil, Jilly couldn't decide if her sister meant her screaming "junkie whore" or the shrieking of butchered haints. "Happens to all of us. Except, I thought, maybe you. I guess not."

Liam cleared his throat. "Maybe he seems benevolent, but Corvus—Blackbird, as you call him—is very dangerous."

Dory nodded. "Sometimes you need that on your side, you know?" Her gaze shifted back to Jilly and widened with contrived innocence.

Jilly couldn't even roll her eyes back. Look whom she'd tied herself to. Inadvertently, maybe. To save her skin, perhaps. But she'd known what Liam was—powerful, demanding, and, yes, dangerous—and she'd reveled in him.

What ten kinds of hypocrite was she to judge? Black-bird might've made the monsters, but Liam unmade them with the same lack of mercy. She pushed to her feet and paced the width of the room. "Who is he, this Blackbird?"

"We killed him." Liam raised his voice so she could hear from her distance, but Dory's gasp was still audible. "Or we thought we did. He created solvo and started spreading it. We had to stop him."

"Solvo takes away the pain," Dory said. "You shouldn't knock it."

He lifted one eyebrow. "Even you won't take it." When she just scowled, he continued. "Corvus thought solvo would help him conquer the world."

Dory sniffed. "He said in retrospect he should've started with just the South Side and worked his way up from there."

From the glint in Liam's eyes, Jilly recognized that he'd meant that domination quite literally even if Dory was being snide.

Jilly halted her pacing and slumped against the wall. "How do we find him?" Her voice sounded funny, scratchy and broken like warped vinyl. She knew what they would do to him, or what they would try to do. Pre-sumably, he'd return the mayhem, full force.

Dory shook her head. "You can't find him. He's Blackbird. Here and there."

"He has to land sometime." Liam pushed to his feet. "And if not, he leaves his droppings. Where does he deal?"

"Everywhere," Dory started. When Liam gave her a look, she huffed. "Sometimes he hangs near Back of the Yards. And near the pier, but he doesn't deal there. He says he just likes to look out over the water."

Jilly expected Liam to charge from the room, ham-mer swinging, but he surprised her. He settled his hip against the counter and studied Dory. "You're giving Corvus up without much of a fight."

Dory shrugged. "Blackbird likes to talk. He tells us

a lot, even if it doesn't all make sense, and he doesn't mind us talking. It's not like the cops can find him. Or stop him."

"Is that what you think we are? Cops?"

She shifted her gaze to Jilly. "Something like that. Maybe vice."

"Something like that," he repeated softly. "Dory, look at me."

The timbre of his voice shifted, lowered. Jilly found her gaze drawn to him too, though she recognized the demon harmonics for what they were.

Dory hunched like a bedraggled bleached-blond rabbit facing a wolf. "What?"

"What does Corvus hold over you? You and the others we found with you."

"He had a party pack that wouldn't quit, besides solvo."

"You didn't hang with him just for the drugs. You could get that anywhere." He didn't bother pointing out she *had* gotten it plenty.

Dory rocked from side to side in her chair, as if Liam were dragging the words out through some twist in her throat. "He understood."

"Understood what?"

"Us. More than anybody else ever did. He said we could let the darkness out."

Liam sighed, a purely human sigh that broke whatever spell he'd woven.

Dory straightened abruptly, her face scrunched with petulance. "I don't know why anyone cares now. Nobody did before."

Jilly finally found her voice. "I always cared."

After a moment, Dory nodded. "You just couldn't do anything."

"Now I can." The league's basement armory with its walls of weapons called to Jilly as if the new steel in her spine reverberated like a tuning fork to those choices of destruction.

Liam watched her so intently she wondered if he felt it too.

Dory stood, breaking the moment. "You can't keep me here. I haven't done anything." She paused a moment, then gave a harsh bark of laughter. "Well, nothing too bad."

Liam smiled, a calculating expression. "Nothing, huh? I suppose you could always take us to meet your Blackbird."

Dory's amusement faltered. "He's not mine. He won't belong to anybody."

Admiration warmed her voice and set Jilly's hackles up. Especially when her sister looked at her and said, "Kind of like you."

Jilly leaned her head back against the wall. Dory had no idea how far she had sold herself down the river. The Styx, apparently.

Liam cleared his throat. "I need to see how Sera is getting on with our other guests."

"Prisoners," Dory corrected.

He spread his hands. "Such cynicism in one so young."

She flashed him a flirty smile that didn't reach her eyes. "I'm an old soul."

He didn't smile back. "At least it's yours."

When he walked out, he seemed to take the breath out of Jilly's body. She slumped a few inches lower on the wall.

"I can't believe he's your boyfriend," Dory snapped. "He's worse than anything Mom ever brought home."

Her sister's tone straightened Jilly. "He's not my boyfriend." Then she felt compelled to add, "And he's not that bad. Anyway, you seemed to get along with him just fine."

"I know how to deal with guys like that."

"Smile and scoot your neckline down?" She shook her head, half bemused, half in despair. "It's not like I didn't notice."

Dory shrugged.

Jilly rubbed her forehead. "If you think he's so bad, why flash flesh?"

"That's *how* you protect against guys like that. How could you never learn that?"

"By staying *away* from guys you say are like that." Why was she mentally removing Liam from that side of the equation? He was a big, domineering bully. Just because he wanted to save the world didn't change that.

Dory huffed. "You can't get away from them. They're everywhere."

"Like Corvus." Jilly wasn't sure how much more she could get from her sister. Dory had been so out of it. Could anything she said be trusted?

"Blackbird doesn't fuck his girls." Dory frowned. "Actually, I don't think I've ever seen him touch anyone."

The thread of longing in her voice crept along Jilly's spine. When was the last time someone had touched her sister gently, with love?

The chill spread through her skin. When was the last time *she'd* been touched that way?

The memory of Liam's big hand against her demon-marked flesh after that desperate coupling in her apartment threatened her, and she slammed the door on it. Just as she'd slammed the door on any number of helping hands reaching her way—afraid she'd find more like her uncles or her first bad boyfriend—before she'd learned to be the one to reach out. Either she or Dory had to take the first step.

She pushed away from the wall. "Come on. Let's get you some clean clothes."

"I got evicted," Dory said. "And I lost all my stuff. That's why Blackbird gave me . . ." She dropped her gaze.

The drugs. Jilly withheld a sigh. Dory must have been a glaringly obvious candidate for future hainthood. No place to be. No one looking for her.

"Come on," she urged. "We'll find something."

They met a talya in the hall.

"Jonah." Jilly dredged up his name from the aftermath of the salambe attack. "Where would I find extra clothes? You guys must keep stuff around for . . ." She slanted a glance at Dory. "For after work."

He stared at them a moment. The impassive stillness of his expression drew his otherwise handsome face into forbidding lines, like a marble statue of the strictest saint in the calendar. His chisel-sharp gaze flicked over Dory, assessing. No, Jilly thought, worse than that. He'd already made his judgment.

She stretched her fingers, felt the demon move through the fibers of her self. Apparently the aftermath of her encounter with Rico hadn't taught her anything about not throwing down with big, scary males.

Jonah's lips twitched, not a smile, more a sneer. "I have many, many years of unraveling demons behind me, girl. Not to mention righteousness at my side." His voice was so soft and low only her spiked hearing picked up his words.

She replied in kind, keeping Dory out of it. "And I have my unholy pissed-offedness at being called girl."

He snorted at human volume. "I can't imagine how the league will survive the return of your kind."

She folded her arms over her chest. "My kind?"

His gaze flicked to the exposed skin above her crossed arms, then to her hair. His scornful smile widened. "The fairer sex, I was going to say."

"I can see how you'd drive a woman away." She'd meant the insult generically, but she was surprised how abruptly his smirk vanished. "Maybe outlawing us wasn't fair."

"To whom?" he murmured. The faintly antiquated cadence of his voice drifted toward something she'd almost call sorrow. He shook his head, the waves of his sandy blond hair hiding his eyes. "We keep leftovers in the storerooms downstairs. Help yourself."

She didn't think he meant just help herself to the clothes. He managed to brush past them without actually touching them.

Dory glanced after him in consternation. "Is every guy here an asshole?"

Jilly wished she hadn't sensed that unexpected depth to the rude talya. She didn't want to defend him. "I haven't met them all."

"So far, they're all hot as hell too. Can I borrow your lip gloss?"

Jilly refused to dignify that with an answer as she handed over her tube of balm.

In the basement, the weapons room called to her. But she bypassed its high-tech access panel and pushed open a smaller, regular old door, where she found stacks of cotton T-shirts, sweatpants, and socks, enough that she could have supplied a half dozen homeless outreaches. She hoped Liam was getting a great bulk discount.

"Black, black, or black?" She rifled through the piles. "Large or extra large?"

"Extra large," Dory said. "I plan to eat a bunch more omelets before I go." She leaned against the door. "I missed you, Jilly."

Jilly paused, her hands fisted in black cotton. "How about you don't go again?"

Wait, what was she saying? She was an immortal demon-slaying half monster now. She couldn't set any sort of good example.

She wondered what excuses were going through her sister's mind when Dory sighed and shook her head. "I can't help myself."

"Then let me help, okay?" She waited for her sister's faint nod, wondering if the hesitation had to do with the crap job she'd done in the past. But she couldn't exactly explain that helping would prominently feature destroying Corvus—that, at least, *should* be in her demonic power.

Jilly left her sister to shower and hunted the hallways for Liam. A faint buzz through her skin stopped her outside the office where she'd first barged into his league. She pushed open the door. He was leaning behind that oversized desk, arms braced and palms flattened over the curling edges of a big map, like a lion over a kill. Archer, Sera, and a few other talyan clustered around as if waiting for their piece of the action. They all looked up at her, and Liam straightened his stance.

Archer spoke first. "Did you get anything else from her?"

"Just that all talya men are hot." She glanced at Sera apologetically when the males grinned.

The other woman shrugged. "I noticed it too. At the beginning." She punched Archer's shoulder when he glowered. "Maybe immortality refines the pores."

Jilly shrugged. "Maybe the teshuva like pretty boys."

Liam cleared his throat over the male grumbles. "Looking for something useful here?"

Jilly shook her head. "Dory had nothing but good to say about Blackbird. Corvus." Was it a shared failing of theirs, passed from mother to daughters, to fall for any tough male that strode by?

Sera nodded. "That's the impression I get from the others we picked up. They don't know the demon-possessed gladiator Archer and I faced in the tenebraeternum four months ago rejected his own soul, that he abandoned it in the Veil. They just wanted something to kill the pain. They don't see that all that's left is the evil."

"No one ever does," Ecco growled.

"That's why *we're* here," Liam said. "The teshuva allow us to see what others can't believe. And to do something about it."

Jilly studied him. How did he manage to infuse his voice with such conviction when she knew the doubts that plagued him? Did no one else see cracks? They certainly leaned on him as if he could never falter.

She clenched her fist against the sudden urge to drag him away. He would never allow it. And besides, where would they go?

Sera and Archer had wheedled some locations from the other addicts they'd picked up, and the talyan plotted the addresses on the giant map.

Liam leaned over the rumpled, pushpinned paper again. "If we can find the pattern, maybe we'll find Corvus." His hand clenched beside the map, and muscle rippled up to his shoulders.

Despite that strength, he was lean to the point of . . . points. His wrist bone stuck out as if his skeleton had someplace else to be, as if the demon burned too hot in him. She shuddered, remembering how gruesome that could be. But she shouldn't blame the demon. He pushed himself, with the weight of his crew behind him.

He assigned recon to the talyan and they disbanded.

She took his hand and tugged, steeling herself against the quick spark that fanned through her skin. "C'mon."

Despite his height, he moved so smoothly she drew him along like a ghost on a string. "Where are we going?"

"Out. You gave everybody else a task. Now you have one."

"Since when do you assign tasks?"

"Since you dropped the ball on this one." At the faintest resistance in his following, she glanced back. "Oh, I know you had more important things to do, but while we're waiting for the world to end, we can take care of this."

She grabbed a set of keys hanging beside the back door that led out to the Cyclone-fenced lot behind the warehouse. She narrowed her eyes at him. "I'll drive."

He held up both hands, palms out, as if anything else had never occurred to him.

In one of the league's nondescript sedans, he lounged back in the passenger seat. His outstretched arm bridged the gap to her seat. Though he didn't touch her, the back of her neck warmed at his nearness. If she leaned back just a little . . . But she knew everybody liked to lean on him.

So she kept her back ramrod stiff. "How long have you been crew boss here?"

He shrugged one shoulder. "The problem with even

saying I'm boss is that demons tend to choose their victims from the conveniently disenfranchised. Even when they weren't running with scissors, these people never played well with others."

She huffed out an annoyed breath. "How long?"

"A long time." He stared straight ahead. "There's no ceremony to mark the transition. The purely not-honorary title of league chief hellion goes to whomever steps in it."

"How. Long."

He turned a fierce scowl on her. "About a hundred years. Give or take a decade."

"So it's been that long since you had a meal?"

He blinked. "I eat."

"I saw what was in those cabinets."

He shifted uneasily at her dire tone. "Ecco does most of the shopping. Sera's still on the recently possessed talya 'I can eat doughnuts every day and still fit in my demon-slaughtering clothes' diet."

Jilly smiled. "Yeah, I noticed that. Plus, I don't think I'd want to tell her she was stuck with the grocery shopping."

"Archer went there already. And came back quick."

She winced. "Which is why he would not make a good league boss."

Liam sighed. "I tried to give it to him once. He's been possessed almost as long as I have. He comes from the right background."

"Wrong temper."

"Plus he's not an idiot."

The note of bitterness that crept into his voice wasn't directed at the other talya, she knew. "Why'd you take it, then?"

"I'd just joined the league." *Just been possessed* was the unspoken corollary. "Roald, the talya who you would call leader before me, was already . . . drifting."

"What does that mean?"

"He'd been possessed a very long time." He glowered at her. "And don't ask me how long. I have no idea, since

I never asked. That would've been disrespectful." His glower turned more pointed.

"Demons being so well-known for their table manners," she muttered.

He grunted a halfhearted mix of annoyance and assent. "Roald was tired. The demon erases most damage to the body, but the mind, the soul . . . Half the time, he wouldn't surface from the hunt for days. Leading the talyan might be harder than netting poisonous fanged butterflies, but even poisonous fanged butterflies want . . ." He shook his head. "Where was I going with that?"

She didn't think the comparison was apt. If anyone had been cruelly pinned down, it wasn't the wayward talyan; it was Liam. "The league wanted a leader."

"Not wanted, probably."

"Needed." The inescapable truth of the word tasted like iron in her mouth.

He shrugged. "One night, Ro went out on the hunt, and we never saw him again. If he was fatally wounded past the point his teshuva could hold him together, he was old enough his body would've been ashes to ashes, dust to dust, before we even knew where to look."

Jilly wrinkled her nose.

"When it was obvious he wasn't coming back, somebody asked me, since I'd been a blacksmith once, if I knew where he could get the biggest whetstone ever. And thus a not-so-glorified supply clerk was born."

She pulled into the parking lot. "Speaking of supplies."

He glanced out. "Kitchen Komforts? Are Sera and Archer registered here? Is there something those two haven't told me?"

"You used to have good copper pots, you said."

"We lost them all when Corvus destroyed our headquarters."

She patted his hand, behind her on the seat. "He has much to answer for."

Liam nodded gravely.

"I need a stockpot if I'm going to make soup."

He narrowed his eyes in suspicion. "Why are you making soup?"

Under her fingers, the bones of his wrist felt both powerful and exposed. "You want a well-fed fighting team or what?"

"Hell, yeah."

"Then buy me a pot."

CHAPTER 13

He had not been alone with his thoughts for a very long time. Even when the demon rested, Corvus had always been aware of it, if only from the bands of black that snaked up his arms, once broken on the glaring sands of the Colosseum and healed by the powers of darkness. As his demon dragged him through the city, it saddened Corvus, now that he had his thoughts, that his thoughts now were so . . . thoughtless.

Too, he had not imagined being alone would be sad in itself.

Tilting his head so that his rolling eye would align with its more attentive brother, he watched the empty husks arrayed around him as the demon made its rounds. He was more than them, at least, though he wasn't sure why. Most of the solvo blanks faded into listless apathy within a very short time. That he'd kept any wit or awareness after his djinni-riddled soul had been forcibly woven in the Veil between the realms puzzled him. Whether it was a testament to his iron will, his long possession, or some other quirk, he had no idea.

The soul-swiped husks were everywhere now, as he'd seen on the demon's daily forced marches. He could be proud of himself that the powdery distillation of the *desolator numinis* had worked so well.

He was less entranced with the searing darklings of smoke and metal that had begun coalescing around his own demon. As his ill-fit demon yanked him around, the marks on his arms oozed with a spoiled-egg stench that seemed the sweetest nectar to these unfamiliar darklings. Not the old hulking fellows or little darting black monsters that had once trailed in his wake. These new demons consumed whatever they touched.

Without the tempering influence he once exerted, his demon seemed set on a path that would end in the utter devouring of all. Not his original intent, to be sure. Not even his demon had understood they sought release, not obliteration. With some ruin along the way, unavoidably, but certainly not the central aim.

The demon set their feet for the next congregation of husks. He couldn't understand its obsession; once they'd settled, the soulless carcasses never went anywhere. But his lips were chanting something as he walked, and he realized they were headed to one of the newer collections.

"Free her, free her," he was saying.

Now he remembered. There were a few who longed for release as much as he. One of those waited at this place. He'd seen the trapped longing in her eyes, and he'd felt the kinship of the demon-ridden. Oh, demonic powers hadn't actually invaded her soul; her damnation had been self-imposed.

It had been nice to not be alone. Stripping that female talya of half her clothes and most of her teshuva all those months ago had reminded him of the revels of his Roman master. Not that he'd been invited to those, of course. Nero's court glassworker had strutted his prize gladiator on the sands, but hadn't trusted him around the lovely, delicate works of his trade. Not just the glass, but the girls. No brute hands, he'd said—an unfair branding, to Corvus's mind, considering his virtuosity in the Colosseum.

Then he'd been injured, and thrown aside. Even broken glass was valued. But not him. The demon, though, had wanted him, invited him to join it—slagged and reformed him into something more. After that, he had invited himself to the next merrymaking. But then the screaming had rather ruined the night, and the blood overshadowed the beauty of the glass.

In two thousand years, he'd come to realize the demon was no friend to him, and now it had decided to play master without the subterfuge. But maybe, in the depths of his woe, he had found another to share his pain.

Though he'd admit his hands lacked the finesse they'd once had, and she looked as brittle as the ones who had broken under his touch that night in his master's house after his possession.

Still, as the demon propelled him down the street, his rolling eye looked eagerly ahead. And saw.

Though he had no control anymore, still the force of his dismay locked his muscles, and the demon was forced to wait with him.

The marks on his arms dripped poison with its fury. Once again, he and the demon were in accord. Someone had stolen the congregation and, with it, the one who had met his eye.

"Jilly wants something." Archer paced outside the kitchen.

Liam craned his neck past the other man. To think he'd ever underestimated how sometimes playing leader to a bunch of violent, paranoid immortals got in the way of more important things. "Dinner maybe?"

Archer snorted. "Oh, that's not all she wants."

"Just because your mate offered to serve up your choicer bits if you volunteered her for KP duty again doesn't mean all women fear subjugation by slotted spoon."

"I'm telling you, when a woman feeds her man, she has plans."

"I'm not her—" Liam took a deep breath. "Well, I'm not entirely opposed to the idea."

Ecco stumped down the hall. "What ideas are we talking about? And what is that smell? I want that."

Liam fixed Archer with a smug stare. "See? Sometimes it's simple."

"Did you just call me simple?" Ecco shouldered past him. "Out of my way."

One by one, other talyan drifted into the hall. Liam had sent off the addicts—except for a couple who'd refused—to various rehab programs, courtesy of Sera's previous life and hospital connections. With the coming twilight, that left only the prehunt crowd at the warehouse, restless and well aware they, unlike the junkies, had no chance of casting off the compulsions that rode them.

They milled outside the door to the kitchenette, reluctant to edge by him, until Liam fell into Ecco's wake.

Jilly stood at the stove, a cheerful red-and-white-striped towel hanging from the back pocket of her jeans. The knot-work bracelet was shoved high on her forearm. She didn't look around, just said, "Get a bowl."

Ecco stepped up with alacrity. He towered over the petite Jilly with his outstretched bowl like some Oliver Twist on 'roids. She ladled out the soup, and Liam heard the eager inhalation of the talyan behind him as the fragrance rolled over them.

An elbow in his ribs shoved him aside, and the talyan streamed past him to get in line, never mind the usual teshuva-triggered avoidance of close contact. Or, God forbid, a little respect for their leader.

Good thing they'd never find out what a hard time he'd given her about slapping down the platinum card for the stockpot big enough to cook down a feralis. Not that the whiff of chicken and dumplings coming his way had anything to do with demonology. Heaven, maybe.

He waited in the doorway, arms crossed, while his crew filed past the stoves. From the dinky oven, Jilly handed out fist-sized domes of lightly browned biscuit. Almost the same color as her eyes, he noted idly. The tightening in his belly was definitely hunger. Of what sort, he wasn't entirely sure.

He wished he'd held firm at the grocery store when she wanted to get the insanely expensive industrial-sized jar of honey. Not necessary, he'd argued. Talyan didn't need to be sweetened up. Listening to the men's pleased murmurs as they drizzled spoonfuls of the golden glaze over their biscuits, he realized he wanted that all for himself.

As if he'd touched her shoulder, Jilly met his gaze across the long metal table lined with talyan focused on their bowls. She lifted her eyebrows and tipped the pot toward him. Almost empty. She filled a last bowl and slid it across the counter.

After a moment, he pushed away from the door. The clink of spoons against empty bowls accompanied him across the room along with the low murmur of voices as the men leaned back. Content, he realized.

He walked up to Jilly. "Taming the savage beasts?"

"Maybe." She handed him a biscuit.

The dough warmed his palm. "Thanks." He propped his hip on the counter. His mouth watered and he forced himself not to tip the bowl to his lips. No sense acting the savage, half-starved beast.

She hummed to herself. "I used to cook for the kids. I miss it a little, I guess."

A velvety dumpling slipped over his tongue with a hint of rosemary. Despite his pleasure—maybe because of it?—he couldn't take his attention from her. She scanned the room with lips pursed. He imagined her keeping watch over her kids and was half tempted to start a food fight. Except the soup was too good to fling.

When she turned that eagle eye on him, he said, "You know it's good."

She nodded. "The more they come together as a team, the more likely they are to survive."

"I meant your cooking. The halfway house's loss was our gain."

She ran her gaze over him, foot to head. He held himself still though his skin prickled even with his demon dormant again. "A strong wind could blow you over.

Well, assuming it was a demon-driven wind. Which, lately, it has been."

"I'm not Roald. I won't walk off into the ether."

She met his gaze without blinking. "No one intends to wander off."

He put the bowl down gently and said, "I am not one of your wayward youth."

Though she half shuttered her spicy sweet eyes, he felt the spark jump between them. "Yeah. I got that."

The flare of attraction was hot and sudden and pointless. He took a step back to let it sputter out. "Thanks for dinner."

She spun away to wash her hands.

Subtle, he thought.

Around them, the talyan were rising and stretching, ready for the night. Jilly dried her hands and tossed the towel at the sink. "Okay, let's go."

"Go?"

"Find Corvus. It's why you let the other addicts go, isn't it?" She pinned him with a baleful eye. "I suppose they're wearing tracking collars."

He met her gaze. "No. I have talyan following them."

"Fishing."

"Protecting. If they go running back to Corvus, they could be in danger. But I haven't heard anything back from the guards yet."

Ecco walked between them, rinsed his bowl, and put it in the dishwasher. "If Niall fucks up whatever you're talking about, come to me."

"Go, teamwork," Liam said wryly.

"Thank you," she said over him.

Ecco flexed. "He's not the sort to appreciate a real handful of woman."

"Stop while you're ahead," she suggested.

"See you on the street, then." The other talyan, following Ecco's example, cleared their dishes.

Jonah brought up the rear, added soap, and started the machine. "Your sister is still here."

"Is that a problem?" Jilly's tone implied it better not

be, and Liam wondered if he should frisk her for paring knives.

Jonah shook his head. "She'll be safer with us. I heard Sera is bringing her angelic friend to talk to Dory."

Jilly nodded cautiously. "She told me Nanette's ministry has a background with substance abuse."

"Not to mention, she can heal with a touch." Jonah gave a decisive nod. "I hope it works."

When the last talya had gone, Liam huffed. "Anyone else you want to wrap around your finger?"

She glared at him. "Not really."

He walked out, knowing she'd follow.

"Maybe Nanette can help Dory where I can't," she said from behind him. "But I can at least make sure Corvus and his solvo and his salambes won't be waiting for her on the other side."

"We might not find him tonight." Liam cautioned.

"We have forever, but Dory doesn't. We'll find him."

If the determination in her eyes counted for anything, he knew they would. He couldn't leash her. He shouldn't even want to. The league—hell, the world—needed her fire and zeal.

With a thud of bootheels, she matched his pace down the hall. "I want a sword or something."

The fate of the world might be looking up, but he was doomed.

A wind that still stung with winter's bite hissed down the street in front of the warehouse to tug at his coat, and the pull of the hammer made his shoulders ache, though he'd carried it for a century without noticing its weight. Jilly's jab about being like Roald stung.

She was so used to thinking that broken was a problem, she couldn't see that cracks were good camouflage out here. Cracks let the steam out, made him look bigger when all the pieces were spread out. Cracks were good for a lot. He silenced his grumbling when Jilly appeared.

She'd pulled the spikes of blue-striped hair into twin

tufts bristling like antennae on either side of her head. A few errant strands trailed over her wary golden gaze. He eyed her with trepidation and wondered aloud, "What are you packing? I shouldn't have left you down there by yourself. A chain saw? Suitcase nuke?"

She snorted. A flicker in her hands, and she revealed a double-curved weapon only a little wider than his spread fingers. The two half-moon blades overlapped so that the horns of one pointed outward while the horns of the other wrapped back to protect the hand. The middle of one moon was leather wrapped where she gripped it, but the other exposed edges gleamed with sharp-honed perfection.

"It's balanced like a good cleaver." She smiled and flipped the knife in her hand. The edges winked under the streetlights.

He winced. "The demon can't regenerate lost fingers."

"I won't lose anything."

Apparently she didn't count that missing chunk of her soul. He squelched the hollow thought. "Just be careful. The teshuva lends you some natural—supernatural—talent in the mayhem department, but you shouldn't put all your faith in it." He rubbed his forehead. "Never mind faith. I mean you shouldn't take chances with the demon if you don't have to."

The knives disappeared into her pocket. "I won't," she said. "Either one."

Quiet as bats, the talyan left the warehouse. They edged around him and disappeared into the night, their black clothes merging with the gloom as they separated.

"Alone?" Jilly murmured.

"There's too much evil for the good—or at least the repentant—to bunch up. I'll recall them if we have cause."

"You don't sound like we have a chance."

How to explain to her that after a certain number of years—decades, for instance—it was hard to sound like anything? "Finding Corvus isn't something we'll leave to chance. Come on."

"I need to do something first. Can I borrow your phone for a second?" She was scowling at him even as the question "Why?" formed on his lips. So he handed it over without asking, just to prove he could.

She punched in a number, waited. "Dee, it's Jilly." A spate of girlish squeals rang from the phone. Jilly grimaced and held it away from her ear. "I'm fine." She paused. "I know. Yeah, I got another job." She half turned from Liam. "No, I'm sure not all bosses suck as bad as Envers. Listen, can you come down to the alley for a couple minutes before lockout? I'll be there in a few minutes. Bring Iz, okay? And I want my phone back."

Liam studied her after she hung up. "You can't tell them."

"What?"

"Anything. That's why it's easier to let it go. Let them go."

"I let them go all the time. When I can't help them, when I can. They all move on. I get that." But her stiffly held shoulders belied her acceptance.

His tyro fighter didn't accept anything without a fight. Even when she couldn't win.

When their cab pulled up across the street from the halfway house, the two teens were just coming down the stairs. The four of them met around the side of the building, out of sight of the front door.

The girl threw her arms around Jilly with the same delighted squeal Liam recognized from the phone call. Despite her enthusiasm, Dee fixed him over Jilly's shoulder with a stare too knowing for someone her age. "Your new boss is hot," she stage-whispered as she handed over Jilly's cell phone.

Jilly pulled back. "Who says he's my boss?"

"He has that 'you got time to lean, you got time to clean' look."

Jilly snorted. "Yeah, we do a lot of cleaning."

Dee faked a gasp. "But not leaning, I hope?"

"Definitely not." Jilly gave the teens a once-over. "You two doing okay?"

They both nodded, Dee more decisively than Iz.

The young man studied Liam. "You know what happened to Andre. You know that thing we saw in the alley. That's why you wanted to see me and Dee."

Liam lifted one eyebrow. "My advice? Just say no."

Dee snorted, sounding a lot like Jilly. "We're not dumb."

Which didn't really indicate whether she thought drugs were dumb or he was for even bringing up the alternative. When Jilly gave a faint shake of her head, he tightened his jaw against the urge to demand compliance. Did they think they were immortal? On solvo, they would be, without even the ability to regret the choice.

"Andre won't be coming back." The faintest thread of uncertainty wavered in Jilly's tone. "But if you see him around, I want you to stay away from him. No matter what. And then I want you to call me. I'll leave my phone with you, Dee." She programmed in the @1 business number. "And restrict your texting to after class, yeah?"

Dee rolled her eyes but accepted the phone with a nod.

Iz stuffed his hands in his pockets and gazed sidelong at them. "Why'd you leave, Jilly?"

She hesitated, and this time Liam gave her that slight shake of the head. "Nothing to do with you guys, you know that. You already figured out that sometimes real life takes a hard left turn and your only choice is to follow where it leads."

Liam couldn't completely stifle his cough of amusement.

Iz glared at him. "You were the left turn, weren't you?"

Liam shrugged at the flare of antagonism. "Don't worry. She doesn't follow all that blindly."

After a moment, Iz's stance softened. "Sometimes that's good, right?"

"Yeah. Remember that next time some stranger comes around offering you candy."

The teens groaned.

Jilly glanced back at the street. "You guys need to be inside before doors close. Just remember."

After a bit more groaning, the girls hugged again. Iz hovered close, leaving Liam on the outside of the little circle.

He and Jilly waited as the kids made their way back inside. The door latched with an audible click.

Jilly sighed. "They're no safer than before."

"And in no more danger," Liam reminded her. "The boy could be a Bookkeeper someday. He has the eyes for it."

Jilly shuddered. "There's a career path I'll never suggest."

He gritted his teeth at her vehemence. "Right. Wouldn't want to give anyone the chance to help save the world." He strode out of the alley, forcing her to keep up.

"That's our job, remember?"

Despite his stiff jaw, the question slipped out. "And do you still blame me for it, as Iz does?"

She stuffed her hands in her pockets, then winced and pulled one hand out to suck her finger where she'd obviously nicked herself on the crescent-moon blades. "You explained already, my penance trigger was tripped long before I met you."

Her answer no more addressed his question than the kids had agreed to stay away from drugs. But she didn't need to like him to do her job. The more she feared for her hooligans, the harder she'd work. It only weakened his cause to reassure her.

And revealed a weakness in himself that he wanted her reassurance at all. His spine prickled, as if he'd swung his hammer too wildly and left himself undefended. He couldn't afford to expose his doubts about his leadership. The *talyan* had enough monstrous, ceaseless fears to deal with on a nightly basis without his adding to their burden. Of course she blamed him. He blamed himself for not somehow warning her off, even knowing she couldn't have—maybe wouldn't have—listened.

Lucky him, the needs of the league ground on, and didn't care about his momentary lapse. As a poor smithy fleeing starvation, he would've been grateful to know that he'd always have a place. Instead, he suspected she would be less prickly to that smithy than the league leader he had become.

He took them back to the apartment where they'd found the haints. Already, the encrustations of birnenston were sloughing off the walls and ceiling in the absence of the sustaining demonic emanations. The rumble of the L rattled the broken plywood over the windows, and a few beams of light shot across the room.

"What are we looking for?" Jilly frowned down at a pile of dust, all that was left of a burned-out haint.

"Darkness."

"It's already night."

"Call your demon."

"Oh. *That* darkness. What am I—"

He touched her arm to turn her back toward the dust, and all his senses sharpened, slanted.

She stumbled back from the pile when a cloud of scintillating flecks coalesced, their pattern vaguely man-shaped. "Tell me that's not a soul. Or leftover sliced and diced soul."

Throughout the room, other glowing clouds hovered.

"Oh God," she whispered.

"I doubt he's around at the moment."

"What are we going to do?"

"Nothing. We can't repatriate them with their destroyed bodies, although they seem unwavering in the search. And apparently they can't find their way to wherever an unbroken soul should go." He released her to rub his temple. "Just remember how you summoned the teshuva to see. If we can find more, these soulflies could lead us to other haint haunts. I don't like this sense of something smoldering."

"Not these. The bodies are cold dust and gone."

"Yes, but back home, the peat marshes could burn underground, unnoticed, and then blaze up out of control." He let his hand drop to his side. His fingers ached with the pressure of his involuntary fist. "Where there are burned-out haint husks with soulfly smoke, there's bound to be hellfire."

"Salambes. Maybe even Corvus." She shuddered, watching the soul flecks. When she hugged herself, the knot-work bracelet glinted with their reflected emanations. "And he left these shredded souls to wander. Lost. No, trapped. Never to be freed." Her eyes seemed dull as the ashed coals in a cold forge.

Staring down into her stricken face, he frowned. "I'd say they're a little too free." He tugged at her arm to bump her away from the cloud.

Through her jacket, he felt her shiver again. A scent like iron filings chilled his lungs, and gray mists curdled around the edges of his vision.

He tightened his grip as he felt the world shifting around them. "Oh no, you don't. No slipping into the demon realm. Not for them." He dragged her close, as if he could build a cage with his body to keep the bitter frost at bay.

"No hope," she whispered. "No last chance."

He'd thought the same himself, more than once, but to hear the words on her lips tore his heart. For her, he wanted to lie—never mind the fallen angel inside him—and say everything would be all right. "I thought we agreed, no drifting. Jilly?"

But she was gone, into the demon realm on a downward spiral of anguish resonating with the doomed soulflies. So much for her tough riot-grrl attitude. And so much for his antidrifting commandments. What was the good of being boss if even his big hands couldn't hold her?

Ah, but he knew one technique guaranteed to light her golden eyes again.

"For the good of the realm," he murmured. Now he

was lying to himself, because the flare of desire as he lowered his head had nothing at all to do with saving the world.

He kissed her.

Behind his closed lids, the crackle of ice spread, deep through his bones. And still, his body burned with wanting this, wanting her. He gathered her tighter yet, until the twin points of the crescent knife in her pocket dug into his flank.

Her cold lips opened to him.

Even with his eyes shut, brightness sparked around him. The unnerving mélange of ice crystals, embers, and shattered souls swirled between them, to bind them.

Closer and closer, forcing back the threatening freeze even as her blade cut through the heavy canvas of his coat, then his jeans, until the crescent knife scored his skin. Pain spiked over the point of his hip, and the tickle of blood traced down his groin. If he'd faintly hoped poking a hole in himself would direct the flow away from other rampant parts of his anatomy, no luck.

She warmed under his hands, and her breath sighed over his skin. She clutched him, mirroring the strength of his embrace, until, with no distance left between them, the other-realm shine of the soulflies faded. Only the hot pulse of his heavy flesh, the flash of craving as her tongue traced his upper lip, remained. He growled against her mouth as the sensation pushed him closer to the edge.

No, he was supposed to be pulling them *back* from the edge. He forced himself to lift his head, dragging in a pained breath that whistled past his clenched teeth. Jilly's lips were wild red in her honey skin. When she opened her eyes to meet his gaze, she was entirely present with him.

She reached up and touched his temple. "It shines."

The *reven*. Thank God its translucence revealed only glimpses of other-realm and not his brain. He'd hate for her to see the thoughts circling up there. None of it had anything to do with his duties to the league. "What was drawing you away from me?"

"Those lights." She pressed against him. He didn't wince although the knife dug deeper. "You Irish have all the stories of marshlights leading travelers to their deaths."

"Always a bedtime favorite." He cupped his hand around the back of her neck, avoiding the blue spikes of her hair but soothing her disquiet. "We didn't go to these lights, though. They were drawn to us."

She shivered and glanced over her shoulder.

The soul flecks had streamed away from their ash piles, like miniature stars drawn off their celestial course by a black hole. What had drawn them?

Liam laced his fingers through Jilly's and pulled her arm out to the side, as if they were about to waltz.

The flickers of light followed.

"Eh, why don't they stay over there somewhere, like, far away?" She flinched before they touched her. "The bracelet, of course. It did come from a demon."

"And demons do love a lost soul." He let their joined hands drop abruptly, and the soulflies swirled in the back draft of air before resuming their slow descent toward the bracelet again.

"I don't want to be followed by lost souls."

He decided not to point out that she'd certainly made a habit of it before this. Nobody liked hearing she'd walked herself into the trap. "I don't know how far they'll roam from their remains. Or what remains of their remains."

"You knew they were here."

He nodded. "From the haint-dust samples we brought back to the warehouse."

She narrowed her eyes. "How many of these must be floating around the city? Are they all converging on me?"

He shrugged. "So far, it seems they need to be in close proximity to you to be drawn off course from their body hunt. More important, what effect are they having while they're wandering? They're an unnatural by-product of the chemical *desolator numinis*. Imagine the clog in Chicago's spiritual gutters."

"Your compassion knows no bounds."

He stared at her. "What does compassion have to do with ridding the world of evil?"

"Duh."

"We're talking about capital-*E* Evil with long fangs. I can't fight that back with thoughts of loving-kindness and affirmation bumper stickers."

"Paper cuts can be a bitch."

He scowled. "You're the one creeped out by stalker soulflies."

She swung her arm and he ducked as the twinkling cloud passed over him. Free of his grasp, she glanced at him over her shoulder with an impish smile. "Who's creeped out?"

Before he could answer, all his demon senses kicked into high gear. She stiffened at the same time, and her smile vanished under a straining tension. As one, they whirled to face the bashed-out door where they'd entered.

The hall was empty, but ominous vibrations rumbled through the floor.

"What is it?" she gasped. "The salambes?"

He crouched, waiting. "No haints left here." Without haint bodies, salambes would be no threat.

And he just really doubted his night would end so simply.

Not that he felt any satisfaction about his prediction when, in a rush of sulfurous emanations that blew the soulflies apart, the feralis pack burst through the door.

CHAPTER 14

Jilly should have known better by now. Every time she touched Liam, the world went to hell.

The ferales surged forward in a howl and one stinking rush. Liam met them with hammer swinging. The whistle of the weapon through the air raised her hackles. And her demon.

Even as he knocked the first demon away, she jumped forward with the crescent blade in motion, its identical mate in her other hand. She wielded the knives as if she were a contestant in a reality-TV cooking show and the ferales were chicken carcasses standing between her and a million bucks.

Fierce elation swept through her, as keen as the steel edge that diced the first feralis. The teshuva's version of compassion.

"Back to hell with you," she snarled.

Only filleting would keep a feralis down. The hunched rat-troll thing spewed ichor in a fountain. She ducked to avoid the spray, every motion as well plotted and precisely drawn as a panel in a great graphic novel, her demon playing her like a superheroine.

Hero only because the role of villain had already been taken, of course.

Liam knocked another one her way—this demon had

wings. It recoiled from her attack and bounded over her head with a scream, slashing downward as it went.

Claws tangled in her ponytails, but she slipped free. Thank God for cheap slick hair gel. But a second feralis jumped after the first, and against two demons, her blades suddenly looked much smaller than when she'd admired them on the wall in the warehouse basement.

With a whirlwind attack that she owed entirely to the teshuva, she downed one, but the second pushed her back. Away from Liam, she realized. A third appeared, mandibles spread so wide she swore she could see down into the hellfire animating it. Its corpulent, hairless tail swept through a pile of haint dust, and the soul flecks scattered and faded like embers off a spent Fourth of July sparkler.

Unable to see Liam around the bulk of mutated flesh and virulent demonic energy, she darted to one side, farther from the door.

Where was he? Her heart slammed against her chest, a human counterpoint of fear against the demon's beating fury. This is what he meant when he said the teshuva couldn't do it all.

Another rush took her around the third feralis, before it cornered her. But she was definitely being bullied.

And she'd always really hated that.

"Jilly!"

She whirled. There he was, a half-bashed wall at his back. Where she should be.

She flung herself at the feralis, common sense left behind in the speed of her lunge. It recoiled at her sudden attack, and she dodged past its belated swipe.

Liam was already in motion, one hand outstretched to pull her behind him. "Too many. We have to get out."

"Fight through to the door?" She wished she'd brought the chain saw as he'd teased. And maybe a spare chipper-shredder.

"We'll take the back way out."

She hadn't seen a back door. But he tugged her along, and she followed. The dull roar of his hammer and the

hiss of her blades played low and high over the growl of
ferales. They were losing ground, as the demons pressed
them hard toward the outer wall of the apartment. The
closest feralis raised its fleshy beak to the ceiling and
screeched in triumph.

Then it leapt for them.

With a two-handed strike, Liam blasted it from the
air. He continued the arc.

And bashed out the plywood covering the broken
window. The smell of exhaust, cold metal, and night
overpowered the sulfur.

"Let's go." He yanked her to the jagged opening.

"We're three stories up."

"Not down. Over."

To the elevated train tracks.

The feralis called again. Something answered. And
then something else.

"More are coming," Liam said. "You have to go
now!"

Switching the crescent blades into one hand, she
clambered into the window, suspended over the sheer
drop. Not that she looked.

Liam's big hand steadied her. "I'm right behind you."

As if that were consolation when she imagined splat-
ting on the pavement below. She gripped the splintered
wood.

And launched herself across the open space.

She thrust upward, hoping to reach the top platform,
but fell short. For a heartbeat, she flailed in midair with
nothing to grab. Then the crossbeams of the scaffolding
raced toward her.

She hit hard. The knives in her hand clanged against
the metal. She hoped she hadn't broken anything vital—
either bones or blades—and tangled her arm through
the girders. She tightened her grip against the painful
reverberations still zinging up her arm. No *way* was she
losing her weapons.

She'd caught just below the deck of the tracks. It
would be an easy—a relatively easy—scramble down.

Then she actually looked down. And saw the inflowing tide of malice. The oily shadows swamped the base of the pillars, recoiled a moment, then moved back in, as if bracing themselves for the climb.

She knew how they felt.

A solid thud above made her shriek. But it was only Liam, who'd nailed the jump she'd tried to make.

He peered over the edge of the tracks. "Get up here."

Gritting her teeth and wishing she'd done that before she squealed like a little girl, she climbed. Her boots slipped once on the chilly steel. Liam fisted his hand in the back of her jacket and hauled her up the last few feet.

She spared one glance for the gaping window. The ferales milled but didn't jump. "What are they waiting for?"

"Do we really want to know?"

Good point. When he strode off down the tracks, she hurried to catch up. She had to watch where she put each foot. Plummeting off the tracks or stepping on the third rail now would be such a drag. "Are we getting off at the next stop?"

"Not unless we get ahead of them." He gestured down at the blackening of malice that kept pace below.

"What are they doing?"

"Keeping us pinned up here until a train comes along would be sneaky."

She slanted a glance at him. "Not funny."

"No, but effective. I wouldn't want to pit the teshuva against a train." He glanced back. "Not good."

The first feralis had made the leap to the tracks. Liam picked up his speed.

She was eager to do the same and had to keep the toes of her boots off his heels. "I'm starting to feel like I'm being herded."

"Which is more than even those clever little malice are capable of, much less those ferales. So who orchestrated this reunion?"

Her blood froze. "Reunion?"

"He knew I'd come back to the scene of the crime. Damn it."

"Corvus."

"Played right into his hands."

"But why?"

"Because I was an overconfident idiot."

She resisted the urge to slap him. He knew that wasn't what she meant. And she was sick of his pretending when she knew damn well he wasn't that at all. "What does Corvus want with you?"

"Again, do we really want to know?"

She thought he already did. "It's because you're the leader. If one foolproof way to kill a talya is decapitation—you did say that severed limbs don't regenerate—then removing you would destroy the league."

"Hardly."

"Don't be such a—"

He halted and held up a hand. "Shit."

"I wasn't going to be so harsh, but . . ."

"Feel that?"

The subliminal rumble under her feet wasn't even enough to shake the dirt from the rails, but it made her knees weak. "Train coming. Do we—?"

"Run."

But they were running *toward* the train, with the ferales and malice keeping them on track. Or more to the point, keeping them from leaving the track.

In the past she'd been blamed once or twice, maybe three times, for leaping before she looked. This time, though . . . "We have to jump for it."

"We can't lead the ferales into innocents. The slaughter would be appalling." He huffed. "Not to mention the explanations. We have to wait to find the right place."

She didn't have the breath to tell him waiting seemed like a bad idea. With the bad guys pressing so close, the right place could only be the wrong place.

Then the light of the train loomed ahead of them and they were out of time.

Without speaking, they both put on a fresh burst of speed. Up ahead, a work platform jutted off to one side of the tracks. Beyond it, a shuttered storefront was the only break in the solid brick walls lining the path. The roll-down security grille at street level was scrawled with illegible graffiti, but the plate-glass window above was miraculously intact.

Not for long.

The engine bore down on them. Its single light glared like the wrath of some monstrous deity, and the tracks shook in earnest. To an observer, Jilly thought, it must look like they were the two most suicidal people in the city. Unless, of course, the observer had demon-enhanced vision and could see the converging armies of malice and ferales behind them.

Actually, they probably still looked like the most suicidal people in the city.

"Me first this time," Liam shouted.

He flung himself across the gap to the building. Backlit by the oncoming train, his silhouetted duster flared like wings. In midair, he twisted, gathered the coat close— more like a protective chrysalis now—and slammed into the window.

Glass shattered in all directions in a silver spray. He fell into the darkness beyond.

Jilly steeled herself for the jump, giving him a chance to clear the landing pad. Assuming he hadn't slashed a major artery or anything inconvenient like that.

In a moment the train would be on her, and a moment after that—with a smidgen of luck—it would obliterate the ferales. Which would eliminate about half their problems. At least the half with corporeal fangs.

Unless, of course, she didn't move at all and then all her troubles would be over forever.

Silence. Stillness. Sweet escape. For the space between one heartbeat and the next, the thought beckoned to her with chill fingers and breath like ice. Her vision grayed.

Maybe her sister had it right.

But that wasn't her. Never had been.

The roar of the train drowned the whisper of the tenebraeternum. In a rush, the night bounded back into sharp relief around her. Blinded by the oncoming light, she launched toward the black maw of the broken window.

Thanks to Liam's much bigger body, she cleared the opening without a single snag on the jagged remnants of glass. With the demon's instinct, she tucked her shoulder, rolled, and stumbled into a crouch.

The train screeched by outside the window. Or maybe that was the sound of a dozen ferales squished against the rails. A girl could dream.

Liam was already on the move, although he glanced back once. "You still have your knives. Good."

She glanced down at her white knuckles. The sweat-sticky leather straps that bound the handles felt welded to her palm. Probably she'd never be able to let them go. "Seemed like a good idea to hang on to them. You guys are such hard-asses, I'm sure your armory has a crazy late-return fee." She switched one of the crescents to her other hand.

"Better late than . . . Damn it."

"Well, yeah, pretty much anything is better than—" Then she followed his gaze. "That."

The faint swirling stream of soul flecks flowed toward them.

"This is another haint haunt?" She shook her head. "What are the chances?"

"Pretty high, considering we were driven here by demons."

"I most definitely don't like this." She stiffened as the souls spiraled lazily at her, drawn to the bracelet like tiny doomed stars into a black hole.

"They won't hurt you. I don't think."

She scowled. "I meant, I don't like the idea we were pulled here." She waved her arm, disrupting the slow spiral. "Kind of like these things."

"Stop swatting at them. It's disrespectful. They're not

going to follow you far, or you would've been trailing them around like fairy dust ever since your teshuva gave you the bracelet."

"The gift that keeps on giving."

"For eternity, yeah." Liam checked his cell phone. "Still too much interference to get a call out."

And get reinforcements in. She took a breath, not so much to rouse her demon as settle her nerves. The teshuva could only do so much, apparently. "Then we're on our own. Good thing you got me."

She expected him to laugh. Instead he pocketed the phone and nodded. "Good thing." He opened his coat and folded back the front edge to reveal the grip of the hammer. "The tenebrae were so eager to get us here. Let's go see what they wanted us to find."

Together, they left the soulflies behind in a pinwheel of sparks.

As they tracked deeper through the dark building, leaving the lightened square of the broken window behind, Liam longed to leave *her* safely behind. There was no safety to be had—he knew that—but the impulse didn't change. If only he had a Jilly-sized trap where he could lock her away, someplace he'd find his way back to between battles.

Of course, she'd kill him if she caught even an inkling of his thoughts. How convenient the flight for their lives distracted her from the telltale betrayals of capillary-refill rates, pupil dilation, and galvanic skin response that were the demon's version of mind reading.

She had the link to the soulflies, which led to the haint haunts connected to this latest demonic infestation, which would lead, on a twisting path, no doubt—though certain as day led to night—to Corvus. She was anything but safe.

Like the weapons she had chosen, she was all sharp points and deadlier curves. But unlike the leather-wrapped grip of the crescent blades, if there was any safe place to hold her, he had yet to find it.

That didn't stop his hands from remembering the
shape of her, as dangerous—and strangely calming—
as the hammer he released from the anchor inside his
coat.

The third floor of the storefront where he'd broken
through smelled of dust, mouse droppings, and moldy
cardboard. A storage room, of some sort, but, judging
from the strength of the stench, not one in recent use.

He paused at the closed door that led out to the
hall. A stretch of his demon senses picked up the boil
of malice outside on the street and some more distant,
muddled agony. Perhaps the ferales swept along by the
train.

"Something creepy in here," Jilly whispered. "I don't
suppose the graffiti on the front door counts as art to
keep the malice out."

"Depends on how good the artist was and what he
infused into his art. Tags alone won't do it."

"I knew I should've pushed harder for that art-
therapy program at the halfway house, but, speaking
of creeps, Envers was always telling me we didn't have
the money for it. I bet he'd change his tune after a ride-
along with the league."

Regardless of the creep factor, they couldn't stay here.
He turned the knob and let himself out into the hall.

The eerie black lighting of the teshuva in hunt mode
flattened the perspective in the wide, empty hallway. No
birnenston. No etheric smears. So why had the soulflies
gathered? They moved too slowly to have been drawn
to Jilly from outside in the brief time she'd been in the
building. And if the bodies they'd been ripped from
weren't present . . .

"I see you followed my little trail of bread crumbs."

Out of nowhere, a shape coalesced at the end of the
hall, a deeper blackness among the shadows.

Jilly's hand fisted in the back of his coat, and a few
shards of glass fell from the folds with a warning chime.
Liam settled his hand on the hammer. "Corvus."

CHAPTER 15

Liam angled the hammer in a two-handed grasp across his body, Jilly behind him, as the djinn-man took another step down the hall. Despite the teshuva ascending, Liam couldn't make out the djinn-man's features, although the curious tilt to the head was apparent.

"Corvus?" The rough voice slurred. "Barely. Thanks to you."

Corvus stepped into a faint fall of street light that struggled through from an outside room. Soulflies flickered in the air, and Liam's stomach twisted when he wondered how much haint dust was trapped in the grimy creases of the djinn-man's clothing. Only by shuffling his demon senses to the side was Liam able to make out Corvus's face.

Four months ago, Liam had caught the briefest glimpse of the djinn-man. Archer had thrown him from a high-rise, which made visual identification problematic. There hadn't exactly been a lot left to remember. A powerful wrestler's build, a shaved head, a lot of blood. And then the building had collapsed on him in a quite dramatic spray of bricks and demon-realm wind. More concerned with the survival of his talyan, Liam hadn't bothered noting details, since they'd thought Corvus was dead—body, soul, and demon separated forever.

Apparently the demon part had other ideas.

Closer now, in the staggered light, Liam studied the slack face. On that terrible night, spatterings of gray matter had melted holes in the snow, which probably indicated a certain amount of persistent brain damage. What kind of demon could bring a body back from that? And without the soul as anchor.

One of Corvus's faded blue eyes slid sideways, though the other stayed pinned on them. "We had no fight with you, teshuva."

"'We,'" Jilly echoed softly. "I see them both."

She was right. Liam's human eyes saw the corporeal Corvus body, but his teshuva's sight glimpsed the hovering afterimage of the possessing djinni, like an ill-fitting shadow superimposed over the man.

Corvus's demon still rode him, as brutalized as any haint, but the djinni hadn't burned through its chosen body. It possessed the mangled flesh with a delicacy that whispered of eons of refined control. The only sign of its now imperfect merger was Corvus's exposed *reven*. The black lines that climbed both his arms like vicious briars seeped birnenston. The sulfuric poison had eaten away at his sleeves, leaving his strangeness painfully apparent to even the most oblivious human.

And the djinni claimed to have no fight with the league? Liam could only wish that were true.

"You corrupted my Bookkeeper," Liam reminded him. "And then the two of you pierced the Veil to the tenebraeternum to call over a demon that possessed a good woman . . . which made her one of mine. And still, the league and the djinn might have continued as we have since before even you were taken in Nero's day. But then you tried to kill Sera, and her mate did not handle that well."

"So we noticed." Corvus's lips drew up in a terrible rictus. A smile, Liam realized. "But just as you have found a new configuration with that woman, so we have fresh faces." A drop of birnenston leaked from Corvus's wandering eyeball and fell, sizzling through the old linoleum. Corvus—or maybe the demon—lifted one hand to wipe away the smoking tear. "How do you like them?"

"The salambes?" Liam shrugged. "We destroy malice and ferales. Honestly, what's one more enemy?"

"Ah, but their kind have not been free since the Fall. And they are finding their way here now. With some help from us." Another poisonous tear crept down Corvus's cheek.

Liam had known that the salambes were a foe he hadn't encountered before, despite his years in the tenebrae trenches. But hearing the Corvus-djinni confirm that the tides of the battle were shifting again wasn't exactly encouraging news.

That awful lopsided smile returned. "What's more, we learned the trick from you."

Jilly sucked in a breath.

Liam didn't move. "More of Bookie's betrayals?"

Corvus shook his head. The lazy eye rolled, lid flapping. "Your Bookworm gave us the *desolator numinis*, but you talyan fashioned the burning ones. Yet another way you are lately setting the nights on fire, yes?"

The djinn-man gave Liam a leer and lazy-eyed wink, as if he meant to be chummy, but the slyly suggestive accusation chilled Liam to the bone.

And still the slurred drone went on: "You gave shape to the salambes, but what is the other meaning of 'forge,' blacksmith?"

Liam wondered exactly how much bitching about the league Bookie had done with his evil cohort. He could've done without the djinn-man knowing *all* their secrets. "To forge is to fake."

"Ah, so it is. Are you a false leader, then?"

Jilly surged forward. "He would never help you!"

Only Liam's arm, snagged around her waist, kept her from charging the djinn-man. "As much as I appreciate your defending me . . . ," he murmured. He meant to sound wry, but the warmth in his chest was more than the close press of her shoulders could explain. He'd envied those she stuck up for, and now he knew how it felt. Quite good. If only he had time to revel.

Corvus tilted his head to examine her. "I never said it was just him." Before Liam could chase down the ominous echo the words sent tolling through his head, the djinn-man continued. "You are small and sharp. And you used to run alone, just as my darklings did. Free." He shifted a reproachful gaze to Liam. "You, at least, I thought knew better than to fall back into the trap with her."

Liam tightened his grip on Jilly, unwilling to be led astray by Corvus's—or were they the djinni's?—meandering thoughts. No doubt that miasma of insinuation and lies was as perilous as any boggy marsh. "What do you want, djinni? We followed the little path you laid. Now say why you brought us."

"What I suggested to your annoying talya pair before. Leave us be."

"Leave you—?" Liam bit off a harsh laugh. "Archer and Sera stopped you from ripping open the Veil between us and hell. You think I didn't wholeheartedly support them?"

Despite the slackened features, Corvus looked crafty. "What do you know of whole hearts?"

Liam's chest vibrated with Jilly's growl. "I know that's what you destroy with your nasty solvo," she said.

"Just the soul," Corvus corrected.

"Heart," she insisted. "Mind. Life and light."

"Will you say 'love'?" The doubled octaves of Corvus's human throat and demon overlord made the word a curse and a threat.

Jilly hesitated. "Not that. Never that."

She was thinking of Dory, Liam knew.

Corvus's lazy eye rolled back into position, fixed on her. As if, Liam thought uneasily, the man as well as the djinni knew what she was thinking too. "Will the rest of humanity feel that way, do you think, when their loved ones come to them, vicious as ferales, cruel as malice?"

She recoiled. "What—?"

Liam held his hand at her back. Supporting her or ready to stop another ill-considered lunge—he wasn't sure which. "The djinni means when the salambes are running the haints. Without the help of other-realm sight, no one would know that it wasn't their husband, wife, child, or friend. And when that person became a monster . . ."

"Monster is such a judgmental word," Corvus said. "And it's not Judgment Day. Yet. But the solvo is spreading, and behind it widens the desolation."

Jilly straightened. "Then why even bother saying boo to us?"

Corvus spread his hands in a theatrical gesture. Or tried to, but the awkward angle of his elbows looked more like broken wings than a magician's flourish. His tattered sleeves flapped, and soulflies swirled in the backwash. "You are more kin to me than you know."

"Hardly," she snapped.

The djinn-man narrowed his eyes, squeezing out birnenston that burned down his cheeks, though the demon healed the angry red marks as quickly as they appeared. "Still judging. I thought you might understand how it goes. I could show you rebellion such as your young monsters in training only dream of."

Liam let the hammer drop lightly to his side. The low whistle sang descant to his teshuva snarl. "Whatever Dory told you, you don't know Jilly, so stay out of her head."

Corvus gave him another walleyed stare. "And you know her so well?"

Liam stiffened at the note of mockery. His duty was to know all his talyan, their strengths and foibles. So why did he suspect the djinn-man meant something more?

"Never mind." Corvus's voice slurred, and his lazy eye drifted. "Perhaps you don't yet understand, but I am learning so much from you all."

"He's losing it," Jilly hissed. "The djinni doesn't have a solid hold."

Liam moved forward ahead of her, letting his demon vision flicker to keep both Corvus and the wavering shade around him in sight. "Doesn't make them less dangerous."

Still, the Corvus-djinni took a step back. "I'm giving you the chance to join me."

"First, you said leave you alone. Now, join you." Jilly gave a harsh laugh. Her knives flashed in her hands. "We'll *stop* you."

"Jilly," Liam warned.

Before he could say more—such as, "What the fuck are you doing?"—she leapt at Corvus.

Despite her blurred speed, the shadow of the djinni yanked the gladiator's ravaged body back with an unnatural twist, like an invisible hand sweeping aside a puppet. Jilly dropped to a crouch in the space Corvus had been.

Liam, a step behind, saw the soulflies displaced by a swell of demonic emanation. The drifts of tiny lights were crushed up against the walls. The sharp scent of rusting metal flowed over him.

"Incoming." He swung the hammer over his head, barely clearing the ceiling, and charged.

The rush stirred the soulflies into a wake of eerie phosphorescence and outlined a dozen hulking shapes that filled the wide hallway, wall to wall. Off-kilter, upthrust teeth cut like spear points through the remnants of the pale shimmer behind Corvus. Salambes.

Liam aimed his attack at the djinn-man. No point in swinging a hammer against pure ether. Even Jilly wasn't that hopelessly obstinate.

His charge took him into the center of the salambes as they swept past Corvus. Nothing to see, but he felt the congealing on his skin like slimy ice. It sank through him, a thousand times worse than the sting of a malice.

The agony plunged into his heart and slammed him to his knees. Only the hammer braced against the floor kept him upright.

"Liam." Jilly bolted toward him. He held up a hand, warning her back.

"It only hurts because of your soul," Corvus mocked. "Can you let that go?"

Jilly whirled and let fly with both blades.

From the time-distorted depths of his pain, Liam admired the glitter. She at least knew how to let go. He'd have to remember to tell her that sometimes she was right.

The crescent knives spun into Corvus with demon-amped force. He grunted and folded inward, shoulders rounded.

"It only hurts because of your flesh," Jilly snarled. "Let that go, why don't you?"

Had he been living, the twin blows would have ended him. But after a moment, the djinn-man plucked out the knives buried side by side above his heart. Blood and birnenston gushed from the wound.

The blades clattered to the floor and Corvus straightened.

"Jilly, run," Liam said. Or meant to. All that emerged was a grunt as the salambes bore into him, an ever-constricting shell of ether and agony.

He strained toward her, sweat rising on his brow. The moisture flowed into the corner of his eye, blinding him with crimson. Not sweat, but blood pouring from the *reven* at his temple as the salambes' attack on the te-shuva spilled over into his human body.

She crouched over him, her neck exposed to Corvus. Damn it, that was no way to fight. He was going to take her out hunting every night, teach her—assuming they weren't brutally slaughtered in the next few seconds.

She held out her hand, as if she could reach through the prison of salambes. The bracelet gleamed on her wrist, the base metal reflecting an inner light from its own demon-twisted molecules. "Take my hand. Like we did with the malice."

His muscles were locked as the demon in him fought back the invasion of the salambes' emanations. The preter-natural chill of the unbound demons froze the blood to his skin and iced the red tide over his eye. He couldn't move.

But the soulflies that lingered around the Corvus-djinni began their slow spiral to her.

Corvus took a step back.

"Liam," she whispered. Amethyst and gold blazed in her eyes and she locked his gaze. "Touch me."

The next pulse of his heart sent another surge of blood that didn't freeze. He felt the first weakening in the invisible bars that penned him in, pinned him through.

The essence of the salambes was being divided, drawn to Jilly just as the soulflies were.

"Get away," he rasped. The fact he could talk meant she was loosening the invisible chains on him, but he wouldn't allow it, not if she was taking them on herself.

She held out her hand imperiously, as if the etheric grotesqueries around them weren't coming to her already. "Just reach for me."

What responded in him wasn't his teshuva, half paralyzed as it was by the salambes' deadly embrace. It welled up from somewhere deeper, from some purely human need he didn't have time to examine or deny.

With a shout, he broke from his bonds, slapped his palm into hers. Around them, the hall flashed with etheric light, the salambes clearly outlined and the soulflies shining bright enough to make him squint.

She pulled him closer with a flex of her teshuva's strength and her solidly squared shoulders. She touched his face, fingertips at his temple, palm at his cheek. He leaned into the gentle touch, so at odds with the amethyst blaze that turned her gaze to molten rage. Through the hall, a rush of bone-dry wind cleared the stench of rusting metal, the stink of his own blood.

The demon realm.

"Out of the frying pan," he murmured.

Though he had spoken too quietly for anyone to hear, Jilly answered, "And into hell." With the new clarity of his vision, the salambes seemed to be breaking down, shredding around them as if following the soulflies' lead.

He should be trying to pull her back from this dangerous path. This wasn't how the league had outlined its eternal mission. Even Corvus and his djinni—the soulless, brain-damaged, malevolent fiend who wanted to tear down the Veil between hell and earth to pit demons directly against the gates of heaven—had sounded disapproving.

And Liam didn't much care at the moment. With Jilly tucked against his chest, the pain—well, it hadn't disappeared, but he didn't care about that either. In fact, the whole damn world could end right now. . . .

No, not quite yet.

He lowered his head, set his lips softly over Jilly's. The warmth of her breath moved through him and melted the salambe ice. "Now it can end," he murmured.

"But you just started." Her hand slipped down from his face to land above his heart, her gaze focused on him as if demons weren't shredding all around them. "Are you okay?"

Never mind the demons. She was in his arms. "I'm fine." He glanced beyond her. The space around them shifted between dark hallway and ominous gray void. Only her cinnamon-honey eyes half streaked with violet and the blue spikes of her hair maintained their color. Well, and the carnelian of her lips where his mouth had roughened her. If they were lost between the realms . . . "Can you get us back out?"

"Out—?" She followed his gaze. "Uh-oh."

He withheld a smile. "Indeed. The salambes followed the soulflies after you. It would sure be nice to leave them stuck here."

She looked down at the bracelet, pressed between them where her hand lay curled against his chest. The slowly unraveling demon entities swirled closer around them, circling the drain. "The knot work. It's not just a pattern for us to follow. It's a trap in itself."

"Hopefully not for us." Despite his attempt at reassurance, he didn't let go of her. "Its powers are definitely more convoluted than I suspected. Why I didn't guess that with you as its owner . . ." When she wrinkled her nose at him, he gave her an affectionate squeeze. "We're not too deep. I still see the hallway." Barely.

"What do we do?"

"Like last time. In your apartment." He kept his voice even, but his pulse raced, roaring in his ears with an urgency to rival a runaway train.

Her eyes widened, and he could only wonder what his heartbeat, under her hand, felt like. "You want to have sex in the middle of a demon attack?" She shook her head. "I guess it was a demon attack last time too. The teshuva, I mean. Not you."

But it had been almost an assault, desperate and demon fueled. He remembered her body straining under his, breath frantic. Though bending steel railroad tracks would have been easier, he sidelined the memory. "Just like that time, we want to stay on the human side of the Veil."

"You said the league has always reinforced its humanity through wine, women, and war."

"'Wine, women, and song.' The phrase is 'song,' not 'war.' And I'm sure I phrased it less archaically."

"You didn't. Do you have a bottle of fine Irish whiskey on you somewhere?" She skimmed her hands inside his coat. His chest tightened in response, and he bit back a groan. "No? I suppose we could fight each other."

"We already do." He forced his taut muscles to move slowly, to gently touch her cheek, but his hand trembled. He'd been so harried last time, he'd forgotten to savor the moment. "I can't remember how it goes."

"We snipe. We kiss. We snipe some more." She sounded breathless.

"I would have done anything to bring you through possession."

"And you'll do anything now to bring us out." The gray void leached the emotion from her voice, and hurt darkened her eyes.

She was twisting his words. "Damn it. Stop sniping."

"But that only leaves—"

He silenced her with his mouth.

Archaic, indeed. He sank his fingers into her spiked hair, drew her upright. Somewhere, the hammer fell with a faint, unheeded thud. He tasted sweat, sweet cherries, blood. Archaic? Downright primitive. His heart, which had been just this side of a demon's frozen dinner a minute ago, raged in his chest until he thought they could follow its beat back to the human world.

Her hands inside his coat traced over his ribs and locked behind him. Her fingers dug into the muscles of his back, would have scored him had he been naked. If only. She was small enough to tuck under his chin and when she leaned into him, her breasts yielded with soft seduction, but God, she matched his grip with a clasp every bit as furious.

Alone in a foreign land, ersatz father to his pack of lost boys, he had given up any dream of passion even before the demon had come to him. That the dangers of hell itself gave him a second chance was the definition of absurd.

And he couldn't get enough of her. As he slanted his mouth over hers—hot, wet, hard—the hunger in him had nothing to do with his ravager demon, nothing to do with her discord demon running roughshod over his discipline. No, it was her, her alone. Her fearless temper, her flashing eyes, her quick tongue. Ah, her tongue, darting, teasing him ... He wanted her beyond all sense, never mind his worries about Archer's willingness to sacrifice the world for this feeling, never mind Corvus's oblique warnings and the djinni's leer.

This was *more* dangerous than demons.

His head swirled as she matched him, breath for gasping breath. Or was that the churned remnants of the salambes, torn apart by this woman? What was she that she could rip through the demons' defenses—through his own—with a wave of her hand?

And what the hell was he thinking, whipping up the frenzy?

Not thinking. For once, the ceaseless uncertainties in

his brain, the doubts in his soul, all were swept away by the raw desire singing through his veins.

He savored the weight of her, canted against him. The kiss shifted, deepened, and he fit her curves to his body like working molten metal against an anvil. Ah, except *he* was the one getting harder. And she didn't rest quietly in his hands. She twined around him, molded *him* to her wishes until he couldn't be sure where his craving ended and hers began. Didn't care, because they were one and the same.

Her rebellion challenged his restraint, set him free. And it felt good, as good as her body rocking against his. She did not allow him to box away his feelings; she needled him until he exploded. Her grasp shifted, raking down his back to clutch fistfuls of denim and his ass, and she yanked his hips tight to her belly. His arousal surged at the friction, and he panted against her mouth.

He was going to explode if he didn't have her. All of her. Now. No common sense, no self-preservation, no enduring quest—*nothing*—would stop him.

Her hand in the middle of his chest set him back on his haunches. He caught himself before he tipped over.

Cold, dank air rushed between them. The abrupt separation seared his senses worse than the teshuva's alien intrusion. He ached all over, as if the bolt of longing that went through him had left him torn apart in ways even hell's torturers shuddered to contemplate. To add insult, he had the uncomfortable sensation that his hand, braced behind him, had landed in mouse turds.

"All done," she murmured.

The hallway was dark and empty except for them. *Welcome back to the world.*

CHAPTER 16

Jilly bit her lip. Not that such a tiny sting could obliterate the sensation of Liam's mouth crushing hers.

Her whole body tingled, as if his mouth had been all over her. No wonder the demon realm had tossed them back; even hell recognized the unacceptable temptation between them.

He was her boss. And an arrogant jerk most of the time. Plus, he hadn't really wanted to kiss her.

Not true, her body screamed. Even the most unrepentant demon with its cozening lies couldn't have faked that erection. He'd wanted it, and by God, she wanted him to admit it. He couldn't just keep using this intense chemistry between them as the flash powder in his demon skirmishes. Too many more scorching kisses like that and she'd blow up too.

Yeah, hell so didn't want any part of *this* battle.

"They're gone." Liam rose to his feet, graceful as always, as if they hadn't just wrestled free of the demon realm. Tongue wrestling apparently counted.

But he was right about the gone part. Nothing remained in the hallway except the two crescent knives on the floor, smeared in blood and birnenston. Corvus, the salambes, even the sparkle of slivered souls, gone. "Was Corvus sucked into the trap?"

Liam shook his head. "If the djinni had been, the body would still be here."

He held a hand out to her and pulled her to her feet. He kept her hand in his and gently twisted her wrist so the bracelet winked at them. The crevices of the knot work gleamed with a strange iridescence. "Like ichor stuck in its teeth," he murmured thoughtfully. "The mouth of the trap. And the throat led back to the tenebraeternum to swallow them all. My ever-hungry ravager is suitably impressed."

"And I'm a little . . . unsettled," Jilly said. Admitting as much rankled, but she'd seen he didn't bear the weight of command lightly. "Why did this come to me? I'm the last person on earth who ever wanted to trap anyone."

"Who better to be in charge of it?"

"Um, you? You're clan chieftain of the league anyway."

"It's too narrow a torque to fit around my neck. For whatever reason—the teshuva's reason—the power came to you, Jilly."

What did she fear? The power the bracelet gave her over evil? Or the implied power that Liam, as chief evil fighter, had over her? She was totally willing to hand him the knot-work trap, and she trusted him with the fate of the world, yet still her heart raced when he touched her.

His blue eyes turned unfathomable, and he released her to collect his hammer. "The commitments never waver. And neither can we."

When he straightened, he seemed taller than ever. She stiffened her spine to match him. Tentatively, she reached out with her demon senses, not much different from trying to sniff out the first whiff of something burning on the stove. "No tenebrae left in the building. The malice outside are gone too."

"Escaped or sucked down." He pulled out his cell phone. Over the hiss of a bad connection, he spoke quickly.

She bent to retrieve her knives and wipe them on

her jeans. When she straightened to stick them in her pocket, the hallway blurred around her, and for a moment she thought the demon realm was rising around them again.

"Easy." Liam grabbed her, and she realized she'd tipped far to one side. "Too much for you?"

She wanted to scoff, make a smart-ass comment about how he might be six-foot-and-did-it-matter-after-that, but he was definitely nothing she couldn't handle. But he wasn't talking about himself, and then she'd just reveal that she had thoughts about his too-much self.

Before she could figure out what her next smart-ass comment should be, he swung her into his arms.

She'd always thought petite sucked. People thought less of her because there was less of her. But cradled against his chest, she wondered if she'd been blind to the bennies.

"You're worse than me," he murmured. "I called Archer to bring a car."

Finally, she found her voice. "I can walk." Not much of a smart-ass comment. Sounded kind of weak, actually. Especially muffled against the expanse of his chest.

"All the way back to the warehouse?" He tightened his grip.

"I was just dizzy for a second." Where she curled her fist in the shadow of his coat lapel, the bracelet glimmered. "It's kind of pretty, huh?"

"Pretty dangerous." He started down the hallway without releasing her.

She tucked in her feet to keep from scuffing on the walls down the stairs. "That wasn't business as usual, was it?"

His jaw flexed. "Sera has a connection to the tenebraeternum that seems unique in league annals. Archer did a piss-poor job of describing it, but it sounded nothing like that. I wouldn't have guessed there'd be worse."

Great, she was uniquely dangerous. She was always telling her kids that playing the lone-gunman rebel off on a wild tear was a bad idea. She even thought she'd walked the talk. At the moment, though, she wasn't walking at all, and despite the strong arms wrapped around her, she felt very much alone again. "Could we catch Corvus the same way? Could we sweep all demons out of the city?"

He shook his head. "I still don't know how this fits."

And by "this" he meant her. There was no "we." She was just another cog in his cosmic battle machine. How'd she keep managing to forget that? He certainly never did. The whole time his kiss had wiped her mind, he'd been plotting strategies and doing crosswords.

How desperate was she? She didn't want to answer that.

At the bottom of the stairs, she struggled out of his grasp. He had to put her down or risk dumping her.

Couldn't dump her when they'd never been steady, her helpful brain reminded her. Sure, now it was back online with smart-ass comments directed at herself.

The main floor of the building was a vacant convenience store with only dust behemoths on the empty shelves. Liam easily broke the locks on the roll-down security gate and wrenched up the steel curtain. The screech and stink of rusty metal made her stiffen, demon senses scanning for salambes.

Liam slanted a glance at her. "We're okay now."

"Now," she muttered.

The rush of colder air swept the room, and the dust behemoths tumbled in frantic circles like they couldn't wait to get out either. Liam stepped out onto the street, his face lifted to the night, his hand near the grip of his hammer despite his reassurances.

Demon sign streaked the sidewalk and the stanchions for the L as if black-light paint. But that was it. Even the psychic screams left behind when the teshuva overwhelmed their prey were missing.

Liam's gaze was shuttered. "You got rid of them all."

Which, last she heard, was a good thing, so why the wary look? Unless he thought he was next. After her shamelessly soliciting his kiss, she couldn't blame him for sensing a trap. Ironic, considering that was her hang-up.

She kept a chunk of space between them as she lifted her hand near a smear of ether on a light post. It matched the unearthly phosphorescence deep in the weave of the knot-work bracelet. "What sign does a fleeing djinni leave?"

"It's still riding Corvus's body, so big footprints, half-smoked cigarette butts, getaway cars. The usual bad-guy spoor."

She surveyed the cracked concrete with its scattering of trash. Down the urban canyon of buildings, the rumble of another train sounded. "Not going to help us tonight, is it?"

He shook his head. "Not now that it's obvious we won't listen to his pitch about joining the dark side."

"You wanted to keep him talking?"

"Little harder to keep up his end of the conversation after you put two knives in his chest."

"What did you really think you'd learn? That he's a bad guy?"

"And you're a badass." Liam shrugged. "The djinni-possessed and the talyan have always walked separate paths, the djinn to greater dissolution, the teshuva to repentance. Why did he seek us out? What does he think is changing?" His expression darkened. "He said he has learned something from us. I shudder to think that we've given him any insight or advantage."

"He's probably just trying to make us doubt ourselves. Isn't that the devil's MO?"

Liam studied her, blue eyes as shadowed as when he spoke of Corvus. "Doubt has never stopped you, though, has it? I find myself drawn to that."

She bit the inside of her lip as she tried to unravel the compliment—was it a compliment? Damn it, now he was making her doubt. "I thought we did good. We practically burned a hole through hell."

"Is that what we've shown the djinni?" He closed his coat, tucking away his hammer—and any other evidence that he'd ever been drawn to her. "Corvus had marginal control over the ferales when we tangled with him last fall. Now he has this new species of tenebrae, and he's able to manipulate the salambes. This is not a comforting progression."

She touched the bracelet. "But you have—the league has—more weapons now too."

He hesitated. "Right."

She bristled. "What? I'm not a worthy addition to your crew?"

"I don't know what you are. Or Sera either, for that matter. All I know is that she and Archer do scary things together, things that, as far as I've seen, have driven us closer to the edge, not eased us back. You don't unleash a nuclear weapon when you still think you can save the world. And as for you—"

"Us," she insisted. "You were right there with me, remember? In the demon realm." She lifted her chin. Let him deny it. "Kissing me."

But of course he didn't deny it. He was too good for that. Instead, he just took a half step back. Right. Just denying *her*. Though she hadn't moved, she felt as if the pocketed blades had gone through her jacket into her belly.

"There've been no female talyan for two thousand years or more." His voice was low, almost lost in the approaching rumble of the train. "Maybe there was a reason the mated-talyan bond went extinct."

Not just denying her, but her whole gender. Or subspecies or essence or whatever.

"Or maybe the males were just fucking blind," she snapped, "and doomed the world to rampant evil rather than admit . . ." Admit what? That they had something together? Had what? "Rather than admit they needed each other. Why have a real team when you can always rustle up a tribunal to ask if women even have souls?" Her voice rose over the clatter of the train on the tracks above them. "Let's just burn the witch, make her cover her hair, deny her the vote, or pay her less for equal work. Screw you and your sexist demon. Maybe I don't need you either."

A wind, cold as winter iron, dry as charcoal ashes, hissed around them. Centered on her. She held up her hand. Whether the bracelet was the source or lodestone of the wind, she couldn't tell, but the knot work gleamed with preternatural intensity in the light of the train passing above.

One long step and Liam was in her face, his fingers locked around her wrist, blue eyes overlaid with demonic violet. "Don't you dare."

The heat of his skin shorted out the impulse beating in her chest like wings. She swallowed hard and tasted blood where his wounded *reven* had marked her too, streaked across her face during their wild, realm-spanning kiss. She kept her gaze fixed on his. Because she might be unnerved, but she wasn't going to let him see that.

He stared down at her. "You done with your rant?"

"Since I'm so dangerous, you done pissing me off?"

"Probably not." He'd already made clear he wouldn't get any closer, but he managed to tower over her without taking another step. "And you're not dangerous enough to take me on."

She thrust out her hand, palm flattened to hold him at bay, and opened her mouth to keep arguing. But nothing came to her. The nothingness was almost as brilliant as the shock of his touch when he grabbed her wrist as if he thought she was going to strike him or run away.

She waited for her habitual flash of outrage, but found nothing there too. Just a realization that she could keep fighting, but he wasn't really the enemy. Finally she offered tentatively, "Hard as it is to believe, we're not in the demon realm anymore."

His jaw worked, as if he couldn't find anything to say either. After a moment, the barely-there dimple appeared as he smiled. "You never cease to surprise me, Jilly Chan. Just when I expect a left out of you, you go right." He didn't let her go but shifted his grip. His fingertips brushed the bracelet as he cradled her fist in his palm.

She sighed and opened her hand in his, trying to ignore the cold burn of the bracelet. "And whenever I think you think you're always right, you go left."

"A meeting in the middle, then?" He tangled his fingers through hers.

She had to angle her neck to gaze up at him; he was so much taller. Did he honestly believe they could find a place they could both stand, with her big boots running roughshod over his big plans?

Before she could answer, the headlights of an approaching car caught them in their little tableau. The hatchback angled across the street and stopped, faced into oncoming traffic, had there been any.

Sera leaned out the driver's window. "Archer said to come get you. Just in time, I see."

Liam held Jilly's hand another heartbeat. As if he was waiting for her, as if she was supposed to make a choice with him still streaked in blood, her still twitching at the memory of demons and soulflies and his fierce kiss. Her lips felt tender from the weight of his mouth, like they might be inclined to say something that the tougher part of her would never allow. She'd bite her tongue, but then she'd just taste him again. And a mere taste wasn't ever enough.

The tenebrae herding her into a train had been more subtle. She stepped back, though the loss of his touch let in a cold the demon realm couldn't match.

He let her go. The scowl he turned on Sera was forbidding. "I see you've been taking driving lessons from Archer."

She blinked. "It's the middle of the night. The demon hour. No one's coming."

Liam opened the back door of the car. "You could still get a ticket." He gestured Jilly in, his face as stone set as that of any cop collaring a perp.

"Luckily, At-One always takes care of its loyal employees' little transgressions. And the teshuva are responsible for the big ones." Sera glanced back as Jilly climbed in. "You two look rough."

Jilly settled back. "So do you. Unless those are jelly-doughnut stains and not demon guts. Busy night?"

"Yeah, very." Sera returned her attention to Liam, who'd claimed shotgun. "Where to, boss?"

"Jilly's apartment."

Jilly hunched in her seat. "I'm being sent to bed without supper. I didn't know you could get fired from possession."

"No, no," Sera said. "It's fires *of* possession."

The grind of Liam's teeth was audible in the small car. "I want survival tips, ladies, not a Smothers Brothers outtake."

"Smothers Sisters," Sera said. "Who listens to them anymore anyway?"

Jilly gave her a ghost of a smile in the rearview mirror. "Survival tips from who?"

"Your neighbor seemed to know a lot about the bracelet."

Jilly frowned. "You can't wake Lau-lau. It's the middle of the night. She'll be terrified."

He stared forward. "We'll see." Then he asked Sera for a rundown of her demon encounters for the night, and that was the end of that conversation.

With her jacket scrunched uncomfortably to avoid poking herself on her weapons, Jilly huddled in the backseat. The heat from the blowers up front didn't quite reach her. Or anyway, she couldn't get warm.

What had happened between her and Liam? Together, they'd snared the salambes. And the severed souls of the haints had vanished too. When she'd vowed to find out what happened to Andre and then to get solvo off the streets, she hadn't quite figured on becoming a trap herself, a menace not so different from the sort she'd fought all her life. Sure, she intended to use her powers for good. But then there was that whole possessed-by-evil thing....

She realized the silence had spread to the front seat too.

Liam's resigned sigh carried less air than the straining heater, but Jilly heard it. "So, Sera, what haven't you told me about this mated-talyan bond?"

Jilly cleared her throat. "I might've already let slip that wild demonic sex makes for a fun night of possession."

Sera glanced back at her. "How'd he take it?"

"About like you'd expect."

"Hmm. Archer got over it."

"Undoubtedly," Liam snapped. "I know you've been in the league archives. What have you found?"

Sera squirmed. "Nothing specific, nothing definitive, or I would have told you."

His low growl held demonic double octaves.

"But," she went on hurriedly, "I think the teshuva got scared."

Jilly leaned forward, arms braced on the seat in front of her. "Demons get scared?"

Sera shrugged. "Maybe I'm reading too much into it. But there are oblique references to secret meetings between league leaders. They apparently decided the mated bond ran counter to the mission of the teshuva and unbalanced the human/demon link with potentially catastrophic results. I'm guessing, from supply manifests and armory inventories, that they outlawed relationships between talyan, then split the leagues into male and female factions."

Jilly scooted farther forward. "What happened to the girls-only leagues?"

"Unknown. After all, I'm reading the bad ol' boys' club version of events. And I didn't get the sense they were really eager to talk about it. You know how men are."

Liam cleared his throat.

"But it's obvious," Sera said, "over the centuries, the leagues lost touch, not just with their female counterparts, but with each other." She glanced at Liam. "It's only lately that there's been any communication at all. Thanks mostly to you, Liam."

He grunted. "Lot of stubborn, old-fashioned, rule-bound autocrats."

Jilly snorted.

He glared over his shoulder at her. "Put your seat belt on."

She ignored him. "So there could be more of us out there."

Sera gripped the steering wheel tighter. "Maybe. It might be worth exploring. In all our free time, when we're not fighting off evil incarnate in a desperate attempt to prevent the powers of darkness from sneakily—and lately not so sneakily—transforming our realm into a destination getaway for vacationing hell dwellers."

"Or maybe we'll leave it alone," Liam snapped. "Considering our predecessors thought there was an excellent chance you all would destroy us, maybe the world, with your heretical demon-slaying—"

"Doesn't that sound off to you?" Jilly mused. "How can destroying evil be heretical?"

Liam ignored her, his attention on Sera. "Then tell me why I shouldn't separate you and Archer."

Any semblance of warmth deserted the car.

Sera's voice echoed with demonic lows. "Because you can't."

"That begs the question."

"No begging," Sera demurred. "You just can't."

"He thinks we're dangerous," Jilly added helpfully. She sat back and clipped on her seat belt when Liam swiveled his head to glare at her again.

"He's right," Sera said. "And the only thing that keeps me from being dangerous *and* destructively psychotic from the knowledge that an eternity of war spreads ahead of me"—her hazel eyes gleamed with enough violet to refract in the windshield—"is Ferris."

Liam shook his head. "So either way, with Archer or without, the fate of the world lies in the balance?"

"Damned if you do . . . ," Jilly offered, ready for his glare this time.

"My world was always at stake," Sera said softly. "I just forgot I cared. Until I loved him."

Despite the grumble of the old engine, the breathy whistle of wind past the poorly sealed door, her words fell in a hush. Jilly wanted to swear, open the window to let in the night, do something to break that stillness before she looked into it and saw . . .

"Never mind," Liam said curtly. "It's too late now anyway. Whatever Corvus has figured out, we can't put the djinni back in the bottle."

Sera startled. "Corvus?"

"Watch the road, damn it. I'll fill everyone in after dawn. Pull over there."

Jilly felt another chill as the car rolled to a stop. Lau-lau's light was on. What would her elderly landlady be doing up at this time of night?

"Imagine that," Liam murmured. "Another known unknown with odd hours."

Out of the car, Jilly fell into step behind Liam as he approached the door, Sera a step behind that. Liam tried the door. It was unlocked.

"That's unnerving," Sera murmured.

A dank, earthy scent spiced with ginger rolled out, turning to steam on the cold air before dissipating. The shop was deserted, but from the back, Lau-lau's voice rang out, "That you, *xiao*-Jilly? If you're someone else, the *qilin* will kill you, so get out."

Liam froze.

"A *qilin* is a Chinese unicorn." Jilly gestured at the small cinnabar statue almost lost in the clutter on the counter. "So I wouldn't worry about it."

"Speak for yourself," he muttered.

Jilly glanced in disbelief at Sera.

The other woman shrugged. "I didn't believe in demons either."

Jilly huffed out a breath. "It's me, Lau-lau. With friends."

"Your dragon-man?" Lau-lau poked her head through

the curtain that shielded the back room. Her thin hair was rolled in curlers. "Ah. My tea was good, yes?"

He nodded. "Quite restorative."

She cackled. "Such a gentleman." She turned a curious glance on Sera. "It's good Jilly has found friends her own age."

Jilly sighed. Was immortal her own age? "We need some help, Lau-lau."

"Yes. The demons are out in force tonight."

The three talyan stared at the old woman.

She peered back, black eyes crinkling. "You are not the only force fighting evil in this city, you know."

After a moment, Liam shook his head. "We seemed very alone."

Lau-lau waved her hand. "More powerful, perhaps, but not the oldest, and not alone."

"This is too weird," Jilly said. "I just happen to get possessed by a demon, and my landlady just happens to be a secret commando in the war on evil?"

Lau-lau scoffed. "'Just' nothing. Why do you think I rented to you?"

"But I didn't know anything about demons then."

The wrinkles in Lau-lau's face deepened around her down-turned mouth. "The shadow was on you already."

"Your penance trigger," Sera said softly. "It set you on this path a long time ago."

Lau-lau nested her hands, one fist inside the other, her gnarled knuckles white. "I'm sorry that I could not turn you aside on your path."

For an instant, Jilly envisioned that divergence. A different life. An actual life, with death and everything. A life without ever discovering the league. Or Liam. The instant, bone-deep denial of the thought shook her. "I wouldn't have listened."

"Maybe you shouldn't have." Lau-lau gestured for them to follow her into the back.

At the small kitchen stove, Lau-lau stirred a huge cast-iron pot. Despite her hair rollers and housecoat, she obviously hadn't been to bed yet. The redolence of fresh ginger burned in Jilly's sinuses, and she rubbed her nose to hold back a sneeze.

Lau-lau angled the spoon to display the watery paste. "Strengthens the *Po*. Demon repellent."

Sera peered over the older woman's shoulder. "Does it work?"

"You can try it. Since you are Jilly's friend, I'll give you a big discount." Lau-lau grinned at her.

"There's a market for this stuff?"

Lau-lau's grin sharpened. "There will be."

Liam stood in the beaded doorway, a concession to the small room. With his arms crossed over his chest, he still took up more than his fair share of the space. "You could have told us earlier you knew."

"You had other business," Lau-lau reminded him. "Thanks to my tea."

His expression didn't change. "So tell us— plainly, please—about Jilly's bracelet."

"I explained, the knot work is a trap. The labyrinth has always held secrets. And dangers."

He stiffened, and beads clacked around his shoulders. "Dangers for who?"

"The demons. And you, of course." She narrowed her eyes. "Doesn't it always work that way?"

He pushed away from the doorway. "Maybe you have a balm to counteract that."

She shook her head. "Just as butterflies fly in the strong winds, fate is not washed away by even the strongest tea."

Jilly broke in, her frustration mounting with Liam's. "If we knew more about how to set the trap, bait it, spring it . . ."

"I sell herbs, *xiao*-Jilly. I am not a warrior with all the wisdom you seek." Lau-lau swept a fretful hand down the front of her housecoat. In a voice more bitter than anything in her apothecary cabinet, she said, "Once, we all held pieces of the great mysteries. We are shrunken now, and old, forgetful. We have lost track of each other and the mysteries we guarded. Tricks and hints are all we have left."

Jilly drew a breath to argue, but Sera shot her a silencing glance and dragged her wallet from her back pocket. "One good trick can shut up the toughest audience. I'd like some of that repellent. You take plastic?"

"Cash only," Lau-lau said primly.

While they bottled up the unguent, Liam returned to the shop. Jilly followed and watched him prowl the tight space. She took a few steps in, narrowing his restless paces.

He half turned away from her, his expression distant, and poked at the impulse buys scattered across the countertop by the register. Suddenly, his gaze sharpened, and with one long finger, he separated a small tube from the rest. "You use this one. Cherry blossoms."

She spared one glance for the lip balm. "How did you know she was something else?"

"I guessed. Things happen around you female talyan. Patterns shift. Forces realign." His fingers grazed the *reven* at his temple before he raked his fingers through his hair. "Corvus started this, you know. He wanted to punch a hole through the Veil, and his efforts, with the help of my Bookkeeper, brought through a demon. The demon that possessed Sera, that would have given him access to the weakness in the Veil. Except Sera controls it now, in some strange way she can't explain to me. So I'm sitting on a major threat to the status quo that has been maintained since the first Fall. And now you."

"Me what?" She tightened her fists.

"You're even harder to sit on." He shook his head. "We're headed to hell—do not pass go, do not collect handbasket—on my watch."

She lifted one eyebrow, not sure if she should be more amused or disgusted at his arrogance. "So this is all about you? About your conceit that you have to be the best damn leader?"

"Damned is right," he snapped at her.

"You're just pissed that you can't control Sera, can't control me. You are no better than Corvus."

The words sprang out of her as if she'd whipped the half-moon knives from her pocket. But she couldn't blame it on the demon's reflexes.

Liam's blue gaze shuttered over his reaction, if he felt anything at all. "I have no more choice than you."

She wanted to rail at him, force a crack in that cool facade. "I don't know why, but I thought you were different." She'd started thinking he was strong and wise and, oh God, a superhero from one of her childhood comic books, come to save her from all those wrong-way turns.

That had been just another of her mistakes. Like leaving home. Like confronting Rico. Like thinking she could help those homeless kids when half the time they didn't even want her help, and the other half of the time they vanished before she could steer them toward the light.

Liam didn't really want help either. He had his own thing going, as deep in denial as any of the angry boys she'd worked with.

Trying to go her own way, she'd ended up possessed. Thinking she could forge a connection with Liam, she'd end up . . . Forget it. She wasn't going there.

Maybe those long-lost talya sisters hadn't been banished. Maybe they'd left freely, if not happily. Their souls were forfeit, but at least they knew their own minds.

And they weren't going to lose their hearts too.

CHAPTER 17

For once, Jilly had no smart remarks. Which riled Liam more than her accusation that he was worse than Corvus. Had she given up that easily, decided he couldn't be redeemed? Just as she'd let go of his hand when he'd offered a truce.

He drove away from her apartment with Sera in the front passenger seat cradling her stinking jar of goo. A glance in the rearview mirror showed him Jilly staring out her window, her expression utterly closed. As if she were the wronged party.

Didn't she understand that she—all right, *they*—had crossed a line when they played in the demon zone? Bad enough to be infested with a teshuva. He'd resigned himself to that long ago. But he wasn't going to compound his sin by risking the barrier that protected the world.

He'd seen the change in Archer when Sera came, the shift in focus. More than once, he'd wondered if he would have to intervene and separate them. Even nonchalantly voicing the thought to Sera had garnered exactly the reaction he feared.

Insisting on twin beds probably wouldn't be enough, not when they had risked the world for each other already.

If that devil-may-care recklessness was the result of the mated-talyan bond, no wonder the early league leaders had run screaming in the other direction. With the fate of the league and what remained of the talyan's souls on his head, he could never allow himself the same indulgence as Archer. He had to accept the price he'd paid and remain faithful to the commitments he'd made, that all the other talyan made, night after night.

Regardless of the desires that came to him in his dreams.

Still he couldn't help trying to force her gaze in the mirror. He almost missed the exit onto Lower Wacker and had to swerve to avoid the concrete pylon that marked the entrance to the bottom deck.

"About those moving violations," Sera muttered. He gave her the mildest glance and she subsided.

Abruptly, from the backseat, Jilly said, "We should go back to the bar."

"It was that kind of night," Sera agreed.

Jilly didn't crack a smile. "Not to drink. If solvo dealers are still selling out of the Coil, I bet I can pick up a trail of soulflies there. Maybe they'll lead us to Corvus again."

"Soulflies?" Sera sat straighter.

"Never mind and no," Liam ground out. "This round with Corvus was a wash. Let's quit while we're not too far behind."

"Quit?" Sera boggled at him. "Since when—?"

"Since Corvus can call down on command more tenebrae than we've ever dealt with at once. Since Jilly and I—" He gritted his teeth. "Since I said so."

After a moment, Sera nodded. "Oh. Right. Since then."

Liam realized Jilly was finally looking at him. Despite the intermittent flashes of the overhead fluorescent streetlights, her golden eyes were hidden.

"So you're not going to unleash me to do what I can?" Her voice was low, but with no echo of the demon. Like she wasn't even upset. But he noticed she didn't include him in who'd contributed what to the night's cluster-fuck.

He tried for a small smile, but it made his jaw ache. "I'm just not the unleashing kind of guy. When we have another chance—a chance that won't make things worse than they are now—we'll take it. But not before then."

She didn't move and his demon was dormant, so he couldn't possibly have sensed the minute shift of air. Nevertheless, he felt her withdrawal.

Well, she'd heard Sera. With all their girl talk, she must know as well as he did that was what had to be. They didn't have to beat it out like dull iron just to make the necessary severing edge.

Dawn was coming. Between the support pillars on the open side of the tunnel, the river reflected the silvering sky. Even with his enhanced sight, the demon sign by which the teshuva hunted would be harder to see as daylight banished the creatures that prowled the night through all the ages.

Although lately those creatures had been coming out of the shadows. A circumstance that was only slightly more terrifying than female talyan.

Once again, he was flailing, out of his depth. But this time, the weapon at his disposal was more devastating than the war.

Disposal. The word appalled him. Jilly wasn't disposable. And yet she had to be, just like all the talyan were. For all intents, despite their immortality, they were already dead to the world. They were fated to die for the teshuva's cause.

In the cold spring light, the grungy warehouse windows reflected nothing back, gray as the demon realm. He pulled the car around back, glad to see most of the league's vehicles accounted for. He wanted to hear the night's reports, bring them up to speed—if a confused standstill could be called speed—and then climb into a shower hot enough to burn away even a salambe's chill.

He parked, and his passengers got out. He sat a moment, until Sera leaned in. "You coming?"

"Yeah." He forced his hands off the steering wheel. The poor hatchback couldn't carry him far enough to escape this. Why he'd even think it . . . ?

He remembered what Jilly had said about trying to get away. It hadn't worked for her either.

Liam followed the women to the warehouse.

Sera held up the jar, peering at the greenish glow in the morning light. "Jilly, if you could get your landlady to give up the recipe, maybe I could find a reference in the league records. They tend to be rather snide about lay interpretations of evil and folk remedies against it, but it couldn't hurt to look."

For a heartbeat, Liam wondered if he should allow Sera's continued access to the archives. Previous male talyan had closed ranks once before; he had a duty to ensure their sacrifices weren't in vain. But since Bookie's betrayal over the winter, he'd had no time to recruit a new Bookkeeper. Sera's modern medical background was the closest thing he had to scientific expertise. If anyone was going to make a breakthrough on that front, it would be her.

Whether that would be to the league's benefit was the question.

Before he decided, Jilly shrugged. "I'm not sure she'll ever give up her ancient Chinese secrets. How about we find out if it works first?"

One of the docking-bay doors was open. The talyan had gathered inside, most of them still streaked with blood and ichor. Rank sulfur wreathed the gathering. Which explained the open door.

Liam surveyed the weary faces and wondered if his own looked as drawn. "Place your bets on who had the crappiest night?"

The set of broad shoulders softened with muted laughter, and a few of the men pulled out chairs to sit, letting go of some of their tension.

"Pull that door closed, somebody, and kick the heater." He pulled off his coat and slung it over an unclaimed chair. The hammer clanged. "No sense freezing off the half of our asses that wasn't handed to us."

From across the room, Perrin piped up. "I had more than half." He turned to display the brutal tear down his back that had shredded his shirt and jeans, though he'd managed to cinch up his belt to maintain decency. The raking claw marks had continued down into skin, but his teshuva's healing had made that mostly decent too. "Three ferales, attacking in a pack. Remember when they used to hunt alone, like us?" He tilted his head with a good-old-days sigh.

A smattering of applause and a wolf whistle from Ecco made Liam wince. When he'd invited them to re-hash their night, he hadn't meant for them to share quite so intimately.

But Lex stood, head up, arms straight at his sides, as if he were participating in a spelling bee. "I got mobbed by probably a gross of malice."

"They're gross, all right," someone quipped.

Lex grinned and rolled up his sleeves where malice slime had left marks like frostbite. "I couldn't drain them fast enough. If Ecco hadn't come along, my te-shuva would've been overwhelmed instead."

"You know how I like my malice," Ecco drawled.

Liam cocked one eyebrow. "Over easy?"

Sera spoke up from where she'd tucked herself under Archer's arm despite the ichor smeared down his sleeve. "I bet Liam and Jilly win the office pool with their Corvus encounter."

Instantly, the room sobered, and all eyes swiveled to Liam. His amusement at the camaraderie, if not the casualties, withered.

He gave a quick rundown from the time they'd gone back to the haint apartment building, not glancing at Jilly as he left out the part about their side trip into the tenebraeternum. And the kiss wasn't exactly relevant either, so he skipped that too.

He'd barely paused for breath when the questions started.

"So all the tenebrae are under Corvus's control?"

"How are we supposed to destroy every solvo haint in the city?"

"What else is out there waiting for us?" And a dozen more.

He let the questions peter out. "I think the fact Corvus—or, more accurately, his djinni—lured us in and wanted to deal means he doesn't have the kind of control he wants, that he's still not sure he can work around us."

"Yet," Ecco said.

"Yet," Liam agreed. "But while he's escalated the confrontation, it doesn't change our mission."

From the back of the room, Archer pointed out, "Just makes it irrelevant." When the other talyan glanced at him, he continued. "If Corvus is still trying to tear open the Veil, how often can we hope to sweep up the aftermath?"

Liam kept himself from bristling. After almost two centuries, the futility of their eternal task had maddened Archer. Though Sera had tempered his solitary, suicidal ferocity, his disgust with what he'd derisively called their supernatural-garbage-men status remained. Sera's involvement in the league's Bookkeeper duties had brought Archer back into the fold—a mixed blessing.

"We bested Corvus once." Liam gave Archer a long, level stare. "But the cost was high."

He'd heard Archer's report of that night four months ago in Corvus's lair—although now he was discovering that Archer hadn't shared everything either—but he'd decided at the time not to relay too much detail to the other talyan. It was enough for them to know that after millennia of separate paths, the league and one djinni were on a collision course. Now that inevitable collision seemed closer than ever.

To a man—and woman, apparently—the talyan were a fierce and volatile crowd. Their immortality made them rash, and their damaged souls meant they didn't necessarily care. He'd taken it upon himself to make sure those demon-riddled souls had every chance possible to recover some measure of salvation. Which wouldn't be theirs if they strayed from their mission.

In a low, relentless voice, he made his point. "We survived the battle, but we lost a Bookkeeper and a good fighter when we never have enough. We had to abandon our home, and when Corvus's high-rise blew, we skirted too close to revealing our presence to the whole city. You think it's tough now draining tenebrae bloated on everyday spite and decay? Imagine if you have to work around the terror and mayhem of a populace that learns evil walks incarnate and they can neither see it, believe it, nor fight it off."

He waited while that sank in, then continued. "Corvus has us at a disadvantage, since he is willing to work in plain sight, while we must keep to the shadows. We can't help him make things worse by bringing the horde-tenebrae into the light."

From their set expressions, he could see they were not happy with his assessment, but neither did they disagree.

Until Jilly took a step forward. "But are we saving the city, or just our souls?"

His hands flexed, driven by the reflexive surge of his demon to her challenge. He tamped it down, the heels of his palms hard against his thighs lest he reach for her.

Her gaze burned over him like hot coals, lingered on his fists, as if she thought he would silence her with fingers around her throat. Not that she'd let that stop her.

How could he explain that he didn't want to silence her, but save her—never mind the city—from herself?

Her stare burned deeper. "I always wanted the kids at the halfway house to know until they addressed their problems honestly, they'd always feel like outsiders, outcast even from themselves."

"Is this a 'face your demons' speech?" Ecco asked.

She glanced at the other talya but didn't smile. "What if everyone did? Not just us, but everyone in the city?"

Sera stepped up beside Jilly. "I've wondered the

same. If there are people like Jilly's landlady, regular humans, who are fighting the demons, maybe we should find them and join forces. There's no reason we have to be alone in this."

With his demon hovering halfway to attack, Liam felt the talyan weighing the words as clearly as if they'd picked up stones, hefted the burdens in their hands. They didn't appreciate how their calling was fragile as glass, that every night they walked one wrong step away from hell.

They also didn't know that he and Jilly had been dancing right there on the edge. If they found out, they'd never listen to him, and he dreaded the day he watched them ridden down by the darkness of the world, weighed down by the darkness in their souls.

"There's one reason." At the demon lows in his voice, violet flickered in the eyes around him as the others responded to the implied threat.

Only Jilly's gaze was clear. "What?"

He touched his temple, drawing attention to the most obvious sign of the demon rampant. The *reven* smoldered beneath his fingers, his human flesh incompatible with the other-realm marking, even though they were inextricably intertwined.

And that was the reason. "We are alone because we are marked as damned, and we must atone. That is our only mission, our only fight."

The harsh conviction rolled through them as if those stones had backfired.

"You're the one who pointed it out to me," he reminded Jilly softly. "I am soul brother to Corvus. And so are we all."

Despite the roaring propane heater in the ceiling, the warehouse had gone chill. One wrong touch and they would all shatter. The ravager in him coiled and uncoiled. It knew jagged edges made better weapons.

Even more softly, knowing they would hear, he said, "But we *will* fight. I promise you." His heart bled to hear the ring of truth.

After a moment, Jonah nodded. "The way to repentance is between you and your God." A bitter smile twisted his lips. "Or your demon, as the case may be. It is no longer our place to convert others."

Ecco snorted. "Converting was always your deal, missionary man, not mine. I don't care what Corvus has in mind—bashed in like it is—as long as I get plenty of slaughter time. It'll all come out in the wash." He snorted again. "Well, not all of it. Unless you use bleach. Whatever. I'm beat. Wake me up if tomorrow doesn't get here."

His exit broke the pained tableau. Archer touched Sera's shoulder, drawing her away, but not before she murmured something to Jilly, who didn't respond.

A palace coup? Liam couldn't dredge up the interest to care as he talked to a few more talyan on their way out. They'd all had bad nights, their clashes with tenebrae fiercer than ever. Underneath their murmured reaffirmations that they'd made it through in one piece—or at least pieces that could be put back together—was the unspoken echo to the question Archer had raised: Did it matter?

Their doubt drained him as he subtly reinforced their focus. Their intensity he never questioned, and their strength. But those sterling attributes could become glittering knives turned against the world if ever they lost track of their mission, like he'd indulged the spiraling dark obsession with Jilly.

Though undercurrents of unease still swirled in violet eyes, exhaustion took them to their rooms. The end times offered that advantage, at least: keeping the union of supernatural killers too busy with overtime to review their retirement policy.

When he was alone in the docking bay, he turned off the heater and the lights. He stood in the empty, cavernous space for a moment, but not even the flicker of a lone soulfly disturbed the darkness.

He went inside.

The halls were every bit as empty, but a subdued clatter drew him to the kitchen.

Jilly. Of course. He leaned in the doorway.

She'd only turned on the counter light, leaving her adrift in the otherwise murky room. A pile of neatly split eggshells glistened whitely at her elbow. She didn't look around at him as she cracked another egg. "I'm not trying to win friends and influence people, but the crew will need something for breakfast."

"Maybe you can mix in some of Lau-lau's repellent."

She finally glanced over at him, uncertainty in the hunch of her shoulders. "I didn't think you'd even talk to me."

"Why? Just because you're trying to destroy the league from within?"

"I'm not—" She grabbed a bowl and began whisking furiously.

"You're about to tell me a discord demon can't make omelets without breaking some eggs."

"I'm not making omelets again. I'm making quiche. It'll keep until tomorrow when everyone gets up."

"Jilly," he said softly as he walked toward her

She put the bowl down with a decisive thump, as if she didn't want to be tempted to throw it at him. "I am not the teshuva, not just discord."

"It chose you for a reason."

"But I'm not trying to challenge you," she said. When he snorted, she pursed her lips with a wry tilt of her head but didn't back down as he closed the distance between them. "Not challenge you for responsibility to the league, anyway. I have no illusions what kind of leader I'd be. Still, I really believe I can make a difference."

"That's what I'm afraid of." He lifted one hand when she started to protest. "Your life has been about going a different way. That's why you got involved with the halfway house, to keep the kids out of the sort of trouble you grew up in. But you can't save the talyan by ending this fight. Only in the fighting can we be saved."

She stared at him.

"You think I'm blind, but I'm not." Involuntarily, he touched his temple with the pointed knuckles of his hard-clenched fist. "I see very clearly. I see that we are caught for eternity in this battle. That is the contract we inadvertently signed in our possession. But seeing clearly doesn't mean there's a way out of the trap."

She gently bumped aside his fist to lay her palm against his cheekbone, her fingertips just grazing his *reven*. The combination of her soft touch and even-softer eyes nearly ruined him. Just when he thought she only wanted his head on a pike, she offered him instead a chance to lay his head in her lap. The temptation trumped any the demon had ever conjured.

He half closed his eyes. Then his gaze snagged on her bracelet. Other-realm ethers still glimmered in the woven bands, a mute reminder of lurking threats trapped but not vanquished.

He took a step back, and she paled as if he'd slapped her. But there were only so many pieces of him that could be caught in so many traps before there wouldn't be anything left.

And he had to wonder if that would be so bad.

"I'll go so you can finish," he said stiffly.

"Liam," she said.

But he didn't look back.

CHAPTER 18

Jilly slept until noon. Thanks to the teshuva, she needed less sleep. But she didn't want to face Liam again.

And hiding in her bedroom was oh-so mature. When she couldn't stand her own cowardice anymore, she sneaked across the hall to her sister's room.

Dory answered her knock, looking more rumpled and tired than Jilly'd felt after a night of being chased by demons. "Hey."

She supposed Dory had been fleeing her own. "Hey. Can I come in?"

In the short time she'd been in residence, Dory had trashed the place. Her assortment of clothes from the league's castoffs covered more space than seemed possible. The desk was strewn with paper and markers.

"You're coloring." The words popped out of Jilly in her surprise; then she winced. It sounded like an accusation.

Dory shrugged. "Sera's friend, the church lady Nanette, said sometimes it helps her get what's inside out."

Jilly gestured at the table. "Can I . . . ?"

Dory shrugged again.

She hadn't hoped for puppies and flowers, but Jilly's heart skittered at the dozen pages crammed with Corvus's blunt features.

"I can't get him out of my system." Dory's voice was dull. "After she gave me the pens, she wanted to hold hands and pray, and I told her to get lost." She waved her hand when Jilly frowned. "In a nice way. But it isn't going to work with me. I tried that twelve-step shit."

Jilly had suggested AA to enough kids to be familiar with the resistance. "You have to keep working the steps, Dory. It's not a quick fix."

Dory sat on the bed, her lank blond hair swinging forward to hide her face. "I heard you saw Blackbird last night."

The talyan must have been talking. Jilly hoped they hadn't said anything totally inappropriate. Hard enough to explain her situation to her sister without getting into demonic possession.

Dory stared at her. "Your boyfriend said you tried to kill Blackbird once."

"The league did, but that was before I got together with Liam." Jilly realized she couldn't explain the league either. She reached for a shirt to fold instead. "I told you, he's not my boyfriend."

Dory gave her a practiced adolescent eye roll. "Did you hurt him?"

"I'd like to," Jilly murmured. She wasn't sure if Dory meant Liam or Corvus. "Blackbird attacked us."

Emotions, darker and older than the calculated insubordination, sleeted over Dory's face, too quick to catalog. "Still, you all lived to fight another day."

Once again, Jilly couldn't tell if her sister was glad for her or for Corvus. "Something like that. Dory, with Sera's connections, we can get you a bed in a good program." She hesitated and set the neatened shirt aside. "It's inpatient and out of state, but—"

Dory was already shaking her head. "I don't want to be locked up."

"It's not a prison."

"You've never been," Dory burst out. "Why you think those kids never listen to you? They know you never been there."

The honest fear in her sister's voice beat in Jilly's chest. She steeled herself. "I had my year in juvie. It's not a badge of honor."

Dory shook her head violently. "Not the place-place. The mind. You've never been stuck in there. You always knew you'd find the way out. And I always knew that's why you couldn't get me out too."

Jilly pressed her arm against her stomach, to hold in the sorrow and affection that tried to well up and choke her. "Dory, I'm sorry for . . ." Where to start? "Everything. I'm not myself lately, and I just don't know . . ." Where to start? "Anything."

Dory blinked at her. "That's more than you could've admitted before."

Jilly winced. "Am I such a bitch?"

"A 'babe in total control of herself.' That's what it stands for, you know. 'Bitch.' That's what Mom's boyfriends did to you. You escaped, but not untouched, no more than me."

Her life hardly seemed to compare with Dory's experiences. But then Jilly thought a moment. What had she missed over the years, hidden behind her walls of defiant self-reliance?

Dory interrupted her reverie. "I saw Leroy, a while back. He wanted me to join that crazy cult of his. Said he could get me off the drugs too." She eyed Jilly with a touch of mockery. "No prayers or tough-love lockdown, though. They use herbs and acupuncture or some shit. Sounds way better."

Jilly wondered if she'd be trying for a second intervention soon. The group's front-gate greeters had booted her off the premises quick enough the time she'd gone. But those gates would be no obstacle to her new demonic powers. "But you didn't stay."

Dory shrugged. "Had things to do."

Jilly pictured her brother succumbing to the cult's allure, her sister snared by drugs. And herself, with her self-imposed walls that had only kept her neatly corralled for a teshuva with exploitation on its mind. She wondered who deserved the hardest slap. "God, how'd we grow up still so stuck?"

"Blackbird had an answer," Dory said. "Ask him."

"Maybe I will." Jilly could guess what Liam would say to that. Because he was as stuck as the rest of them.

But maybe it was time to get unstuck.

In the daylight, the Mortal Coil looked like a stiletto-heeled stylista after a long night of sweating off ten-dollar martinis: listing, stained, and vastly the poorer. Jilly let the teshuva flow unfettered, but found nothing untoward.

Which was almost odd in itself, considering the talya reports about rampant tenebrae activity the night before.

The front door was locked so she walked the long block to the alley. Sheltered between the Dumpsters, she amped the demon a little higher and gave the locked back door a hard tug. Not locked anymore. Iz would be so proud of her.

The door opened into the bathroom hallway. Where all the best drug deals took place, Jilly knew. She prowled down the hall. Just one soulfly, one hint, was all she wanted.

She stiffened when she sensed the approach.

"Thought I heard someone come in."

Jilly turned to see Bella.

The club owner leaned in the office doorway, arms crossed. She was dressed in another red baby-doll tee that clashed with her hair, but the beehive was in a loose knot at her nape.

"Thanks for not bringing the double-barreled shot-gun," Jilly said.

Bella patted her hip. "We saloon girls use something smaller and tidier on thieves and varmints these days."

Whether it was a Taser or Mace or something worse, Jilly didn't doubt the blind Bella could drill a dime at twenty paces. "Good thing I didn't come to steal any-thing. As for the infestation . . . well, I won't leave any-thing behind."

Bella made a noncommittal noise. "Does Liam know you're here?"

"He's right behind me." Jilly kept her tone bland. She figured there was a fair-to-middling chance she wasn't even lying. "I thought I'd just get started."

"On . . . ?"

"Finding leftovers from those solvo dealers."

Bella half closed her pale eyes. "We keep them out."

"Oh, I don't mind helping out one of Liam's friends, looking around to make sure you're good. You know, clear." No, they both knew she meant good.

Bella's lip curled, but she took a step back into her office, clearing the way down the hall. She tagged along behind Jilly into the gloomy cavern of the empty night-club. "I'm surprised Liam let you come on ahead. He likes to be on top . . . of things."

Oh, subtle. "I hadn't really noticed."

Fluorescents lit the three bars, but other than that, the club was dark, the high ceiling invisible in the shadows except for the occasional wink of colored spotlight gels like demon eyes as she prowled through the space. Not that her skin prickled with any of that lurking-malice alert.

Bella trailed her around the dance-floor rail. "He'll do anything for his band of merry men. I'm sure you have noticed that."

"It's hard to miss." Jilly wished the woman would stop talking. Made it hard to crush down the impulse to ask questions. Like, how often Liam stopped in. And how often he left alone.

"He pays me well to let the boys burn off their extra energy here. No price is too high."

Jilly worked her way around a corner banquette backed by a smoky mirror. It looked perfect for the clandestine passing of illegal substances. "Funny. I got the impression they did plenty of burning at the office."

Bella slid into the banquette and gave her head a pitying shake. "Well, it's hard to know someone just from work hours."

Jilly forced a laugh. "Not when all they are is work."

Bella's expression soured, and Jilly wondered why. It wasn't like Jilly had anything going with Liam, if that was the problem. That much must be obvious even to a blind woman.

It was also obvious there was no hint of solvo-shredded soulflies anywhere. Maybe she'd been wrong about the club and its owner; the Coil had seemed like such a great place to find trouble.

Disheartened, she slumped into the banquette across from Bella. "Look." Then she winced. "Sorry. I guess you've known Liam a long time." Not as long as she herself would, of course. "I'm just trying to put a stop to the solvo. That's a good thing for all of us." Meaning, like, the world.

Bella sighed. "Shit like solvo takes all the joy out of drinking and dancing and fighting."

"Right." Whatever got the club owner on her side. Or off her back anyway. "Well, at least the guys have the drinking and fighting part down."

"Archer dances now. Thanks to Sera. Anyway, he prowls around the dance floor. We count that. And he needs it."

Jilly's lips twitched. "I'm trying to imagine the moody broody bad boy getting his groove on."

Bella closed her eyes and smiled back. "Yeah, I try to picture it too." She opened her eyes again, and her pale gaze fixed hard on Jilly despite her alleged disability. "*Your* boots sound awfully heavy for dancing."

In the mirror behind Bella's head, Jilly caught a flash of violet. She blinked, wrestling back the teshuva. "A waitress like you should understand. I like comfortable shoes."

"Yes, ruts are like that, aren't they?" Bella put her elbow on the banquette table and propped her cheek on her fist. "I don't dance either. Tell me, Jilly Chan, what rut were you stuck in before Liam rescued you?"

Jilly wondered which should offend her more, to know that Bella had sniffed around enough to come up with her last name, or the idea that Liam had rescued her from anything. But she wondered at the curiosity when it was so clear the other woman didn't like her. "I wasn't in a rut. I had a very rewarding job working with homeless and at-risk youth."

Bella chuckled. "No wonder Liam chose you. Ah well, he makes a fine boss."

Jilly opened her mouth to correct the club owner on the choosing, then realized how close she'd come to spilling secrets that weren't hers. "Yeah. The at-risk part crosses over especially well."

She didn't even bother addressing the boss part, but she had to admit Liam was dedicated to his crew in a way Envers had never been with the kids. That had been the start of her conversion, she realized; whatever else he was that drove her crazy, he cared. Deeply and in an all-consuming way. And she was becoming part of it. Sinking into the secrets, becoming part of the league. Becoming Liam's. She waited for the expected surge of outrage, spiced with claustrophobia.

And waited.

Bella drummed her long nails on the tabletop. "You know, if the league really wanted to put your nose to the ground tracking solvo, you should start at Back of the Yards."

Diverted, Jilly sat back in the cushions. Dory had mentioned the area too. The old stockyards were long gone, but its rough, industrial history leached through to the modern name. "What's there?"

"The start," Bella said laconically.

Wasn't everyone full of mystery these days? "Thanks for the tip." She rose and turned to go.

"I'm going to have to charge you for that lock you jimmied."

As Jilly strode away, she tossed over her shoulder, "Put it on the boss's tab."

She was already gone. Liam knew that even as he walked into the Mortal Coil. The club felt dead, which wouldn't be the case if Jilly's vibrant self were anywhere in the vicinity.

How he'd know that he didn't want to contemplate.

But Bella was already approaching, and he couldn't just stalk away.

She cocked her head, as if she was studying him. "You're all fired up about something." She smiled to herself slightly, as if the words amused her.

"Did Jilly mention where she was off to next?"

"I figured you'd know, since she said you were right behind her." Bella's smile tightened. "I guess she meant you were playing catch-up."

He rubbed his forehead. "Jilly?"

"She's looking for the source of all things evil. Solvo," she clarified when he looked up sharply. "I suggested a good place to score."

Liam's hands clenched, though he kept his voice mild. "You might have stalled her."

"She didn't seem interested in waiting around. Quite unwilling to heed orders, I'd say. Must be maddening."

"Yeah," he muttered.

Mad didn't even begin to cover it. Furious. Outraged. Those sounded better.

He found himself out on the street and realized he wasn't sure he'd said good-bye to Bella. Something about an addition to his tab. He'd send her a fat check and hope that covered everything. He didn't have time to flow Bella and Lau-lau into his understanding, not when Jilly's every move threw him another twist.

Why did it not surprise him that a knot-work demon had chosen her?

He knew Jilly hadn't taken a vehicle from the league lot, and the outskirts of the old stockyard district were close enough to walk. She wasn't that far ahead of him that he couldn't catch up in his car and drag her home.

He wove through traffic with more than a few honked horns, wondering how he could call a warehouse of mismatched antiques home. And why did he think to stop her from pursuing her last purpose in life? Even before the demon possessed her, she'd been a vigilante crusader.

His only task should be to aim her like the weapon she now was. Of course, he needed to have the weapon in hand to aim it.

Never mind how badly he wanted her in hand.

He skirted the L with a wary eye. Full daylight was no guarantee of protection from the tenebrae, but at least they still seemed to prefer the night. The human-clad demons, however, went about in all weather.

The elevated tracks turned away from the road, and he drove straight into the bland industrial park. He rolled down the windows, the ravager demon's senses blown wide.

The stockyards had closed long ago, gone with the railway lines that had once fed cows and immigrants into the massive killing sheds. Even the limestone arch that had marked the yards as "slaughterhouse to the world" was gone, relocated to the historical museum where it stood in much more genteel surrounds.

And still Liam swore the smell of blood and shit lingered over the concrete.

He slicked one hand down the prickling hair at his nape. Not his demon, just bad memories. He cruised the main streets. It was Sunday, he realized, which explained the empty parking lots. Less traffic, fewer witnesses; always good. How hard could it be to find one short but curvy tyro demon-killer in an empty industrial park?

His nostrils flared at a bitter drift, and he peered out the passenger window at a plume of smoke curling from behind one of the buildings.

That might be a reasonable place to start.

CHAPTER 19

Liam slalomed the car around the back side of the building and found himself in a confusing maze of stacked truck trailers. Though his pulse tried to leap ahead, he slowed the car. Wouldn't want to careen around a steel box and flatten Jilly. Although she'd deserve it.

Rising above the roofline, the whorl of smoke was now a widespread black wing. Why stop with the bad news of ferales frolicking in the daylight when they could attract attention with smoke signals too? What the hell had she gotten herself into?

And he knew it was her. Where there was smoke, there'd be his fiery female talya, no doubt.

His.

Damn it.

He saw an opening between the trailers and gunned the car past the last obstacles. In the middle of the barren space, glittering with the urban confetti of broken glass, Jilly stood, arms wrapped around herself, facing a smoking mound of debris.

He was out of the car and at her side in a heartbeat. "What happened?"

"Nothing." She gestured at the pile. "I found them like this."

"They" were bodies, charred and crumbling even as

he watched. The smoke was half dust, spiraling into the sky.

"Haints." Jilly's voice was dull. "No sign of anything else. If you squint, you can almost see the soulflies against the black."

Fury rose up in him, far blacker than the smoke and dust. "And what if there had been something else? Say, Corvus, lying in wait for you to blunder in."

She shook her head. "He was as freaked by our last encounter as we were. I think that's what happened here." She gestured at the pile. "He was cleaning house. This is just the garbage he left behind." She clutched herself tighter. "Just garbage."

Already, the black smoke was thinning as the haints crumbled. If anyone had seen the alarming sign in the empty park and called it in, there'd be nothing left by the time a police cruiser was dispatched to check it out.

"If he is gone," Liam made sure his tone indicated he wasn't willing to give her that pass, "then it was only a short time ago. The fact there's anything left of these bodies at all means the salambes abandoned these bodies recently."

They witnessed in silence. Just as she'd said, if he glanced to one side, he glimpsed the translucent shards of soul matter. At first, the flecks held a vaguely columnar shape, but as the bodies flaked away and the dust lifted on the breeze, the soulflies wandered off. Truly lost souls.

A thin stream of them began to spiral down toward Jilly and that damned bracelet, but she continued to stare into the ashes, oblivious.

"Why would you leave the warehouse?" He kept his voice neutral.

"Because I have to do something and everyone else seemed occupied. You know, sharpening their swords for tonight and whatnot."

"*I* wasn't sharpening any sword," he said tightly. "I do all weapons prep before I sleep."

She shot him a glance piercing enough to shame the

well-honed tips of her crescent knives. "You said we should stay away from each other."

"That was not what I said." He was fairly certain it hadn't been that. At least not so bluntly.

"That was the logical extension of what you said."

"Since when are you logical?" He tried to rein in his temper, but the lingering sour stench of burn made him edgy. "Logical would not lead you to believe that Bella has your best interests at heart."

"I think it's likely she has no heart." Jilly turned her face to the sky. "I suppose I could find out." She glanced back at him. "She wants you, and not just because of the cat-and-mouse fun of the who-knows-what game you're playing together."

"She wants what seems like my money," he corrected. "And maybe the power she senses. Not exactly the basis for a long-lasting relationship—even without the demonic-immortality angle."

"I've seen worse reasons to fall in love."

That word again. He didn't like how it kept popping up around him, a pretty package with an undertow of pain like a candy-coated malice.

"The quiche was great," he said. Anything to get off the other subject.

Her lips twitched. "Also not a reason to fall in love, whatever Lau-lau might say."

He scowled. "What is it with you females and love?"

Her smile faded. "Nothing. Not a damn thing." She stalked away from him.

He had to take three long steps to catch up with her. "Where are you going?"

"To find what I came for. Corvus's hideaway. Dory said he liked to deal from here. What if there's a stash of solvo, or a lab, somewhere in all these buildings?"

"We don't know how Corvus makes it. Bookie took that secret into his soulless funk."

"Then now's a good time to find out how they did it. And stop it. Maybe even reverse it." She avoided the smoldering mound. "For some."

"You really think you can put a soul back in its body?"

She halted and turned her considering gaze on him. "The body is just another trap. Isn't that why your touch brings me back to myself when the demon realm is all around us?"

A strange heat lanced through him, half satisfaction that she would admit he'd affected her, half anger that she considered it a trap.

Oblivious, she continued. "Why shouldn't we be able to lure the soul back, just as we lured the salambes?"

He shook his head, trying to fling off his internal mayhem and evaluate her words. Considering how she fretted over her hoodlum charges, he shouldn't be surprised she would bulldoze any pesky obstacle—like, oh, cold hard reality—that stumbled into her path. Still, it was one thing to talk a young gangbanger into considering college, and something else again to trick a spirit into its shell.

On the other hand, if anyone could do it . . .

Your touch brings me back to myself.

He gestured for her to proceed.

She searched his face, one hand restlessly twisting the bracelet around her wrist. "You don't even believe me. You don't have to come along."

He gave her a long look but didn't speak. When she strode off, he stayed close on her heels.

They quartered the nearest buildings in the hopes of finding a sign of demon activity, a thread of birnenston, something. But the few remaining soulflies dissipated, lacking even the will to follow Jilly.

"Nothing." He smoothed a hand down the back of his neck. "A dead end. Let's get out of here."

Jilly propped her hands on her hips. "But you feel it too?"

"Feel what? That we're wasting our time?"

"The creep."

"If we found a few creeps, we wouldn't be wasting our time."

"Stop being so bossy and just listen a minute." She put her hand on his arm, halting him in his tracks.

God, just that little touch sent ripples through his senses. Not calming, not at all, but clearing somehow, like a wind that swept the dreck away.

"If there's nothing here, why are you so nervy?" She trailed her touch down his arm, wrapped her fingers around his wrist in a loose manacle. "The demon would be jumping out of your skin if it wasn't tacked down in your soul."

"I've always hated this place." The admission blurted from him, drawn out as if her touch was the lure.

She glanced around at the identical beige buildings with their antiglare windows and the bare brown hollows of empty retention ponds. "What's not to hate?"

He gave her a ghost of a smile. "This is better than what it was."

She considered. "You knew the stockyards when they were still running."

He jerked his head in a nod. "As a stinking off-the-boat immigrant with one eye, if you couldn't do anything else, you could always work the slaughterhouses. They didn't ask awkward questions."

"Like, how come you had only one eye?"

"Like, 'How did you get here?' I didn't have any papers."

"A lot of people left Ireland during the famine. Was it so hard to get documentation?"

"It was if you were a murderer."

Had he expected her to recoil? She just looked more thoughtful as they started hiking across the no-man's-land of empty parking lot to the next set of ugly buildings. "The boy who died when you were breaking down fences in Ireland? But that wasn't your fault."

"Not then. Later."

She cast a sidelong glance at him that flicked over his *reven*, but she kept walking. "From running with a gang of rural hoodlums to one-eyed murderer. You've led a more rebellious life than I gave you credit for."

"Rebellious?" He couldn't contain a harsh bark of laughter. "Hardly. I'd learned my lesson about breaking rules after I saw that boy trampled into the mud. I kept my head down, never bent another thing besides nails, and even those I forged again. Never got hotheaded unless I was working too close to the fire. And still I managed to kill a man."

There was nothing in this place to trigger memories of his last days at home. No heather and mist and peat smoke.

Just the woman with steady golden eyes, drawing the past from him like poison from a wound. "What happened?"

He shoved his hands in his pockets. The hammer at his side swung counterpoint to his speeded step. With any luck, the next buildings over would be infested with salambes and this conversation would be over. "Just more of the same. Only worse. By then, I was working as the village blacksmith. Some local boys had broken into a British granary, stole barley. When the regiment came to town, I said the tools that did the deed were mine."

"You didn't want a repeat of what happened before. So, just like you always do, you took the lead."

He clenched his teeth against the surge of remembered dread, barely dimmed. His temple throbbed. "I wasn't going to let another boy die when I had a chance to stop it. I just wanted to talk, but one of the soldiers hit me with the butt of his rifle. The blood pouring into my eye blinded me, left my hands slick. When I grappled with him, the gun went off. And he was dead."

"So you don't even know whose finger pulled the trigger?"

He gave her a hard look. "Beside the point."

"Not legally."

"The demon didn't come to me with a briefcase and power tie. That night was my penance trigger, the moment that had started all those years before when I ran through the darkness, yanking down fences with the boys, and has fated all the nights since." His belly cramped. Youthful hunger for justice had morphed to just hunger. Naive rage had hollowed him into an empty vessel, perfect for the teshuva.

A worried line etched her brow. "The soldiers could have killed you."

He paused and lifted his head to scan the buildings around them. "Are you sensing anything?"

She copied his stance, then shook her head and slanted a glance at him. "Just you avoiding the conversation."

He walked on, a little faster, as if he could outpace her unasked question, the concern he felt from her. Concern for him, ages too late and as irrelevant now as then. "Would I have chosen that instead if I'd known what would come? Struggled just a little harder when they threw me in the cell along with the boys?"

"Would you?" she challenged.

Ah, there was the Jilly he knew. After a moment, he shook his head. "They confiscated everything I had, of course. But they didn't notice the fine nails stuck in the sole of my boot."

A grin chased across her lips. "You picked the lock. Why, boss, I'd never have guessed it of you. Iz would be so proud."

He shrugged, though her teasing eased the pain in his gut. "I got the boys out, but where is safe in a hungry, occupied land with a price on your head?"

"You got them here."

He squelched her admiring tone. "Not all. The oldest, Patrick, took fever during the passage. We'd bribed our way on board, but I couldn't provide even enough water. So starving, fleeing, guilty as charged, and now dying of thirst."

She hunched her shoulders. "I can't imagine how terrible it was."

"I was in charge, Jilly." He met her gaze squarely. "When he passed, I dumped him off the back of the boat in the dead of night, afraid the quartermaster I'd paid would think we carried sickness and throw us all overboard. I told myself I would do anything if I could get the rest of them here, and keep them alive."

"And you did."

He strode away from her. "This is the place I brought them. From the green hills of Ireland, to the killing fields of Chicago." He couldn't curtail the native lilt that had all but deserted him, and his lips curled back, as if the stench too had come back to haunt him. "We lived in a Back of the Yards boardinghouse. I tracked the filth in every night, and slept with the taste of blood in my mouth. I thought if I just worked harder, I could get us down south to a farm, something more like where we'd come from. I took a third shift, stole scraps for the boys."

"No wonder you're worn thin," she murmured. "The starvation continued."

He rubbed his temple this time, feeling the old ache. "I was blind on this side from the soldier's strike, and it slowed me enough that the foreman always passed me over, even though my blacksmithing skills carried, in some ways, to butchering. I was desperate, exhausted."

"Understandably," she said.

They stopped just beyond the sidewalk to the next building. He met her gaze. "Could you understand if I said I wanted to leave the boys?" He didn't wait for her to answer. "By myself, I could have made it. With the four of them that remained, impossible."

"But you didn't leave them," she said softly.

How could she be so sure about him? "Worse. I betrayed them. Good Catholic boys, they looked up to me. And I came home after one really fucked-up night possessed by the devil."

"What did it promise you?" Her voice was scarcely above a whisper.

"That those I led would never die." His lips twisted. "I forgot the devil says what we want to hear. I never thought how 'never die' wasn't the same as 'couldn't be killed.' "

"You couldn't know."

"One of the boys did. The youngest, Sean, would have been a fine priest."

"Except for the stealing-barley part," Jilly broke in. "But I know how that goes."

He smiled, surprised at how easily her irreverence lightened his memories and his heart. "Sean said he went along just to forgive them." His smile slipped. "But he couldn't forgive me. I couldn't ask him to."

"Which one? He couldn't, or you couldn't? Those are two different things."

He waved his hand. "I should never have gone back after Roald brought me into the league. But I couldn't just abandon the boys. Sean wouldn't let me in, though. He *saw* what I was, and he was afraid I would take all their souls. I was . . ." He cleared his throat. "I worried they'd be lost without me. But Ro said he'd make sure they survived as long as I didn't betray the league. Not as I'd betrayed the boys." The old leader hadn't accused him of any such betrayal, of course, but the memory of guilt still had teeth.

"What happened to them?"

This was when she would turn away from him. "I don't know. I never went back again."

She lifted her eyebrows knowingly. "Never ever?"

Her perception made him shift from one foot to the other before he could stop himself, like any boy caught out in a lie. "Once," he admitted. "A woman was staying with them. Sean had told her what I was. She wouldn't let me see them either. I left." When Jilly took another breath, he added repressively, "For good."

And it had been. For their good, as well as his own. He stared up at the building before him. They could be standing right where the old tenements had been. In those days, he had staggered back to the boys each night in a black oblivion, making his way by animal instinct alone. Now even the concrete and steel pylons that had guided the stock cars this far into the yards were gone.

Everything was gone. Which didn't explain his lingering unease. He turned a slow circle, scanning.

Jilly stiffened and set herself to guard his back. "What is it?"

"There's nothing here."

"We've established that."

"Nothing remains from that time, and yet I can't shake the memories." Even though he very much wanted to.

"They dozed the place flat."

He straightened with a twinge of hunter's thrill. "Flat. Of course. But they didn't get everything. This way."

He loped away from the building with Jilly on his heels.

"What's up?" she called.

"Not up. Down." He headed for the retention dredge that would handle melting snow or overflow water in a storm. The gaping mouth of a concrete culvert poked out of the shallow bank. "All that filth had to go somewhere."

Jilly peered past him at the sewer. "You're not thinking . . ."

"Where better to hide the psychic stench of evil than under a century of old blood?" He tracked the line of the culvert back along the street. Halfway down the block, he stopped at a manhole cover. He toed the tufts of brittle brown grass grown around the edges. "Stay here while I—"

"Oh, please." She leaned down and with one hand overturned the solid steel disk. "Got your demon eyes on?"

Before the clang of metal on concrete died in his ears, she stepped into the black hole.

CHAPTER 20

Jilly straightened in the stinking dark, her hand braced on the curve of the wall. Cold concrete scraped against her palm.

That jump would've been way cooler if she hadn't landed in ankle-deep sludge and spattered it all over her jeans. "Yuck."

Liam executed a controlled slide down the rickety ladder she hadn't been sure would hold even her weight much less his six-foot self. Of course, he was such a lean cuisine, as Dee liked to call the boys.

He stepped off the last rung. His precisely placed boot barely made a ripple in the goo. "How convenient nothing waited down here to gut you."

"I figured I had the advantage of surprise. And splatter." She lifted one foot with a grimace. "No birnenston or ichor streamers here. Deeper?"

The passageway barely cleared her head. Liam had to hunch to avoid touching the concrete dome. He brought out his hammer, though she wondered how he'd find room to swing. She took the crescent knives from her pocket and fanned them in her left hand, leaving her right free to trail near the wall.

Her demon-amped vision captured the last photons of light coming from the open culvert at the end of the tunnel. When they rounded a curve, even that petered out.

Her fingers bumped against an outcropping in the wall. "The tunnel just changed to brick."

"We joined up with the old sewer system." The stone made his voice hollow. "They flushed the offal right out into the waterway."

They walked on. She guessed they must be well under the buildings now although the sewer showed no signs of use. Even the trickle of backwash had dried up. Her skin puckered at the thought of the rivers of blood and worse that had poured where they were walking, soaked red on red into the bricks. No, wait. That wasn't the reason her skin was crawling. "Do you see that?"

"Yeah."

The sickly yellow tendrils snaking down the corridor made a hell of a welcome mat. The key word being "hell," of course.

She switched one knife to her free hand.

The tunnel vaulted abruptly into a central hub the size of a large room with other tunnels trailing away into the deeps. The ceiling was high enough for Liam to stand up despite the crusting of birnenston that hadn't quite engulfed the entire space.

"Home, bitter home," she murmured as they circled the jumble of overturned shelves and shattered glass, so violently destroyed that one metal bracket was embedded in the bricks, and the pulverized glass sparkled like glitter over the thick gluey ropes of birnenston. She booted a broken-necked flask, and it rolled away through a scattering of matte white powder. The binder, she guessed, that they'd used to give solvo substance in the human realm.

She'd been in a meth lab once, pulling out one of her kids, and she knew she'd never forget the unique stench, like cat piss and diesel spiked with ugly desperation.

But this . . . Under the birnenston stench was a sweeter fragrance. "It smells like the first minute of a spring rain."

"Washes everything away, Corvus promised. Memories. Pain." His voice petered out.

She grimaced. "Your soul."

"That attitude'll get you kicked off the marketing team." He prodded a vein of birnenston with his hammer, and the substance crumbled, released a cloud of sulfurous rot that overwhelmed the rain. "Who's in charge of quality control around here?"

She edged around the tumbled shelves but found no raw materials, no finished vials of solvo, and no convenient cookbook with the damning recipe. "Corvus didn't have much time to close up shop. He burned up haints doing it, but there must not have been much to move either. Why? Does he have another lab somewhere?"

Liam stood tall in the center of the hub. "Or does he have everything he needs to make his move?"

She thought for a moment. "Which is worse? That'll probably be our answer."

A faint smile flickered across his face. "That's the spirit."

"Spirits are exactly the problem." She pocketed her knives again. "You were right the first time. There's nothing here. Damn it."

"Not quite nothing." He pointed above his head.

She followed the line of his hammer. Almost lost in the embedded tangle of birnenston threads was a small beaker, miraculously intact and gleaming like a tiny strung pearl.

They made their way back to the surface. The beaker of raw solvo nestled in Jilly's puffed pocket, and she walked gingerly, as if she carried a rain-sweet bomb. Not that there'd been any explosions, but she figured the day was young. "I can't believe they missed it."

"The downside of an army of smoke-heads led by the brain damaged. Details may get overlooked."

"What are we going to do with it?"

He let out a long breath. "I haven't worked that out yet. Right now, it's just another twist." His gaze drifted toward violet, and she wondered if he was angry with her, his newest recruit leading him astray and once again twisting, wrinkling, and denting his precious SOP.

Then he blinked as he faced the sun, and his demon was gone. "Let's get back to the warehouse. It's going to be another busy night."

The trek back to the car was silent. Only as they climbed in did she ask, "Why'd you come after me?"

"What should I have done instead?"

"You were pretty explicit that there's no place for any . . ." She hesitated, testing the awkward word. "Any bond between us."

"That doesn't mean the league doesn't need you."

Oh. The league. Of course.

Her expression must have given her away, because he said softly, "That's all I am now, Jilly. The leader of the league of teshuva. Those who would repent. If not for that, I'd be nothing."

Silence descended again as they drove through the bright day.

When they returned to the industrial area around the warehouse, they had to dodge delivery trucks and bustling forklifts. Only the salvage building was still, the league's inhabitants not yet roused for their night's work. Liam parked in the back lot with the other well-used cars. Side by side, they walked through the quiet corridors made narrow by the leftovers and castoffs of other people's lives.

The dust of the past tightened Jilly's throat. Here they'd finally had a victory—a little victory, about the size of a test tube, actually, but still—and she was moping because . . . because some blind throwback of a saloon girl said she couldn't dance?

Staring at her booted feet, she realized she'd dogged Liam's footsteps right up to his room.

He stopped, hand on the doorknob, and looked down at her, eyebrows raised in polite inquiry.

Her cheeks burned. "Bella says the guys should dance more."

"Bella sells more drinks to sweaty people."

An image sheeted through her mind, straight off a comic book cover—Liam, as he might have been in happier days with some no-doubt practical implement taking shape under his hammer, perspiring at his forge, iron thewed, and clad in a leather apron.

She narrowed her eyes.

No *way* had *that* been pictured in any of her favorite childhood rags. Plus, even a half-witted blacksmith wouldn't work half clad around a hot forge if he wanted to keep his leg hair and other bits, especially when he was . . . happy.

"Jilly?" His brows dropped into a concerned line, and he cupped her chin to raise her gaze to his. "Where did you go just then? Not the demon realm?"

She felt herself canting forward to rest in his hand as she stared up into his blue searching eyes. "I'm not drifting," she protested.

Not at all. Falling wasn't drifting.

"Come here." He opened the door to his room and shepherded her inside with one hand behind her shoulders. "Take off your jacket." Without waiting for her to obey, he tugged at the nape of her coat.

"What?" She unzipped and shrugged out of the sleeves before he strangled her in his impatience.

"The birnenston exposure in the tunnel must have offlined your teshuva. You aren't making sense." He framed her face in his hands again. The rough caress of his calluses made her shiver. "Don't go there without me."

"I wasn't going there without you." She wasn't thinking about the demon realm.

Though he'd been the one to tell his story, she was the one who felt exposed, as if his words had chipped away at her defenses. He'd risen above his bad choices as a boy only to fall back deeper into the muddle, for all the right reasons, just to end up damned. His past was her nightmare scenario for every kid she'd ever watched walk out of the halfway house. And yet look what he'd become.

She reached up with one hand to echo his touch, her fingertips brushing back a lock of his black hair to reveal the even blacker mark of the demon. The *reven* that curled under her breast and over her heart ached, not a pain to be avoided, but in a plea to be touched.

"What are you doing, Jilly?" His voice was a soft rasp. "No need to weave our way into the tenebraeternum. We're in no danger here. Not with the energy sinks in place, a dozen vicious talyan ready to charge in if we shout."

"Then we won't make a sound." She pulled herself up onto her toes—thank heavens for the extra inch and a half of rubber and steel—and kissed him.

Desire didn't have to ride pillion with danger. She was more than the mark that made her his tyro talya. She'd show him. And he wasn't nothing without it.

With the tip of her tongue, she traced the firm line of his lower lip, sucked it softly between her own. He groaned against her mouth, and before she could warn him about the cry that would bring his men barging in, he pulled her to his chest.

The teasing rushed out on her breath, crushed by the strength of his grasp as he drew her up to slant the kiss, hard and deep. A blacksmith's iron thews had so many benefits, she decided, when he swung her up into his arms, never faltering with his kiss.

Pillows, full and scented of heather, yielded under her as he laid her on his big carved bed. She stared up at him as he shed his clothing. "I thought I'd have to convince you."

His gaze never left hers. "You did."

She smiled. "Ah, the kiss. My irresistible touch."

"The threat of dancing." When she held her hand out to him, he came to kneel at her side. "We do work well together," he admitted.

She wrinkled her nose at the reluctance in his voice and tugged him over her hip. Caught off balance on the soft mattress, he tumbled over her. She pounced to straddle him.

Under her hands, his broad shoulders flexed, then relaxed, sinking deeper into the pillows.

"So this is practice?" She dipped her head to flick her tongue into the hollow of his throat.

His Adam's apple bobbed as he swallowed hard. "For the good of the league."

For once, the thought didn't pierce her. Maybe because of the dimple in his cheek, maybe because he was already skimming the shirt up over her head, filling his hands with her, bringing her breast to his mouth, his long fingers hiding both *reven* and butterfly tattoo, so there was no sign of what had marked her.

Other than him. Hot and moist, his tongue left an invisible trail around her nipple that puckered her flesh. Still on her knees straddling him, she braced her forearms against the headboard as down he went between her breasts and over her belly, the path where he'd been now cooling until she shivered with the desire for more. His tongue dipped into her navel and she clutched at the fat-bottomed angels carved into the wood, which was oh-so wrong. But then he went lower still, his grip on her buttocks bringing her hips to his mouth, and that was oh-so right. She leaned into him with a moan. Suddenly, she was very glad he prided himself on bringing such focused intensity to all his responsibilities.

"So demanding," he whispered against her thigh. He grazed his teeth along the sensitive inner tendon and she bucked. He laughed, a warm gust across her center that opened something inside her—oh, not just her sex, which was open and yearning enough with wanting him, but something more hesitant and wistful. She wanted to make him laugh more, to see his eyes shine, and not with purple.

She pushed away from the headboard and sat back, her ass balanced on his thighs with his erection jutting up to tease her cleft. She closed her eyes and swallowed hard. When she looked at him again, his smile was downright devilish.

"Something I can do for you?" he asked, all solicitous.

"You've done enough for the moment." She closed her fingers around the lean ropes of muscle in his shoulders. "Time to share the torture."

"Torture?" His tone turned indignant. "I hadn't even begun."

"Well, I'll be in charge of the end."

He crossed his arms behind his head and smiled again. "Do your worst."

She did, with hands, tongue, and teeth, until her lips closed softly over the blunt head of his cock. He shuddered and his groan seemed ripped from the depths of his soul. She cupped the weight of his tight-drawn balls and circled her fingers round the base of his shaft, stoking him higher. One, two, three. Then he dragged her up, his big hands strong as ever but awkward with his eagerness.

It was her turn to shiver when her nipples brushed over his chest. Her kiss was more a gasp when she pressed her lips to the *reven* decorating his temple. His fingers sank into her hips, and he murmured against her throat, "Ah, *xiao*-Jilly, I can take no more."

She licked her lips and tasted the truth of his words, salt-tinged and musky. "I'll take you, then."

Centered over him, she sank down, holding his shoulders and his gaze. His blue eyes went deep and smoky, and his body under her was as honed, hard, and potent as anything she'd find in the league's basement armory. He raised his hips to fill her and finally—finally—eased the ache inside.

As their breathing matched and slowed, Jilly rested her head on Liam's shoulder. "This is the ugliest bed I've ever seen. I mean, really? Cupids? Who has sex in a bed carved with cupids?"

"I prefer to think of them as cherubim." His low, sleepy voice rumbled under her ear. "Cherubim are a species of angel, and if devils are fallen angels, then these could be demonic cupids."

She tilted her face up to see if he was kidding, but his eyes were closed. "How is that better?"

"We just had sex under them. I like to think demonic cupids would be more indulgent."

She traced her fingers down his chest, and he sighed out, his breath gusting her hair. "Indulgent, right. Well, they obviously consumed their fair share of doughnuts. But they didn't burn off the calories like you said the teshuva would."

His arm tightened around her. "There are other ways to burn calories." When she sniffed, he continued. "Fighting the tenebrae, for example."

She tweaked the fine line of chest hair down his middle. "Or other ways."

He brushed his lips over her crown. "If it bothers you, I'm sure I can find another bed here somewhere, unless the men have absconded with them all."

"What would they do with beds?"

"Nothing like what we just did, I assure you." His tone turned pensive. "Most of them have hideaways elsewhere, sanctuaries where they go to lick their wounds, be alone. Archer has a conservatory, I recently discovered."

Curiosity spurred her tongue before she could bite it. "Do you have a secret place?"

He hesitated, and disappointment tugged at her chest. "I shouldn't have asked," she said. "Then it wouldn't be secret, would it?"

But when his arm clenched this time, it felt more like a man grasping for a last chance. "No, I don't have a place, not besides this. Or wherever the league is. It didn't seem right. How can I ask them to keep coming back to this if I'm not here, always?"

She closed her eyes. The steady thud of his heart under her palm marked out the moments.

It was so easy to watch the resolute, unwavering leader, standing tall against the darkness, and think power and arrogance drove him. But he was neither the heavy-handed chief for her to rail against nor some fantasy comic book hero. He was a man. A man who tempted her in ways no demon had ever imagined. Hearing the need in his voice, she felt as if she'd turned another corner through the complicated paths of him, getting closer.

But for every step that way, she knew she was getting farther from herself. She'd wanted to show him that they could have something together, that they *made* something together—two halves of a whole, standing together. How could she hold him when that meant dividing him from what he was? Her uncles had dominated with cruelty, while her mother manipulated with weakness. She refused to lead Liam by the strings of their attachment.

When he sighed with a depth that made her realize he'd fallen asleep, she rose, dressed in her possibly birnenston-stained, teshuva-addling clothes—if only she could believe that was explanation enough—and crept out of his room.

The sound of a slamming car door drew her to the loading bay, where Ecco was unloading bags of groceries with Dory.

He leaned against the back of the truck as she approached. "Hey, look, it's the cook."

Jilly crossed her arms. "Think that's going to keep me out of trouble?"

"Going to keep us from starving," Ecco said. "Since it's your fault that Corvus"—he rolled his eyes at the oblivious Dory—"and his minions are all riled up."

"My fault?" Jilly stared at him.

Ecco waved his hand. "You females."

Dory hefted a couple bags. "Females? God, these guys are worse than Mom's. You really know how to pick 'em, Jill, don't you?"

Jilly felt as if the glass vial cradled in her pocket had exploded against her stomach.

Her "uncles" had been domineering, egotistical, and violent. Liam *was* more of a threat than they had ever been, because for all their conceits, they'd been weak men.

And because she'd always been immune to those others.

Dory dumped the groceries in Jilly's arms, and she had to scramble to keep the heavy load from crushing the solvo in her pocket. They trooped into the kitchen to unload the goods.

"Where is Liam?" Ecco tossed a bakery box across the counter. "I need to stay out of his way till after he sees the receipt. Vegan doughnuts don't come cheap."

"He's, uh, sleeping. I think." Jilly winced internally as she felt the heat creeping into her cheeks. "I have to . . ." She edged away from the counter. "Be right back."

Ecco straightened and gave her a hard look, though nothing as sharp as the gaze Dory pinned on her. "I'll get something started for dinner," Dory said. "But I'll need your help."

"Right, right." Jilly escaped, cursing herself. Now who looked like the addict?

She avoided the bedroom hall and made her way to the basement, where Sera had her little temporary lab. It reminded Jilly uncomfortably of the sewer. What if Liam was right? What if, like his last Bookkeeper, she and Sera were guiding the league down a terrible path? She was carrying a soul-stealing monstrosity in her pocket, after all.

And she found herself very willing to seduce the leader of the league away from his duties.

She realized she'd been standing blindly in the doorway when Sera nudged past her. "Jilly. Just who I wanted to see. Well, actually, I was looking for Liam, but he's not around, so you can give him the message."

Jilly's face heated again. The ridiculousness of it made her bristle. "Why does everyone think I'm in charge of big, bad Liam Niall?"

"Because you're sleeping with him." Sera scooted a chair up to the computer terminal where multiple external hard drives were stacked in precarious towers. "The archives finally coughed up a reference to salambes."

Curious despite her annoyance, Jilly dragged a chair

beside Sera. "Took long enough." Then she winced.
"Sorry. I don't mean to be bitchy. Not your fault."

"Yeah, it's Liam's fault if he's not balancing you better than that." When Jilly sputtered, Sera shot her a
quick grin. "Ferris and I think that might have been one
of the reasons for the talyan-pair bond. Talya and teshuva are supposed to come to an accord during the first
ascension, and the immediacy of sex is a perfect way to
keep the human body in tune with this realm. Regular
tune-ups only make sense."

"A balance and a tune-up, huh? I didn't get the extended warranty in Liam's fleet-vehicle maintenance
plan," Jilly said stiffly.

"Too bad. Have you seen the crap they drive around
these days? Turns out their last Bookkeeper siphoned
off league assets as well as souls before he ended up
soulless himself. Apparently haints can't remember
bank-account numbers, and Ferris hasn't been able to
track the money transfers once they left the country."
Sera clicked down the page. "Ah, here it is. The reference is from an image-to-text scan of an old, handwrit-
ten league manuscript. Don't know the date, but it was
old enough that they wrote their descending *s*'s a lot like
f's. So the computer wasn't recognizing the word." She
pointed at the screen where the reddish brown ink on
the yellowed paper appeared to read "falambes."

"How'd you know to look here?"

Sera rubbed the back of her neck. "Funnily enough,
Bella pointed me in the right direction. After talking to
your landlady, I've been wondering about these other
women who seem to know more than we do. So I went
to the Coil for a drink, sat down at the bar, and sort of
idly asked her where she might look for things that burn.
She said s'mores, urinary-tract infections, and witches.
Needless to say, the league archives didn't have a lot on
Girl Scout outings or UTIs, but witch burnings . . ."

Jilly eyed the text. "You speak German?"

"No, I ran it through an online translator. Maybe

an official league Bookkeeper would have more resources, but I haven't had time to track down anyone
trustworthy."

"Which wouldn't be Bella," Jilly acknowledged.

Sera nodded. "Those women seem to know more
than us, and they seem strangely reluctant to cough it
all up. To make things worse, the German is actually a
translation of a passage in Dutch, so the whole thing is
just a half-assed pidgin garble." She popped open a new
page. "But here's what we got."

Some of the words hadn't translated at all—including
"falambes"—and the syntax was not proper English, but
Jilly's blood ran cold at the words she could read. "A
witch trial. More than sixty people burned at the stake.
Yeah, I imagine salambes would consider that quite the
party."

"Keep reading," Sera urged. "It gets better. Or worse."

"'Unseen beast is the fiery salamander of legend'?"
Jilly shook her head. "Is this from *Ye Olde National
Enquirer*?"

"I searched on 'fire salamander.' Folklorists say that
salamanders living in damp logs would scatter when the
firewood was laid in the hot hearth, thus freaking out
the nice people gathered around the fire into thinking
that salamanders were fire demons. But I find it a little
hard to believe that even people back in the sixteen
hundreds confused a newt with this." Sera clicked to a
second page.

The intricate woodcut had overly stylized the flames,
but Jilly recognized the misshapen, asymmetrically
horned creatures frolicking around the burning fag-
gots. Half buried in the piles of kindling, the victims—
men and women both, judging from the costumes and
hairstyles—writhed, contorted partners in the macabre
dance.

Jilly's throat seized in disgust, as if the ghost of
scorched hair had drifted through the lab. She pushed
away from the screen. "So the last extant reference to

salambes was from the days of burning witches? How
not reassuring that they're back right when female talyan return to the scene."

"Whoa, there's nothing to associate the salambes
with us," Sera objected. "Witch burning was sporting for
hundreds of years in the middle of the last millennium,
and we think the last female talya was gone well before
that. Besides, there are women *and* men both in this picture, tied back-to-back, their arms interlocked."

"Exactly." Jilly didn't look at the illustration again. She
remembered the feel of Liam's arms wrapped around
her, the heat of his passion slick on her skin. "The ele-
ment of fire has always been associated with desire and
sin. The mated-talyan bond has all that in spades." She
dragged her hands through her hair. Liam's habitual gesture. She finally understood where he was coming from.
"The Corvus-djinni said we'd brought this on ourselves."

"Of course the devil says that," Sera snapped.

"That's what I told Liam," Jilly murmured. And yet
now, without him around to challenge, she questioned
whether she was taking the easy way out. The devil might
delight in lies, but it was the grain of truth, like the dust
in the center of the pearl, that made the lie ring true.

Was Liam right that the bond between male and female talyan had been deemed too dangerous? What if
the preternatural desire of two wounded talya souls had
drawn the salambes, with their affinity for invading and
destroying any empty vessel, through the Veil into the
human realm?

What if, once again, her choice of lovers was toxic, not
just to herself this time, but to the world?

The ugliness of the question—no, the *wrongness* of
it—ripped through her, sharper than any demonic tooth
or blade. Her "fight the power" defiance lost all relevance
when Liam—demon-ridden though he was—so carefully
wielded his power for the good of his men, the oblivious
people of the city, for *her*. That ardent focus and hammer-
blunt strength he'd used to form and refine the league.
The power of the ravager inside him he'd turned only on

the darkness. And on himself. Liam Niall might be all the things she feared, but only because she doubted herself, tangled up in the way he made her feel.

She straightened, casting off the urge to follow the thread of that thought until she came to the center of what, exactly, he made her feel. The damned discord demon had her tied in more knots than her bracelet. She pulled the solvo from her pocket. "I'm just here to drop this off."

Sera took the beaker and headed into the lab. "Just because I have a soul cleaver myself, he thinks I know what to do with the pure stuff?"

Jilly blinked. "You have one?" She'd thought possessing a demon-warped trap was proof enough of trafficking with the devil. How could a soul cleaver ever lend itself to the fight against evil?

"Long story. Corvus and Bookie playing around with a formula in this realm is what called my demon through the Veil." Sera touched the pendant hanging around her neck. The gray stone glimmered faintly, like a cheap opal. "I ended up with this." She must have sensed the disapproval because her gaze narrowed on Jilly's bracelet. "Kind of like how you ended up with that."

Everything she'd ever fought against was here in this building, in one form or another. And half of it no longer seemed wrong. Jilly almost reeled at the wave of moral vertigo. "What are we?" she whispered.

Sera spun away from her. "Not whiners, that's for damn sure."

The confident scorn bolstered Jilly's spirits a bit. Still . . . "I don't want to be responsible for destroying the world."

"God, aren't you special?" Sera clunked the beaker down on the table with more force than was really necessary. "What makes you think the world needs you for that?"

Jilly winced. "Liam."

"Figures. He thinks the sun goes down on his command so he can start the hunt."

The urge to defend him welled up, but Jilly settled for "That's a bitchy thing to say."

"And yet so true. Jilly, good and evil go on without us."

"But we're supposed to be here to tip the balance toward the good." Jilly gestured at the pearlescent matter in the beaker. "We have to be willing to use *that* to get the upper hand?"

"You're already possessed by a demon. Did you really think this was going to be a bloodless—scratch that—soulless war?"

Jilly stared down. "If I sold my soul once, I didn't think I'd have to do it again and again."

Sera flattened her palm over the pendant. Or above her heart, Jilly wasn't sure which. "The *desolator numinis* isn't evil by itself. It's all in how it's used."

Jilly snorted. "How many times has the world heard that one?"

"Yet it's so true," Sera repeated with a touch of asperity. "The only soul I ever took was Corvus's. And I tried to give it back." She shook her head when Jilly drew breath to ask more. "Yes, your soul is suspect, sold and shattered. Stop mourning that. What matters now is what's in your heart."

Jilly managed not to recoil as if Sera's words had hit her somewhere midchest. "I just want to stop Corvus from turning more of the people I care for into salambe flambé. I need my brain, muscles, and a sharp knife for that. Never mind my heart."

Sera eyed her, and Jilly shifted uncomfortably under what felt a lot like pity. "He's afraid, Jilly."

She didn't pretend to misunderstand, but she snorted. "Liam isn't afraid of anything. Except failing the league." A failure made more likely by the discord she spread like a plague.

"What do you think it would be, if he tried for your heart and fell short?"

Jilly shifted. "Weren't we talking about the fate of the world?"

Sera gestured at the bracelet, then wrapped her hand around her necklace. "In our case, it's all connected, all tangled up. That's what the mated-talyan bond is about."

"No wonder he isn't interested." That wasn't fair, she knew. He was very interested. She could take off her shirt or take down a feralis and he was right there beside her. But through it all, a part of him was walled off, and every step she took toward him seemed to lead her farther from where she was trying to go. And she couldn't even blame him, since she so staunchly defended her own walls—not a maze, but a barricade.

Sera frowned, running the pendant back and forth on its chain. "It's not like he has a choice."

Jilly yanked her gaze off the teasing glint of opal fire. "We always have a choice."

"But the broken pieces of you fit together in ways no one else's ever could. That's the strength of the bond. It must be killing him not to reach out to you."

"Not so's you'd notice." And once he found out salambes might indeed have risen out of the energies of the talya bond, he wouldn't allow himself to merely fret about their connection; he'd feel duty-bound to sever it. Pain ripped from her insides through her heart to lodge in her throat, like being gutted.

Jilly held out one hand, the one without the bracelet, hoping it wouldn't visibly shake, to block more interrogation. "I didn't come down here to talk about him. . . . That. I just wanted to bring you the solvo."

"I know as much about reverse engineering as I do about girl talk. Which is apparently nothing." Sera sighed. "Just leave it."

Jilly spun on her heel and started to walk away, then paused. "Thanks for bringing your angel friend in to talk to Dory."

Sera lifted one shoulder in a shrug. "Nanette was by again this afternoon. I didn't get the impression it went much better than last time. She can't control her healing touch."

Jilly figured since she couldn't control her destructive one, she couldn't really complain. "Still, thanks."

Returning upstairs, she followed the clatter of pans back to the kitchen.

Dory was rummaging through the cabinets but smiled over her shoulder. "I watched you do this often enough, with less food than we got here now. I should at least be able to throw a bunch of stuff in a pot and make stew, shouldn't I?"

That was the attitude their mother had had. Throw a punch and the kid should obey, right? Throw enough love at her men and they should stick around, right? Throw away everything in the end and nothing would hurt, right? How wrong she'd been.

Jilly eyed the cluttered counter. "Let's brown some onions while we see what we have." Whatever else happened, they still had to eat. And chopped onions would at least explain the redness of her eyes.

Dory and Ecco had been enthusiastic in their shopping, if not exactly rational, though the economy-sized brownie mix and jumbo bag of miniature chocolate chips seemed like a blatant cry for help. Jilly inventoried, stocked, and found a little calm as the counter cleared.

With the big stockpot simmering on the stove, she wiped down while Dory sat at the table, mixing chocolate chips into the brownie batter. "So, Nanette was here again."

Dory didn't look up from her stirring. "She's nice, but clueless. We prayed some more. I told her exorcism is my only hope."

Jilly glanced sharply at her, but Dory seemed oblivious to the truth of her words. Had she overheard something, or was she picking up the not particularly subtle vibe around the warehouse? Jilly tossed the towel aside and sat across from her sister. "Dory, would you think I was crazy if I told you demons are real?"

Dory scooped a fingerful of batter from the bowl and stuck it in her mouth, eyes wide as she finally looked up. The pose struck Jilly as too innocent to believe.

Exactly how secret was this war the angels and djinn were fighting, with the teshuva in the middle?

She took a breath. "Dor, you really are in trouble. And so am I."

Dory nodded. "It's always been that way. We've always been on this path. That's why Leroy hooked up with those self-help nuts, you know. They told him he could make his own future. After he cut himself off from everything else and followed their path, of course." She gave an asthmatic smoker's laugh.

Jilly cut over the coarse sound. "Corvus is a devil. An honest-to-God being from hell. He's making the city over in his image, one soul at a time."

Dory looked down, a faint smile playing over her lips. "And you think Nanette's praying will help?"

"No," Jilly snapped, disturbed by that secret smile. "Which is why I'm part of this team that's going to kill Corvus. But I want you to be okay." She held her voice steady against a threatening waver. "This won't be worth it if you're not okay."

Dory raised her gaze, her expression somber again. "And what about you?"

Before Jilly could answer, Ecco stumped by in the hall, then stuck his head into the kitchen, hair slicked back wetly and gauntlets shining. His gaze fixed on Dory. "Brownies."

Jilly rose. "Only if we come back alive."

Dory wrinkled her nose. "Only if I don't eat them all first."

Jilly was grateful that meant her sister would stay. After one last glance back at Dory, she joined the exodus of other talyan.

They gathered again in the warehouse truck bay. No one had turned on the heater. This was no cozy debriefing. The men stood, wrapped in dark coats, heavy with weaponry, violet eyed. They were all so tall, it was easy for her to duck behind them. Not that she was hiding. Just being as politely circumspect as Liam had been, letting her sneak out of his bed.

Liam paced the raised concrete dock. "I want a salambe, and I want a haint. Separate and intact."

Ecco spoke up. "We starting a petting zoo?"

Over the scatter of chuckles, Liam continued. "Con-
taining an unoccupied haint should be simple enough.
Tie a string around one and lead it here. The salambe . . .
If you corner one, try the same technique as bottling a
malice."

"You can stuff a malice in an empty beer bottle as
long as it's blessed," Jonah said.

Ecco interrupted. "What do you know about empty
beer bottles, missionary man?"

Jonah shot him a flat glance. "We're going to need a
sanctified fifty-gallon drum for a salambe."

"Nanette was kind enough to put her touch on a fairly
large fishbowl this afternoon." When no one spoke, Liam
added, "It's a nice old antique from the storeroom. Very
sturdy. Comes with a wrought iron stand, even."

"Oh well, then," someone muttered with asperity. "If
the Holy Roller laid hands on a fishbowl, what could go
wrong?"

Jilly stepped up. "I'll take it." If she didn't trust Nanette's blessing, how could she believe Dory would be
saved?

"Jilly." For the first time since she'd entered the room,
Liam's deep blue gaze fixed on her.

What did she see in there? How far would she have
to go to find out?

"I'll help," Sera echoed. Behind her, her mate was a
tall, dark, expressionless statue. Who did not speak
against her volunteering.

"Hell," Ecco said. "Might as well make a night of it.
Let's all go."

Chapter 21

In the end, Liam limited the bag-and-tag team to a half dozen plus himself—Jilly, Sera and Archer, Ecco, who had the most experience bottling malice, Jonah and his penchant for preaching, and Perrin, a quiet talya whose affinity for curbing the poison birnenston had earned him a spot on more than one cleanup crew. With another team of seven on close standby in the event they ran into something more substantial than a free-ranging salambe, Liam figured he'd made the outing as foolproof as possible.

Except for himself, of course.

He was a hundred kinds of fool for not simply assigning the task to Ecco. He should have known Jilly would leap at the chance to get into trouble, leaving him no choice but to jump behind her.

And he'd been damn quick about it when the jumping had been into bed.

When had he lost control of his league? How had he lost control over himself?

He wasn't such a fool that he didn't know the answer to both questions was riding in the far backseat of the passenger van. Jilly was talking to Sera in a voice so low that even though he tweaked his teshuva, he couldn't eavesdrop over the sound of the engine. But even that faintest murmur of her voice distracted him from Ecco's running commentary on the joys of thumb wrestling malice. Something about—"And if you get too much of one under your fingernails, when you try to stuff it in the bottle, the ether will snap back at you like a freakin' rubber band smacking you in the balls."

"Maybe if you kept your pants zipped while you hunt," Archer suggested drily.

"Since you're the only one with a girlfriend around here, I think you better keep your mouth zipped," Ecco started. Then his gaze slid toward Liam, who stared pointedly forward.

Perrin's voice from the middle seat across from Archer was even more to the point. "Anybody else picking up that eau de birnenston?"

Silence prickled in the car, and Liam's temple throbbed once with the sensation of demons rousing around him.

"You're the one with the touch for it, Perrin." Liam rolled the windows down. "Guide us in."

"Take a left here." The talya leaned forward between the front seats. His head swiveled from the driver-side window to passenger and back again. "A right up at the stop sign."

The lingering stench of rotting eggs caught Liam as he rounded the corner. At this time of night—well past even the most belated Valentine's Day emergency shopper—Jewelers Row was empty. The security grilles over the windows glistened brighter than the low-value merchandise left in the windows after the shopkeepers had locked the rest away for the night. Even without the diamonds on display, the street, with its quaint lamp-posts and tidy flower bunkers of quailing early-spring flowers, spoke of satisfied wealth. The office suites on the floors above were closed and mostly dark.

Invisible to the human eye but a neon scream to the teshuva's, the etheric smears of demon sign etched the sidewalks and a few parked cars.

Liam cast a wary eye upward at the L tracks that rose

on steel girders above the van. The setting was very similar to where he and Jilly had desperately leapt to escape a certain locomotive misfortune. And he'd always hated flashbacks. "The marks on the cars are fresh. Keep an eye out."

Abruptly, Perrin came halfway out of his seat and gripped Liam's arm as he peered through the windshield. "Penthouse. Birnenston thread. Been there long enough for part to harden."

Thick encrusted tendrils snaked out around the peaked copper arch surrounding a large window on the seventh floor. Streaks like slow flames crawled down the limestone facade, but winked out before they touched the ground.

Liam growled, "And we didn't notice this earlier because . . ."

"Because the angelic folk patrol these streets." Jonah tapped his fingers restlessly on the back of the seat. "At least I thought they did. I've been turned back from here before."

"Me too," Ecco said. "But we have plenty of other hunting grounds, so what did I care?"

Liam rubbed his forehead. "Nobody to turn us back tonight."

Would he have been grateful to see the subtle shine of an angelic possessed striding to the assist? Or would he have had an interrealm incident on his hands when he right-hooked the slacker for allowing something hellish to take root so deeply?

As Archer called the backup team to explain their find, he parked the van in front of the possessed building. No point being sneaky. The demons that had inhabited the place certainly weren't shy about their presence.

The six of them climbed out of the van. Ecco toted the blessed fishbowl, looking—with the exception of the bowl—like a medieval Mafia heavy with his slicked-back hair and exposed gauntlets.

"I do not have a good feeling about this," Perrin muttered as he collected the two slender eight-foot spears that were his preferred weapons.

Liam didn't doubt it. His own feel for birnenston was muted at best, though the poisonous aspects affected him as much as any talya. For the sensitive Perrin, the raw streams of birnenston must be nearly torture. Conveniently, they were all used to torture.

"We're here for a salambe," he said. "The third team is picking up a haint. If we don't find what we want, we're out."

Archer paced him. "Remember when the league was just 'pain plus drain equals slain'? Whatever happened to standard operating procedure and business as usual?"

"Business as unusual voted me down." Liam couldn't even summon righteous indignation. As the walk down slaughter memory lane with Jilly had reminded him, he'd always known he was a terrible leader. And not Genghis Khan terrible. Just terrible straight up with a side of suckage.

The chill inside him was there even before the night soaked through his coat.

"Let's go in through the back," Jilly said.

She did like her alleyways, he knew. Falling into a wary line, the talyan followed him around to the service entrance. The alley was clean and well lit, which only served to emphasize the streaks of birnenston leaking down from the upper floor.

"This is most definitely the place," Perrin said.

The door was unlocked.

"Ooh, bad sign," Sera murmured.

They crossed the threshold, and Liam felt his teshuva hunker down, driven deeper by the poison of the birnenston. Perrin blanched, as if his demon had taken most of his blood with it.

"Lots of demon sign." Archer unleashed his axe, a vicious recurved weapon. Sera drew a much smaller but seriously serrated knife. "No sign of actual demons."

For all the unreadable hieroglyphics of ether etched on the walls and the bone-cold stench of the tenebraeternum, they were alone. He would have preferred to be alone, rather than leading his team into unknown peril.

"There was plenty of known peril to go around," he muttered.

"Up," Perrin said.

Though the doors stood open to the vintage wrought iron lift in the lobby, they searched out the narrow, enclosed back stairs. Either way seemed ripe for a trap, and Liam flexed his fingers over the hammer's grip.

Jilly stared uneasily up into the darkness.

"Don't tense up," he murmured. "With your teshuva repressed by the birnenston, you won't be able to recover as quickly. You have to be able to let it flow."

She rolled her head back along her shoulders once and flicked him a smile that faded after one step. He realized Archer was watching, so he gave the other talya a curt nod that sent him to the front of the line.

Liam put Jilly right behind him and gave the others the signal—hand up, fingers spread—to string themselves out single file, not close enough to be caught in one attack, but not too far to be separated when the attack came.

But none did. Even as the other-realm stench thickened, they gained the seventh-floor landing without incident.

"Don't get tense," Jilly whispered from behind him.

He shook out his arm, where the weight of hammer had tightened his muscles, and glanced back with a faint grin. "Feels better when you just attack."

As soon as he said it, the words seemed to crystallize in his mouth, realization drying the smile on his lips. That's why he kept egging on the conflict between them; he could fall into the familiar patterns of parry and thrust, keeping her at a distance and avoiding any pain. With the tenebrae, no one could fault his strategy, but with her . . .

And now was really not the time to turn his attention inward. Once more, his obligations to the league came to the rescue.

Her answering smile didn't quite erase the strain around her eyes, but she flashed her crescent knives at him. "Ready to go."

Of course she was, but was he?

Archer pushed open the door into the penthouse. Whatever—whoever—had occupied the space before was lost in the obliterating tangle of birnenston. The thick threads bristled with the embedded remains of feralis mutations, and the air itself trembled with the unheard echoes of malice cries.

"Did something attack them here?" Sera kept her voice low. "If it was angelic warriors, they do a crappy cleanup."

"That's what us garbage men are for," Archer said.

"No angel has been through here." Jonah sounded convinced.

Perrin said simply, "Up."

They took the last flight of stairs to the roof.

The bare open stretch of asphalt roof blended into the night sky, except for the glowing glass cube at the other end.

"A greenhouse?" Sera took a step forward, but stopped with Archer's hand on her shoulder.

"No hothouse flowers in there," he said. "Unless you mean hot as hell."

"Just what we've been looking for." Liam led the way across the roof, the six talyan spread like wings on either side.

Rust bloomed on the metal frame of the shed-sized structure, but the glass was intact. Acid rain and pigeon shit smudged the surface. Behind the glass, smoky outlines spun like slow-motion dirty laundry.

"Hey, the salambes bottled themselves," Ecco said. "Too bad we can't take the whole thing home with us."

"Why would they bottle themselves?" Perrin circled the hothouse, his expression puckered with professional curiosity. "Birnenston is toxic to all the tenebrae, same as it is to us. Ah, look, every pane is etched with it, and the vents are sealed. No wonder they can't get out. It's the demonic equivalent of the blessed fishbowl."

The poisonous emanations leaked from the base of the hothouse and clogged the corroded blades of the big fan that had once regulated temperatures inside the shed. In the sickly yellowish glow, only the blue streaks of Jilly's hair held color.

"Somebody else trapped them," Jilly said, half to herself. "Corvus? Does he have haints and salambes cached like weapons all over the city?"

Breaking into the hothouse and snagging just one of the salambes was going to be like opening a can of worms. If worms were superfast, incorporeal, and demonic.

"No haints here, at least," Liam said. "But the salambes may scatter, like they did when they exhausted the bodies at the apartment den."

"We'll get one." Jilly twisted the bracelet around her wrist. When she caught him looking at her, she cocked one eyebrow and rattled the bracelet. The knot-work metal bent the repellent light of the hothouse into silver glints.

The chill in his gut deepened. "No."

Ecco glanced over. "No what?"

"I'll be the one doing the catching." She had caught everyone's attention at least. She faced them, leaving Liam to stare at the squared set of her shoulders.

Even when she was jacked up in her thick-soled boots, those shoulders barely reached his sternum. He wanted to wrap his arms around her, pull her back from the brink, where she threw herself with such unholy zest.

But the league was the only wall between the world and the brink.

"Some of the tenebrae are attracted to the bracelet." As if she felt his measuring gaze, she drew herself up another few inches onto her toes. "To me. When we crack open the glass, I think I can keep one's attention long enough for Ecco to get it in the bowl."

Ecco stroked his chin. "Snagging a malice isn't exactly fun. The jellyfish-sting/rat-bite combo is enough to make you just want to drain it and be done. This'll be worse."

She nodded once. "I've had a little experience. I got through it."

"Got through it?" The words burst from Liam, as if

she'd driven her shoulder into his chest. She was talking about when they'd come together to trap the demons. She meant she'd "gotten through" their kiss.

She cast a fleeting glance back at him that didn't quite meet his eyes. "Just open the glass."

"The sheer amount of birnenston is going to make this messy." Perrin rattled his spears with restless tension. "It's collected to a potent dose, which is why the salambes haven't been able to force the seal. My te-shuva has a taste for it and gives me some immunity, but you won't be able to stay in contact long without risking some serious damage."

"I think this won't take long at all." Liam swung the hammer over his head and smashed through the glass.

Brittle with age, the thick panes shattered. Gelatinous ropes of birnenston held a few shards suspended, but the demonic seal was broken. The salambes boiled out, taking their looming, horned, insubstantial form as they hit the night air.

As quick as they were, the birnenston-enforced captivity had obviously weakened them, and the talyan were quicker.

With the ends of his spears, Perrin scooped up birnenston. He wound the sticky, frayed filaments around the leaf-shaped blades like some vile cotton candy. In the presence of so much unleashed etheric energy, the birnenston flared to torch brightness. Perrin drove a few salambes between the two spears with all the skill of a street performer wielding juggling sticks on fire. Half smoke they might be, but the salambes cringed away from the birnenston-coated spears. Perrin angled them toward Jilly and her bracelet trap. Ecco stood with the fishbowl at the ready, Jonah with the blessed seal in hand.

Sera stood with Archer behind her, his hands on her shoulders, as if they were watching the whole crazed carnival. But her eyes were closed and his sparked with violet power, and the bone-dust scent of the tenebraeternum was on the wind as they broke all the rules of the league with their mated bond.

Liam focused on Jilly. His muscles tightened again, with the urge to go to her, to stand at her back, her head tucked beneath his chin. But whatever nerves had plagued her before, her calm expression made clear she'd found a centered place. With his brute hammer, Liam had never felt more useless.

So to his disgust, his ravager heart actually lifted in delight when the squadron of winged ferales rose over the edge of the roofline, clearly intent on joining the fight.

Well, so was he.

With a shouted warning, he whirled to face the newcomers. The ferales had feasted well on the animal remains in the city. Most sported at least two pairs of wings, and they swept through the salambes, maneuvering like lice-infested Apache attack helicopters.

This, the hammer was good for.

Etched steel snarled through the air, and the Apaches became more like mosquitoes. Though the toxic slop of the birnenston sapped his teshuva, purely human fury energized his every swing. In the corner of his vision, Jilly centered herself under a salambe Perrin had cornered with his smoldering birnenston-tipped spears. Ecco and Jonah lurked nearby with the bowl and seal.

Next to the three powerful talyan, she looked small, and despite them, she looked alone. Vulnerable, with her knives pocketed as she reached up toward the salambe, the bracelet on her wrist a sullen silver glow.

Even as he methodically decommissioned the ferales, a part of Liam screamed to abandon the fight and go to her. He should be standing beside her, keeping watch while she worked her magic.

With a last vicious sweep, he cleared the roof of ferales. Bashed bodies were piled high, and the last few functioning demons circled the rooftop, screeching. Loose feathers drifted across the asphalt to snag in the ooze of birnenston.

He'd had his chance with her. And the urge to forget everything just to be with her reminded him why he'd refused to take that chance. Holding the world together meant he couldn't hold her. Not the way he wanted to. She was his weapon, not his woman.

He waited, hammer held loosely at the ready. The salambes—except for the one Perrin had pinned in place—swirled around the rooftop. Ether trailed behind them in agitated contrails.

Jilly had almost lured Perrin's salambe into her grasp. The upper part of it still had some definition, its single nonsymmetrical tooth horn thrashing in desperation. But its lower half dissolved into unformed ether that funneled toward Jilly's outstretched hand.

Liam didn't like the look of the straining demon. When he and Jilly had done ... whatever they'd done, the tenebrae had seemed to come willingly to their doom. They'd spiraled down peacefully. This one struggled to escape, tearing off smoky bits of ether in its flailing.

The closer it fell to Jilly's fingertips, the more frantic it became. In just another heartbeat, it would be within her grasp.

Liam's breath stopped in his throat. This was wrong. He was too far away if anything happened.

He was already moving when it did.

The first trailing edge of ether touched Jilly's hand. Before he could shout, the salambe engulfed her.

With the haints, the salambes had hovered half in, half out of the soul-emptied bodies. Jilly was already occupied—double occupancy really—so it only coated her like an ill-fitting skin. But Liam had no doubt the pain of demonic energies clashing was a thousand times worse than any malice sting.

Jilly, her face white with strain, punched through the enveloping skin of the salambe. She peeled it back. Her puffy coat began to shred around her as if the other-realm energy had rotted it past cohesion. The crescent knives clattered out of her disintegrating pocket. She stood in her T-shirt, skin exposed to the salambe and the elements. Beneath the hem and above the neck-line, the dark lines of her *reven* blazed violet. The flesh around it shimmered translucent as her teshuva waged its half of the battle.

He was almost across the roof, still too far. But she didn't need him. She mastered the salambe, gathered it between her hands. Whipped on other-realm winds, her blue-striped hair stood in a dark corona around her pale face. When she gestured Perrin back and turned to Ecco and Jonah, her eyes were pure amethyst.

In the conflicting energies, the fishbowl glowed the faint gold of angelic blessing. The gleam brightened as Jilly forced the salambe toward it. The piercing shriek from the demon—pain and rage and fear—thrust aural talons into Liam's spine. But that didn't stop his race to Jilly. He shouted her name.

The salambes that had clouded over the roof seemed drawn as to a lightning rod. Even as he leapt, they streamed down on their trapped kin. Their cyclone drew the remaining ferales into the demonic mix. The air on the roof crackled with sleeting demon ethers—the dark powers of teshuva, salambes and shrieking ferales, and birnenston in a maddening clash.

Jilly thrust the salambe into the bowl in Ecco's hands. Jonah slapped the foil seal over the opening. The glass flared gold just as the downward arrow of salambes reached it.

Angel blessing and hellish fury touched.

And the rooftop exploded.

CHAPTER 22

So cold she burned, Jilly watched Jonah seal the bowl. Finally.

Then all hell broke loose.

The downward pressure of other-realm wind almost flattened her, and she glanced up to see the salambes plunging toward them. She turned to make sure Ecco had the bowl securely tucked under his meaty arm. No way were the demons taking it back.

Liam shouted something. Probably good advice she didn't have time to decipher.

She tried to reach into herself again for the teshuva's slanting energies, to deflect the coming onslaught. But she couldn't even catch her breath, the first time since her possession that the knife wound had bothered her.

The birnenston, she realized, was killing her slowly. The teshuva sputtered in her veins.

In a fury, the tangled mess of salambes and ferales broke over the rooftop.

Like a lightning rod, Perrin's spears shattered in a spray of shrapnel and knocked him away. Jilly flinched at another sharp pain that lanced through her side, like a runner's cramp. The backlash tumbled her, boots over head. Ferales slammed down against the asphalt, driven as hard as the talyan by the salambes' force.

The salambes whirled together again, sucking up the shrieking, flapping ferales. Jilly's skin crawled as the collection of malevolence seemed to find its focus.

And plunged straight at them.

Ecco ducked and covered, clutching the bowl. Jonah screamed a warning. She raised her fist, the knotwork bracelet tight around the clenched muscles of her forearm.

For a heartbeat, the demonic cyclone seemed to hesitate. They remembered what had happened to their trapped kin.

Then the cyclone split and hit the rooftop to either side of her. The asphalt buckled and bowed in one violent contraction.

She was flying. She had a hazy moment to wonder if a winged feralis had grabbed her, and thought maybe she could convince it that they should escape together; then she crashed down. Glass shattered an arm's length away, and she realized she'd just missed smashing into the ruins of the hothouse. Lucky her, something softer had broken her fall.

Then the birnenston began to congeal around her.

"Jilly, get up. Get out of there."

Shaking off her daze, she realized the shattering glass had been Jonah, blown on a trajectory only a few feet from hers. He'd hit the wreckage of the hothouse. The twisted metal frame had collapsed around him, leaving him half in, half out of the shed. And a guillotine of plate glass hung above him.

She met Jonah's clear gaze. No fear. No telltale violet either. His teshuva had been driven deep by the poison that had leaked out of the hothouse all around them.

Wildly, Jilly called out, but her voice broke. Too far away, Archer and Sera were driving ferales away from Perrin, who was on his knees. Not ten feet away, Ecco's bulk was slumped over. Dead? Jilly prayed he still held the fishbowl in the curve of his body. She didn't see Liam at all. Suddenly, prayer seemed pointless.

Thick ropes of ooze clung to her knees as she struggled upright. She tried to tear free, but her boots were hopelessly mired. She remembered the haints embedded in the stalagmites, trapped and dying.

There was a glint on the asphalt. Her crescent knives, fallen from her dissolving coat. If she could cut her bootlaces open . . .

She scrabbled toward them, contorted by her trapped legs. Her reach fell short.

Ah, to be a few inches taller. Or if only she'd been wearing nice pumps she could've slipped out of.

A piercing tingle traced through the birnenston wounds. Her teshuva's version of a warning she didn't need. The nearest ferales flapped in tattered circles around the rooftop, broken, but the salambes were regathering.

The ventilation fan, knocked half loose from its moorings, began to turn. To her horror, Jilly realized that the salambes, lacking corporeal shells, would use anything at hand to destroy their enemy.

The smoky ether of the salambes twined through the blades, whirling them into a blur. The bang of loosened metal pounded in Jilly's head. When the fan jolted loose, the shearing weight of it would chew through anything in its path. Like Ecco, Jonah, and her.

She strained for her knives. "Liam," she screamed. And tore one boot almost loose.

She reached an inch farther. But her other boot was utterly swamped in birnenston. Her hands slid through the greasy slicks of it, and the corrosive poison ate at the skin between her fingers. Impossible. She had no fight left.

The deafening clatter of the fan told her only seconds remained before the salambes worried it free. She flinched at another crash of metal, closer. As if the threat could be any more immediate.

Again, Jonah threw his weight against the twisted metal cage that held him. He heaved again and again, with enormous strength despite being pinned with his whole arm in the wreckage. The thick plate of broken glass above him quivered.

"Stop!" Jilly cried.

He didn't. He wrenched free. But not quick enough, his teshuva almost dormant.

The glass sheeted down. Jonah tumbled back with one agonized scream and a fountain of crimson.

Even as he fell, he angled toward her and slapped her knives across the asphalt with the raw bone of his severed wrist.

Sobbing, Jilly snatched the blood-drenched handles and sliced through her bootlaces in one blow. She bolted out of the birnenston, her stocking feet suctioning out of the dissolving leather of her boots, and grabbed for Jonah's arm. What was left of it.

"Ecco," he gasped. "The bowl."

Who cared about the fucking fishbowl? With her hand clamped around the arterial spray of his brutal amputation, they staggered to Ecco and tugged him into the shelter behind the ruined hothouse just as the salambe-driven fan burst from its foundations.

The fan blades tangled in the confusion of bent framing. Jilly covered her head, but the squeal of metal and the musical explosion of glass rang in her ears. To her shocked gaze, the hothouse looked like a version of her bracelet writ large and distorted, with the weave of metal and the gleam of ether trapped within.

"Where's the bowl?" Ecco rasped. Blood—his or Jonah's, Jilly didn't know—streamed down his face.

"You don't have it?" Jonah's voice was a moan as Jilly knotted her socks in a tourniquet around his forearm.

Halfway across the roof, Jilly saw Liam, in pursuit of the sturdy glass bowl, tumbling and half invisible in a swirl of salambes.

And behind him were the last of the ferales.

The putrid stench of birnenston had flatlined all her senses except horror, and she could barely keep track

of which way was up. But she knew the edge of the roof
was all around.

And only a shallow lip ringed the edge.

If the salambes pushed the bowl over, it would smash
open on the sidewalk below. Blessed it might be, but it
was still only glass. Who knew demons would be so keen
on protecting one another?

God knew, the teshuva couldn't pull it off.

Doubling back like a snake of smoke, the salambes
left the bowl, which continued to roll toward the edge.
Liam didn't stop and he was swallowed in the cloud of
ether. Jilly recoiled at the memory of that unrelenting
agony. He'd been through it once, and he'd just done it
again. Only this time, the ferales would close in and finish the job.

She bolted to her bare feet.

Out of nowhere, Archer, Sera right behind him,
jumped into the ferales' fray. A half step behind them,
Perrin leapt at the bowl with a warrior cry.

The salambes echoed the scream. Their shrieks lifted
a scintillating cloud of pulverized glass and birnenston.
Half a rooftop away, Jilly gagged on the nose-searing
scent and tasted blood in her throat. The salambes
whirled off Liam, who staggered but did not fall.

Perrin had claimed some immunity from the birnenston, and he used it now. The jump carried him over the
rolling fishbowl.

"No," Jilly whispered.

The bowl tumbled closer to the drop. The salambe
cloud darted beneath Perrin and lifted the glass sphere
a foot or more into the air. It would clear the knee-high
roof lip easily.

But Perrin stabbed the yard-long shards of his spears
down into the asphalt—one, two, three—in a circle
around his prize. The tripod of stakes pinned a rough
tepee over the glass, holding it in place.

For a single breath, the salambes fell silent.

Then with a thunderous roar, they swept Perrin off
the roof.

Liam straightened as if one of the stakes had gone through him. Jilly thought she might have cried out, an anguished shout she knew he would never release. Or maybe the ringing in her ears was only the salambes' shriek as they rose to thread between the ferales circling on the wing. In a churning mass, the tenebrae vanished into the darkness, abandoning their trapped kin.

The other-realm wind stilled. Liam was already racing across the roof, back to the access door.

Jilly took a step after him and fell to her knees after one bloody footprint. But her heart hurt too bad for her to feel her blistered soles.

Sera crouched beside their little decimated trio. "Oh no," she murmured. "Jonah."

He recoiled at her touch. "Save it for Perrin, death singer."

Lips tight, she glanced at Ecco, but he shook his head, eyes bleak. "Nothing for me either, solace bringer. I dropped the ball, or the bowl, and Perrin paid."

Archer stood with the fishbowl in arms. The sputtering *reven* on his hand flared in counterpoint to the roil of greasy demon smoke inside. "Enough. We need to get you all out of here so the teshuva can heal you up, do their job."

"We did the job, all right." Jilly's ears still rang and her words sounded hollow, as if her head were stuffed in the fishbowl along with the salambe. "It's all about the job."

Sera levered her upright. "Stop it." Her voice was gentler but as firm as Archer's. "You know that's not true."

But it was. Jilly stared down, stomach churning not at the sight of her flayed feet but at the memory of marching up to Liam and demanding to be part of the team. If she hadn't volunteered her demon-trapping self, would the night have gone so terribly wrong? Except for the inescapable pull of the knot-work bracelet, the salambes would have fled. The talyan would have been frustrated . . . but alive and intact.

She'd wanted to prove herself, forgetting that a rebel without a chance shouldn't drag others down into the abyss with her.

Without Liam to ride herd with his curt hand signals, they clustered silently together, Archer and Ecco supporting Jonah, Sera next to Jilly. One feralis could've thrashed them all, but their muffled footsteps roused nothing. The rough treads ground against Jilly's bare heels and she staggered.

Before Sera could catch her, she straightened with a guilty look back at Jonah. If he could walk at all, it was the least she could do. Holding her voice at a mere whisper, she asked, "Shouldn't we have tried to find his . . . his arm?"

Sera shook her head. "Did you see the wreckage the fan left?"

"But isn't that the teshuva's promise, to keep us alive and well? Whole isn't part of the bargain?"

"It took part of our souls, Jilly. Do you think it really cares about whole?"

Her legs still wobbled, but her feet and the birnenston blisters on her hands stopped bleeding by the time they reached the ground floor. The front door hung open, askew on its hinges where Liam had busted through without even the pretense of subtlety.

For a moment, Jilly wished she could just walk out through the open door and keep going. But she resisted when Sera started to lead them down the street to the van. "Don't."

Archer rumbled low in his throat but paced behind them.

They turned the other direction, to the side of the building where Perrin had fallen.

Liam stood on the empty sidewalk. He had removed his long coat, and was laying it over the still form crumpled in the flower bed.

But not before Jilly saw that Perrin must have hit the beams of the L or the lamppost before he landed. Blood speckled the early snowdrops. She looked down. The

skin on her hands was slowly smoothing over. Perrin's
wounds never would. "What's the point?"

"We get immortality, not indestructibility," Sera reminded her.

Considering what they were up against, Jilly wondered if immortality was enough.

Jonah lifted his head, staring at the covered body.
"His demon is gone."

"Sneaking bastards, all of them," Ecco muttered. "I'd
like to stuff them, each and every one, in a fishbowl and
lock it with enough angels' blood and brimstone to last
past the end of the world."

"We should have let it go," Jilly burst out. She hadn't
known the angelic seal was primed with the blood of
an angel's host. She definitely didn't want to know how
much was needed, though it couldn't be even half as
much as had poured from Jonah's arm. "We could always have tried again."

"Exactly," Archer said. "And Perrin might've died—
finally—then instead."

"Jilly." Sera's voice was gentle. "This is what we do."

"But I'm the one who wanted to do it. He shouldn't
have had to make the sacrifice for me."

Liam finally straightened and turned to face them.
His *reven* guttered, the ravager still struggling out from
under the birnenston poisoning. "It wasn't for you."

For the cause. Of course. She closed her hands into
fists. The slowly healing flesh stung as if she'd grabbed
sharpened steel.

Despite her silence—or maybe because of it—Liam
continued. "Sometimes you don't get to make the call
who sacrifices."

She lifted her chin. "If not me, when it was my idea,
then who? The teshuva?"

"Me." With a nod, he sent Ecco and Jonah to the van.
He bent and lifted Perrin's body over his shoulder. Jilly
shuddered, remembering that simple, blunt strength
when he'd lifted her.

Ecco was behind the wheel. Jonah slumped in the passenger seat beside him, unconscious, his breath hitching, the demon unable to save him from the agony even in oblivion. Archer and Sera had climbed into the far back, Archer with his arm around his mate. Jilly settled into the middle seat, arms around herself to push back the cold. Her palms and soles throbbed with returning life, which seemed vulgar with Perrin's body behind them.

Her morbid thoughts were derailed when Liam sat beside her. He gestured for Ecco to drive, then leaned back and put his arm around her shoulders. She realized she was shivering.

"I never thought to stock the fleet with spare blankets." His tone was thoughtful, as if they were discussing placing an order with Martha Stewart.

But despite her own wounded chill and the fact he at least still had his long-sleeved button-down shirt, pure ice radiated off him. Carefully, she wrapped her arm around his chest.

This was nothing like his cupid-carved bed. That moment of respite seemed a thousand years away. Her breath hitched in dismay when she realized, for some, like Blackbird, that wasn't even an exaggeration.

Liam's grip tightened, almost to the point of pain, then abruptly relaxed. "Let me see your hands."

"I'm fine."

He stared down at her, blue eyes unblinking.

She untucked her hand from his waist. The skin was still marked with rings of white scars like water droplets in a pond, but even those were fading. "See?"

"So where's all the blood from?" Without waiting for an answer, he set her to one side and nudged up the bottom of her T-shirt.

"Hey." She pushed at his hands.

"Stay still."

She hissed when his fingers probed her side. "It's probably Jonah's."

"No, not fine." He lifted her T-shirt. Under her breast, the black lines of her *reven* were quiescent with the demon dormant. "Relax. No one can see here."

"I'm not— Never mind." She wasn't tense because she was prudish. It just wasn't right that her demon had faltered when she most needed it. Perrin had died, Jonah had had to make a terrible choice, and here she was, wishing . . . wishing things that didn't have anything to do with death or not dying. She wanted. . . .

She just wanted. Again.

He let out a breath. "It missed all the important parts."

"Don't we always," she murmured.

He glanced up. This time there was a flicker of violet in his gaze.

She didn't look away. "Perrin died because of us."

"Perrin died because of the salambes."

She shook her head. "If you and I had worked together, we could have bottled the salambe before the others descended."

From the way his jaw worked, she knew he agreed. But he said, "If we did what we do, we could have opened a rift in the Veil that let through worse demons than the salambes." When she flinched, he nodded. "Sera told me about the reference she found. Corvus said he learned something from us. We can't afford to teach him any more bad habits."

"Then I'm useless to you." When he drew a breath, she took his hand. "I'm not strong enough to take them on my own, which is how you want to hunt."

"You're stronger than you know."

She tried to smile. "Oh, I have a very high opinion of myself. But I know when I'm not going to make it."

"Bullshit. When have you given up?"

She stared at him. "Ask my mother. Ask Dee and Iz and the other kids who are probably wondering what happened to me."

"Neither of those were your fault."

"Ask Jonah."

He tried to ease his hand free from hers. "You don't get to take that on either."

She kept a grip. "Because that's yours too?"

"Yes, damn it. You've been overstepping your bounds, talya. I lost a fighter tonight. It has happened before and it will happen again." He leaned over her, gaze flat and still. "And you will stay out of it."

"Stay out of which part? The being guilty? Or the dying?"

Or did he just not want to mourn *with* her? His arm over her shoulder could've been simply sharing what precious body heat remained between them.

After all, he couldn't want a weapon that backfired on him. She'd sown discord in the fragile team he'd built, which was nothing a bowl of soup could fix. And what little they knew about female talyan made it seem like there was no hope for any fix.

"I'm sorry," she said at last.

He didn't answer.

By the time they made it back to the warehouse, all the talyan knew what had happened. One at a time, they returned to drift through the dock where Liam had laid Perrin's body on a stack of pallets. Jonah stood at the dead talya's head, his arm tucked under the front of his crimson-soaked coat. His teshuva might have stopped his bleeding, but from the white lines of strain around his mouth that the demon hadn't smoothed over, it was clear only sheer human obstinacy kept him upright.

The same bone-deep weariness left her swaying on her bare feet, but Jilly couldn't bring herself to leave the dock. She stood at a slight distance. Though she didn't look around, she knew Liam lingered behind her.

"We have to be done here." Archer stalked by them. "He's been possessed a long time. The body'll be dust and bones before dawn."

Sera snagged him by the arm and dragged him to a halt. "Let them be. They need to see. They need this time."

"Ghoul," he hissed at her. But his body curved toward hers.

"Healing," she countered. She touched his shoulder. "Go inside. Eat some of what Jilly made. They'll follow you, and then we can take care of Perrin. Lex volunteered to make the drive out to the burial ground down south. Even if the league has never fully explained what happens to the talya soul after death, we know what's left of his body will find a beautiful place to rest."

Archer watched her a moment, eyes half lidded. Though he didn't move, Jilly's skin prickled as she felt the demon rising in him, as if just the thought of walking away from his mate was a threat. After a tense moment, he nodded, and his exit did pull a few other talyan into his wake.

Sera joined Jilly. They watched Jonah, who bent his head over the body, as if in prayer.

"They don't lose a brother often," Sera murmured. "In some ways, that makes it harder for them."

Jilly slanted a glance at her. "Who wants to practice at losing just so you won't cry when the time comes?"

"Who said anything about not crying?" Sera shrugged. "Violence only sharpens the edge of the pain."

Liam's voice rumbled behind them. "Violence, properly wielded, also takes care of what's causing your pain." He inclined his head at Ecco, who nodded and finally dragged Jonah away.

Jilly winced at their matched halting steps. "With all that's coming at the league, I'm surprised there isn't a funeral a day."

"The teshuva are almost always strong enough to repair the damage from malice and ferales," Liam said. "It's the others that have been the problem."

"The salambes." Jilly gripped the blanket tighter around her shoulders. "And the djinn."

But Sera gave him a narrower glance. "And you still wonder about the demons that choose a woman, don't you?"

He met her accusing glare without any sign of regret, his arms loose at his sides. "I never believed you were evil. Either of you."

Jilly wondered if she'd ever be warm again. "Just dangerous."

He didn't answer, and Sera prodded, "In the last four months, you've lost two talyan. When was the last before that?"

"Check league archives."

"I don't need to." Sera's voice was low. "I know you remember every one."

He gave her a level look. "Does it matter? I gained a talya for each one I lost."

His nonanswer was answer enough. And Jilly didn't want to be a replacement part. "We should go."

He nodded. "Get something to eat. The teshuva might not care, but your body still does."

Now he cared about her body. "I mean, Sera and I should leave the league."

They stared at her, with flickering violet in their eyes and demonic lows in their voices when they both said, "No."

"Something dangerous happens when we . . . when we touch." She looked at Liam. "You said it yourself. What happens between us might not be evil, but it isn't good."

His jaw tightened. "So we won't touch." A scant heartbeat later, he added, "Except when we can use it, control it."

"You two speak for yourselves," Sera snapped. "If Archer heard this, he'd break something."

"We're already breaking the league," Jilly said. "One man at a time."

"That's what happens when you won't bend to changes." Sera cast a hard look at Liam. "Even brain-damaged, soulless Corvus figured that out."

"Maybe that made it easier," Jilly said. "All he had left was his heart."

"And his demon," Liam growled. "We paid a high price, but we have a salambe to dissect, clues to unravel, and the end of the world to avert. No one is leaving."

His vehemence silenced them until Archer strode up, stark lines drawing his face into a hard mask. "Your sister's gone."

As if the cold was just too much, Jilly's heart went still in her chest. So much for nobody leaving. "Maybe she needed something for the kitchen. Frosting for the brownies. Maybe—"

"And she took the last of the solvo."

CHAPTER 23

As the sun came up, Corvus eased back on the musty mattress. When his demon went dormant, it tended to forget to position his body in ways that wouldn't leave him aching and stiff. After all their years together—centuries, actually, not that he could remember them—it now treated him like a rag doll it had not quite outgrown.

Which made him wonder when it would need him no longer.

Almost without his awareness, his hand crept across the dirty sheet to touch the first faint beam of light. No warmth yet, but spring was coming. He smelled it sometimes, when the wind was right.

He sighed.

A gentle hand reached out to stroke his brow. "You okay?"

"Never better." The slur in his voice ever since he'd fallen should have belied his words. But it was true.

How right it would be that when the blooming season came, the last of those vile talyan who'd left him crushed under the tons of brick and glass would be gone.

He rolled his head carefully against the pillow. The djinni had knit up the flattened bones of his skull, but sometimes he imagined what was left inside rattled a bit.

"Never better," he repeated, though he wondered if that made him sound like the idiot he was now.

But the woman beside him smiled as if he'd said something profound. The light of the sun and the smile gave life to the otherwise gaunt lines of her face. In his time, the women had been round, soft, but these days everything seemed to have become tighter and sharper. One of the many reasons destroying it all had seemed so reasonable. Oh, he supposed he could always find a rounder woman. Like the newest female talya.

But that one wasn't soft at all. He frowned as the woman beside him traced her finger down his chest, lingering a moment on the faint parallel scars, as if someone had tried to open him on the dotted line. "She did that to me," he said.

"Who did, baby?"

"Your sister."

Dory's eyes widened, though even in the brighter light, her pupils never changed size. "What?"

"She stabbed me."

Dory sat back, dragging the sheet up to shield her naked breasts. "I didn't know—"

He smiled. "Don't fret. I am not angry."

The sheet sagged. "You're not?" A bit of animal cunning returned to her pinched features. "At her? Or at me?"

He chuckled, a grating sound. "Either. Remember how I said you must let go your hurts before you can move on?" When she nodded, he tucked a strand of her lank blond hair behind her ear. He moved slowly, lest he accidentally poke out her eye with his clumsy hands. He who had once wielded swords finely enough to carve birds on the wing. "Let it go, Dory."

She leaned into his touch, and let go.

"Into thin air," Archer growled.

Liam spiked his fingers through his hair. In the brilliant—and frigid—March light, his teshuva's sensitivity to the dark side was less powerful. But to not pick up a single trace of Dory's passage?

"No signs of struggle," he said at last. "She went willingly."

Ecco nodded. A white thread was all that remained of the jagged wound at his hairline. "A feralis on the wing could have plucked her up any time in the night if it knew where to find her. If she summoned it."

"She's a confused woman," Jilly objected. "Not some djinni witch."

Liam had planned the search to rendezvous at Grant Park after quartering the area near the warehouse and then expanding in concentric rings through the morning, jumping ever farther afield as they found nothing.

Under the bright sun, the lake sparkled, and the white breasts of the wheeling seagulls soared like foam whipped from the whitecaps. Dozens of people braved the cold to stroll in the light.

"She told me Corvus liked to come down here," Jilly said. "This was my last idea."

"We don't know that she went to Corvus," Liam cautioned.

They all, even Jilly, stared at him until he shrugged, hoping he'd wrestled down the flush of embarrassment on his face. Of course his teshuva-ridden talyan had seen through his lie.

Jilly paced with jerky movements. Liam watched the pulse of amethyst in her eyes as the demon sputtered in and out of her control. She was exhausted. They all were.

And they couldn't afford any more mistakes. "We're going home."

The others turned to head back to their vehicles, but Jilly stiffened. "We're abandoning her?"

He didn't see any way to soften the decision. "For now."

"Go, then. I'll keep looking."

"We're all going." He kept his voice even.

She spun to face him, golden eyes flaring pure violet. "You told me no one was leaving," she mocked. "But you couldn't keep one weak human woman from sneaking out. How will you stop me?"

The other talyan melted back. While he appreciated their discretion, he half suspected a touch of wariness drove their tactful retreat.

Having lost her puffy jacket in the salambes' attack, Jilly had borrowed Sera's coat, which was enough like Archer's coat that it had always made Liam think of matching velour tracksuits. Except now the sleek red leather, hanging on Jilly long enough to touch the ground if it weren't for her brand-new shit-kicker boots, made him think of concubines.

He realized his own thoughts were none too coherent, so he shouldn't blame her for challenging him. Even if his demon, hovering unnecessarily close to the surface as his control slipped, made such a challenge particularly unwise.

In the face of his silence, she bristled. Literally. The crescent knives appeared in her hand, fanned to array all four forward points at him.

He kept his hands at his sides. "That really what you want to do? Right here on the pier with everyone watching?"

The demon flash in her eyes clashed with her coat. "I just want to find Dory."

For a second, he contemplated lying again. But he thought that just might set those blades in motion.

So instead he reached out and touched her face, just a fleeting glance of his fingertips against her skin. When he stepped closer, the knife tips prodded at tender places, but he let out a breath and gave himself some room. "Remember what I told you. You can only take on so much before you risk getting taken over." He should know.

Despite the cold, a faint blush rose on her cheek where his touch had passed. She closed her eyes for a moment, and when she opened them again, the violet had leached away as purely human pain surpassed the demon's barriers. "I thought I had another chance," she whispered. The gleaming points of the knives dipped away from his groin. "Why would she leave?"

"Maybe she wasn't ready for another chance." Now she might not get a third, but he didn't think he needed to add salt to Jilly's wounds.

"I just can't believe she went back to him. She kept riding me what trouble you were, but then she went back to Corvus."

Her words twisted in him, sharper than the knives. "So maybe you shouldn't listen to her." She glanced up, and he realized abruptly how much of the grievance was in his tone. "Maybe you should let the talyan get some rest, which you know they can't do if you won't call a halt."

She swayed on her feet and glanced around her, as if she couldn't quite remember where she was. As if she didn't quite realize what it meant to be in charge of other people's fate, balancing one against another.

When she finally looked back at him, her throat worked in a hard swallow. She put away the knives. Without a word, she followed the other talyan away from him.

He stood for one more moment, between the lake and his league. Except for Jilly in her wild red, their sleek dark clothes, so suitable for night hunting, made them outcasts on the sunny pier. The afternoon of rest he would give them was no vacation—more like purgatory, waiting for the burning to begin.

He turned his back on the water and headed for his men. And woman.

He ignored the one last flare of his demon at that thought.

At the warehouse, Liam followed Jilly to her room, feeling like the black shadow of doom hovering behind her.

"I'm not going to double back to continue the search," she said, her voice dull.

"I know." He pushed open the door and she edged past him.

It took her a full heartbeat before she realized he'd followed her in.

Her gaze snapped. He could almost see her shove her weariness away. Next she'd be shoving him away. "I said I wasn't going to leave."

"And I said I know." He went to the window to pull the curtain against the sun. Still, enough light leached around the edges of the fabric that he didn't have to summon his demon to see as he sat on the chair to pull off his boots.

"What are you doing?"

"Taking my boots off."

"Don't fuck with me." She huddled in her long borrowed coat, which took some of the threat out of her words.

"Truly, I'm too tired." But now that she'd said it, some of his fatigue lifted. Which was unfortunate. Just so long as nothing else lifted, he'd be fine.

"Perrin is dead, Jonah mutilated, my sister missing." She took an agitated step, prelude to pacing.

He caught her arm. "Sleep."

She stiffened against his hold. "No demon mind tricks."

"No such thing. And the demon's got nothing to do with it." Recklessness loosened his tongue. "Wouldn't it be easier if it did? Then we could deny what's between us with a righteous heart, knowing we were denying sin itself."

"It is a demon," she whispered.

He stood, barefoot, and stripped the shirt over his head. Then he faced her. "I don't see the demon in your eyes."

But he was playing with some kind of fire. He called himself a hundred kinds of fool as he took a step nearer and closed his fingers around cool red leather.

He slid the coat over her shoulder, down her arms. He trapped her there for a heartbeat, felt her sway toward him. He steeled himself for a head butt. Instead, her cinnamon-honey eyes were half closed, as if she were falling asleep in his arms.

He gave the borrowed coat another nudge, and it pooled in crimson at her feet. Underneath, she was in the same unrelieved black as his other people.

But she wasn't like the others. And that's what would get him in trouble. That's what would destroy the world.

Still he could not release her.

Instead, he knelt, trailing his hands down her arms. His knuckles brushed the outer curves of her breasts, and she trembled. Down he went, pausing at her midline. He lifted the bottom of her T-shirt. The shrapnel gash in her side had knit to tender flesh, her *reven* swirled around to encompass the fading scar with the inky darkness of dormant demon.

With a flick of his thumb, he unfastened the button of her low-rider jeans and eased the denim over her thighs. Good little talya. Even her underwear was black.

He lifted her feet, one at a time, from the loosened laces of her boots. She braced her hands on his shoulders and looked down at him.

And he stopped cold.

He'd seen her charge salambes, leap across voids, tease the Veil that separated the realms, without fear. In her eyes now he saw the fear that he would hurt her, that he would not be what she needed.

And she was right to be afraid. Not of herself, or what she could do. Of him.

He didn't speak, only rose to his full height and swept her into his arms. She didn't resist. He carried her to the bed and laid her down. It was all his muscles doing the resisting as he tucked her against his side without desiring more. Or at least without reaching for more.

"Just sleep." He didn't recognize his own voice.

For a long minute, he listened to the grind of her

teeth. But finally her fist, hard as a rock on his chest, loosened, and her breathing smoothed into sleep.

Gingerly, so as not to wake her, he smoothed her fingers over his heart. He stared into the dark as his pulse matched itself to hers.

CHAPTER 24

Jilly awoke at a cool breeze running along the small of her back, like fingers.

That better not *be* anyone's fingers.

She bolted upright, wrestling a moment in the covers that had been tucked around her. She wasn't exactly cool, she realized; she'd just been warmer before. With that comforting weight at her back.

Liam eyed her warily from across the room, where he had pulled back the curtain just a bit. He reached for his shirt. She'd seen enough when he'd taken the shirt off, so she knew she should avert her gaze as he dressed. It wasn't like he was some great work of manly art. The lean length of him was more whipcord than stud, and the wild tangle of his hair was definitely the work of demons rather than modern haute couture.

And yet she didn't look away. Her fingers tightened on the sheet with the ancient-by-now memory of gripping his flanks as he eased into her. Only the faintest evening light trickled into the room, but traceries of old scars glimmered on his skin as her demon roused to the coming darkness. And the tripping pulse of her heart.

He did up the buttons of his shirt with quick fingers, as if it were some kind of armor. "I was hoping you'd sleep a little longer so I could change before I had to come back and make sure you didn't run off."

"You could tie me down."

He paused, his stillness taking on a predatory air. Her breath caught.

Then she narrowed her eyes when she wondered if he might be taking her seriously. "Don't even try it," she warned. "Not when you won't listen to any of my other suggestions."

"Whatever keeps the rest of my crew safe."

He didn't make a sound, but she knew by the change of air pressure, by the whispered scent that was just his, that he had come over to the bedside. His voice was a low murmur that barely reached her ears. "I'd chain you to me if I had to."

He might have come to lead the league by default, but he didn't shirk his duty. His never-ending, undying—until he was summarily executed by some vicious hell beast—duty. And he didn't have to say that she could get him killed too, just as Perrin had lost what was left of his life. The chill that had started in her spine when he'd left the bed enveloped her like the black lines of the *reven* that curled toward her heart.

"I won't go anywhere." She looked up at him so he could see the truth in her eyes.

The touch of violet lent his blue eyes a searchlight brightness as he studied her.

"I might find Dory without you," she continued, never dropping his gaze. "But whatever else you think of me, I'm not stupid enough to believe I can take Corvus by myself."

Still he did not speak.

So she added, "I don't want to be bound to you any more than you want to be bound to me."

She gave him a chance to say he *did* want it—wanted her. Instead, he stiffened, almost imperceptibly, but with her focus on him, she saw it. She knew it had been a cheap shot, but she didn't really care. He couldn't have his arrogant, dictatorial league-leader cake and eat her too.

She kicked back the covers, ignoring the flash of skin she was giving him. He'd already made clear he wasn't going there, so what did it matter?

He averted his gaze—more than she'd done for him—as she grabbed her jeans. It was the same pair she'd worn looking for Dory, the same as she'd worn in the hunt for the salambe. The denim was soiled with birnenston, shards of glass, and blood.

She dropped it. "Go. I just want to shower. I'll be here to hunt tonight, no worries."

She turned away, stripping off her T-shirt, and heard him scramble. She huffed out a breath. She'd scared away men before, but not usually at this point. What an ego buster.

The bathroom wasn't much nicer than a utility closet, her skin sallow in the humming fluorescents, but the water scalded away the filth and the worst sting of the past twelve hours.

Not that she expected the memory of Perrin's broken body or Jonah's spurting blood would ever go away. And ever was a very long time now.

She didn't linger, and she barged back into her room wrapped in a towel, determined to shock her boss once and for all.

But Liam was gone. As were her dirty clothes. Fresh blacks were laid out on the crisply made bed.

"Sure knows how to wipe away all the evidence," she muttered. "Like he was never even here."

She dressed, wincing when she bumped the tender skin on her side. The demon was taking its sweet time patching her up. Although she supposed if she compared it with her recovery time after her stabbing, she should be grateful. No sense being all unappreciative just because she had to sell her soul. Her health insurance plan hadn't been that great before either.

She pulled on the clean jeans. They were sized for her ass but a little too long in the leg, so she rolled the cuffs.

Her new boots smelled of fresh leather, and her throat tightened briefly with ridiculous sadness. Her old boots had been perfectly broken in.

As she walked out into the hallway and closed the door to her room, she contemplated leaving the warehouse. But no, that was something best left to the clueless chick running toward danger, usually with her pants off. She'd keep her promise to Liam, since she'd already laced up her boots, so it was a little late to get half naked and full-on stupid. The moment for that had come and gone last night.

She passed the kitchen on her way out and saw a dozen talyan eating leftovers. A few looked up and nodded as she went by. She nodded back. She'd have to find some way to get the KP duties taken care of on a regular basis. The league didn't offer a golden parachute—she blanked the image of Perrin going over the roof—so it could damn well provide a prep cook. She banished the memory of her sister at the counter too.

At this rate, she wouldn't have many memories left.

The basement lab was dark except for one bright construction light clamped above the central table. Sera and Ecco hunched over an empty glass-walled container bracketed with metal electrodes. Off in the shadows, the fishbowl lay open, its angelic glow exhausted.

Jilly froze. "Did it get out?"

They glanced at her. Ecco lifted his hands, speckled with faint scarring like hers after she'd wrestled the salambe. "Had to take it apart, but we got a good shred."

In the harsh light, Sera's face was pale and drawn under her lopsided blond ponytail. Jilly wondered if she'd slept at all. "I have no idea what I'm doing. I dissected worms in high school biology. After that, it was mostly theory and philosophy." She clenched her hands, as battle bruised as Ecco's.

"So what's your philosophical theory now?" Jilly edged closer to the table.

Sera reached around to rub her shoulder, knocking

the ponytail farther askew. "We've already seen how the salambes seem to occupy a morphology somewhere between the incorporeal malice, which feed off of but never invade living flesh, and the ferales, which convert dead-animal matter into working husks for themselves." She clicked off the desk lamp beside her and pushed a button on the side of the glass box.

Jilly blinked in the sudden dark, poised to rally her teshuva. But the electrodes on the box began to glow. A pulse crossed the glass. And the salambe within roiled into view.

"Dim the lights, send a few positive ions through— the same kind of energy that drives the Santa Ana winds that make people crazy and the opposite of the negative ions at the beach that seem to calm people down—and voilà," Sera said. "Cool light show and absolutely no practical application."

Jilly walked around to the other side. At closer range, she could see the solder gleamed with gold flecks. Some angelic force infused the box where Sera and Ecco had basically recreated the hothouse under more secure conditions.

The salambe's coiling energy mesmerized her. She shook off the trance as the electrode pulse faded and the salambe dimmed again. Ecco turned the lamp back on. The salambe was all but invisible in the bright light.

"So the salambes occupy the same place in a haint as the soul used to," Jilly mused.

Sera shrugged. "Nothing in league archives offers any clue. There are references to a vaster array of tenebrae than what we've seen, but previous Bookkeepers seemed to think everyone must already know what they were talking about." She hissed out a breath. "Overconfident snobs. They thought they'd always be walking the same path, not necessarily winning the war against evil, but not challenged either. Now, when we most need that information, I don't even know where to start looking." She glared at Jilly through red-rimmed eyes. "Do you have any idea what sort of paper trail gets left in a handful of millennia? More like a paper mountain."

"Still," Jilly insisted. "The salambes obviously can't use a human with the soul on board. When I was fully engulfed, I could feel it chewing at me." She kept her voice even, as if that horror were no worse than a few mosquito bites. "Maybe given enough time and a few more friends, it could have forced my soul out and taken over. But the solvo makes room for the salambe by removing the soul, so it's reasonable to assume that the salambe is operating some of the same mechanisms as the soul."

Ecco stared at her. "You make it sound like puppetry."

She gave him a bitter glance. "Isn't that what we are now? Puppets for the teshuva?"

He shook his head. "I fight because I want to. The teshuva just makes the fun last longer."

She studied him. Did he honestly believe that? But he was far more experienced than she, and she couldn't call her demon into fine enough focus to call him out as a liar. Plus, that'd probably just be a really bad idea.

She huffed. "Forget it. Never mind what we are. It's what the salambes can do that matters. If they offer a guide into the ruined pathways of the abandoned soul, we could put an end to solvo addiction." What had seemed so worth getting fired over when she imagined Andre, lost on the street, had become a miniature feralis clawing at her heart when she imagined her sister, not lost, but found. By Corvus.

Sera tilted her head. "The league would at least be back to the same place it was before Corvus set his sights on destroying us."

A small foam-lined casket stood open on the table behind Sera, the shards of a broken glass vial upended in the place of dishonor.

Jilly studied the debris. "Dory stole the solvo out of there?"

Sera nodded. "Smash and grab."

Just beyond the reach of the lamp, the fragments still glimmered with a pearlescent sheen. Even the dust of the raw solvo she and Liam had retrieved from the sewer possessed a luminescent beauty completely at odds with the bare-bones lab, its seething box of trapped evil, and three worn fighters.

She pointed at the glass sliver. "Put that in with the salambe."

Sera hummed under her breath. "Interesting."

Ecco stared at Jilly under wrinkled brows. "They used to let you work around children?" He directed the incredulous look at Sera. "And poor dying people? You're like mad-scientist girls."

Sera steepled her fingers in a serious pose, but she winked at Jilly. Who would've guessed she'd find an ally in the crew's good girl?

Jilly turned a fierce, challenging smile on Ecco. "C'mon, now. Who's going to get hurt, after all?"

"Um, us?" But he leaned forward curiously as Sera plucked a shard from its resting place.

The faintest scent of rain teased them. They all inhaled.

"Okay, that's just wrong," Ecco said. "Sulfur, rotting dead things, even rusty metal, I was okay with that. But a quiet night's walk in the forest primeval? Very wrong."

Jilly stared at the glimmering glass. "I wonder what it tastes like." She winced when Ecco punched her shoulder.

"Stop it." His voice was harsh. "That sort of drifting is what gets a talya killed."

She blinked at him. "I wasn't—"

"You start wondering what it's like to check out, and that's the end of you," he said. "Oh, you might not die right away, what with being immortal and all, but your existence becomes pointless, and even if you never take the solvo, your soul will be lost."

The word bounced cruelly around the hollow space, and even the beguiling scent of the solvo couldn't dampen it. Jilly lifted her chin, studying the big talya. "Projecting much?"

Ecco flushed, the white thread of his new scar more obvious against his red face.

Sera cleared her throat. "Let's just agree we're not going to be checking out any time soon. I think Jilly's experiment sounds"—she lifted her eyebrows—"fun. You should appreciate that, Ecco."

He scowled. Then shrugged. "Yeah, okay. Do it."

Sera tweezered the solvo-dusted splinter of glass and held it up at eye level. "Not enough to get anybody high," she said doubtfully.

"But maybe enough to steal a soul." Jilly shifted to the balls of her feet and noticed Ecco looked similarly prepared.

Working through a small, gold-lined portal in the glass container, Sera tapped the shard into the salambe's cage.

Nothing.

"Not as fun as I thought," Ecco said.

"Hit the ion pulse," Jilly said. "People take solvo when they are hurting. If the positive ions re-create that experience—"

Sera pushed the button.

The electrodes gleamed. The salambe flared to life for a heartbeat.

Then the angel-blessed glass ignited.

CHAPTER 25

"What? The explosion on the roof wasn't enough for you? Losing Perrin and Jonah's arm wasn't enough?"

Liam paced in front of the three miscreant amateur metaphysics professors, pausing at the turn just long enough to glare at them. His temple throbbed with fury, and the demon burned in every muscle, begging him to unleash on something, someone.

Jilly.

He froze in front of her, deafened by the angry pound of his heart in his chest. She'd said she wouldn't go anywhere, and yet she'd managed to find the worst sort of trouble in the only stronghold he had left. She defied him even while obeying his orders.

Ecco cleared his throat as he picked at a shard of glass embedded in his cheek. "Admittedly, it wasn't as much fun as we'd anticipated—"

Sera and Jilly winced as Liam wheeled on the other male. "Fun?" His voice throbbed with demonic lows.

For once, Ecco didn't respond by summoning his own demon. He just settled deeper in his chair. "Did I mention it was Jilly's idea?"

Liam clenched his fists until his whole body was just one aching desire to detonate.

Although they hadn't seen fit to invite him to that *fun*.

"The results support my theory." Eagerness rose in Jilly's tone as if she didn't notice—didn't care about—his edging into violence. "If solvo shreds souls and salambes, then maybe souls and salambes are more alike than we know."

"So what?"

She narrowed her eyes thoughtfully. "So you should be glad we discovered that solvo destroys salambes."

"Are we going to become pushers ourselves? Manufacture more of the stuff?" He stalked closer to her. "Will we become what we most hate?"

She tilted her face up. "You mean more like."

He didn't recoil, but her point struck home. Why did he want to hold to the old ways? Where had it ever gotten them? Except further behind, as he lost his already-too-few men to Corvus's new threats. Why did he keep thinking he had any place left at the head of this fight?

He should drift away gracefully as Roald had before him, make room for the young and hungrier.

Damn it, no. No matter how much easier it might seem to step aside, he knew better than most what sort of trouble the young and hungry got into.

He glared at Sera. "You at least I trusted to know better. As our interim Bookkeeper, you should have come to me before trying anything extreme."

She stared at him, but not in challenge. More with pity. "You can't do it all, Liam. That's how a team works."

"And I am still leader." But they must know how close he was to losing it. Especially Sera, who had been kidnapped by her frantic mate when she'd volunteered to sacrifice herself—with Liam's sanction—to save the world. If he ran off, would he do so to escape the league, or to avoid chancing Jilly as he'd risked another talya's mate?

Once again, he pushed away the impossible question. He glanced sharply at the broken vial of solvo. The larger portion of the sample was gone, thanks to Dory, and still the stuff was a hazard. "Seal those pieces," he snapped. "It's a bad influence, obviously. Ecco, clean up this mess. Sera, Archer wants to talk to you." He speared her with a glance when she grumbled. "Jilly, come with me."

He wasn't amused when Ecco wiped his brow with exaggerated relief.

Liam stalked out, leaving Jilly to follow. He'd trust the same self-preservation instincts that had made her duck away from the worst of the exploding glass would make sure she followed immediately and silently.

He should have known better.

In the stairwell, the drag of her steps behind him made him grit his teeth. "I can finish chewing you out in front of the others, or you can pick up your feet and take your licks in private."

She gave a short, low laugh. "Why start now?" When he whirled to glare at her, she just glared back. "Lay a hand on me, and you will regret it for the rest of your suddenly very short life."

A protest sprang to the tip of his tongue that he would never lay a hand on her, but that's exactly what he wanted to do. He was so tired of the dance. It was worse than fighting, this circling around what was between them.

If he just indulged it . . .

No, that was sin itself talking. And he didn't even have the excuse of the raw, exposed solvo nearby.

He tightened his fists against the urge to reach for her. "I want just one peaceful night of destroying tenebrae. Is that too much to ask?"

"No one's stopping you," she snapped. "Oh, wait. Except Corvus."

He glowered at her. "And you."

The stairwell was as uncomfortable a place for seduction as he could imagine—other than the middle of a tenebrae attack—and still his body yearned toward her. And here he'd always thought he had the inevitable talya death wish firmly under control.

He had nothing under control when he was with Jilly.

He took a long breath and let it out even more slowly. "I don't want to fight with you again."

"And yet we do it so well, remember?"

He couldn't help but smile at the wry note that crept into her voice. "Yeah."

"You told me not to go out, and I didn't." When he opened his mouth to point out that she'd found plenty of trouble anyway, she pinned him with a glare. "I get at least a few points for that."

"You get minus points for destroying company property." He held up one hand. "But I'll count you back at zero if you aren't around any more explosions for the rest of the night."

She huffed as if his request was a huge imposition. "If we had enough raw solvo, we could launch it into a room of salambes—maybe even use it against malice and ferales—from a distance, and no one would get hurt."

He gave her a reproving glance. "Except for anyone caught in the resulting cataclysmic blast. You said Sera used just the smallest bit of leftover solvo, and look what it did."

Jilly chewed at her lip and looked away. "But we wouldn't have to risk anyone in the hand-to-hand again. If it works, the talyan could overcome the tenebrae without having to get close enough to match their demons against each other."

Knowing he shouldn't, he reached out to touch her cheek, to bring her gaze up to his. "Losing Perrin was bad," he said softly. "But we can't fix it, can't bring him back, by avoiding our mission."

He expected her to pull away, assuming she didn't just snap off his head—and maybe his hand. Instead, she rested a moment against his touch. The blue streaks of her hair hung down without their customary gel, straight and soft against the backs of his fingers.

"I just can't seem to make anything better," she murmured. "My family. The kids at the halfway house. I manage to make things worse even when I'm fighting evil incarnate and it seems like there's no way things *could* get worse."

"We all have our special skills," he said. She rewarded him with a fleeting smile, compelling him to remind her, "I wanted more for the boys under my watch too, so I know how you feel."

He wished he could make it better. For her. Never mind the world's battle against evil. If he could ease her hurt, even for a moment, maybe that would be the first step to making up for all his failures over the many long years.

After all, he did know how she felt. He just wanted to feel more of her.

He leaned down, very slowly, giving her time to protest. She only stared up, her eyes half closed and her lips parted.

Softly, he closed his mouth over hers. Spicy and sweet. The sigh of her breath warmed the damp joining of their lips and spread with a curling rush through the rest of him. He stroked his tongue against hers, felt her melt as the heat rose between them.

He pulled her up against his chest, the clean cotton of the black T-shirt he'd laid out for her—the whole time imagining her bare, wet, hot skin in the shower—rumpling under his clenched fingers. He'd like to see that skin, taste it, mark it with his presence, a warning more clear than even a flashing *reven* to any who would hurt her again.

A clang from somewhere down in the basement made him lift his head.

But she didn't draw away. "I thought we weren't going to do this again."

He brushed a twined strand of blue and black hair behind her ear. "If it's this or fight . . ."

Her hand rested in the middle of his chest, rising and falling with his slightly harried breath. "We can't do anything by halves, can we? But that's all we are anymore. Half of a soul, half demon."

His grip on her tightened involuntarily. Because he didn't feel divided at the moment.

Oh no, definitely all of him wanted all of her.

She might think of herself as somehow lessened, but he knew better.

"You said it was my fault we lost Perrin, and I agreed. But I didn't say why." The confession ripped out of him. "If I'd been with you, we could have staved off the salambes' attack, at least long enough to confine the one and make our escape."

Under his hand, he felt the imperceptible stiffening of her spine. "What do you mean?"

He pulled her closer again. "This. This power that binds us. I've denied it, thinking it would do more harm than good. But as you pointed out, how can we sink any deeper?"

She'd gone utterly still in his grasp, and he realized he could've offered a more impassioned appeal to her senses before pointing out the cold practicality of their joining. He tilted his head, gaze fixed on her mouth, ready to make up for the error.

But she pulled back, exerting no little amount of her teshuva's strength. "So you think one kiss seals the deal?"

"No," he murmured. "I figure two or three should do it."

This time she was not amused, he saw. Under the black weave of her T-shirt, her muscles rippled as she amped the demon higher. "So we're going to hook up to save the league."

He had to let her go or risk an undignified wrestling match on the cold metal stairs. "I thought you understood. You noticed it yourself, before I did; we're two halves of a whole, mirror images."

"Matter and antimatter," she countered.

"And if we handle the explosion right, we'll only take the evil in the world with us."

She took a long step back from him, until her heels hovered near the edge of the stairs, as if she'd rather tumble back down than be near him. "You're the one who said no more explosions."

"I was hasty." He grimaced. "You bring that out in me. Just another way we're different."

"Just another way we'll kill each other before we could drain a single malice."

Frustration rose up in him. "You want to fight. You've been pushing to take this to the next level."

She stared at him, her golden eyes opaque with some secretive veil that hid more dangers than the barrier guarding the human realm from the demon. "I don't want to be just another weapon in your hands."

Her refusal hung in the air between them like a double-edged sword with no grip.

He had no choice but to take it, never mind the blood and pain. "That's what we are, Jilly, weapons. And when we're not together, we're half the weapon we could be. Which makes us useless in this war."

He knew the point of her weakness, her impulse to come to the rescue of hopeless cases. Though the underhanded ploy caught in his throat, he added, "How can you deny us—deny the world—this chance to be saved?"

Her brows drew hard together, as if she sought to rally her defenses, but when she opened her mouth, no sound emerged.

From below them, Ecco clanged up the stairs, grumbling to himself. When he saw them on the landing, he stopped to stare between them. "What? Did you beat her? It wasn't that big a mess." Then he shoved past them out into the warehouse.

Liam rubbed at his temple. Beat her? He hadn't pushed her that hard. Had he?

Her stricken expression had blanked when Ecco interrupted. Her arms, which had been wrapped around herself, fell to her sides. "Of course. Whatever we have to do to stop Corvus. Shall we hunt?"

He should have felt the thrill of victory, that perfect bone-deep righteousness when the hammer haft smacked into his palm. But he felt nothing.

As he gestured her ahead of him out of the stairwell, he didn't feel as if he'd found another weapon. No, somehow he knew he'd lost here.

CHAPTER 26

The creeping chill that had invaded Jilly with each of Liam's sensible words hadn't abated by the time the talyan hit the streets. Liam had announced at their pre-hunt docking-bay gathering that he would not—would *not*, he said—lose another man.

They were traveling on foot, en masse, and yet Jilly had never felt so alone.

Their black ghosting shapes, *reven* flickering, were strung far enough apart as to seem completely unrelated, just a few more random, artless tags on the cityscape. She didn't even have a sense of what they were doing tonight. Every word had seemed to come at her from a distance, wrapped in gauze. Gauze would've been nice over Liam's needle-sharp words earlier.

He didn't even know how he'd stabbed her. It was all so clear to him. She'd been a fool to ever think there could be more than saving the world for him.

Certainly she wasn't enough.

And yet she couldn't accuse *him* of a talya's massive conceit when she was the one who wanted to be put ahead of the world in his estimations. He was right; there was nothing more important than what they'd been chosen to do.

And if she had to give up herself to a man who was

interested in her only as a tool, well, it hadn't killed her
mother. Only drained her soul. And Jilly had already
given that up.

A hand on her arm distracted her. Sera peered into
her eyes. "You okay?"

"Yeah," Jilly said. The talyan were spread out enough
that none would overhear. Not that she would have said
anything else anyway.

"You look a little out of it."

"Sorry." Jilly drew in a shallow breath. "I won't let
anyone else die because of me."

Sera frowned. "I didn't mean—"

"Never mind." Jilly shoved her hands in her pockets,
for once not having to avoid the nick of the crescent
blades. There'd been a new jacket waiting for her when
she joined the talyan in the docking bay. The puffy silver
wasn't like anything the other talyan were wearing, but
sewn into the interior were clever, secret sheaths for her
knives.

She knew whom the jacket had come from. With the
way she was going through clothing, she should be glad
the league had a uniform allowance.

Despite her silence, Sera didn't pull away. Instead,
her sidelong glance seemed to study her like an Arctic-
core sample. "How are you and Liam getting along?"

"Does it matter?"

Sera seemed to take the question at face value.
"Maybe. There aren't enough league records to know if
the mated-talyan bond was always by choice."

"You'd think institutionalized rape would be a bad
way to fight evil."

Sera recoiled. "Liam would never—"

Jilly hunched her shoulders. "No. Of course not. I'm
just . . ."

"Feeling shanghaied again." Sera nodded. "Like you
were thrust into a life—signed, sealed, and delivered—
with a man you don't even know." Her hazel gaze was
sharp. "With a man you might not even have chosen."

Jilly had thought she didn't want to talk about it, but

curiosity pricked her. "You and Archer get along so well."

Sera smiled. "When Ferris was a rich landowner's son a long time ago, he would have shown me to the servants' entrance. When I was a thanatologist helping people accept their coming deaths, I would have happily booted him along the way. But there's something between us. . . ."

"Compulsion." Jilly ticked the word off on her thumb and continued with, "Stockholm syndrome. Masochism. Oh, insanity . . ."

Sera tapped her chin thoughtfully. "So you're saying you guys aren't getting along real well?"

"He sees nothing but the league. I'm nothing to him but a weapon."

Sera shook her head in disagreement. "More than that."

"Right. A potentially backfiring weapon. So not even one he can trust."

"If he doesn't trust someone, it's himself. I've seen him looking at you."

Jilly rolled her eyes, but some of the deep freeze in her veins melted. "I won't play those high school games."

"Why? You didn't learn anything from the kids you worked with?"

"Learn? I taught them those sorts of games can get you in big trouble."

Sera sniffed. "You know, you're as bad as he is. No wonder you're meant to be together." When Jilly prickled, Sera added, "I bet by the time those street kids came to you, they'd figured out that sometimes being alone and on their own isn't as romantic as it seems. Sometimes it is just lonely."

"Nobody thinks being alone is romantic," Jilly objected. "They ran because they were scared, abused, unwise, tired of being unwanted."

Sera just looked at her. "Sound familiar?"

Jilly tried to summon up a suitable glare, but her lips twitched with reluctant amusement. "Didn't you give up your counseling day job? And anyway, I'm not dying. Although I suppose the night is young."

Sera smiled back without restraint. "That's the thing these bullyboys don't understand. You're possessed, not gone. You're still you."

"Nobody wanted me for who I was then either." Jilly bit her tongue. She hadn't meant for *that* to slip out.

But Sera just nodded. "I think that awareness of being alone must be an effect of the penance trigger. As if others can sense the flaw that runs through us from then on, that cracks us apart. They know they won't be able to bridge the gap and fill the void. Only one man will be able to do that."

Jilly stared at her. "Your talya mate." Her tone fell flat. All this time, when her friends from work and her meager social life had teased her about being too picky, actually there'd been only *one* man. One she would've said was totally wrong for her.

Not to mention totally uninterested.

She peered at Sera. "You haven't told Archer any of this, have you?"

Sera hunched her shoulders. "He's a little sensitive about entwined fates and destinies, crap like that. I love him, but seriously, I imagine men like him are the reason the league has lost track of its feminine counterpart. Talk about commitment issues."

"Well, you can forget it if you think Liam is leading the charge back in the other direction."

"You can't let the bond fail," Sera insisted.

"Yeah, yeah, fate of the world." Jilly waved her hand. She tried to sound flippant.

Sera opened her mouth to protest, but her cell phone rang with an insistent beep.

"Better get that," Jilly said. "The world thing can wait."

Sera scowled as she snapped open the phone. She listened a moment, then handed it to Jilly. "For you. It's the world calling."

Jilly frowned at her and took the phone.

"Jilly," Liam said curtly. "This call routed through the At-One number."

"Dee," she said. He didn't answer; the call was already clicking through.

"Hello? Jilly?" The teen's voice sounded younger than it ever did in person.

"What's wrong, Dee?"

"You said to call. . . ."

When the girl didn't continue, Jilly's blood congealed. "Andre? Is he there?"

"No. Iz saw something outside. Like that thing in the alley."

Shit. "Is it there now?"

"I don't think so. Iz said it left. With ol' Downunder."

For a moment, Jilly couldn't make sense of the comment. Then she remembered the kids' nickname for Dan Envers. She just hadn't expected to hear the director of the halfway house associated with a feralis.

Except now that Dee said it, the connection seemed so easy.

"We're coming," she told Dee. "Stay inside. And for God's sake, don't let Iz follow them."

"He already said if anybody's taking that thing on, it's your new boss."

"Then there's hope for him yet." She added a few more reassurances and warnings before she hung up and turned to Sera. "Instead of just wandering around in the dark, you want to go thrash some demon ass?"

"Now you're leading the charge?" The voice behind her was cool.

She didn't glance back. "Archer, Dee called. There was a feralis sniffing around the halfway house. And the director was with it."

Archer processed a moment. "You got the pink slip. The director got slipped the solvo."

"Worse," she said. "I would have noticed if he'd gone all vague on me. He might still have his soul in the literal sense, but what if he's selling out kids to Corvus and friends?"

She expected more hassle, but the talya only nod-ded once. "It's not far. Let's go." He faded back, his cell phone at his ear.

In the charged silence, she felt the talyan reflow around her, on their new course into the night. A course she'd chosen.

Was this what Liam felt, sending his people into dan-ger on a word?

She froze.

Sera, who'd paced her, took another step, then glanced back. Talyan ranged ahead of and behind them, keeping to the shadows, half shadow themselves in their dark hunting gear.

Jilly's skin prickled. The old stab wound flared and the warning ache spread around. She imagined the *reven* raced with violet sparks. Her demon was rousing.

In response to what?

She didn't turn in a pointless circle, just cast her senses wide. The street flickered to the black-light hunt-er's sight.

"What have you got?" Sera's voice was cool, the ear-lier cajoling notes gone. She was all business. "The half-way house is almost a mile away."

"Do you feel it?"

"No. I'm not— Wait." She raised her head, eyes half closed so only a slit of violet gleamed under her lashes.

From out of nowhere, Archer was beside Sera. His hand settled at the small of her back. "Did you want something, darling?" A faint Southern drawl made the word more threat than endearment. The demon's mark across his knuckles pulsed, and Jilly didn't doubt that if he grabbed a malice in that hand, he'd drain its energy in a single beat of his heart.

Sera leaned into him, as if that touch was all she'd been waiting for. "Jilly picked up on it. I'm still getting a lock."

Archer glanced around, though his hand never left Sera. "Where's Liam to tweak her?"

"He can tweak this." Jilly lifted the relevant finger.

Archer grinned at her wolfishly. "Not like that, you naughty girl. Not here anyway. Save it for the stairwell."

Jilly rubbed her forehead. "Ecco's such a gossip."

Sera settled closer to her mate. "The boost is something we've been working on."

Archer's grip tightened with blatant possessiveness. "'We' meaning me and her. No one else."

"Of course," Sera soothed. She turned her attention back to Jilly. "You must have felt it when you touched him."

Whatever vague menace needled her from their surroundings was nothing compared with the threat Sera's words conjured. "I felt like maybe I was setting myself up for a major heartbreak, if that's what you mean." She didn't even care that Archer was listening. He knew everything anyway. Not that there was anything to know.

She took a breath to clear her annoyance. It was messing with the reception of everything going on around her. She had to get out of her own head.

Maybe that's what Liam's hand on her skin was supposed to help her do.

Well, she didn't have that at the moment. And damn it, she didn't want it.

Didn't want it just for this.

Gritting her teeth, she tried to rip through the fuzz of her own distraction. No pain, but it was much harder than tearing through the salambe's enveloping ether. The tenebrae had just been trying to eat its way into her. This soul-clouding haze of doubt and despair was something she'd imposed on herself.

"I thought I felt something, like when I was in the sewer tunnel with Liam." Had her conversation with Sera just got her thinking back to a moment when she and Liam had been oh-so briefly in accord? "Maybe it was nothing."

"Right." Archer's curt tone let her know he didn't believe her for a second. His restless gaze scanned the street. "So, back to my point, where's Liam? Why isn't he with you?"

"He was up at the front," Sera said.

"Jilly's more important." Archer's voice was matter-of-fact. He snagged a passing talya. "Lex, find Liam and send him back to me."

The talya's gaze flicked among them, and his eyes flickered violet as if he was keyed to their roused demons. He nodded once, then slipped away.

Sera prodded Jilly, "What did you find in the tunnel that you're picking up on now?"

"Birnenston," Archer said. "Rat shit."

"Solvo. That's what it was." Jilly wheeled back the way they'd come. She ranged back along the sidewalk, casting for the rain-sweet scent. Archer and Sera followed as she cut through an alley and popped out on the next street over.

She kicked herself for not catching the association right away. This was what they were out here for, not for angsting. Liam was right about that.

At the mouth of a blind alley, she paused. She peered into the darkness, so deep she needed the teshuva's help to see the end.

"This is where I met Liam," she said. "This is where Iz and Dee brought me when we were looking for Andre."

Sera paused beside her. "You said Andre was dealing solvo. This is the right kind of neighborhood. Or wrong kind, I suppose."

"Corvus isn't stupid enough—or anyway his djinni isn't—to keep a solvo-manufacturing operation open here after a talya almost stumbled over it." Archer hummed thoughtfully. "I wonder if that near miss started him closing up shop all over town, the tunnel under the slaughter yards included."

Jilly took a step forward. "Let's go see what he left behind this time."

"Hold up, talya," Archer said. "Wait for your mate."

She glanced back at him, wishing she could summon enough violet glare to wither him on the spot. "He is not my mate. He is not even a partner."

"I'm still your boss."

The three of them stiffened when Liam appeared so silently he'd triggered none of their alarms.

"Don't get so focused on what's in front of you that you forget to look behind," he admonished. "I could have been some big baddie."

Jilly bit her lip on the curt response that jumped to her tongue. Something obvious, along the lines of he *was* a big baddie.

Archer looked almost as annoyed as she felt, although he snapped, "Luckily it was just you."

Liam gave him a deceptively mild look. "Luckily." His gaze arrowed down the alley, then back to Jilly. "A stroll down memory lane?"

Thank God they weren't a couple or they'd have to retell at all their eternal anniversary parties the story of how they met in a stinking alley over a feralis head. "Shall we?"

He held out his hand. Not a courtly gentleman's gesture. An invitation to linked-demon mayhem.

Well, she just happened to be in the mood.

When she threaded her fingers through his, she knew she'd been lying to Sera and herself when she'd played dumb about the power of touching him. Her senses came alive, leaving the demon's amplified sensitivity behind in the dust. Her every nerve sang, outward and in, so that the alley around her shimmered with secrets revealed. And her heart seemed equally exposed.

Just hers, of course, not his. But when she tried to squelch the link, to keep it all business, Liam squeezed her hand warningly. "Hunt."

She didn't like the feeling he was hunting her heart, but she steeled herself against the fear. They had bigger game than their petty feelings. He'd made that clear.

"Focus," he murmured.

She took a breath and settled into the bond as gingerly as curling up on a bed of nails.

"You were wandering off without me again," he murmured as they walked down the alley.

Was he trying to make the bed of nails as uncomfortable as possible? "I had Archer with me."

Liam's fingers closed tightly on hers. "Not the right answer."

"And I'm not into possessive men, remember?"

The shrug of his shoulder lifted their joined hands. "I'm possessed."

"That's no excuse. Sera says we're still ourselves." She lifted her chin but didn't look at him. "We still deserve some basic human consideration. That's why you bury the talya dead, even though a few minutes' procrastination would turn them into dust and you could just sweep them under the rug."

"Never."

They stopped at the end of the alley, where Iz and Dee had climbed the fire escape to the roof.

"As traps go, this is a simple one," Liam said. "One way in. No way out."

"Iz and Dee got out," she reminded him.

"You didn't."

No. She'd escaped the ferales with his help, but the demon already had her. Sera might say no one escaped fate, but of course a thanatologist would think that.

Jilly glanced around the alley. "I don't see anything. And I still don't smell that solvo rain." She felt her cheeks heat. Had she been attracted here only by her memory of meeting him?

Liam released her hand, and she wondered if he'd read her thoughts somehow. He wouldn't appreciate being misled from his task. "We've gone up before. And we've gone down. This time, let's go through."

The hammer was in his hands in a heartbeat, and then he was swinging. Splinters of brick flew, and she skipped back to escape the spray.

Sera and Archer had completed a slower sweep and

caught up with them. "Oh, the subtle method," Sera said, observing Liam.

"Nice technique," Archer commented.

Jilly paced just out of reach of the shrapnel. "I don't even know what he's— Oh."

Liam broke through the wall.

CHAPTER 27

It felt so good to be attacking something solid, something that would fly apart beneath him. And he didn't have to feel guilty about it. Just smash.

The wall came down too quickly for his satisfaction.

The bricks crumbled before him, and then he was through. The sudden glare of white light cast halos in his sensitized vision, and he brandished the hammer against the surge of tenebrae he half expected. After all, he'd said the alley made a good trap.

But the attack didn't come. He squinted until the teshuva backed down a notch.

Inside, the walls glowed pearlescent and the wash of sweet rain made all of them inhale.

"Now we know why Corvus switched to sewers for production," Archer said. "Much easier to erase the evidence."

Liam took a step into the room. Though the place was absolutely empty, the walls were glazed with solvo dust, like the inside of the vial Dory had broken. No sign of birnenston or recent demonic activity of any kind remained. "Did the solvo destroy everything demonic?"

"It shreds souls, not demons," Sera said.

"We saw what it did to the salambes." Liam glanced around. "For God's sake, don't touch anything and lick your fingers. Our souls are precariously balanced enough."

Sera crowded behind him. "If we can scrape these walls, we've got enough for a hell of an explosion."

He snorted. "Have you been talking to Jilly?"

"Yes." Sera glanced up at him with a guilty expression and sidled away. "Not about you or anything. Much."

There was a mystery he didn't want to unravel. "Jilly," he called. When she approached, he reached out for her. "I'm not picking up anything demonic at all. You?"

She hesitated, her gaze fixed on his hand. The small rejection speared him with unnecessary force. He did not betray his reaction; the muscles in his face were too stiff for any expression. But she shifted beside him, facing the room. The back of her hand bumped his; then her fingers slipped into his grasp.

"Sensing anything? Besides us?" Her breath hummed out in a faint sigh. After a moment, she shook her head. "At least we know what happened to Andre."

He didn't disagree. There was no way a human had been in such close proximity to solvo for any length of time without succumbing to its whispered promise of peace. Even with his demon riding high, he felt the distant urge to just sink to his knees, to let the effort flow out of him.

Along with his soul, of course. And the teshuva wouldn't allow that. He could imagine the giant red "fail" on a fallen angel's scorecard to lose its human mount to the dark side.

Right next to the big black check mark of doom for ravaging the Veil and crossing into the demon realm, of course.

Gently, he disengaged his hand. "I'm sorry we couldn't help him." He gave her shoulder a light squeeze, one talya to another. But her warmth lingered in his flesh. Unfair, that hellfire promised such pleasure.

He prowled the abandoned room. "All right. We'll leave a few talyan here to harvest." He shot a glance at Jilly. "But we won't be blowing anything up tonight."

The four of them backed out of the subtly glowing space. After the soft fragrance of the solvo, the alley seemed even more ugly and pungent. He paused to give directions to Ecco to pass along to the others, sending half the crew onward to recon the halfway house, then joined his wayward trio on the street.

"We're not getting anywhere." Archer's frustration bounced off the brick wall. "Corvus has gone to ground. Either his head wasn't as bashed in as we thought, or his djinni isn't interested in risking his immortality again."

"Yet another question," Sera murmured. "Why should the djinni care what body it inhabits? Without the anchor of the soul, it can jump anywhere."

"Maybe it's not as much fun and games as you think." Jilly stared past them, focused on nothing. "Being alone."

Sera leaned sideways a few inches so her shoulder pressed against Archer's. Liam wondered if that touch relieved the kind of tightness that seized his chest at Jilly's words. Finally, he nodded. "Corvus and his djinni have been together a very long time."

"Yeah, true love," Archer growled. He winced when Sera elbowed him. "Meanwhile, where are we going to find him?"

Jilly straightened, and Liam glanced at her. "What is it?"

"True love," she repeated. "Dory wanted Corvus that much. So where would a drug-addicted prostitute and her evil lover go?"

Archer shook his head. "We already checked her old apartment."

Jilly hung her head. "Not where she lived. Where she turned tricks. Where I got stabbed."

Liam ached to reach out to her. But he couldn't take away her pain with a touch. He'd only made it worse. But as far as walks down memory lane went, this one was a real bitch.

*   *   *

Anyone who hunted evil for a living ended up in bad neighborhoods. Not that evil was limited to bad neighborhoods, of course, but bashing the shit out of evil tended to be less frowned upon in places where people were scared to look out their windows.

And somehow, it had always seemed more righteous to Liam that the league be most heavily dispatched among the places where people cared the least.

So police tape, cars on blocks, security grilles, and the smell of old blood were nothing new to him. And yet the street Jilly led them to offered horrors deeper yet.

Malice sign was everywhere, etheric hieroglyphics etched into the brick and cement. Faint smears of ichor glowed under his teshuva's vision, marking where ferales had drooled over their prey. Maybe the bestial demons had snagged just cockroaches and pigeons, but Liam feared the worst.

Or maybe around here, a quick, violent death was less unspeakable horror and more business as usual.

Jilly stopped on a corner beneath a busted lamp and stared down the street. "That's it, down there. This is as far as I got after Rico stabbed me."

His teshuva shifted, tasting the passage of innumerable malice that had followed the riot of negative emotions that swirled on the street. However much of her blood had been spilled here, though, it had been trodden away by many careless boots.

"You made it a good long way." Liam wondered whom he was trying to soothe, her with her pained memory or himself with his present fury. As if breaking into the Cook County prison to remove her attacker's lung was justice. Still, his fist clenched at the thought.

She cast him an indecipherable glance. "Yeah, I made it all the way into the demon's arms."

They'd been his arms. Or the teshuva had taken his appearance anyway. He knew her one glimpse of him before the demon came to her hadn't been the seed of her possession, just a symptom. But he wondered if she could ever forgive that essential betrayal.

Actually, how could she, when he continued to lead her deeper into danger and damnation? He wouldn't forgive himself, even if this time she was leading.

She shook off her hesitation. "This way."

He glanced back at the couple dozen talyan ranging behind, awaiting his command. Would they find a battle with Corvus and his minions? Or just a strung-out frightened girl? "Let's go."

The flophouse actually wasn't the worst on the street. It sat back from the sidewalk a short ways beyond a wrought iron fence. Someone had stuck red plastic daisies along the walk. The gate was open.

The scent of the rusting metal caught in the back of his throat, though he didn't sense the presence of salambes. Traces of ichor were well aged, though malice sign smeared the place thick enough he could almost taste the despair himself.

Archer prowled past him. "If Corvus's djinni is dormant, we're not going to pick it up. He'll be just another wretched human."

Liam drew breath to correct Archer's harsh interpretation, but let it go. Since it seemed fairly accurate. "Once we're in, the djinni won't be dormant long."

Archer inclined his head in agreement. "Flush the Blackbird?"

Ecco approached on the last words. "Did someone say flush? This place is the toilet to do it."

Liam rubbed his forehead and sighed. He knew now was not the time for a lesson in compassion. Not that men possessed by demons had much room for compassion. "It's not a big building. Teams of two. Door-to-door. No need to call out. We'll know if you find him."

Liam held Jilly back with a hand at her elbow as the rest broke along their preferred lines and filed into the building. She tensed against him, not hard enough to yank free, just enough to let him know she begrudged the restraint.

"You're afraid," he said. At her hard glance, he tsked. "For Dory, I know. But don't add your negative emotions to the maelstrom. Even if you don't bring a malice storm down on us, you'll still cloud your view."

She took in a breath, and though she didn't meet his gaze again, for just a moment, she leaned into his touch. Then she set her shoulders back and gave a stiff nod. "Right. Can we go now?"

"Do you know which room was hers?"

"The girls didn't have their own rooms, just took whatever was available."

He blew the demon's senses wide as they proceeded between the daisies. From the mingled strains of lust and disgust soiling the general pall of apathy and consumption, he guessed the building was still a bordello in daily use. The miasma was so thick, he couldn't tell if Dory or Corvus had come through. No drifting scent of rain washed the air.

Maybe if he was touching Jilly . . . but that was just an excuse. They'd find out soon enough.

The talyan spread through the building, their soft footfalls lost beneath the creak of bedsprings, muttered curses, and the draft that moved through the shabby halls.

"Come on." He headed down an empty hall.

Jilly followed. "Maybe this is pointless."

"Maybe." He figured she knew that, on some level, she didn't want to find out what happened to Dory. Because it wouldn't be good.

He flattened his hand against the first door and spurred the teshuva higher. The walls and ceiling pulsed with old energy signatures, malice and human, but nothing else. He knocked anyway. No answer.

Jilly stood a few steps away, her head cocked and gaze fixed on the stairway at the end of the hall. "Let's go up."

"But . . ." He stopped himself. "All right."

They had just started toward the stairs when the scream rang out.

Jilly bolted ahead of him. Despite his burst of speed, she was already up to the landing before he caught her arm.

"Let me go." Her voice vibrated with the demon. "That was Dory."

"I know." He didn't let her go, but he hauled her along as he strode for the source of the shriek.

Lex hovered in the hall, staring into an open doorway. He took a step forward just as a body came flying backward through the door. Talya, Liam guessed, by the black clothes, but moving too fast to identify. He shoved Jilly behind him and leapt to the fight.

He had only a brief impression of nicotine-stained walls, and then the etheric blaze of Corvus's djinni blinded him. He continued forward in a rush. But he left the hammer sheathed. He couldn't risk hitting Dory, even though she was screaming loud enough to track if she'd stop racing from corner to corner like a panicked rat.

He closed with Corvus in a blunt collision that rattled his bones. For all the damage done to him in the building collapse earlier in the winter, Corvus was still a powerful man, his body honed from many lifetimes of battle.

Liam knew he couldn't sap the teshuva or he'd have no chance against the djinni, but he couldn't clear the demonic dazzle from his vision.

Damn, but Corvus was strong. The djinn-man's hands closed around his skull, and Liam wrenched backward to prevent Corvus from twisting his head off.

"Liam!" Jilly's cry was a clarion call in the darkness. With a sudden shock, his vision snapped into hunter's light. Eerie tracers of etheric energy patterned the room. If only he could turn those tracers into bonds to trap the ascendant djinni.

Instead, he jolted forward again to head-butt Corvus. The *reven* at his temple flared, bright enough that even he could see the violet gleam blazing from the interrealm rift that marked him as possessed.

Corvus staggered back. He reached for Dory as he fell.

"No, you don't," Liam growled.

But Dory held out her arms, wrapping herself around the windmilling djinn-man. They went down in a tangle. That looked like a setup. Liam released the hammer.

Jilly dragged at his elbow. "Don't hit her."

Like he'd done the salambe-ridden woman in the haint-haunted apartment. He'd known that moment would come back to get him.

In a heartbeat, the djinni rose in a smoky yellow column. It dragged Corvus up behind it more quickly than any human could have moved. Dory was knocked aside in a loose-limbed sprawl.

With Jilly crowding close, Liam couldn't swing without risk. Corvus gave him a single meaningful look, his lazy eye rolling as if in sympathy. Then the half-loose djinni yanked him backward out the window.

"Damn it," Liam growled. "Not again."

The glass shattered. Corvus disappeared, with that faint teasing grin still on his lips.

Liam raced to the window. He could hope for a terrible splatter, but they were only on the second story. An easy fall for a powerful djinn-man.

Sure enough, Corvus landed on an abandoned car. His impact knocked the cement blocks out from under it and the dent in the roof was impressive, but he swung himself down and landed on his feet.

He glanced up once, meeting Liam's gaze, and then he ran.

Liam pulled himself into the window frame, ignoring the shattered glass.

"Oh no." Jilly's cry drew him back. "No."

He paused for a moment, torn. Literally and figuratively, judging by the amount of blood pouring from his hands.

He went to Jilly.

She was cradling Dory. "Not again," she moaned, echoing his words.

No, not again. This time it was worse.

The faint whiff of rain clung to Dory, and her smile was vague.

Unlike angels and djinn, the teshuva had lost the ability to see souls when they were exiled from both heaven and hell. But Liam didn't need that dubious talent. He knew what he wouldn't see.

Dory had lost her soul.

CHAPTER 28

Jilly guessed she must be crying because she saw the spatter of wet on her hands as she clutched Dory, but she didn't feel anything. "Too late," she whispered.

Dory blinked up at her. "Jilly." Her voice was thick, and her words came slowly. "Hey. Is it late? That must be why I'm so tired."

"Yeah." Jilly knew the other talyan had gathered. A few had gone in pursuit of Corvus. She'd heard Liam issue the order. But he'd stayed.

So had Sera, and with her, Archer, who hovered near the window as if he'd rather be out on the street. "You'd think Corvus would've developed a healthy fear of heights after I threw him out the last window."

Sera shushed him.

Jilly could have told her his flippancy didn't bother her. Nothing hurt her. "Dory, where's the rest of the solvo?"

"I took it all. He said then we could be together."

"He's gone," Jilly pointed out.

"No. We're together."

Jilly supposed her sister was right, in a way. Soulless together. She glanced at Liam. "We have to get her somewhere safe, somewhere the salambes can't find her."

He hustled them out of the apartment and down the

hall, his fingers firm around her arm. She didn't protest. His grip steadied her. No, more than that, held her together.

She'd had to attend court dates with her kids, and once, identify a body of a young man who'd passed through the halfway house. She'd done it with tears—half sorrow, half frustration—burning in her eyes.

Escorting her sister's upright cadaver, she summoned the strict control Liam had pushed so hard. She placed her boots with precision, side by side with his, her eyes dry as the tenebraeternum's bone-dust wind.

One tenant peered out as they passed, her salt-and-pepper hair in rollers. "That's right. You empty that trash out of here."

Sera wrinkled her nose. "She's no worse than the rest."

The old woman returned the grimace with a snarl. "Oh, she's the emptiest kind of all." She slammed her door.

Jilly tried to summon up some curiosity about whether the woman was another like Lau-lau, mysteriously cognizant of the war around them. But it was hard to care when she couldn't feel.

The league had been on foot, and there was no way they were going to summon a cab in this neighborhood. They made it only halfway down the block.

"I'm tired," Dory repeated.

Liam glanced at Archer. "Find us a ride."

"Around here, they're probably already stolen anyway." Archer disappeared down a side street with Sera in his wake.

Liam settled himself on Dory's other side. "Let's keep moving. I don't like the way those malice are gathering."

Jilly glanced up, the first hint of feeling coming back to her. A feeling of fear. "Can they get to Dory?"

"Without her soul, I don't know why they would. Which is what's worrying me."

Jilly shook her head, trying to get some sense back.

Of course he was right. The malice fed on negative emotions. Dory was just one limp noodle of indifference, not a meal at all.

Still, she kept an eye on the flittering oily shadows that paced them down the street. "I got in the way, didn't I?"

"You were worried about Dory."

She noticed he hadn't said no. "I should have been focused on Corvus."

He kept scanning the shadows. "Your impulsiveness is no more changeable than . . ." He hesitated. "I was going to say your eye color, but of course that changes, even more often than your hair, I imagine." He rubbed his temple. "Don't blame yourself."

"Do you blame me?" Her voice sounded small in her own ears.

He was silent a moment. "Maybe I don't know any more why we're doing this. Is it to save our souls? The world? Or to save people like your sister?" He shook his head. "I'm as lost as you are, Jilly."

And that *was* her fault, she knew. He'd led the league fine, one fight, one night at a time. Then she'd come barging in.

"I won't make that mistake again." She didn't add that she had no more reasons to make that mistake. "I'll be the perfect talya. I'll do whatever you say."

She bit back what sounded awfully like a sob. No need for her feelings to come back now. Just as well if they'd stay dead forever.

Liam didn't respond, his gaze fixed on a car turning the corner ahead. "There's Archer."

She sagged, relieved he didn't scoff. She wouldn't blame him for deciding she was more trouble than she was worth.

The late-model Cadillac that pulled up next to them sparkled more than anything on the street, obviously well loved.

"There were plenty less flashy," Sera was saying as Liam opened the door.

"Yes." Archer drew the syllable out with teasing patience. "But he said he had anything I could possibly want. I wanted his car."

"He meant the drugs or possibly that girl on his arm, obviously." Sera quieted when Dory moaned. "How's she doing?"

"You have solvo?" Dory's voice was pitiful.

The pointless surge of fury almost made Jilly drop her sister into the car. She steeled her demon-amped muscles to guide the bowed blond head past the doorframe. "No more, Dory."

Maybe she was worse than Corvus now, to withhold the only thing that would soothe her sister. A faster slide and deeper descent into nothingness.

There was plenty of room for the three women in the back, even with Dory sprawled across the seat. Jilly held her sister's hand, but between the two of them, she doubted they could have melted an ice cube, given the coldness of their joined hands.

She let the cold seep deeper. Maybe it would kill the ache. Maybe it would finally harden her, sharpen her into the weapon Liam wanted her to be. "Stop at Lau-lau's."

Liam glanced at her. "The energy sinks around the warehouse should keep the salambes out."

She didn't call him on the "should." "The league doesn't care about soul-struck humans. If anyone can help, it will be someone like Lau-lau, another human who knows what we're up against." Jilly wasn't that person—wasn't even *a* person anymore.

Be hard, she reminded herself. Sharp. Don't notice the way he stiffened. She wasn't accusing him. He had his own fight. And she'd been on the wrong side of it too long already.

Liam nodded at Archer, who turned the car to Chinatown.

The light in Lau-lau's shop window spilled djinni-yellow across the street. Jilly wasn't surprised. How had she not noticed her landlady's odd hours? Not like the strange smells and weird displays were such a great disguise. No, she'd just been oblivious. Because she had enough problems of her own. She smiled mirthlessly at her ignorance.

Archer parked in front of the shop. Liam helped ease Dory out from the backseat. She moaned but made no effort to hold herself upright.

Jilly scrambled out. "I've got her."

Liam didn't release his hold. "Get the door."

She set her jaw. "I know you want to go after Corvus."

Archer didn't actually rev the engine in agreement, but he might as well have. Liam never moved. "Archer, Sera, recall a talya with a scour-class teshuva and get a line on Corvus's trail. Jilly, you get the damn door."

With a muttered curse, she did, calling out a greeting as she went in. She pushed a smoking brazier out of the doorway. The ginger-scented unguent inside looked like the mess Lau-lau had been cooking down earlier. Jilly hoped it was having some effect on keeping demons at bay.

Liam followed, with Dory swung up into his arms. Jilly knew the strength and comfort of that embrace. Just as she knew it wasn't doing her sister any good at all.

Lau-lau emerged from the back room. Her expression was nearly as blank as any haint's. "Why have you brought her here?"

Jilly stumbled over her own feet, weariness and shock at the rejection almost bringing her to her knees. And Liam already had his hands full. But he stepped forward. "She needs help."

"She needs a soul," Lau-lau snapped. "Wouldn't have hurt to have a spine earlier either."

Liam shook his head. "Don't judge, *wu-po*."

Lau-lau narrowed her eyes. "You've been doing your homework."

"I like to know what I'm up against."

A sudden grin split the old woman's mask of censure.

"'Witch' is such an old-fashioned word. But there might be hope for you yet."

Jilly shifted impatiently. "Done?"

Lau-lau glanced at her. "You already guessed I might not be able to help."

"Better than nothing." Jilly knew the weak exhaustion was in her tone. But if she couldn't let her guard down here, she might as well walk out onto the street and open herself to the malice.

"Nothing is right, all right," Lau-lau said. But she gestured for Liam to slide Dory into the office chair behind the counter. Dory slumped there, jaundiced and pallid as the burn-etched bone fetish beads hanging by the register.

While Lau-lau poked at Dory, Jilly rounded on Liam. She hissed, "You thought calling her a witch would inspire her to help us?"

"I thought calling her a witch only made sense, since she is one. Plus, she obviously thinks it's cute that I'm trying to learn your ways."

"My ways? Would that be the demon slaying? But you already knew those ways—better than me. My abject failures? You already knew that too." More cruel words caught in her throat and she choked. He reached out for her—as if the Heimlich maneuver could dislodge her demon or the lump in her throat—but she flinched away. "You can go now. There's nothing more you can do." He had to go before she lost it completely.

He dropped his hand to his side in a fist. "There's nothing you can do either. So we'll stay until we know for sure what nothingness looks like."

But he went to the door, staring out into the night. Maybe watching for salambes or something worse, she thought. Or maybe wishing he could go. In tense silence, they waited for Lau-lau to finish her exam. Although what there was to see, Jilly didn't know.

Lau-lau shuffled into the back room for a few minutes, waving away Jilly's anxious questions. When she returned, she carried a small wand.

Witch. Liam mouthed the word at Jilly.

Lau-lau held the wand over Dory. "In some black magics, sorcerers draw the soul from the body and prevent its return using charmed objects."

"Dory had nothing on her," Jilly said. "She didn't even have a coat."

"Nothing *on* her," Lau-lau murmured.

It wasn't really a wand, Jilly saw, but more like a dowsing rod, bent slightly off the true. Lau-lau balanced the rod between her fingers. The end dipped toward Dory's forehead.

The furrowed skin at Dory's brow split. But instead of blood, a gleam of white ichor beaded like a pearl.

"Solvo." Jilly's breath caught painfully as the bead welled up, broke, and wept across Dory's forehead. The solvo hardened into a small asymmetrical star. "Can you get it all out?"

"I don't know." Lau-lau let the rod wander again. It brushed over Dory's chest and hovered above her heart.

Dory arched upward, and Jilly closed her eyes. She didn't have to see Lau-lau nudge aside the neckline of Dory's shirt to picture the spreading rays of solvo.

A tug at her arm made her open her eyes. Liam was staring down at her. "Come on."

She resisted. "Where?"

"Just come sit with me." He led her to one of the planter stands and pressed her down before pulling over another of the heavy ceramic stools. He handled it as if it weighed nothing. Which, of course, it didn't. Not to him. Nothing stood in his way or resisted his might. How nice for him. How nice for the world, even if it didn't know about him.

How nice for her, if she could stand to let go of her own obstinacy.

The crowded shelves blocked her view of Dory, and as her visceral horror eased a bit, she realized that had been his intent. "I'm fine."

"I wasn't." He rubbed his temple, then seemed to realize what he was doing. He settled his hands on the grip of the war hammer half veiled in his coat. "The solvo has marked her just as we are marked by the teshuva coming up through the flesh."

Did that mean an eternity for Dory, locked in soulless limbo? "And I thought being damned was bad," Jilly murmured.

"There are fates worse than death." Liam's voice was low and grim.

He stared blindly ahead. Where the *reven* reached the corner of his eye, pale violet sparks arced across his pupil. Never at rest. That was a terrible fate.

Straining against the ache in her body, as if unshed tears had frozen in her muscles, she reached across the space between their stools. She took his hand from the cold steel and laced her fingers through his.

That focused him.

"No demons," she murmured. "Just us."

He squeezed her hand, and his gaze was purely blue.

They sat in silence like that until Lau-lau came over. "I lured out a few more strands of solvo." She gestured vaguely at her forehead, navel, and pelvis. "But the dowser never stopped moving. It's still in there."

Jilly stood to pace. "Because good news just might stop my heart." She wrapped her arms around herself, her hand—still warm from Liam's—pressed under her breast.

"And only the good die young." Liam rose to stand behind the older woman. "Do you have any other secrets for us?"

Lau-lau shrugged. "I'm old."

Jilly scowled. What was that supposed to mean? That her landlady was one of the bad guys? Liam let it pass with a nod, so she just huffed out a breath. "Then what next? How do we retrieve Dory's soul?"

He stared at her. "You've seen the soulflies. There's no way we could hunt them all down around the city, capture and reassemble them. Presupposing that's even possible."

She set her jaw. "If we can help Dory, we can stop the salambes. Stop Corvus."

She knew she was reaching. Who said there was a connection anymore between Dory and Corvus? Just because Dory imagined herself in love with an immortal demon-ridden gladiator didn't mean the feeling was mutual. How could a being of pure evil and the soulless body it inhabited even feel love?

Lau-lau sighed. "I'll see what I can find. Most cultures believe that lost souls are always drawn back to their homes."

Liam chuckled without humor. "Most cultures also think higher forces are keeping watch, trying to save them. Which just goes to show you."

Lau-lau raised one eyebrow and swept him head to toe with a glance. "And aren't they right?" She blew out a long breath that hollowed her cheeks. "There's nothing more I can do for her. Go now. And put the brazier back. Who knows what else will blow in tonight without it?"

She turned away, looking more like an old woman than Jilly had ever seen. She bit her lip and glanced at Liam. He shook his head and went to lift her sister from the chair. Dory's bleached hair tumbled around her face to hide the solvo that marked her as blatantly as the te-shuva's *reven*.

"We'll take her upstairs to your apartment," he said.

Jilly hesitated. She should be glad to be home, just like those lost souls Lau-lau had mentioned. But it didn't feel right anymore. "Let's go back to the warehouse."

He studied her a moment in silence, then nodded.

Since he'd put all his people on the hunt, Jilly called for a cab. As they headed out to the sidewalk, she glanced three stories up over her shoulder at her apartment window with its peeling red trim and wondered if she'd ever see it the same way again.

Or if she'd ever see it again, period.

She played the drunk girl with passed-out friend for

the cabbie's benefit as they settled in the backseat with Dory. Liam pulled her close for maximum show.

He brushed his lips over the crown of her head. "Almost there."

Almost home. A bubble of laughter caught in her throat. She choked it down for fear it might sound hysterical. Home. All that awaited them was a jumbled maze of old furniture and even older and more-confusing demon-fighting warriors.

But she couldn't stop herself from leaning into the shelter of his embrace.

The warehouse was quiet and dark. Since Liam hadn't taken any calls, she guessed the Corvus chase and tracking Envers and his feralis had been an absolute bust.

They took Dory to her old room. Liam bent the window frame so it wouldn't open, in case Dory thought to reunite with her lover, while Jilly redressed her sister in a clean T-shirt. Dory was smaller than some of the teens whose bruises, tears, and rages Jilly had tended at the halfway house, as if her very presence had been sucked inward by the solvo that gleamed with eerie beauty, strung along her median line like tiny starfish made of pearls.

Jilly stood back with a sigh. Liam guided her out of the room and locked the door behind her. Side by side, they walked to the kitchen. He flicked on the light and went to the stove.

Jilly contemplated the dirty dishes in the sink. She'd have to put up a sign pointing to the dishwasher. Not that the technique had helped with her siblings. Maybe this time she'd decorate it with pictures of her pointy knives.

A minute later, Liam retrieved her from her paralysis. He seated her with a cup of coffee and a brownie. "We'll do whatever we can."

She twisted the words back at him. "We can't do anything."

He reached out and took her hands to wrap them

around the coffee cup until her fingers warmed between the ceramic and his skin.

"Liam?" Jonah stood in the doorway, his thickly bandaged arm in a sling. "Thank God you're back."

Liam stood. Jilly was half a heartbeat behind him. "What is it? You found Corvus?"

"Oh yeah." Jonah's lips curled. "He's out front on the street. And he brought his army."

CHAPTER 29

Liam leaned over the edge of the warehouse roof. The wind tugged at his coat, worried at his hair. He hadn't had good luck with roofs lately, but it was the best location to get a feel for the scope of what Corvus had arrayed against them.

On the street below, the haints stood in ragged rows straggling out into the shadows, a dozen deep. Salambes smoked between them, their numbers unclear as they phased in and out. The oily ink of malice formed a black-curtain backdrop to the whole display, while pinpricks of perfect light—aimless soulflies—highlighted the scene.

"It's like a Bollywood dance number," Ecco noted. "But with way-less-cool costumes."

"Could be worse," Liam muttered.

Ecco slanted a glance at him. "Than a musical in hell?"

"Could be on ice." As he spoke, a soft rain began to fall.

Ecco laughed.

The rain closed in around them, isolating the warehouse from the rest of the city. An illusion, Liam knew, yet painfully accurate. No one would be coming to help them.

But it had always been that way. They were trapped with no escape.

The line of haints peeled back to leave a clearing in their center. Corvus stepped into the void. To Liam's roused teshuva, Corvus's shaved head reflected the flicker of the salambes' unholy light.

"Take a note," Liam said to no one in particular. "The league needs to invest in rocket launchers."

Such mundane methods wouldn't disrupt demonic emanations—might even feed them—but a well-placed cluster bomb would take care of the haints. He couldn't let himself remember that they'd been human once. And that he had been too.

Corvus stared upward. He threw back his head, arms spread wide. "Where is my better half? Bring me my woman."

Augmented by the djinni, its powers unfettered by the anchor of a human soul, his voice vaporized the rain so his words carried to the warehouse in a cone of coiling smoke.

"Good special effects for Ice Capades," Ecco said. "I can't believe even djinn-men have girlfriends these days. What does he have that I don't? At least I have half my soul." When no one answered, he sighed. "Should I get Dory?"

Liam had left Jilly with her sister. "Of course not."

Jonah, silent until now on Liam's other side, shifted. "If that's all he wants, we might give her to him and hope he goes away. She got herself—and now us—into this mess, believing she loved him. We can't stand against that crowd. We are too few."

Ecco punched Jonah's shoulder, not lightly. "If you think Corvus is bad, imagine facing Jilly when you say you're taking her sister away. She'll tear off your other arm."

Liam winced, though he couldn't decide which was worse, Ecco's insensitivity or the clear picture in his mind of Jilly's reaction to Jonah's expedience. "Armageddon," he murmured.

"Damn straight," Ecco said. "And while you're thinking Armageddon, you should also ask yourself why Corvus and the djinni both desire poor deluded Dory of the dreadful decision making. Can't be true love alone."

"His better half." Jonah gave an ugly laugh. "You're offering marital counseling to a soulless, brain-damaged husk and the bottomless evil jerking him around and the drug-addict prostitute they tag teamed? We're the only thing standing between a rogue djinn-man and the rest of the world. If we fall here—"

Liam kept his voice soft, with none of Corvus's theatrics. "No. We make a stand."

Ecco nodded, but Jonah looked unconvinced. "Is that the leader of the Chicago league speaking? Or a mate who fears betraying his bond?"

Liam straightened to look Jonah hard in the eye. "I say it."

Jonah inclined his head.

But the question gnawed at Liam. His qualifications had always been suspect. Now there was just an obvious reason to doubt him.

Again Corvus bellowed, "Where is she?"

Liam pitched his own demon to carry his voice. "She is not yours."

"You have yours already, talya. Don't thieve."

Liam smiled bitterly. "As you have stolen Dory's soul? Stolen all those souls?"

"Released," Corvus cried. "Freed as I have been."

Ecco huffed thoughtfully. "Ever notice how 'evil' is 'love' spelled backward with one different letter? It's like we're just one fucked-up spell checker away from eternal doom."

Corvus lifted his arms, and the djinni rose above him. The poisonous yellow edges of it bled into the rain so it seemed to fill half the street, rising as high as the second story of the warehouse.

"Oh shit," Ecco said. "That's no good."

Jilly sat beside Dory's bed. Her sister twisted restlessly until the sheets wound around her like a burial shroud.

On her sweat-beaded brow, the solvo glistened. Jilly wanted to tear it out, never mind the violence.

Out in the hall, the thud of boots distracted her. Harsh male voices called to one another in low tones, as if they didn't want to disturb her.

Too late. She was officially disturbed.

She rose from the bedside and looked down at her sister. Too late indeed. She wanted to weep, but her eyes were dry, as if the night had carved her down to bare, ether-etched bone. She touched Dory's cheek gently and went to the door.

The talyan were returning, pounding up the stairs from the basement, laden with weapons.

Archer had two in each fist. She stopped him. "Hand it over."

He paused as the other talyan rushed past, and gave her a superior sniff.

She waggled her fingers in a give-it-here motion. He tossed her the mace.

She hefted the short-handled weapon, admired the glint of light off the dozens of steel points. "It goes with my hair."

Archer grinned. "Yeah. Come on, then."

She hesitated, then shook her head. "I'm going to find Liam."

He nodded. "What you gotta do. He's up top." Then he was gone with the others, heading for the front walk, where the talyan would meet the enemy head-on.

Leaving her to realize that had always been her problem, doing what others said she had to do. She and authority had never gotten along, and fucked-up fate was just another force telling her how fast to dance.

But somewhere along the way, she'd started believing in fate.

Maybe about the time she learned demons were real. So what other mystical, magical powers of the universe had she been refusing to let sway her?

She needed to find Liam. She'd meet her own demons head-on too.

*   *   *

Liam stiffened as the first of his talyan burst from the warehouse to confront Corvus's army. "Let's get down there."

"Wait a minute," Jonah cautioned. "Once you're in the thick of it, you won't have this overview. See what they're going to do, how they're going to fight. Then go down."

"They'll fight like demons, I bet," Ecco said. "I'm on it." He turned to go, then rocked back on his heels, jolting Liam. "Oh, baby."

Liam glanced over his shoulder and froze.

When avenging angels of the cupid size fell, they could only hope they looked half as badass as his reluctant tyro.

From spiked hair to spiked mace to the wide stance of her booted feet, Jilly exuded warrior maiden. Not maiden, his body reminded him with sudden inappropriateness. Those small but steady hands had been wrapped around him not so long ago.

He cleared his throat. "I thought you were with your sister."

"I can't help her." Jilly raised her chin. "But I can help you."

Liam stiffened. "Whatever you're proposing—" And he could guess, considering her purposeful grip on the mace.

"Okay, then, we're going." Ecco hauled Jonah behind him. "Maybe we'll leave a few malice, just for fun."

Liam ignored them. He couldn't look away from the gold and amethyst sparkle of her eyes, the diamonds of misted rain in her hair. How could he stand beside her when he was a starving ex-blacksmith who'd only worked in iron and steel, base and dull? And even that had been a long time ago. These dark nights, he was master only of blood and ichor.

She shifted the mace to one hand and let it swing down to her side. "The league needs *us*."

He didn't pretend to misunderstand her. There wasn't

time for that either. "I don't know what I have to give."
Not anymore.

"Me," she said simply.

His bones turned to rain. He held himself straight by
will alone. "I wouldn't give him Dory. Corvus won't get
you either."

"I'm more than he can handle." She bit her lip, and
the carnelian flush made him wish he'd been the cause.
"Together, we might be more than he can survive."

So this would bring her to him—violence and the
promise of revenge. He supposed he should be glad
it was so simple and clear. The ravager in him roused
willingly to face the tenebrae, but a deeper impulse remained to take her hand and run, somewhere the league
didn't matter because evil didn't exist. He couldn't guess
where that might be, since he'd never known such a
place, even as a boy. So he imagined his big, ugly bed,
minus the voyeur cherubim. Wrapped in her fierce embrace, body and soul, he'd take her hand and ask her,
would she have him now? With life and death, heaven
and hell, damnation and salvation out of the way, would
she still have him?

Here in the world, though, evil still existed, and gave
no quarter for such irrelevant questions. Plus, she was
shivering in the cold rain, the diamond droplets melting
into the blue streaks of her hair.

How could she not hate him for making her a pawn in
this war? She'd spent all her life refusing to be confined
by fate, yet her possession had been inescapable, and
he was the figurehead for that damnation. He wouldn't
have blamed her for rebelling. Instead, she'd thrown
herself into his fray with all her might. He admired her
fortitude, needed her help, and had no defense against
her touch, even when she reached out to him with the
end of the world in her eyes. He'd never break free of
her. And he'd never want to.

Besides, he couldn't stand to see her cold. He pulled
her under his arm and wrapped the edge of his duster

around her. Her skin was chiller than the metal of her weapon.

"Nice mace," he murmured.

"It's nothing," she said. "No, really, compared to what we're going to do, it's nothing." She tilted her face up, her gaze fixed on his. "Kiss me."

"*Xiao*-Jilly." He couldn't stop himself.

"Don't," she said. "Just . . . kiss me."

He thought the world would shift to gray around them, tumble them into the demon realm. But he felt only the soft parting of her lips, the warm exhalation of her breath, the yearning in his flesh.

She drew back, her gaze sliding away. "Take me down."

Oh, he wanted to. Right there in the puddles gathering on the asphalt. But that's not what she meant. Down to the battle. Only in close quarters could they unleash their joined power. The danger was incalculable. But when she slipped free of his embrace, when they chose the league and its eternal mission instead of running for that imaginary place without evil, he knew the price had already been paid.

Chapter 30

Despite her puffy coat, Jilly was cold inside. Fear, she told herself, as she and Liam raced through the warehouse to the front door. Fear of the tenebrae army, fear of Corvus's power, fear of death.

And foremost, fear of the tall, lean man at her side and what his hands on her could do.

And she wasn't worrying about falling into the demon realm either.

They burst through the front doors, out onto the sidewalk, where the talyan were fully engaged, moving like a hundred men. But the ranks of haints and salambes were like a thousand.

As each haint fell, the salambe phased to a new husk before the talya fighting it could get close to drain the demonic emanations. The salambes kept the talyan going in a merry dance. Without the merry part.

With the first stumble, the first sign of exhaustion, the salambe/haint pairings would move in and finish the talyan. That stumble hadn't come yet. But it would.

Liam cursed and reached to pull her behind him.

She resisted and moved instead to stand in front of him, facing him. "Together. Remember?"

"No. You stay here. We need to regroup, remember our formations."

"We don't have time for that. Let them do what you've trained them to do."

"I'm supposed to lead them."

His gaze was fixed over her head, on the battle. He wanted to be in the midst of it, she knew, keeping his men safe. She was holding him back. No, she had to believe that while he might not want her as his bonded mate, he would always do anything for the league.

"I can't do this alone." She flattened her palm in the middle of his chest. The bracelet winked, flaring with each shout or otherworldly shriek in the clashes behind her, as if drawing that energy. She hoped it would. Liam had told her she must take control of it, and she would, but she needed him, his strength and certainty.

The sound of battle was right behind her, but she didn't turn. Of all her secret doubts, she never doubted Liam would have her back.

He dragged his gaze down to her. "Jilly?" His voice sounded far away. Then he clamped his hand over hers.

At the touch of his skin, as always, the thrill flared in her. She stiffened, waiting for the remembered sense of danger, of losing herself. But unlike last time, now she felt only a fierce joy, a resonant echo through her being, as if part of her had been calling out, and finally heard a reply.

With Liam beside her, she felt she could bend hell itself into a puzzle no demon would ever escape. She had one heartbeat to contemplate that maybe she still had something to learn from him about reining in her bravado, and then the tenebraeternum closed around them.

As if the rain had become a shell, enveloping them apart from all the rest, the featureless gray spread in all directions. It had never felt so vast, and she realized her connection with Liam had never been so complete.

Too bad it had taken this extreme to bind them. Ah well, what did she know about steady relationships anyway?

She didn't want to step away from him, not with the

infinite nothingness all around. Only her bracelet—the demon's knot-work trap—glinted. Somehow, she knew a misstep would be the end of her, led by marshlights into the mist, never to return. Even Liam the Irishman with his hammer couldn't bash through this gloom.

Ominous blooms of smoked orange managed to make the otherwise featureless gray even more threatening. "The salambes," Liam said. "The tenebraeternum exists parallel to our world with only the Veil keeping us separate, which is why when we shift between the realms, we're still 'here.' The salambes are using that overlap to phase through the tenebraeternum as they jump from haint to haint."

"No wonder they're so fast."

Frustration sharpened his voice. "And the talyan can't touch them while they're out of the human realm."

She curled her hand to tangle her fingers with his. "Then it's a good thing we're here."

He looked down at her and his lips twitched in the beginning of a smile. "Yeah, good thing we're in hell." Gently, he untangled himself and ran his fingers down her wrist to the bracelet. "Let's see who else you can trap back on this side."

She hoped somebody, since she'd epic failed with him. But she'd always known what he wanted her for. As for her wanting more . . . well, as his weapon, she'd still have his hands all over her. So she took a breath and sank into the gray, mesmerized by the faint glowing weave of the bracelet.

When she and Sera had been watching over Dory, the other talya had explained, haltingly, how she and her mate had found themselves in the demon realm. A near-death experience in Sera's childhood and her work as a thanatologist had given her a unique slanting view of the other-realms even before Corvus's attempts to destroy the Veil had summoned her teshuva. Battling Corvus, Archer had almost lost what remained of his soul, and only Sera, wielding the soul-cleaver pendant, had been able to patch the Veil.

Jilly looked up at Liam, wishing . . . No, she'd never felt herself to be the kind of person who patched things up. "I can get them lost."

That's where all this had led her. To the realization that she'd run so hard from entanglements, she'd barred anyone from holding her. No wonder the kids had related to her; she'd never had a clue. And no wonder Envers at the halfway house had cut her loose. He might have been in the pay of the devil himself, but even the kids knew, at some point, it was time to grow up and face her fears.

Thanks to her teshuva, now she'd never grow up. But maybe a rebel without a chance could still face all the world's fears.

The first flecks of wayward soul scraps wavered through the patches of gray and intermittent orange, their light as white and pure as solvo. The lights danced around her, drawn into patterns as intricate as the whorls of the bracelet. The demon talisman froze her arm, stealing energy from the part of her spirit-self existing in this realm just as it drew ether from the tenebrae.

If she could just attract enough of the salambes, the talyan out in the world would have a chance.

The first orange glow began to take shape. Hulking, crescent-horned, scimitar-clawed shape. Then another, following the glittering trail of soulflies into the pattern that was the trap ending in the tenebraeternum, where they belonged.

"Jilly." Liam's grip on her tightened. He covered the bracelet, his hand hot on her skin, as if he could burn away the chill. And stop what they'd set in motion. "I'm thinking this is a bad idea."

"It's the only way."

"No. There are many paths. That's what you always told the kids."

"Many paths, yes. And they're all leading here. To the end."

He dragged her deeper into the gloom, the soulflies

strung out behind them. "You have to listen to me for once."

"I did. And you said this was all for the league. For the mission. For the world."

Anguish twisted his features. "Don't listen to that part. There's more than that. There's you, and me—"

The first of the salambes overtook the swarm of soul bits, swatting them aside in a contrail swirl. Liam gave a shout and leapt for it even as it attacked. She expected him to blow through it, as Ecco had during their first encounter with the incorporeal tenebrae. But Liam and the salambe collided with a force that knocked the soulflies into another swirling confusion. Jilly gasped; she knew his emanation in the demon realm wasn't his physical self—still, destruction was possible. Maybe even more perilous, since whatever happened to the demon-mottled soul of a talya after death, its chances couldn't be improved this close to the deeper nether-world of hell.

More salambes were phasing into the gray, their shapes clearer now than in the real world, as if the compatible energy gave them extra power. How unfair.

She gritted her teeth. Hell, like life, might not be fair, but she had a demon of her own, after all. She lifted her arm, the bracelet lofted high. The soulflies spiraled in, slowly at first, then making her dizzy with their quickening whirl.

The league wasn't going to win. There were too many against them, her force and Liam's split from the other talyan—split from each other—just when Corvus had found a way to bring the forces of evil together in a real army.

The soulflies were like a path, leading her farther down into the gray. She had to follow, to trap them in that spiral where they couldn't hurt anyone anymore. Where they themselves couldn't be hurt.

Because that's what she'd always believed. She'd gotten trapped in her own pain and sadness. It was just easier, safer, to stay locked inside. Wasn't Liam always telling her to be safe?

Since when had she ever done what *he* said?

At the thought of him, her heart contracted, and she realized, dimly, that it hadn't done that for a while. That beating thing. Was she dying down here in the gray? She would've thought it would hurt more.

She didn't want to hurt, and it hurt to love Liam when she wasn't sure he could love her back. Not that she'd taken the chance to ask.

Love. The word lanced through her awareness, brighter than soulflies, straight and true.

Perhaps a path out, if she was brave enough to take it.

Somewhere in the gathering darkness, the thought welled up inside her, the reminder that he didn't want her. He had a love already, the league, the mission.

Sink, the darkness whispered to her. Fall through the cracks. Get lost in the shadows.

She'd never get out.

Never have a chance to tell Liam, give him the chance to love her too.

The lost souls around her pulled her down. All those people who hadn't found hope or strength or love. Just the solace of emptiness. The weight of those tiny shards was overwhelming.

"No thanks," she whispered. "I'm not going to start listening now. I know what I want." And whom she wanted.

If ever she was going to use her defiance for her own good . . .

She pushed back. The soulflies—so gently drifting in the human realm—were a cyclone around her now, the white blur of them lightening the gray. She remembered how the black malice cyclone had spun around her and Liam, and how they'd busted free together.

She'd always wanted to go it alone, but now she needed to take a lesson from the way she'd always harped at the wary kids who'd been too disappointed, too hurt by the life that had come before.

She didn't want to be trapped in her own shit anymore. Time to get over it.

"Liam!" She didn't reach for the demon lows; instead she dredged up all the longing and entreaty she'd never voiced and flung it out to the void.

A palm slapped over hers, and strong fingers slid down to wrap around her wrist, tighter even than the band of the bracelet.

From between the shadows, first one broad shoulder, then the rest of Liam appeared. He pulled her close. "Stay with me."

At the feel of him, sturdy and real, tears welled in her eyes. She blinked hard. "I will."

He must have heard the sincerity, and the extra note of something more. He looked down at her, brow furrowed. She touched his jaw, and the confusion in his eyes vanished. He leaned down to kiss her forehead.

When he lifted his head, the other salambes had phased almost to the point of solidity and marched forward in a line. Their single upthrust teeth glinted in the soulflies' glow. Jilly didn't want to test whether her etheric body could be ripped apart by those teeth, as Dory had been bisected, to her everlasting damnation, by the pearly white line of solvo.

The closest salambe swiped at them, and Liam swung her out of the way. Her outflung arm, the knot-work bracelet a sullen gleam, trailed a churning backwash of soulflies.

As one, the salambes flinched back.

"The bracelet," she gasped as Liam danced her backward out of reach. "They're afraid of the bracelet."

"You were lucky to catch one on the rooftop using the knot-work trap," he reminded her. "The rest of them will get us before we can get them all."

She shuddered at the memory of Perrin disappearing over the ledge. Hovering in the tenebraeternum, she and Liam were even closer to a much more terrifying descent.

The soulflies gathered closer to her again, and the salambes crept closer too, until Jilly was choking on the rusted stench of them. If only salambes were as drifty and quiescent as Dory without her soul. Rain-sweet wouldn't hurt either.

But the demons didn't have souls, so the pretty white poison of solvo would have zero effect on them. Their soullessness and the haints' was what made their pairing so powerfully evil and evilly powerful.

Liam retreated another step. He wouldn't have, except for her, she knew. He couldn't wield his hammer when she was in his arms.

She was supposed to be his weapon, but she'd lost Perrin, his demon slipping away with his soul, just as she'd lost Andre, lost Dory's soul, unable to lead her sister back from the darkness that trapped her.

Damn, just when she would give her own soul to Liam to prove she was willing, she found it worth less than the tiny flecks whirling around her, which at least had the advantage of forming a shimmering pale shield between them and the salambes.

Such a thin, insubstantial shield . . .

She clutched Liam's arm. "It's not the bracelet scaring the salambes. It's the soulflies."

She twisted in his arms and dragged him forward a step. The wandering souls followed. And the salambes retreated.

"Dory and the haints are vulnerable without their souls," she started.

Liam finished her thought, "And the salambes would be vulnerable with them. Trapped in one body, just like we are."

Keeping her sheltered under his arm, he strode forward. The soulfly shield belled out ahead of them. "Hey, badass rebel girl, how about you wave them a nice 'fuck you'?"

She grinned at the bright gleam in his eye and did as he asked. At the upward sweep of her braceleted arm, the soulflies swirled out toward the salambes, which scattered in all directions.

Liam closed his grasp around her upraised fist and brought her hand to his mouth. His teeth clicked against the woven metal; then his breath was hot on her palm as he kissed the pulse point of her wrist. His gaze never left hers. "You want to show them who's really boss?"

Her heart skipped at the appearance of the faint dimple in his cheek. She nodded.

His mouth descended on hers like an avenging angel, soft as feathers and white-hot. She clutched the bunched muscles of his back, and under her hand, he felt real, unyielding, worldly. She wanted to survive this. To take her chance with him.

Behind her closed eyes, the tempest of the soulflies twinkled like a frozen sea of stars from when the universe was newly born.

Liam whispered her name against her lips.

In a heart-stopping reverberation, the white glow burst, and the real world returned, harsh and bright with color even in the dark of night.

In this realm, the tenebrae—malice, ferales, and salambes—were a wild tangle of ether and distorted flesh. The talyan struggled on all sides.

Jilly slipped from Liam's arms even as he unleashed the hammer in a single move of lethal beauty. She flattened her palm between his shoulder blades, and her pulse raced at the deadly sensuality of his blacksmith strength pitted against a foe that he would bend and break.

She fisted her hand in his coat as he swung, and the hammer swept the soulflies on a tsunami of etheric energy, blasting them toward the salambes. The salambes fled ahead of the bright flecks to bury themselves in the empty haint husks.

The soulflies, drawn in tow, stuck, half melted in the haints.

One salambe, embedded in its haint, shrieked. The malice took up the chant. But they backed away. The salambe, its smoking orange leaking into the night, strained to jump free as Liam approached, hammer at the ready.

But it couldn't get away, locked down by the shredded scrap of soul, shining on the haint's forehead like an echo of the solvo stars that had blossomed over Dory's empty flesh.

Down the line, the haints staggered drunkenly as the trapped salambes struggled to free themselves. Liam swung again, Jilly lending her teshuva's strength, to arc another wave of soulflies across the battlefield of the street.

A few salambes fled to the shadows, malice in a black tide around them.

They split and wove around one huge form that did not flee.

"I will not be trapped," Corvus cried. "Not by these."

His djinni—half again as tall as any of the salambes—towered over him, a poisonous yellow mushroom cloud that pushed the soulflies away.

But the tiny white flecks crept closer to the trembling gladiator body.

Ferales, never the sharpest pins in the voodoo doll of demonic influence, flailed through the fight, inattentive to the turning tide. The talyan attacked with renewed vigor. With the salambes trapped inside the faltering haint bodies, the talyan were able to close and bring their teshuva to bear to drain the tenebrae. The clashing demonic emanations shivered the rain as it fell.

Liam advanced on Corvus. Jilly followed close, her shroud of soulflies lighting the night.

"You've lost." Liam's voice thrummed with demonic lows.

Corvus snarled. "That never stops your teshuva." He threw up his hands, a thrust of ether that scattered the flecks of soul.

But they returned, aimless yet tenacious as butterflies in the wind.

Corvus recoiled. "You can't win. There are not enough of you to stand against my darkness."

Jilly stepped forward. "We have each other."

Corvus's lip curled in disdain. "As we took your sister for our own, we will take that too. Have you talyan not yet discovered the name of this power that pierces the Veil? But you taught it to us, this love that is a weapon to span heaven and hell."

He meant to wound her, weaken her. Liam drew her close, his hand wrapped around her to cradle the *reven*, the place where the knife had sunk and severed her—though she hadn't known it at the time—from the life she'd had before.

She straightened her shoulders against Liam's chest. "You can't take from me what I've lost myself. *I* brought me here. And I choose a new path."

To Liam, Jilly's soft words felt straight and sharp as a freshly honed blade, cutting him to the quick. Did she think she'd lost all chance at love? God, hadn't he believed that when he'd come to understand all the forces arrayed against the league? But he wanted to be beside her, whatever she chose. And wasn't that love?

There was so much in the way, though. He circled, drawing her with him, and the net of soulflies tightened.

"You'll never find the way." Despite his words, Corvus lowered his head and took another lumbering step back. "Just as your teshuva can't stop fighting after they've lost, we've watched you talyan chase what you can't have." He glowered at them, but his lazy eye wept, and the tear was sheer as glass, only human. "What you shouldn't have."

Hearing words he'd said spoken in the djinn-man's lisping grunt made Liam's skin crawl. Under his hand, Jilly wavered as if she felt it too, a shudder that went deep into bone. The pale curtain of soulflies shivered and parted, letting through a glimpse of darkness that threatened beyond, a hell on earth always waiting. Corvus smiled.

Both the djinn-man's eyes pinned Liam with vicious

glee. Liam read the satisfaction in that glance that said he'd brought this trouble on himself.

But he'd finally figured out he was happy when trouble came in a *xiao*-pixie package with badass boots. And the tenebraeternum wasn't so tough when he had a rebel of his own at his side.

He smiled back at Corvus, feeling like they understood each other better now. "Shouldn't? Maybe. But I want it. And come teshuva, league, and all your armies of shadows, I won't be afraid to ask if she can love me in return."

Corvus roared and leapt, the djinni in the fore.

Liam met the leap halfway. He swung the hammer with all his human and teshuva force. Hammer and djinni collided, and the night blew apart in a shower of soulflies and stars.

Chapter 31

Liam rolled. Shards of slagged metal clanked around him. His head rang with a hollow sound, and his hands stung and burned. Had his forge exploded?

The street around him was a shambles. Street? Not the forge, then. Light posts bent. Concrete and asphalt buckled. Bodies lay strewn. . . .

In a cold sheet of terror, the drifting memories of his past vaporized.

"Jilly!"

He staggered to his feet, looking around wildly.

There, just a few steps away—a glint of blue against the silver rain.

He dropped to his knees, oblivious to the figures rising around them. Friend or foe, he didn't know, didn't care. Not if she didn't open those golden eyes and light his darkness.

Because none of this mattered without her.

He turned her face up to the rain. Her dusky skin was blanched, even her lips leached of color. Her silver jacket had been ripped open. A trickle of blood joined the marks of her *reven* to add intricacy to the butterfly tattooed above her breast.

He touched the spot. It was just a shallow wound, not

fatal. But she didn't rouse. Though she lay in his arms, he couldn't find her with his demon senses.

Where had she gone?

"Ah, Jilly." His voice was ragged. "What have you done to me?"

A form loomed over him. He didn't glance up as he stripped out of his coat and swathed her gently in its folds.

"Niall?" Archer crouched beside him. "We need to—"

"Take care of it."

"But—"

Liam snarled. "I have given enough. I will not give her too."

Archer backed away, moving closer to Sera.

Liam didn't miss the knowing light in their eyes. Nor did he care that he was following the talya bond down a path that led he knew not where. Since the soldier's gun had smashed into his temple and blinded him, he'd never seen so clearly, not even with the teshuva's power. He would make his way to the heart, never mind the risk.

He wrapped his fingers around her wrist below the bracelet, feeling for her pulse. Thready, distant. Since she'd been resonating with the energies the bracelet stole from the tenebrae, the shock wave of his clash with Corvus's djinni must have hit her with terrible force. "Come back," he whispered. "Without you, this means nothing."

He pressed her cold hand under his shirt, against his chest, closing the gap between them. He lowered his head to her parted lips.

So far away. He'd kept her at that distance, with his fear. Fear not just for the world but for his heart. She wasn't merely lost to some metaphysical labyrinth—they'd been there and won through already—so he couldn't rally his teshuva to the rescue this time.

This time, he'd have to go himself.

No enhanced senses, no amped strength. Just his need for her, spun through the shadows, seeking respite.

Every morning of his long-ago life, he'd breathed over the black coals of his cold forge, rousing them to the fiery intensity that had been his livelihood. To fail then had been to go hungry, which was nothing compared with what he risked now.

So he coaxed Jilly from the abyss, with his touch, with the words he'd feared to say.

"My weapon. My woman. My heart."

Her lips warmed under his, and the breath she finally sucked down was his.

He pulled her up tight against him when she cried out, "Where—?"

"Hush. I'm here. I'm always here for you."

She clutched him. "I was trapped. I didn't think I'd find my way out."

"Who better than a blacksmith to make the key? But now you're stuck with me."

She gazed up at him, and the frantic whirl of violet calmed.

"Forever." He kissed her again, long and lingering. With eternity ahead of him, he vowed he would awaken her so every new morning. "Forever, if you will."

She lifted her hand from where he'd still held it tucked against his chest, and drew his arm forward. Snug around his right bicep, a torque gleamed with twisting threads that matched the strange glow of her bracelet. "Looks like I already did."

He rotated his elbow, admiring the seamless silvery flow that circled his arm. "The recoil when the hammer hit the djinni . . ."

"What a tangled web of soulflies, demon bits, and shattered hammer."

She curved against him with a weary sigh, and he leaned close to shelter her from the rain. "Still," he said, "the tenebraeternum armed me with a matching band, but it did not give me you." He tilted her chin up to gaze into her honey-cinnamon eyes. An endless feast for his body and heart, yes, but only if she spoke the words.

After he did, of course. He was still the leader. Though it counted to him only if she was willing to follow. With her beside him, he could go on forever. "I do love you."

He felt the shudder rip through her, and for a heart-stopping moment, he feared he'd opened some abyss worse than anything the league had documented.

But she only smiled at him. "You say it with such conviction, just like you do everything else." A sheen lit her golden eyes.

Not just rain, he realized, tears. His rebel tyro cried because of him. A hammer blow to the chest would have been less shocking. "Trust me, Jilly, this is like nothing else. You are like no one else."

Her smile deepened. "I love you."

He would've stayed happily trapped in the moment, locked the world out. But around them, the bone-chill wind of the tenebraeternum whispered as Archer and Sera joined forces to shepherd the defeated demons back through the Veil. A malice screamed somewhere in the darkness, its ether unraveling, then fell silent.

Jilly touched his temple, bringing his attention back to her. "Where's Corvus?"

He rested his head against her hand. "I don't know. I was only looking for you."

"Well, the league won this battle, if not the war. We'll get him next time."

"We?" He settled on the concrete as if they had all the time in the world—which they did—and there was no place he'd rather be. Which there wasn't.

"I realized there was something bigger than me," she said.

"That'd be me."

She nudged him, gently. "Not just you. Us." A jerk of her chin indicated the other talyan, the warehouse, the league. "I get that now. The rebel finally has a cause."

"But the cause is not enough, is it? You showed me that." He tucked back wayward blue strands of her hair, softened in the rain. "Everything I know the league should stand for—salvation for the city, redemption for the teshuva, hope for the talyan—all of it doesn't matter if there's not a place for this, for you and me."

She blinked, tears spiking her lashes, and he kissed them because he knew his tyro talya would always have her spikes, and he loved her for it. Her hand dropped to his chest and fisted in his shirt as if she'd never let him go. "Why did we have to take such a winding path to get here?"

"I had to quit drifting," he said, "and you had to come out from behind that maze of walls you built around you."

"I couldn't have, not without you. You came over the walls for me."

"Through," he said. "Through the walls. Hammers are a good weapon for that. But you followed me out."

"I will always follow you." She tucked her head under his chin. "As long as you don't do anything colossally arrogant."

"Not with you around to save me from myself."

She untucked enough to peer up at him. "This won't be easy, you know. *I* won't be easy." When she bit her lip uncertainly, he caught a quick scent of sweet cherries, as if the wild wind had blown in an early spring.

He pressed his lips to her brow and closed his eyes for a moment. "Then I'll be the center of your storm."

He stood, lifting her to her feet with him. They turned to face the ruined street and the salvage warehouse with its windows cracked and ichor smears, the talyan standing in ragged ranks.

She slipped her hand through the crook of his elbow and leaned close, the torque pressed against the *reven* that curled over her breast. He smiled down at her, his heart light—and his soul too—as if they wanted to spiral in on the woman beside him, now that they'd finally found their place. "Welcome home."

Epilogue

"How convenient the league keeps a warehouse full of architectural salvage." Jilly tweaked her teshuva to heft the heavy stained-glass window into the gaping hole left by the "unexplained gas-line-leak explosion." The city inspector had eagerly latched onto that excuse, which Liam had offered without a single betraying blink. The only other explanation for such devastation would be an all-out war of some sort.

And who would believe a war existed between evil incarnate and . . . well, not good guys, but repentant demons? Plus, Liam had promised to pay for the street, although Jilly wondered if they'd have to sell the last of the aging fleet to pay for it.

"Convenient? Hardly." Sera held up her end with equal ease despite the impatient April wind that pushed at the bright patchwork of glass. "The league just has a tendency to need replacement pieces." Then she winced and cast a sidelong glance at the talya fitting the shims at the base of the window. "Oh, Jonah, damn it. I'm sorry. I might be sharing half my soul with Archer, but I shouldn't let him take my discretion too."

Jonah, his arm stump held tight against his body, didn't acknowledge her apology. "We should have abandoned this place, like we left our hotel last time we lost to the djinn-man. We can't let the league's mission be revealed."

From the doorway across the room, Liam said, "The league's mission remains. But it's past time to make a few changes, which includes standing up to the fight." Jilly's breath caught at the sight of him, tall and focused as ever, yet with a conviction now that drew her irresistibly. Good thing she was holding a window or she might just embarrass them both. He crossed to her side with a smile, as if he knew her thoughts. "Corvus and his djinni won't find us so alone next time."

Jonah rammed the shims under the frame, all crooked, and walked away.

Archer, who had arrived with Liam, stood to block him until Liam gave a small shake of his head. The blond talya shouldered past Archer into the hall, the crack of his boots on the linoleum louder than any demon worth its repenting would ever allow.

Sera winced. "So who got the discretion? Nobody here so obviously. He's still hurting."

"The teshuva healed the wound," Archer said.

Jilly shook her head. "But he is still alone."

In silence, Liam adjusted the shims while Archer fixed the window in place.

They stood back to survey their work. The plaster was broken in raw chunks and the metal fins of the window frame stuck out, but the spring sun blazed in riotous color across the floor.

"Pretty," Sera announced at the same time Archer said, "Last one." They leaned into each other with matching smiles.

Liam gathered Jilly even closer. "You got Dory settled in with the others?"

"That's why I couldn't come to bed. I know we're back on the hunt tonight, but I saw Jonah couldn't handle the window by himself, and . . ." She leaned her head against his chest, taking comfort in the steady thud of his heart. "And there were just so many. I don't know how Nanette will cope, even if she says she has other angelic possessed willing to work with Lau-lau's dowsing technique."

He smoothed his hand over her hair, then lifted her chin to meet her gaze. "Maybe they can extract all the solvo, but there's no guarantee all the pieces of her lost soul will find her again."

"And no promise the soul can take up residence in the body—I know. Nanette explained."

He brushed a tear from her cheek with the edge of his thumb. "Still, there's a chance, so there's hope."

"That's what the mated-talyan bond gives us," Sera said, her tone pensive.

"A piece of our soul back?" Archer asked. "Since apparently discretion is nontransferable."

But Jilly understood. It was all she'd ever wanted to give the kids she'd worked with, all she'd wanted for herself. "A chance at hope." She traced one finger down the lead solder in the stained glass, the dull metal holding such beauty together.

"Is that what Corvus learned from us?" Liam mused. "Where there's love, there is hope?"

Archer snorted. "What does evil hope for?" When Sera frowned thoughtfully and took a breath to answer, he ran the tip of one finger over her lip. "Never mind. I'm sure we'll find out. Later."

Sera nipped at him, then sighed. "Still so much we can't answer."

"Together," Liam said simply, "we will."

Jilly pulled her hand back from the window when her thumbnail dented the soft lead, gray as the demon realm. The tenebraeternum wouldn't be so easily mastered. But if anyone could do it ... She gave her man, her mate, a brash smile and pulled him down for a kiss. "Evil doesn't stand a chance."

Glossary of Terms
from the @I Archives

ascendant: The rise of a demon within a possessed human; refers to the initial incident of possession and subsequent risings.

birnenston: Also known as brimstone. A sulfuric compound leached from some demonic emanations interacting with the human realm.

desolator numinis: "Soul cleaver"; a demonic weapon.

djinni: *djinn* (pl.) Upper echelon of demonkind; fallen angels who are content to stay fallen.

djinn-man: A human possessed by a djinni.

ether: The elemental energy of spiritual and demonic emanations.

feralis: *ferales* (pl.) Lesser demonic emanation encased in a physical shell of mutated human-realm material. Physically strong but not so impressive in the brains department.

ichor: A physical by-product of demonic emanations not compatible with the human realm.

league: Isolated clusters of possessed fighters assigned to high-density human population areas with the mission of reducing demonic activity.

legion-tenebrae: Blanket term for lesser demonic emanations, including malice, ferales, and salambes. Also *tenebrae*.

malice: Incorporeal lesser emanation from the demon realm, typically small and animalistic in shape with protohuman intelligence.

mated-talyan bond: The synergistic combination of male and female possessed powers.

reven: The permanent visible epidermal mark left by an ascended demon.

salambe: Highly emanating demonic form from the same subspecies as malice.

solvo: A chemical version of the *desolator numinis*; produces opiatelike effects in humans while splitting off the soul.

talya: *talyan* (pl.) 1. Sacrificial lamb, a young man, Aramaic. 2. A human, typically male, possessed by a repentant demon.

tenebrae: Blanket term for lesser demonic emanations, including malice, ferales, and salambes. Also *legiontenebrae*.

tenebraeternum: The demon realm, separated from the human realm by the Veil.

teshuva: A repentant demon seeking to return to a state of grace.

Veil: An etheric barrier between the human and demon realms composed of captured souls.

*As a Chicago heat wave threatens to melt even
concrete and steel, the city's underground league
of demon-possessed warriors readies for the final
battle against a rogue djinni seeking to unleash
hell on earth.*

*Ex-missionary Jonah Walker lost his wife, his faith,
and his soul when his demon came to him. Maimed
in the league's last djinni encounter, he'll do anything
to join in a talya bond, to find a new right hand
to continue the fight.*

*Too bad that right hand comes attached to the sexy
curves and smart mouth of a down-and-out stripper
whose touch is the spark that will burn him alive.*

Continue reading for a preview of Jessa Slade's
next Marked Souls novel,

VOWED IN SHADOWS

Available from Signet Eclipse in April 2011

His congregation would have died—again—seeing him in a place like this.

Jonah Sterlings Walker kept his arms crossed so he wouldn't inadvertently touch anything. He'd learned that lesson the first night at the Shimmy Shack when his elbow had stuck to the tabletop. Presumably the tacky substance had been the congealed spill of some previous customer, but whether the spill was a beverage . . . If he could've kept both feet off the floor, he would've done that too.

Unfortunately, the repentant demon that had shattered his soul in return for vicious fighting skills against evil hadn't gifted him with the power of levitation.

Or invisibility. From the gloom beyond the stage curtain, the woman's gaze weighed on him like lead anchors. Violet-tinted lead anchors, a sign that her demon—which had been circling her without her awareness for more than a week by the league's calculations and finally settled in three nights ago—was on the verge of its virgin ascension.

The only thing virginal about her.

The volume of the unrelenting din they called music dropped as the deejay exhorted them, "Put your hands together. . . . Scratch that, put 'em in your pocket—not your front pockets, you filthy jag-offs, your back pocket, and start pulling out those Lincolns for ... our naughty Nymphette!"

A few men hooted as told; a half dozen others tipped back their drinks as if suddenly very thirsty. She stepped onto the stage, bare as the day she was born. Barer, since even newborns slid into the world with more body hair than that.

The costumes earlier in the week had been bad enough. Layers of vinyl and gauze, links of chain, strings of white eyelet lace from another century, adding insult to injury. And he'd suffered injury aplenty, with every knock of his cock against the back side of his zipper.

At least the ridiculousness of the schoolgirl knee-socks, the maid's apron, a *kimono* of all things, patently unsuited for the feral tangle of her dreadlocked hair, allowed him to steel himself—in more ways than one—against the inevitable fleshly display.

Jonah snapped his eyes closed. Too late. Under the harsh lights, her dusky skin glowed, sleek as the snake threaded across her outstretched arms. The shine off her shoulders, the snake's coils, and—ah, dear God in heaven—the fullness of her breasts burned on the insides of his eyelids. Unfair that she could invade his defenses with nothing more than ... nothing.

He might as well see his oncoming destruction. He opened his eyes.

She glided across the floor toward him, her bare feet silent on the parquet. But she timed each footfall for every other beat of the music, so even though her approach was slow, his heartbeat quickened against his will to echo the incessant bass.

Which made him wonder, exactly how repentant was his demon?

As always, she moved with an almost agonizing grace, a difference from the other dancers he attributed to the forty pounds of reptile hung around her body. Sweat glistened across the skin of her chest, but her spread arms were unfaltering under the weight. Only her rounded hips marked the cadence.

After the gyrations and jiggling of the others and the gleeful flinging of G-strings, her prolonged tension unsettled the room. Jonah stiffened against the twist inside him that tightened his muscles and sharpened his senses: the demon reacting to the changing ambience, the first whiff of threat.

Where was the teasing smile? The bustier and the stockings? He felt the uncertain shift in the men around him. Here were the tits and ass they had come for, and yet this was not their fantasy. This was too raw, too wild.

The ropes of her dreads slid across her breasts, hiding, then revealing her dark areolas, and the blunt ends lashĕd the high upper curve of her buttocks. Achingly slow, she raised her arms, and the snake eased from her shoulders to spiral across her torso. The scales, colored in shades from chocolate to sand, rippled down her body. Its blunt diamond head poised for a moment like an earthy jewel centered above her navel, then continued lower.

Her hands tracked its descent, easing over her breasts, lingering at the flare of her hips. She tipped her head back, throat exposed, and her dreads swung loose as the snake coiled down her thighs.

It pooled at her feet like a shed skin. Unfettered, she stood exposed, her taut curves the same tawny brown as the middling tones of the scales, an illusion of snake to woman. Hell on the herpetological half shell.

Jonah's pulse thundered in his ears and he realized he hadn't taken a breath in too long. When he finally did, it sounded like a gasp.

In the middle of the stage, the lights aimed with such salacious focus not a single shadow remained on her; not the faintest female mystery was left to the imagination. And yet somehow, he knew he wasn't seeing all of her. The purple smudges around her eyes seemed to absorb the light, but her gaze fixed on him, still and predatory behind the unnatural thicket of her lashes.

The demon was rising in her, and it called to him, teasing him to reach out.

There'd been a time when he believed wholeheartedly in converting the heathens. Not that he'd had much luck. And it seemed neither he nor the world had come very far.

He clenched his fists. Fist. His missing hand burned as if he held it out toward open flame. Rather like he was doing with what was left of his soul by coming to her now.

The djinni that had taken his hand six months ago had taken with it his certainty that the fight for good would prevail. He would do anything to tip the balance back in favor of his belief.

He stared at the Nymphette.

Anything.

The beat bled awkwardly from one song to the next, and she knelt to retrieve the snake, but instead of beginning her next dance, she crossed toward him and stepped out onto the bar that surrounded the stage. The gawkers rumbled, a sound somewhere between approval and consternation at the break in their routine.

Another step and she was standing on a barstool. The three-legged chair wobbled, and at his table, Jonah planted both feet on the floor, half rising to catch her should she fall. But she crouched, one hand steady on the bar, the other on the snake, and continued toward him, as if neither furniture nor elevation changes would get in her way.

Dimly, he heard the deejay squawk for the next dancer, the Nymphette having abandoned the stage. Though her hands were busy rearranging the snake across her shoulders, her violet-tinged gaze never left his.

He'd been stalked before, but this made every hair on his body prickle in alarm.

She glided right up to him, right between his legs. He leaned back, arms still crossed, thankful the height of the stool gave him a slight vantage point to look down at her.

She didn't touch him, but the heat of her naked body radiated through his jeans, sank into his thighs. "You want a dance, Cap'n?"

Her voice hummed through him with the demon's double lows, and the scent of the snake—a sharp, loamy tang—made him shudder. But the league's leader had explained what would happen, in a conversation as excruciatingly vague and embarrassing as heard by any bride on her wedding night.

Not that Jonah wanted in any way to compare this moment to his wedding night.

The pain and rage that swept through him brought his demon screaming from his depths and should have made the woman before him step back. Surely her rising demon would sense the violence in him.

Instead, she canted her head forward, a dare. "Assuming you can swing it." Her gaze angled down to his crotch. "The price, I mean."

She had no idea what this was costing him. "In private, if you'd oblige." His voice sounded hoarse to his own ears.

She eyed him. "VIP lap dance? Well, look at you, coming on strong now."

He stood abruptly, forcing her back a step. "Yeah, that's me. Coming strong." He closed his fingers around her wrist.

"Don't touch," she hissed.

"It's a strip club." But he released her when the snake hissed too.

"And I'm stripped, in case you hadn't noticed. But no touching."

"Ludicrous," he mumbled. But he waved her ahead of him toward the hall that led to the back rooms he'd scouted earlier.

She eased around him. "You paid eight bucks for a Power Slug. You'd know ludicrous." She nodded to the bartender, who popped the tab on a small aluminum can and slid it across the countertop toward them. "Have another; I get a percentage of the bar."

Jonah took the proffered energy drink as they passed. When they stepped into the back hallway, the pounding music dulled to a merely irritating headache. The AC pushed the stale odors of cigarettes and damp cardboard boxes but offered little in the way of coolness. "Are you always so . . . flattering of your patrons?"

"Only on the first date. You and me, we've been dancing around this thing for a week now. Time for flattery is long past."

He lifted one eyebrow. "A week is a long time?"

"You owe me for all those long stares. With all that looking and no paying, you're giving Mobi a complex."

"Moby? Ah, of course. The snake. Curious choice of names. The obsession angle works, but I'd suppose it would be hard to dance with a white whale around your shoulders."

She cast a glance back at him. In the unlit hallway, her eyes glimmered with only human reflections, the demon's drive waning for the moment. "Mobi as in Möbius strip, going round and around, always ending up back in the same place."

The brooding tenor of her words struck something inside him.

Before he could speak, she ducked behind a curtain. He followed her into the small cubicle. The VIP lounge lacked any features that might have identified it as important or a lounge. A single hard-backed chair faced into the cubby's corner, as if it had been pushed hastily awry. He pulled the shabby red curtain closed behind them.

She spun the chair toward him. "The only Mopey Dick I expect to see here is yours. And I can make that all better."

Jonah took a pull off the Slug. The sweeteners and caffeine buzzed through him as his demon-boosted metabolism dealt with the chemical brew. At least the task distracted the creature of evil inside him.

She plucked the can from his hand and tossed it aside. The spilled liquid fizzed for a moment. Under the lone incandescent lightbulb, her small smile was hard enough to dash hearts upon, were any imprudent enough to somehow find their way to this place. "So tell me what you want, Cap'n."

Jonah sat and crossed his arms. He needed her demon ascendant before he made his move. She wouldn't believe his story otherwise. "Dance for me, Nymphette." He knew physical stress triggered the demon's rise. The newly possessed males traditionally drank and fought their way to balance with the other-realm emanations coursing through their bodies. He'd heard it worked differently with the females.

"Call me Nim." Her voice turned husky, not with the demon, just a come-on. She swayed closer. "Nymphette is such a mouthful. And maybe you want me to save my mouth for ... other things, right, Captain?"

"Don't call me captain."

Her eyes narrowed at his brusque tone, but she didn't speak. She sidled toward his chair and slowly, muscles flexing, sank to her knees between his legs. Her gaze rested straight ahead, and his flesh, already strung tight, lifted like a marionette. Her mouth—that wide, generous mouth—was such a short distance from his zipper. He ached all over at her closeness, his erection straining toward her, his jaw clenched against giving in.

She unwrapped the snake from her shoulders and laid it at his feet. The weight of the beast was surprisingly heavy and hot through the leather of his boots as it wound around his ankles. He couldn't hold back a grunt of dismay.

Nim smiled at him, crookedly but with the first hint of honest emotion he'd seen in her. Amusement, at his expense. "Don't want you sneaking away early, like you've been doing all week."

"Hadn't planned on it." Anyway, not until her demon was firmly rooted in her soul and she'd been brought into the league fold as its latest possessed fighter.

She rose smoothly, so close between his thighs he felt the passage of air against the denim of his jeans, but she never touched him. The way she used her body was sinful, but he had to admit, she kept it as brutally honed as any warrior maintained his weapons. A demon could choose worse than to take such a dwelling.

She turned within the confines of his spread knees and set her back to him. She ran her hands up her torso, over her shoulders, and through the dreads of her hair. With a single twist, she bound her hair into a thick knot at her crown.

She leaned to one side, and he couldn't stop his gaze from following the sinuous curve of her spine, down between the points of her shoulder blades to the twin dimples framing her tailbone. His hand twitched to see if his spread fingers would span the distance.

Just as well it was the phantom hand.

She glanced over her shoulder. "No touching."

"So you said." He knew he hadn't given himself away. Couldn't, considering his maiming. But she obviously didn't think that would stop him.

Her fog-on-the-water gaze traced him. "You aren't here with lust on the mind. No lusting man could have lasted that whole week. Definitely couldn't last now." She straddled his knee, again without touching him, and dipped low in a slow-motion grind that never quite brushed his jeans. "You're so strong. Crazy strong." Her voice was a purr. "Is that because of the ring?"

His left hand, tucked against his ribs, tightened into a fist. He smoothed the pad of his thumb over the gold band. "No. Not because of the ring."

She tilted her hips and slid one hand back to ride above the shadowed cleft between her buttocks. Where he'd wanted to put his hand. "Because of the hook?"

The metal tip drove into his bicep. How could she ask so casually? "Aren't you supposed to be dancing?"

She bent backward, an impossible contortion without touching him. And yet she managed, even her hair suspended above his lap, teasing without touch. She stared at him from her inverted pose. "You're supposed to be pulling out something."

"You said no touching. Presumably that means myself as well."

"Your wallet is exempt from the no-touching rule."

He sighed, aggrieved, and uncrossed his arm to shift to one hip and reach for his back pocket. "At least this is on an expense account."

"All business. I like that in a man. We're practically soul mates."

A cold anger swept him. "Don't say that."

"Bosom buddies, then." She turned again to straddle his other leg, facing him. Her arms crossed in a low X across her belly pushed her breasts into tempting handfuls. Another supple writhe brought her down low, so low and close her nipples would've grazed his lips. If not for her oft-stated no-touching rule, of course.

"You have no idea how close we'll be," he said.

ALSO AVAILABLE
from

Jessa Slade

Seduced by Shadows
A Novel of the Marked Souls

When Sera Littlejohn meets a violet-eyed stranger, he reveals a supernatural battle veiled in the shadows, and Sera is tempted to the edge of madness by a dangerous desire. Ferris Archer takes Sera under his wing, now that she is a talya—possessed by a repentant demon with hellish powers. Archer's league of warriors have never fought beside a female before, and never in all his centuries has Archer found a woman who captivates him like Sera.

With the balance shifting between good and evil, passion and possession, Sera and Archer must defy the darkness and dare to embrace a love that will mark them forever.

"Wonderfully addictive."
—*New York Times* bestselling author
Gena Showalter

Available wherever books are sold or at
penguin.com

S0068

Penguin Group (USA) Online

What will you be reading tomorrow?

Tom Clancy, Patricia Cornwell, W.E.B. Griffin,
Nora Roberts, William Gibson, Robin Cook,
Brian Jacques, Catherine Coulter, Stephen King,
Dean Koontz, Ken Follett, Clive Cussler,
Eric Jerome Dickey, John Sandford,
Terry McMillan, Sue Monk Kidd, Amy Tan,
J. R. Ward, Laurell K. Hamilton,
Charlaine Harris, Christine Feehan...

You'll find them all at
penguin.com

*Read excerpts and newsletters,
find tour schedules and reading group guides,
and enter contests.*

Subscribe to Penguin Group (USA) newsletters
and get an exclusive inside look
at exciting new titles and the authors you love
long before everyone else does.

PENGUIN GROUP (USA)
us.penguingroup.com